International Tour

PART TWO OF TOUR SERIES

LUCI FER

Trigger Warning

This story contains content that might be troubling to some readers, including, but not limited to, sexual harassment, grooming and post traumatic stress disorder. Please be mindful of these and other possible triggers, particularly during Chapters Eight and Nine. Please seek assistance or medical advice if needed.

This book is dedicated to the dreamers... let your soul sing.

I bounced excitedly on my toes, down centre stage, the tingling vibrations of the music started to invade my being. I stepped forward, and the strobe light vanished like it was never there in the first place. There was no trace of the vibrant reds, oranges, or other colours. The thrumming of the drums had turned into a chirping, startling my senses alive. *The bloody alarm clock! How was it morning already?!* "Well, fuck."

The frost of the air conditioner saturated the bedroom, and I tugged the duvet higher, seeking the warmth. Drowsy dreaming gave way to creative sparks and new ideas, which set my mind adrift to all we had accomplished since our Regional Tour. Abandoned Bygone had finally broken the charts, and with the heightened success came notoriety I had often dreamt about. Becoming famous later on in our journey afforded us the maturity to navigate the media-induced storms more clearly. My band and the songs became the beating heart within me. We found the ability to speak strongly through our music and inevitably emerged as industry leaders. Our renown grew broader, and so did our smiles. It was what we worked so hard for. And, as our fans pulsed around us, we became electric… a frenzy of action. We didn't just *hear* the tunes any longer. We fed off their vibes, thriving at the apex of our craft.

After our Regional Tour, we returned to the studio and worked solidly on our new album, *Bold Fortune*. Like the first, *Mile End*, it quickly became a smash hit. The debut song, "Private Destiny," reached diamond in the first month. With multiple Platinum awards and over ten million streams, it was now our highest-selling track. This was what we were born to do; we couldn't escape that. It was our *destiny*. There was no denying Charlie was the anchor to help me thrive. She brought calm to my life. Her soul complimented my own. I learned to love myself and find balance. I could be a pillar for others because I was able to heal in the space she had given me. The alarm screeched across the room again, causing me to toss in the bed and seek refuge. I felt like I'd barely slept. The boys and I had worked painstakingly in the recording booths, with multiple awards shows and performances to promote the album threaded through our studio schedule. And, as if that wasn't enough, just before we wrapped up a few hours ago, Mark reminded us of an urgent meeting called by the studio executives later this morning.

"Make it stop, Cutie," I mumbled into my sheets. I tried to get comfortable again, fluffing the pillow several times before throwing it over my head. Finally, Charlie turned it off, and I felt her shuffle in the bed, fussing with the down comforter before releasing a sigh of contentment.

"What time did you finish last night, Batman? I didn't hear you get home." Charlie's morning voice flooded the room. I wrapped my arm around her waist and pulled her closer, enjoying the warmth of her body.

"Late," I sighed heavily. "I feel like I just went to bed." Seconds later, her soft fingers stroked my face, her nails running up into my hair, shrouding me in a comfort only she could provide. "Mhm, that's nice."

She asked, "when's the meeting," and I quickly racked my brain before telling her, "Eleven."

"I'll call you an hour before and ensure you're up." I nodded but didn't open my eyes. The physical exhaustion had hit me like a right hook to the jaw. "Ring the home phone. My mobile's on Do Not Disturb."

"Alright," she promised. "I've got to get showered and ready for work, my uber will be here in an hour. I love you. Go back to sleep."

"Love you, too," I whispered, still not opening my eyes. I pushed my lips out, signalling I wanted a kiss. I didn't have to wait long before I felt the soft skin of her hand on my cheek again and the smooth deliciousness of her lips skimming over my own.

She was gone too quickly, and the bed felt void of familiarity. Before I could register much, I nodded back to sleep. A few hours later, I woke to the phone chirping beside me and drowsily reached for it. I knew it was just Evil Midget with my wake-up call, so when I answered, I was quick to moan rather sexily, "Talk dirty to me, Cutie."

"Sorry, bro. I don't feel that way about you." *Fuck! Of course, it was Chester.* I groaned, "You're supposed to be Charlie," his amusement was blatant. "Yeah. I got that, but I'm your wake-up call instead. She's stuck in a meeting. So, still want me to give you some sexy time?"

"Nope!" I shut him down fast, adding, "I'm good. I'm up."

"Damn... I'm better than I thought if you already have a hard-on!" His wild laughter filtered through the receiver, earning a head shake from me.

Twenty minutes later, I was showered, caffeinated, dressed—including fresh kicks—and driving into town. After expertly navigating the gridlocked traffic, I walked inside the studio, stopping to greet many of the staff before strolling up to Charlie's office. I stuck my head around the doorframe, and an empty room greeted me. I decided to walk back out for a smoke and messaged her. "Cutie, I'm here on time, and I'm exhausted. You're not even around to greet me?" For good measure, I threw in a raised eyebrow emoji, highlighting my disappointment.

"I'm two minutes away, babe," she replied. "I promise I'll take care of you tonight." A full-body thrill ripped through me. I continued the rest of her message, which read, "early dinner, a bath, then into bed for a nude massage." I had barely finished when I saw another one come through the bright screen.

"That was a *nice* massage. Damn, autocorrect." The eye-roll she included at the end had me amused. I didn't hesitate to point out I was okay with the nude massage, too, and then I quickly tapped into my phone. "We have an appointment at four. I forgot to tell you." Charlie asked where we were going, and I was about to reply when I saw her walk into view.

She was a ray of sunshine amongst the already bustling Sydney streets. Dressed in a black and white plaid mini skirt and a knitted dark sweater, her luscious legs were drawing me in. Coupled with her beautiful golden hair, which was down as I loved it, I still couldn't believe my luck. I pushed off the concrete wall and went to greet her. Bending at the knees to meet her tiny stature, I moved in to give her a deep kiss, caressing her hip and giving it a gentle squeeze. "Hi, you look gorgeous."

"Thanks." Charlie beamed. She kissed me again, then enquired, "Where are we going at four?" With her arm looped around my waist, we strolled the short distance to the studio. I told her it was a surprise and heard my Cutie suck her teeth. "Like that, is it?" She shook her head, feigning annoyance at my secrecy. "Such a shame. If I knew what it was and I liked it, I could've had *all day* to plan that nude massage for you." She stepped away from me and walked backwards to her office, waving with a wicked grin. "Hope your meeting goes well, babe. Come find me afterwards."

"Evil Midget!" I shook my head, feeling tormented by her. "It's not nice to tease a man like that." She smirked, and I blew her another kiss before heading to the boardroom. After everyone greeted me, Shane mumbled that it was *about time*. "Shut up, man. It's not even eleven yet."

"Gives you time to clean Midget's lip gloss off then." *For fuck's sake!* Chester had to point that out, throwing in a wiggle of his eyebrows to match. I quickly wiped my mouth, and Mark highlighted his disappointment.

"I don't know. I was pretty drawn to your lips. You should've kept it on." We laughed as I ran over and started humping Mark in his chair. Of course, just as I hit my groove, the glass-panelled door ricocheted open, alerting us to the arrival of Marcus and the board of executives. The remaining guys were tickled as I sheepishly took my seat. After the recent long nights in the studio, I was mentally fucked when we drudged out of the meeting two and a half hours later. I had a few things to sort before reconvening with Charlie for our appointment, so I hauled ass down to the basement to get cracking. I returned around twenty past three and went straight to her office. She was there, busily working away on her computer, wholly absorbed in her screens, so much so that she didn't even notice me standing in her door-frame.

"Hey Cutie, wanna go for a ride?" My voice piqued her attention. Charlie's face erupted into that million-dollar smile she reserved just for me, and I greeted her with a provocative wink in return. She was also fast off the mark in asking how the meeting went. "Good. I promise to fill you in, but we've gotta get going right now." I tapped my wristwatch impatiently.

"Alright, babe. Let me pack up." She closed her laptop and stood. "Are you gonna tell me where we're going yet?"

"On the way," I vaguely offered, trying to dismiss her curiosity for as long as possible. "It's only about thirty minutes." Charlie finished tidying up, and I took her delicate hand in mine, guiding her out of the studio. I had barely found my spot in the maze of peak hour traffic when she turned to quiz me about the meeting again. I reached over and placed my hand on her leg, rubbing the tenderly soft skin. Even after all this time, I loved the feel of her pins under my fingers. "It was great, but I need to ask what your upcoming schedule looks like?" Her face frowned and the confusion set in, so I continued. "Can you clear it for six weeks?"

"Agh, I'd have to check, babe." Her nose scrunched as she tried to search the catalogue of work stored in her pretty head. "Why's that?"

I turned from the road briefly to face her. "What do you think about Canada?"

"Love to go! Especially to watch hockey." A smile instantly broke across my face. I seriously loved this girl. Everything was so easy with her. "What's that got to do with the meeting, though?" Her question snapped me back to the present. "Are you thinking of taking a break now the album release is out of the way?"

"Not quite," I said. "After all, we still have the media hype surrounding us." Charlie glared at me, unimpressed, much to my amusement.

"Dude! Why are you being so cryptic?"

Now that made me laugh! "Why have I been demoted to *dude*?"

"Brax!" Charlie whined. "The meeting?"

"Okay... Well, we're going on tour again." I let that linger while her elation filtered the vehicle before adding, "To Canada." I loved her shared passion for what I did, but the squeal that came next sounded like nails dragging down a chalkboard.

"Seriously?" Her voice was still peaking, and I nodded to her, indicating '*yes*'. "That's fantastic for you guys! I'm so proud of you!"

"Marcus negotiated so we could take our photographer from the last tour. After all, it was our biggest success." Barely able to contain her excitement, she twisted in her seat faster than a spinning top. "Are you fucking with me?"

"You think I'd leave you for six weeks? You're out of your damn mind, woman."

"Holy shit, Brax!" She bounced in her seat, and I looked at her, my eyes ablaze with the passion she stirred within me. "We can go to a hockey game, right?" I cracked up again while also promising we would see a match. Charlie reached for my hand on her leg and entwined our fingers, squeezing them. The smile on her face was everything. I just hoped she would be as happy when she saw the next surprise. "So, where are we going anyway?" she murmured as if sensing my thoughts.

"There's a property I need you to take photos of."

"Are you considering using it for one of your video clips or photoshoots?"

"Yeah... something like that," I muttered, not wanting to give too much away. She nodded her acceptance of my vague explanation and looked out the window as we continued our journey.

After we pulled up, Charlie grabbed her camera as I walked around to help her out of the car. We made our way down the cobbled driveway to an expansive architecturally-designed, industrial-inspired home. From the road, it appeared to be one level. It was built in reverse, so the lower floor was concealed and opened up onto a pool, spa, and entertainment area, providing needed privacy from the surrounding suburb. As instructed, I went to the lockbox, removed the keys, and escorted her inside to look around. I watched her twirl through the rooms, breathing it all in, and a loving glow engulfed my face. Her camera clicked rapidly, taking various pictures, and once she had finished inside, I led her out the back via the lower level.

"Holy shit! These views are breathtaking, Brax!" The infinity pool and spa were sculpted perfectly to encapsulate the forest backdrop. The fact there were no prying neighbours behind was also a welcomed bonus. "I didn't realise it was two levels when we came in." She pointed over her shoulder to the entrance. "It's built down, instead of up, and quite deceiving."

I nodded, observing intently, before asking her what she thought. "Reckon you could make this work?"

"Oh, sure," she replied before breaking out into a chuckle.

"Why are you laughing?"

"We've spoken about our dream home at length, and this pretty much ticks every box. It has the privacy of being on a bigger block with no houses behind. It's not too far from the city, but just enough to have rural views. The industrial yet modern feel of the interior...." I listened intently as she mentally went through the tick boxes. "Pool and spa, plus the downstairs level–which is perfect if we have to work from home." Her eyes lit up suddenly as if a lightbulb had just switched on. "You could even have that studio you always wanted!"

"So, when do you wanna move in?" *Yeah, I deliberately slipped that in casually.* Charlie didn't register what I'd said for a few seconds, and then her eyes bugged out. I loved catching her off guard, the shock that adorned her face melted my heart.

"S-say that again." She stumbled slightly on her words, confusion present.

"Charlotte Bancroft," I said, stepping closer to her, "when do you wanna move in?" My words were slow and deliberate, leaving little room for uncertainty. I was now close enough to wrap her in my arms and pull her into me. "We had a tough time figuring out where to live when we first moved in together." It was hard to believe that it had been eight months ago. "And I don't want you to feel as if you're living at *my* place, so why not rent it out as we did with yours? Let's move into *our* home." Charlie scrunched her nose, the way she always had when I hit her in the feels. And in turn, she knocked the wind out of me again. She was the most adorable thing ever in my eyes.

"You wanna buy a house with me, Brax?" she quietly questioned. "I found our dream home, babe. All that's left is your signature on the paperwork, and it's ours in thirty days."

"Just when I thought I couldn't love you any more." She slid her hand up my arm, easing over my collar and around my neck. Applying a bit of pressure, she pulled my head down to meet hers, and our lips found their way to each other. We moved as one, getting lost in the sensuality of our embrace.

I eventually pulled back and looked down into her eyes.

"So, is that a yes?"

Charlie nodded her head frantically, never breaking eye contact.

"It's a yes, Batman."

"I love you."

Smashing our lips together, I picked her up off the ground. She gripped my neck tightly, passionately accepting my tongue between her lips. Starved for air, we pulled apart and stared into each other's eyes while I continued holding her. She stroked my cheek, cradling my face and smiling at me,"You're getting laid tonight."

"You're fucking amazing, baby. I can't wait to call this our home." I saw the spark spread across her face, and I was overcome with the same feeling I'd been experiencing since the moment we met. It was as if my soul had stopped the search it had been on for my entire life. No longer did I wander. Finally, I was sitting atop the hill, basking in the glory. Charlie reached me in a place no one else ever could with her eyes, voice, touch, and presence. Before her, no one had been able to unlock my soul. It's not that I didn't want them to; I've wished for a love like this forever. Maybe they just didn't have the key. Charlie had it; perhaps the universe guided us without speaking. In a way, when I met her, I was stunned. I'd been alone for so long, it was almost unsettling at first to need someone so much. Now, she consumed my entire being. It had been on my mind since I found this house for us. So, when we returned from Canada, I had every intention to make her my wife... *if* I could bite my tongue that long!

Chapter Two

CHARLIE

Home was a sense of serenity in the soul, so anywhere I was with Brax had become residence to me. However, five weeks ago, he surprised me by finding the house of our dreams. We penned our signatures to the contract the same day, and after a long thirty-day wait, took possession of it last week. As we settled in, I was eager to make it a kaleidoscope of memories, a treasure trove of the life we were creating for ourselves. While the move had been mayhem, we'd never been happier. And tonight, we were hosting a housewarming party with our friends and family. It was also a chance to celebrate with everyone before we left for Canada next week.

"Babe! You don't need that long in the bathroom," Brax hollered, making his way into our bedroom and moving closer to the ensuite. "You're gorgeous already. Now let me have a damn shower."

"Okay," I conceded before pinching my nose teasingly. "And yeah, you need a wash."

Brax had been working around the house all day, helping to prepare everything for tonight. I watched in the mirror with lust-filled eyes as he started to strip out of his clothes. Noticing my thirsty glance, he pressed into me from behind, and inched his fingers along my hips, kissing my neck mumbling against my skin.

"You're beautiful," he whispered. My head lolled into him between enticing caresses, appreciating the loving words he lavished on me. "Wanna bend over for me?" he added. "I promise I'll be quick."

"How about you have a shower first so that it sounds more appealing?" I scrunched my nostrils with the pretence of a foul odour filling them.

"Rude!" He smirked and slapped me on the ass. "If someone didn't have me working my backside off all day, I wouldn't stink." I laughed and told him I may have exaggerated; it wasn't too bad.

"So you'll bend over for me then?" he begged, trying his luck again.

"No."

Brax finally jumped in the shower, and I finished my hair and makeup before heading out to get changed.

While he was still in the bathroom, and knowing people would arrive soon, I decided to take the drinks out to the cooler box. After switching the music on, I made my way back inside. That's when I saw him sitting on the lounge downstairs, about to open a beer already.

"Don't do it, mister!" I warned.

Brax glanced up when I spoke, and after giving me a quick once over, he immediately started whining.

"Why, Charlie?" My brows knitted as I glanced at him. "Why you gotta do me like this, babe? Now all I wanna do is fuck your brains out." He waved his hands up and down like a man in pain.

"Who said you couldn't?" I relished the chance to torment him. When he groaned that he meant right now, I brushed him off. "Give over already. You're such a hormonal adolescent sometimes."

He leapt over the coffee table and raced at me before I could move. When I cracked up, he grabbed my waist and pulled my body closer, firmly pressing his hips to mine. "Does this feel like a teenage boy to you?"

I was in hysterics as he vigorously ground his groin against me. When he didn't try to stop, I playfully pushed him away.

"Get off already, you baboon."

"No baboon tonight, baby. It's all caveman."

Brax bent down, wrapping his hands under my backside, before picking me up and throwing me over his shoulder. I squealed gleefully and tried to wiggle from his hold when he took the chance to give me a light spanking across the ass. His intention was obvious by this stage, but the echo of our intercom system rang through the property, stopping him in his tracks.

The bell saved me!

This man was definitely on his way back to bed!

"Put me down so I can get the door!"

When Brax groped me again and said I was lucky, I didn't argue; I already knew this.

Chester's hyperactive nature was on display when I greeted him, so when he bellowed "Midget," I stumbled back.

Brax yelled from downstairs, "Monkey Nuts!"

"Midget Fucker!"

The rest of the band found it comical, having come to expect nothing less of Chester, although it earned an eye roll from me.

"Where are you, bro?"

"Downstairs, asshole!" Brax shouted directions back. Chester looked shocked as he stepped in and gazed around the house.

"How much do you fuckers get paid! You have a two-storey house?"

Giving him a gentle nudge, I told the little shit to watch himself and get inside already.

I greeted all the guys but spent extra time saying hello to Kendall and Mace. "So how long are you here for, Kendall?"

"Well, that's a loaded question," she said with a familiar smile, perhaps even a hidden story behind it.

"How about we grab a drink and chat before everyone arrives?"

Mace suggested and we moved to the downstairs bar to fetch some glasses and a bottle of wine. When I shouted to Brax to keep an ear out for the doorbell so we could talk, it was Monkey that answered.

"Fuck, that didn't take you long. When don't you girls chatter?"

"Didn't realise we needed your permission, Chester," Kendall shot back at him.

"That's my girl," Shane proudly replied.

The boys were eager to have a quick smoke first, knowing we would probably be longer than them, so when they all started begging, I could hardly say '*no*'.

"Alright, chop-chop."

I clapped my hands, ushering the band to get a move on. I was growing impatient, wanting to hear more about how Kendall ended up in the city.

"Yeah, that's what we are doing. Going for a chop, a cone, a smoke. Same same, baby."

Before Chester could register, Brax kicked him in the side of the thigh, much to my entertainment.

"Fuck! Sorry, Sweet Cheeks," he apologised to me, furiously rubbing the cork to his muscle. Then turning back around, "You're a prick, bro!"

"Also, you fool, I meant chop-chop, as in getting your jog on, and not get distracted."

He started clicking his fingers at me, leaning forward on the bar.

"Speaking of distraction, is that a bra or a boob tube under your top?"

When Brax groaned and tried to kick his legs out again, they ended up in a headlock wrestling each other.

"He seriously needs to find a girl." I nodded at Mace's observation. "Hopefully, one that can tame his wild ass!"

I poured us all a drink and grabbed a blunt to share. The guys finally came back to swap spots with us. Of course, Brax made no secret of grabbing my ass as I passed him. "Quit it, you sex pest!" I wiggled away with a grin spreading across my face.

"It's those damn pants! They're so sexy." He turned to the boys looking for some support. "You should feel them." When Chester agreed and jumped up to run at me, Brax stepped into his tracks, "Stop! I just realised what I said. Don't touch her!"

The girls and I headed outside and sat on our outdoor settee to spark up. I swiftly returned to pressing them both for further information, Kendall was the first to go.

"Well, apart from next week, I guess the biggest question is, can you put up with me for six weeks?" Kendall waited for my answer.

"You mean you're coming to Canada, too?" She nodded, confirming my hopes.

"Agh!" My squeal of delight sent the boys racing to the glass bifold doors, sticking their heads out, concerned expressions painted across their faces.

"Babe? What is it?" Brax hurriedly quizzed me. "What's wrong?"

"Oh, nothing. It was good news." I shrugged my shoulders, trying to look innocent, "Oops!"

"Fucking women when they gasbag."

Kendall immediately turned on Shane telling him to "watch your mouth if you don't want to sleep in the spare room tonight."

"You will. I'll sleep in my bed, woman." The guys all snickered and encouraged him.

That was until Kendall asked him, "repeat that again, Shane," and stood up.

"Nothing, babe." And when he backed the fuck down, it was Mace and I laughing.

The band headed back in, and we continued our conversation. Kendall confirmed she was here until we left, and after asking her how she managed to get the time off from studying, she explained her University had granted an exemption for correspondence learning this semester. When she said there was even more news, I got super excited.

"Oh my god, you're pregnant!" My eyes brightened, but Kendall was fast to shut me down.

"Fuck no!" she yelled back with an exaggerated shiver. "Jesus, babe, are you trying to give me a heart attack?"

"I know, I'm sorry. My uterus just jumped in front of a bus also."

"The other news is that I am also coming." Mace confirmed.

"Shut the fuck up!" I bounced like a kid in a candy shop. "Yes! I want to scream again!" I clapped my hands with zeal.

"You just did!" Brax yelled back from inside as I flipped him off, even though he couldn't see it. Mace went on to explain she would fly out a few days later than us as she had work commitments she couldn't get out of; before taking some much needed annual leave. It was great to hear I would have female support on this tour and be able to share the band's success collectively.

Just as I did a little happy dance in my seat and mentioned how incredible this would be, I heard Marcus behind me "What's going to be epic?" My head flew, and I jumped up to hug and kiss him on the cheek. "You know, I just saw you yesterday?"

"Quit being an old bitch and come have a smoke with us." With a welcoming smile, he pulled me into a side hug before grabbing a spot with us. The moment he sat down, we heard motormouth Chester at the door.

"Hey! Stop picking favourites! You wouldn't let *us* join you."

"Fuck, you're a sook, man. Just come out already." The rest of the guys followed, and I asked Brax to leave the front door unlocked so people could come in as they arrived. When he finally returned, I shuffled onto his lap, he rubbed his hands over my thighs.

"I think you should wear these pants to bed. I love the feel of them." He pushed me down on his crotch, stroking my legs with more enthusiasm.

"You're such a weirdo." I giggled before wrapping my arm around his neck. We all sat and had a few cones quickly, getting into the partying spirit. I was talking with the girls while we watched the guys fucking around with each other, Chester and Brax doing their usual wrestling shit.

"I love this more than anything," Mace sighed as we watched our slightly dysfunctional family in front of us. I couldn't argue. My friends were by no means perfect, uninhibited, wild and free. They were the wind that flowed effortlessly through my fingers, our connected souls woven together like wires forming the right kind of sparks. They were the stability when the world around us went chaotic. United, we navigated and grew, and if I was fortunate enough to spend the rest of my life surrounded by these people, I was luckier than I could have ever imagined.

"This is home." I looked around the group and released a contented sigh, then heard the splash come from our pool. Of course, Chester and

Brax had been the ones to take their fucking around too far, and all I could do was shake my head. *Yep, this was home—my home.* Chester buckled over, grabbing his stomach. And to be honest, I wasn't far behind. "Oh my God, Brax!" Everyone was soon tittering with us while he swam to the edge and hoisted himself out of the pool.

"Don't suppose you wanna grab me a towel, Cutie?" Knowing I better, I trudged upstairs to grab one, still shaking my head but none too surprised. When I returned and he came to meet me, I put my hand up, indicating for him to stop. "Wet clothes off first, please. I don't want water all through the house."

"Lies!" Chester hollered, and I glared at him. "She's just trying to get you naked, bro."

"You want me to strip, baby?" Brax wiggled his eyebrows as I held up the towel.

"I want you to hurry up, please. Our other guests will be arriving soon." I wrapped it around him, affording some privacy while he peeled his soaking clothes off. The moment he dropped his pants and wiggled out of the drenched shirt, Chester shouted my name. I peered out past Brax just as that Monkey took a photo. "Are you shitting me right now?" He turned his phone, and just as I had suspected, the pic looked dubious. Brax cracked up laughing, realising it appeared, for all intents and purposes, that he was flashing me his junk.

"Send me that photo!" he managed between his muffled laughter.

"No!" I glared at them both. "Delete it now." While Brax ran upstairs to get changed, I collected his soaked clothing and took them to the laundry. *That* would be a job for tomorrow. By the time he returned, more people had arrived - friends from the studio, Tina and her partner Alex, along with many of our wider circle of mates. We excused ourselves and made a point of spending as much time as possible with everyone. After all, with our busy lives, it wasn't often we had this opportunity. We were speaking with some of his friends from football when, out of the corner of my eye, I saw mum walking down our driveway. I tugged lightly on Brax's hand, and we excused ourselves to go and greet her.

"Hi, Mum!"

"Pixie!" My mother had always been one for surprises that made my entire soul smile. When she handed over a housewarming gift, I was fast to hug her, engulfing her in the love she had always shown me. Even through my difficult childhood, mum had always been extraordinary. She helped to pave the way forward for me. As we stared at each other, I felt an overwhelming sense of peace wash over my being. "Brax, how are you, dear?"

"Never better, Carole." They embraced before he took her belongings and guided us inside. "How long are you staying in the city?"

"Just for two nights." She rubbed his arm warmly, and her eyes scanned our home, a sense of joy bathed her welcoming features. "I'm so proud of you both. This is simply stunning." Brax wrapped his arm around my waist, and I couldn't help but look up at him with love. That sentiment was basking on his face also. "And you dear," mum said, placing her gentle hands on both of my cheeks, "just get more beautiful every time I see you." She paused, turning back to Brax, "Thank you for looking after her."

"It's my pleasure." Mum gave his hand a soft squeeze. After he placed her handbag and gift in the dining room, we gave her a guided tour of the home, finishing back where we started.

I was excited to hear what she thought after seeing the whole place. "So what'd you think?"

"Those views are breathtaking." Mum pointed out the glass-panelled wall in our dining room and moved closer, observing it more intently. "Simply stunning," she mumbled softly.

Brax had heard her and whispered delicately to me, "Just like you."

"There's so much space here," mum continued. "So when you get back from Canada, can I expect some grandbabies?" Brax and I both choked and looked like deer in headlights. Mum so casually slipped that in and had utterly caught us off guard! After dropping that grenade, she went to the top of the internal staircase and listened to the merriment of everyone enjoying our home from downstairs. "Now, if I just follow that Monkey's laughter, will I find the rest of the band nearby to say hello?" She started walking down the stairs, and I could have sworn I heard a slight chuckle.

Brax finally turned to me, throwing a thumb over his shoulder. "So... agh, your Mum."

"Yep." I nodded, "I got that one." I met his stare, still bewildered.

"Good chat?" He broke out laughing and hugged me into his chest, gently rocking me from side to side as I exhaled. When he leaned down to kiss my cheek, I wasn't ready for what he was about to say. "It's not the worst idea ever...." My head snapped up faster than he could blink, as a result, I headbutted him on the chin. He grabbed his jaw and rubbed it furiously. "Agh, fuck!"

"Far out!" I grumbled. We both tried to ease the ache from our collision before making eye contact. Seconds passed, and then we burst out laughing. "Are you okay?" I finally managed once I settled down.

"I'm fine. Are you?" I nodded that I was. I suggested we head back to the party. I wanted to shake off what mum had said as quickly as possible. We made our way out, and the moment I felt Brax's hand wander to my backside, I slapped it away just as fast. "Quit it already!" I turned my head over my shoulder to warn him. "My Mum is right over there, and your parents will be here shortly."

"What?" He grinned wickedly, adding, "I'm just trying to please your mother." I stopped in my tracks and turned to face him.

"How is feeling me up all the time going to keep her happy, Brax?" My hands rested on my hips as my eyebrow raised.

"Did you not just hear what she said?" He pointed back upstairs. "How do you think I'll give her the grandchildren she wants?" When he smirked at me, my jaw hit the ground. The horror on my face had a thunderbolt of laughter ripple through him.

"You little fucker!" I couldn't believe he just used that to his advantage. Before I could say any more, Brax swept me into his arms, still amused as he covered my lips with his own.

Chapter Three

BRAX

My parents arrived after Carol, while mum smothered Charlie and me in hugs, dad struggled to get a word in. He mumbled a "hello" and a little wave, and then we gave them a tour upstairs before heading down.

"I'm proud of you, son. You've done well." My father patted my shoulder warmly as he took a good view of the downstairs.

"Thanks, Dad. Do you have a second before we join the rest?"

"Of course." I let Charlie know and pointed upstairs. She nodded and showed mum outside. "What'd you want to talk about, Brax?" Dad spoke first when we both settled back in the upstairs lounge room. I sat across from him and realised my father had always been the firefighter to my troubles. His wisdom helped to bring the calm that I needed, especially lately.

"Dad, I've been thinking a lot about where I go from here…." I looked up, hoping he would understand. "It's not like I can just tour or play gigs forever, right?"

"There's no reason you can't perform for as long as you enjoy it, son," he quickly countered.

"I understand that, but I'm at an age where I want more."

"How so?" he asked. "I thought music was your passion?" Concern painted his aged features, and he leaned forward.

"Yes! Of course, it is. It's everything to me, Dad." He nodded, and a sense of relief flooded his face. "I mean, besides the music," I continued, "what else do I have?"

"Well, for starters, you have a beautiful girl downstairs," he warmly acknowledged before continuing, "who seems to love you just as much as your mother and I do."

"That's my point. We have this incredible home, so what comes next? I don't want our story to stop here."

"What is it, Brax? You know you can always talk to your mother and me."

"I wanna ask Charlie to marry me."

Dad's expression didn't change; I guess he'd expected it. "So? What's stopping you?"

"I keep thinking it's too much, too soon. We just moved in here, we…." I started waffling before adding, "What if she's not ready? What if after everything her father tried to do, it freaks her out? We've never spoken about it, so I don't know how she feels. How do I even have that discussion?" It all rushed out of me like a tidal wave, and I had to suck in a few deep breaths to recover.

Dad slouched back, contemplating what I had just poured out. I studied him intently, anticipating the guidance he had always given me. "Thinking will not overcome fear," he said. "Action will. We can support you, but only you can choose to act, Brax. And if there is one thing I know about my son, he doesn't give up on what he truly wants."

Mum, dad and Carole left after midnight, and we agreed to meet them all for lunch before we flew to Canada. The music was turned up, and the drinks flowed more generously. Charlie and I stood off to the side, swaying away in each other's arms, watching our friends celebrate our new home and upcoming tour. I was soon distracted and found myself wrapping her into me tighter, our bodies gliding smoothly together, encouraged by the hypnotic trance of the music. My mouth wandered to her neck, using my lips and tongue to tease her delicate skin. When I finally glanced up again, I saw Chester's face right in mine. Startled, I pushed Charlie slightly into him and jumped back. "Hungry?" He laughed in my face.

"What do you want, asshole?" I threw sass at him. Charlie looked amused as she straightened herself and moved back closer to me.

"The brunette over there." He pointed to the far corner of the deck, and our gazes followed. "I want her," he said, pointing to one of the administration girls from the studio. "She's playing hard to get, though."

"She's not playing hard to get, Monkey." Charlie laughed at him. "She knows your reputation."

"How? Do we know each other?"

"You dick! She works in Human Resources!" I shook my head at him. "She's been at the studio longer than you have!"

"Help a brother out then!" Chester pleaded, nudging my shoulder.

"No chance."

"Besides, it's fun to watch you struggle." Charlie chuckled and waved Shane and Kendall over, who had just strolled back out with a beer. We took a seat with them, and I was none too surprised that Chester had gravitated to the other side of the deck.

"So, you kept that quiet, Shane?" Charlie quizzed him, returning me to the conversation. I was just as surprised. He hadn't mentioned a word of it.

"You mean Kendall going to Canada with us?"

"You think I'm stupid?" He pointed over his shoulder to Chester. "Like hell I was giving that fucker ammo to carry on with for the last few weeks." We were all amused, knowing he was right. "Plus, I like having her there to watch me perform." The height of success was difficult, and so was everything that came with it, but having the girls around to support us during those times made winning the battle that much sweeter. Love has transformed us to have a deeper emotional perspective, and it helped to shape our latest album too. The maturity in our songs was a direct reflection of the security we now had in our personal lives. The night gave way to the early morning hours, and many of our guests started to leave. Most of my band mates were either in front of the Playstation—some comforts never grew old—or crashed out in one of our guest rooms. I sat on our outdoor lounge with a beer in hand, and soon Charlie, Liam, and Mace joined me. The girls were half asleep, as Liam and I chatted absentmindedly, I noticed the first rays of the new day starting to creep up over the forest behind. The sun's presence graced us with the lullabies of the Rainbow Lorikeets, and the eye-catching strobes of yellow and orange momentarily blinded me. It transported me to those first few moments on stage… when the spotlights come up, and a triumphant eruption fills the air without effort, the sound engulfing every person in the arena.

Liam's voice drew me out of my trance, "Can I tell you something, Brax?"

"What's that?"

"I'm thinking of asking her to move back to the city with me." He glanced down at Mace, who had fallen asleep in his lap, and stroked the trademark purple hair we had all come to love. "When we get back from Canada, of course." It warmed my heart to see that my friends had been as lucky as Charlie and me.

"Honestly, Liam, it was the best decision I ever made." I gazed around the property that we were fortunate enough to call our own.

"You finally look settled, bro." I smiled because he was right. I felt the calm and peace that I had long searched for.

"I know you've always loved what you do," Liam continued "We all enjoy performing and thrive off the buzz from it. But she's what you needed." He pointed to Charlie curled in my lap. Her eyes were closed, finally resting after a long night, and I hugged her a bit tighter to me. "Midget's your natural high."

"She is, mate. We were both silly for so long regarding these girls." He laughed at my reply but didn't deny it.

"It's funny because we all used to push you together since you couldn't see it for yourselves," he said. Charlie adjusted in my arms as I chuckled.

I gloated by highlighting that we used to do the same for him and Mace. "Typical Chester, getting the best of both worlds."

"I thought I was friend-zoned."

"You almost were." Liam's dreads flopped back as the humour overtook him. "How did you guys bring it up? You dragged it on for years."

"It was in Stanthorpe. Remember we were talking about the claw marks Lizzie left on Chester's back?" When he nodded, I continued. "Charlie commented about it being kinky. I made a quip, and she heard it."

"She wasn't the only one, Brax." My head swung in his direction, and he tilted his beer to me before taking a sip.

"Thanks, mate." I sat back, taking a swig of my own. Charlie shuffled again, and I gave her arm a gentle rub.

"Excited to perform again?" he asked, and I gazed over. The spark in his eyes showed a fondness as he reminisced about past gigs.

"Always! No explanation needed." His smile magnified. "I hope it goes quickly."

"Really?" He sounded shocked by my comment, but I understood. We spent considerable time in the studio while constructing an album, and the celebrations only began once we could perform for our supporters.

"I think I'm ready to ask Charlie to marry me." I whispered just above a breath.

"For real?" Liam questioned, sitting up more refined. "That's great, Brax. When are you gonna do it?"

"Well, that's where I need your help." I waited for his undivided attention. "I'm thinking after the tour, to avoid distractions. Hopefully, I can wait that long, though." She twitched in my lap again. For a second, I wondered if she was still awake, but her closed eyes suggested otherwise. "It's all I've been thinking about since we bought this house."

She moved again, and that's when I knew she could hear. Regardless, I pressed on with the conversation. *Why?* I realised it was an opening to approach the subject with her. I wanted this, yet I couldn't lie... I was shitting myself! *Is there any man who wouldn't?*

I later let Liam know I was heading to bed and picked Charlie up.

Her warm breath skimmed the exposed skin above my collar, as her head settled on my shoulder. She spoke up when I used my foot to push our bedroom door open.

"I'm awake." The vibration of my chuckle caused her to smile.

"I'd an inkling."

She opened her eyes and asked, "Then why did you carry me?"

"You were relaxed." I shrugged it off and crossed the room to place her on the bed. I shut our door, remembering to lock it with Chester lurking in the halls. "Plus, it gave me an excuse to get my hands on you."

"Is that so?" Charlie's voice was laced with a not-so-innocent seduction, and she leaned back on her elbows while I strolled to her side. I gestured so she'd lift her hips, and with some confusion, she did, allowing me to undress her. After disposing of my pants and shirt, I chucked them in the linen basket. When I settled behind her in bed, she groaned.

"Could you put the air con on, please? It's too hot!" I knew it was coming and obliged, powering up the remote. "Thanks, Batman."

"You're welcome, baby." I rolled over, and she cuddled closer, pressing her butt against me. I rested my head on her shoulder before asking, "How long were you awake?" She turned and smiled at me, so I rephrased. "Were you even sleeping?"

It didn't surprise me when she shook her head no.

"Why'd you have that talk, then?" she asked, then rolled over when I didn't answer straight away.

I needed a second to collect my thoughts. After pushing up on my elbow, I looked down and brushed loose hair back from her face. "I feel like we need to have this conversation. I want this with you."

Charlie scrunched her nose, and I knew from that little gesture she felt every word. "You don't think it's too much, too soon? We just bought this house." She looked around our bedroom as if to emphasise her point. There were no nerves I could hear.

"It doesn't," I reassured her. "We've said it before, we waited long enough. It's everything I wanted and so much more." She nodded, understanding what I was saying. "This is where I want to be. A life with you is the endgame. Anything else along the way is just a bonus."

We stared at each other while I tried to read how she was feeling. The silence seemed infinite, but she hadn't pulled away from me.

"Tell me what you're thinking," I begged. "Find comfort in our love and know we can work things out together."

"It scares me a little," Charlie whispered.

Confident I already knew the answer, I asked anyway. "Marriage?" She agreed with a slight nod but stayed quiet, so I pulled her closer. "Cutie, you understand it's not like that with us, right? We love each other."

"You're right."

"I wanna spend the rest of my life with my best friend who I'm in love with. Some never find that luck." I twisted further sideways, helping to mould our bodies together. Her breath skimmed my chest, and I brushed my lips along her forehead.

"I want that, too," she said.

"Then that's all I need to know. But you should understand…" I trailed off and placed both hands on her cheeks, then lifted her head to force eye contact. "When the time's right, I'm going to ask you to be my wife."

Our mouths entwined, neither of us wanting to stop. My eyes fluttered open, watching as she licked her lips and sighed.

"Okay, Batman."

I kissed her again, and we embraced to my favourite rhythm. Desire. Passion. Love. Delicate hands danced down my chest, tracing my stomach as they headed towards their intended destination. Her fingertips ran up and down my shaft, watching as I inhaled in anticipation. Charlie loved to tease, and this was the perfect time as the room buzzed with sexual energy.

The assault on my dick began, and her wicked grin met my gaze. "So, you wanna show me how much you love me?"

"Hmm, like you even need to ask," I quipped, replying to her seduction. I twitched against those exploring fingers. She looked at my face, finding it masked with excitement and lust. I was silently begging at this point, but she continued to play with me to rouse a response. I nodded for her to keep going, caught in the erotic thoughts of what would come next. I wanted to see her absorbed in the pleasure we created together, and my pleading gaze was her strongest sign to take this further.

"Do you know how badly I want you, Brax?" Charlie purred against my ear while her hand continued to torment my cock. She ground against my hips, creating a blaze of tension.

"Fuck, you turn me on so much." I moaned, thrusting against her hand and struggling to contain myself. I could tell she was relishing the tease, but I needed more. She gripped my erection as her mouth pressed to my ear, mumbling words that nearly killed me..

"I think I need to suck your cock." Hearing her so wound up had a visceral effect on me. I rolled onto my back, anticipating her moist lips. Her mouth formed a perfect 'O' while bobbing up and down on my dick.

"Fuck, Charlie! You're so good at that, baby." She moaned with me still in her mouth, so I propped up on my elbows. "You like that, don't you? You love when I praise you for looking after me." She answered with a whimper, then went back down between my legs, holding my gaze, but I was too wound up now. *I need more!* She let out a startled squeak as I dragged her over my body. I sat her on my stomach and started rubbing my thumb around her clit. With hands resting on my chest, her head hung forward, causing those golden strands to create a curtain around her face. Her eyes became hooded, and she pressed further when I increased speed.

"Look at me." She did, and I rubbed a little faster. Her fingers gripped my chest tighter, and her knees dug around my sides. "Do you know what a goddess you are?" With one arm around her waist, I pushed up into a sitting position and continued to tease her creamy pussy. Our foreheads pressed together as I worked to please her. "My Calypso." Her eyes lit up hearing the comparison to that song. I kissed across her collarbone and then nibbled her tender skin, causing her head to roll back. "Oh, Brax. Please!"

I moved to her neck and started kissing up the front. "Please what, baby?" I mumbled into her mouth. I dragged fingers down her swollen pussy, waiting for the answer. When she took longer than I wanted, I circled my finger.

"I… aww fuck! I can't." Charlie buried her head in my neck as she started grinding faster.

"You need me as much as I need you. Is that what you're trying to say?"

A muffled "yes" came in reply.

"You feel like the air is being sucked out of your lungs?"

"Yes, Brax," she whimpered against my lips, grinding deeper into my fingers.

"Without my touch, your body aches."

"Yes." Charlie whined as I slid my finger inside. Her nails dug deep into the skin of my shoulders, and she pushed against me, arching her back. "Now you understand why I can't imagine living a day without you." I smashed my lips onto hers and rolled her over, desperate to bury myself in my future.

We finally flew to Canada today!

I was so excited. I'd been up since dawn, pottering around the house while Brax snored his head off. *Oh well, at least I could sleep on the plane.* He finally woke around seven and seemed surprised that I was so alert.

"Why are you up? You hate mornings!"

"I couldn't sleep."

He scrunched his face and mimicked me. "Aww, are you excited?"

"Yes!" I jumped into his arms, squeezing his neck as I rocked from side to side.

"Get off me, you dork!" He mucked around, then pulled me in for a sexy kiss. "I've gotta get sorted. Let me make a quick coffee, Cutie." He patted my backside before placing me on the ground. I offered to fix his drink so I could grab another, and his eyebrow flew up. "I don't think you need any more caffeine. You're already hyperactive." Ignoring that, I went about making them, then joined him on our deck. I placed the drinks on the table and curled up on the couch beside him. I felt giddy and couldn't stop fidgeting. For the first time in my life, endless possibilities surrounded me. I'd found a haven where I could be my complete self and live freely.

"Can you sit still?" He fussed and ripped me out of my thoughts. "What's wrong with you?" Amusement etched his face.

"I don't know." I tried to find the right words to express myself. "I'm just thrilled. There's no other way to describe it." I looked up with a sheepish smile. "The last few weeks have been hectic, and I've loved every minute. I wouldn't change a thing." I shrugged, adding, "This is exactly where I'm supposed to be."

"Me too, Cutie."

After enjoying our coffees, he ran off to have a shower and get dressed. I locked up while I waited, but of course, he double-checked when he came out. We set the security alarm, grabbed our luggage, and were on the road. It took our Uber an hour to navigate the traffic to the airport, causing me to grow rather impatient.

Shane and Kendall greeted us as we made our way to the entrance. I hugged her tightly, feeling comforted that she would be joining us on the tour with Mace. Life on the road could be a rollercoaster ride, but having good friends there certainly made it easier.

"We're lucky bastards, you know?" Shane not-so-quietly whispered to Brax. When we turned, we found the boys smiling like Cheshire cats.

"Fucking oath we are." Brax gave me a quick wink, and the seductive eyes Shane threw to Kendall didn't go unnoticed. She shot her finger at him, much to his amusement.

"Behave yourself," she said, stepping closer. This thrilled him even more.

"Wanna join the mile-high club?" he mused while grabbing her hips. Of course, it was a resounding *no,* which left me humoured he'd even tried to begin with.

"Why are you laughing?" Brax whispered as we continued inside. "I was about to ask you the same thing."

We checked in for our flights, grabbed our onboard luggage and headed to the cafe area, where we'd agreed to meet everyone before heading through customs. Brax and I ordered coffees, then returned to see that Chester, Mark, and Marcus had arrived.

Chester was bouncing in his seat, and I knew I wasn't the only one who had been jittery all morning. A giggle rippled through me before I could stop; he just had that effect on people! Brax felt the vibrations and looked down.

"You were up before the sun and just as hyperactive," he teased.

"She wasn't the only one up in the dark," Chester bantered. The dirty smirk on his face told me exactly what he'd been doing. "Besides, I'm so excited. Nothing can ruin it."

I pointed out the obvious to him. "The entire day is going to be spent on a plane."

"She of little faith." His sly reply had me feeling like he was privy to something we weren't.

Liam finally slouched in, mumbling about the *ridiculous* hour of the morning as he never was one for early starts. We finished our drinks and went down the escalator to the customs line. With a long queue in front of us, Brax and Marcus used the time to discuss the first movements of the tour. I rocked impatiently on my heels as I drifted in and out of their conversation.

"You have two days to recover once we arrive in Toronto," Marcus said, "and then another two to coordinate logistics with Glaze before we hit the road." Glaze was the band they were touring with. "Their manager Nick has booked some studio time, separately and together."

"I'm keen to get in there with Chris," Brax cut in. Chris was Glaze's lead singer, and they'd spent a lot of time on the phone since the tour was announced. "We've been throwing around a few ideas for new material," he added, for the benefit of the band.

"You thinking of a collaboration?" Shane drew the rest of the boys into the conversation, and they fired a million and one questions.

"Chris had an idea, and I think it might work," Brax explained. He looked around at his bandmates. "After this tour, we'll both be working on our following albums, so it's an excellent time to consider doing something a little different, right? We can't miss a chance to work with a band like them." While this revelation seemed to surprise the rest of the boys, the look on Marcus' face implied that he was involved in those discussions on the back end.

Chester whined for the next forty-five minutes, which is how long it took us to get to the front of the queue. By this stage, the adrenaline had long worn off. We made our way through the metal detectors and waited for our handheld luggage to be scanned. My head tilted to better see the screen when it stopped on mine. The customs officer examined it closer before waving to his colleague, so I elbowed Brax and pointed towards them. I didn't know what was happening and yet I still felt nervous! My brain tried to catalogue if I'd packed any prohibited items, but I'd triple-checked that.

"I'm sure it's fine, babe. Did you leave a can of deodorant in there?" I shook my head, positive I hadn't. They released my bag, and the customs officer carried it to an examination bench. Brax and I followed their instructions to join.

"Could you open your bag, please?" When I agreed, he asked, "did you pack it yourself?"

"Yes." I unfastened it and stood back so he could conduct a further inspection. My concerned eyes sought Brax. Sensing my panic, his fingers wrapped around mine, giving them a gentle squeeze for comfort. I was confident he could feel the vibrations of anxiety rippling through my body. The tremors started in my hands, quickly followed by droplets of sweat saturating my palms. "Could you open the front pocket of your luggage for me, Ma'am?" I immediately complied. After a brief search, the customs officer pulled his hand out, holding up the obtrusive instrument. "Are these yours?" A bemused look had now replaced his previously stern features.

I was mortified, frozen to the spot. I couldn't believe this had happened, and in front of everybody! The snickers from the band—mostly Chester— left my head spinning. They'd mock me over this for as long as I lived. He was holding up Ben Wa Balls... removed from *my* bag! Then it clicked... I turned with a deathly stare, and I could have sworn he shrank on the spot for a second.

"Chester!" I squealed.

Thankfully, Brax sorted the situation since I was too embarrassed to string a sentence together. He explained to customs what Chester did, and they shrugged it off with a bit of humour. Apparently, it was a common occurrence. After shaking hands with them and apologising, he returned. Chester stepped out to speak to him when he passed, but Brax effortlessly manoeuvred around him.

"Completely ignore him," Brax instructed me. He wrapped his arm around my shoulders and tugged me closer. We started making our way to the gate, ready for departure. "I don't want you going off when we're at the airport."

"But, Brax," I protested. "He just humiliated me in front of everyone!"

"I saw it, Charlie." His grip on me tightened, and we slowed down for a second. Pulling me in firmer, he placed a comforting kiss on my temple. "That's why I'm gonna get the little fucker back." That sparked my interest immediately, and I looked up at him. "You with me?" His smirk grew wider when I acknowledged our silent understanding. "A long and quiet flight should give him plenty of time to think about it."

After a small wait, we were called to board the plane. Chester was boisterous in his joy, seeing as we could enter the aircraft as a priority. "Fuck yeah! First-class! Now, that's what I'm talking about." He examined his ticket and added, "At least someone knows who I am."

"Yeah, an obnoxious asshole." Brax heard me and turned his head to hide his amusement. Once he arranged our bags in the overhead storage compartment, we settled in the executive pods, pleased with the two-seater. "You know he'll be over here the first chance he gets."

"With any luck, I'll be asleep by then." Brax emphasised his point by swallowing melatonin and taking a swig from his water bottle. Seeing Chester approach, he fussed with his earphones before popping them in and looking in the opposite direction.

"You fucked up this time, mate." Liam's comment made me smile.

"How mad do you think he is?" Chester questioned the others. Shane and Mark soon joined in the banter, but he waved them off. "Nah, he's fine. He has to pretend to side with the missus or she'll give him hell."

"You just focus on yourself," Marcus directed him, flicking his hand to sit down.

"Okay," he mumbled rather deplorably before taking his seat.

"Someone's sounding nervous," I said quietly to Brax, throwing a thumb over my shoulder toward Monkey Nuts.

"Good." His tone was flat, and so was the stare he volleyed over my shoulder.

When I turned discreetly to peek, I noticed Chester's eyes locked on his. My head swivelled back around, but Brax hadn't wavered. I shuffled in my chair, scooting closer to draw his attention from Chester, and his gaze met mine.

"What?" His head tilted sideways to examine me and his face was a picture of confusion. "What's that look for?"

"You're kinda hot when you're being all broody." I let my eyes wander up his toned chest, and when they fell on his lips, I knew why I loved them so much. It was the softness of the words he spoke—not just in song but in private. I reminisced over the salacious words he would hum to me, and my tongue swirled deliciously over my lips. Skilled fingers teased my thigh, he moved closer, burying his face in my neck. His teeth tugged at my skin, and his relentless assault intensified with his hunger. Pulling back, I placed my hands on his stubbly cheeks. I heated under his passion-glazed eyes and smiled. "That mile-high club is sounding tempting."

"Don't tease me, Evil Midget," he muffled through his amusement.

Our mouths embraced again, and our tongues explored one another, allowing ourselves to get lost for a moment. We heard the cabin crew over the speaker, and turned to watch the plane taxi out onto the runway. I rested my head on his shoulder, and he reached across, patting my leg. We gazed out of the window together, watching the last glimpses of home for several weeks. Once in the air and the seatbelt lights were off, I moved across to sit with Brax. "Your adrenaline's worn off, hasn't it?" He nudged me slightly as I made myself comfortable and cuddled into him.

"I'm just gonna have a nap," I mumbled. I settled against his chest with hands tucked under my head. Brax was drawing lazy patterns up my back, his fingers tenderly exploring and caressing me into a peaceful sleep. Chester woke me some time later, trying to get his attention, but I shrugged him off.

"He took melatonin, Monkey. He won't wake."

After a few awkward seconds, he trudged back to his seat, not before adding, "Tell him to come to see me when he's up."

"No problem." I was confident Brax was awake, though, and once the coast was clear, he opened his eyes and grinned at me. "How long are you gonna ignore him?" I whispered, finding the charade entertaining.

"The entire trip."

And that was precisely what he did.

We finally hit the tarmac in Canada, two stops and twenty-six hours later. I was relieved to see it was nine in the evening local time, meaning we wouldn't have to wait long to sleep off the jet-lag. Chester barrelled toward us as we made our way from the plane, and Brax immediately pretended he was on a call.

"What's he doing?" Using my pinkie finger and thumb, I gestured that he was on the phone. "He didn't come and see me?"

"He slept the entire flight," I said, brushing him off with a slight of the head.

We made our way through border control with no fucking around this time, and after collecting all the luggage, we located our vehicles and were on the way to the Airbnb. The crew would sort arrangements for the equipment once cleared through declarations. Aushop found a seven-bedroom house in Downtown Toronto for us to stay in for the first five nights. It was a few minutes' drive from Soundhouse Studio, which was ideal, especially when the band had to meet with Glaze.

It took under half an hour to arrive, and the first thing I noticed was the way the snow hugged the house like a newborn baby. Nature had hushed the street under its frigid duvet. It differed from anything we had experienced before, especially from the tropics, and it was a marvel unto itself. The moment I stepped out, the cold licked at my face and crept under my clothes, spreading across my skin like the lacy tide. With chattering teeth, I gripped my coat tighter as we made our way inside. After familiarising ourselves with the layout, we sat on the white sectional sofas to sort out room allocations. Before Marcus could speak, Brax interjected.

"Can Charlie and I have one far away from Chester, please?" Monkey started cackling. It sounded funny, but I knew Brax was serious.

"Well, there's a separate guest quarter downstairs," Marcus explained. "It has a bedroom and private bathroom. The master suite and the rest of the rooms are upstairs."

Brax stopped him. "We're happy to take downstairs, aren't we?"

He turned to me, and I eagerly agreed. "Right, I need a shower, food, and sleep."

"You lot get sorted. I've gotta race out to meet Nick. He's organised some keys for the studio. It'll be easier for us over the next few days." The boys thanked Marcus as it was crystal clear he'd been more organised on this trip. "I should only be an hour. I'll pick up some dinner on the way back."

Brax nodded. "Sounds good, M. Thanks."

Marcus waved security over, and after some discussion, one of them went with him while the others stayed back to oversee the house. We collected our luggage and moved across the polished timber floors towards our room. Chester was the only one making noise, apart from the clanking of wheels on our suitcases, as he tried to gain Brax's attention one last time.

"You coming back for food, bro?"

Brax continued without acknowledging him, and he turned to me, puzzled. With a casual shoulder shrug, I gestured that I didn't know. After unlocking our room, I heard the whispering behind us. I couldn't define what they said, especially when Liam's laughter ricocheted around the lounge room.

"Fuck, I think he's pissed at me this time, guys." Chester's voice rattled.

Chapter Five

BRAX

I locked the door the moment we were inside, and Charlie headed into the ensuite to shower before Marcus returned with dinner. I pulled out my phone, flopping back on the bed and phoned my manager.

"I'm glad you called," Marcus answered, and before I could say anything, he added, "I've been meaning to speak with you."

"About Chester?" I asked. He confirmed *yes*, so I followed up. "What'd you wanna know?"

"This is an enormous opportunity for you guys." I was aware, but I nodded along, as he stressed the point. "No foolishness like the first tour." He let that linger, and as I had vivid flashbacks, I realised what he was saying.

"No prank wars," I promised.

"Good."

"But," I cut him off before he got too excited, "I wanna make it very clear he's not gonna fuck with us all on tour." And by *us*, I meant Charlie and me. "Let me make a statement, M." He was silent for longer than expected, so I pulled the phone from my ear to check if he'd hung up.

"What are you thinking?" he asked. I explained my idea and asked if he'd go to the shop for me, then pocketed my phone and laid back.

The last thing I remembered was the soft ripples of the mattress as it folded into me. Waking some time later, I checked my phone, surprised that only an hour had passed. I fell back onto the pillows, resting my forearm over my eyes, then heard muffled voices from the common area.

"Where is he, anyway?" Liam asked.

"He'd fallen asleep by the time I'd showered," Charlie answered. "I think he took too much melatonin." Shane mumbled something about not sharing before Liam's laughter prevented me from hearing what they said next. Mark's calm yet inquisitive voice eventually floated through.

"Is he still pissed with Chester?" I turned my head towards the door, trying to hear better from my vantage point.

"I don't think he's pissed—"

"He's only that quiet when annoyed," Shane interrupted before Charlie could finish trying to bluff for me. Liam and Mark didn't hesitate to agree.

"Where's Monkey?" she asked, quickly moving the conversation along. The boys told her he had gone for a shower and that Marcus would be back with dinner soon. "I might get Brax up then."

"That would be a splendid plan," Marcus answered, having just arrived back. "Can you give him this also? He needed supplies from the store." The bedroom door creaked open as I was contemplating whether to jump up and grab my hoodie or stay tucked in the bed's warmth. Knowing it was Charlie, I lay there, eyes closed, and felt the mattress dip. I flinched when her fingers caressed my cheek, and her warm breath tickled my neck seconds later. Those smooth lips skimmed over the stubble on my cheek before she placed a few quick kisses on my lips.

"Brax, it's time to wake up. Marcus' back with food. He also gave me a shopping bag for you."

"I'm awake," I mumbled. I smiled without opening my eyes and heard her chuckle.

"Hi, baby." She moved closer, and our lips glided over one another. I opened my eyes to see her shining down on me. "Would you like me to bring some dinner here instead? You can go straight back to sleep after you eat."

"I'll get up in a minute." Our bodies instinctively combined. The effortless yin and yang moulded intricately yet oh so perfectly.

"What's in the bag, Brax?"

"A gift for Chester." She twisted in my arms, and her sparkling eyes were full of mischief. "Just wait and see." I tapped her nose before swinging my feet off the bed and standing. I stretched my arms over my head, and my cramped bones creaked in torment from all that flying.

"Tell me!" Charlie pleaded when I bent down to pick up my hoodie and jacket.

"I will later," I hinted, pulling the cotton warmth over my head, "after everyone's gone to bed. It requires a stealth attack." I rubbed my eyes and yawned as streaks of light penetrated my vision.

"Let's get coffee," she suggested, as if able to read my thoughts. Once the door was locked, I took her hand as we headed into the lounge room. Liam, Shane and Kendall were about to head outside.

"What are you up to?"

Their heads turned, and Liam waved a blunt.

"Marcus came back from the studio with a smoke," Shane explained. "I'd offer to share, but I don't see melatonin on the table."

We both laughed, and I told him, "All you had to do was ask."

Charlie and I joined them after making our coffee, and the night's freeze slapped me so hard that my skin felt raw and sore to the touch. It wasn't a pleasant coldness, but the kind that made you walk all the faster and brace your head down. No matter how warm the blood in your veins, your face still froze.

We weren't used to this blanket of white Down Under, and it felt criminal to disturb the perfect covering. Charlie passed me the coffee while racing to grab a jacket and blanket.

"Why are you shivering? I thought you loved the cold! You always have the air con on minus ten degrees at home." I exaggerated, to prove my point. Between chattering teeth, Shane expressed his disgust.

"Getting warm's easy. Cooling down is harder." She shrugged us both off.

Sparking up, I felt the harshness of the smoke and cold air hit my lungs, followed by a heavy mist as I exhaled. We heard footsteps on the internal stairs, and a few seconds later, Chester, Mark, and Marcus appeared. Attracted by the pizza boxes, Chester jumped from the bottom step and slid across the floor before grabbing a slice and stuffing more than half of it in his mouth. He made his way outside while demolishing the rest of the portion.

Pulling his jacket higher, he took the vacant seat next to me. "You talking to me yet?"

Confused, I pointed to myself.

"You're ignoring me," he challenged further.

"Pretty sure I was just sleeping, mate." I shrugged, but he pressed on, insisting it was before that.

When I stopped responding, he stood and asked, "Anyone want a joint while I'm grabbing one?" We nodded and he raced inside.

Shane coughed behind his hand once the door shut. "You're pissed with him, aren't you?"

I shook my head, a wry grin presenting. "It's Chester. He's done worse shit." I replied to Shane. Mark laughed and agreed. "But he's gonna learn not to fuck with Charlie."

After another smoke, I noticed everyone sitting around unwinding. The combination of jetlag, melatonin, and the cold had me asleep on Charlie soon after. She barely got me to bed as I fell back on the mattress. Today had worn me out. She groaned in exhaustion while struggling to remove my jacket, boots and everything else. Where possible, I tried to help.

I woke up some time later and checked my phone, finding it was only four in the morning. I flopped back on the pillow, rubbing my eyes, and that's when it hit me. It was the *perfect* time to exact some revenge on Chester. I sat up and switched on the lamp, looking like a deer in headlights as the bright light pierced my half-sleepy state. I moved to the edge of the bed and was pulling on my track pants when I felt the bed dip behind me.

"Sneaking out to your other girlfriend?" Charlie's tired voice mumbled. She reached out, stroking my back.

"I'm sorry. I didn't mean to wake you." She smiled without opening her eyes, then snuggled back down into the pillow, tucking her hands underneath it. "I'm coming back to bed after serving some revenge." My fingers danced across her face, caressing her while she shuffled to get comfortable. "You wanna help?"

That got her attention.

"I'm awake!" A smile erupted as she sat, and her alert eyes flicked open.

"Put something warm on." I chucked one of my hoodies onto the bed, and she pulled it over her head. "We have to be quiet."

Using just the light from our mobile phones, I let her in on the plan while showing the bag's contents.

"Brax," she whispered, her eyes widening. "Marcus will flip out, and you know it."

I laughed before reminding her, "Who purchased it?"

"Oh, and he okayed this?"

When I nodded, she still seemed shocked, even as I assured her it was fine. We crept up the dimly lit internal stairs and, on the third attempt, located Chester's room. Once Charlie had slid under the bed, we set to the task.

Later, as we climbed back into bed, I felt pleased with our execution, especially considering she didn't know the plan until the last minute. I cuddled in behind her, draping my arm across her waist. My face pressed into her neck, and my steady breathing skimmed across her flesh. "Babe, I have a—"

"You know you suck at cuddling, right?" I cut Charlie off before she could finish. The moon's reflective light illuminated the disgust on her face and her head flung at me.

"Are you serious?"

I chuckled, explaining, "You can't just lay there. I'm content cuddling and, with any luck, some more sleep."

She decided to let it go, so I hugged her tighter. A few minutes later I felt her backside grind up on me. She couldn't stand the silence, or maybe she was just aroused? Either way, it had the exact reaction she was hoping for.

"Are you gonna waste that?" Her seduction licked the air. "Or do you wanna get naked with me?"

A sensual sway of our hips ignited when I rolled on top. Taking her hands in mine, I pinned them on either side of her head.

"Evil Midget," I mumbled between hard kisses. "What should I do with you?"

"You could fuck me." Her head lifted off the pillow, allowing our lips to brush as she spoke. I released a feral growl and crushed my mouth on hers, enjoying a passionate moment before drifting back to sleep—sated and relaxed.

Chester's deep roar woke the house some hours later, thundering through the rooms as he sought help. After throwing on some clothes, we raced up the stairs, arriving on the landing at the same time as a sleepy Liam.

"What the fuck's going on?" He scratched his head before Chester's booming voice drew attention again. Charlie hid behind me when he knocked on the door, biting her bottom lip as she quivered in humour.

"It's unlocked!" Chester hollered, almost to hysteria. "Get me the fuck out of here!"

Liam opened the door with grave concern that was soon replaced with amusement at the sight greeting him. He fell to the floor, and his contagious laughter was the perfect response to our handiwork.

He shouted to the rest of the band to check out the scene. Thunderous footsteps alerted us to their arrival, and the reactions didn't disappoint as they joined in the commotion. When Mark started taking photos, I had tears rolling down my cheeks.

"Stop fucking laughing and get me out!" Chester's pleas fueled the fire, and we all buckled over again.

Anchored in place, he could do nothing in his current state besides accept our merriment. Being Saran wrapped in the bed will do that to you.

I sat next to him, and his nervous laugh didn't go unnoticed.

"Alright, dude. I'm sorry." *Now he was.* I wanted to laugh when he said he was "busting for a piss."

"That's unfortunate." He guffawed and apologised again.

I rolled my eyes. "Sounds really sincere."

"What the fuck do you want me to say?" He lifted his head and shrugged his shoulders.

"How about 'Sorry, Brax. I'm an asshole.'"

"I'm a loveable one, right?" I shook my head at the twat. *Fucking joker!*

"It's debatable," I replied, much to Charlie's delight.

He surrendered, muttering the words, "I'm sorry for being a prick."

"Good, man." I patted his cheek. "Now, I want you to think about what you've done. We'll be back soon to let you out."

"I need a piss," he pleaded as I stood up. Charlie giggled and suggested "cross your legs," knowing he couldn't.

"Fine! Keep your fucking hands to yourself in future though, got it?" I leaned in and when Charlie went to fetch a pair of scissors, whispered, "And for the record, she doesn't need Ben Wa balls, if you get what I'm saying." His laughter ricocheted around the room.

"I expect you have this out of your system now?" Marcus asked after we made our way downstairs. When I agreed, he added, "Good. No more shit from either of you."

"When the fuck did you even do that, bro?" Chester interrupted as he jumped off the last step. He flopped back on the couch, awaiting an answer.

"When I knew you wouldn't wake up." *This fool. For over three years, we'd been best friends and bandmates. I knew when to strike.*

We returned to the room to get sorted for the afternoon. Marcus had scheduled a non-negotiable rehearsal with Glaze, and the girls were coming with us. It would be a great chance to grab some photos for social media, plus I enjoyed having her there when I performed. She had a calming presence which brought clarity and fluency to the music. After all, she was my muse for the new album.

"Hey, Chris!" I headed over as I spoke, recognising the leader of Glaze. He was a classic punk rocker wearing skinny, ripped jeans so dark they matched his curly mop-top and moustache. Despite his elevated position in the industry, he was down to earth and welcoming. "It's good to meet you."

"Likewise, Brax." He shook my hand before turning to his bandmates. "This is April and Brett, as well as our crew." Brett was so similar in appearance to Chris that they'd often been mistaken as relatives. He welcomed us to Canada as he went around the group shaking hands. April was talking to the girls. A petite blond with a pixie bob, but her vocals packed a punch.

Everyone started chatting amongst themselves, and Charlie and I soon found ourselves sitting across from Chris. We'd spoken a few times since the tour was announced, brainstorming ideas and bouncing off one another. He was a talented writer, but his ear for tone was unreal. I was excited for us to work with him and saw a real opportunity to learn from Glaze. "Safe trip?" he enquired.

"No hiccups."

"And you must be Charlie." Chris turned to her with a smile, she shook his hand. "I feel like I already know you. Brax speaks fondly of your support and involvement in his career."

"Thank you." She blushed. "I'm very proud of him. And I'm excited to see what you both have in mind for this collaboration."

Seeming shocked, he shifted in his chair, facing me. "So you looked over it?" *What artist would pass up an opportunity to work with Glaze?*

"Mate, Abandoned Bygone is *all* in."

"Let's fucking do it!"

I woke the following day to Brax leaning on me, tickling my cheeks with the strands of my hair. "Quit it, you pest. I'm sleeping." I groaned and tried shrugging him off.

"Are you tired?" The sarcasm saturated his voice.

"Yes."

"Sucks when you're trying to sleep and someone keeps badgering you, doesn't it?"

"Funny fucker."

I snorted, pulling the blanket up further. He wasn't impressed and tore it back before rolling on top of me. Using the stubble on his cheeks, he started tickling my face and chest. I gripped his head, squealing, "Alright, you baboon. I'm awake!" He sat up on my hips, beating his chest and insisting he was a caveman. "You're an idiot. I'm awake, okay. But why?"

"I've got a surprise," he mumbled. He kissed my nose adding, "I need you to come with me to the studio." *You're lucky I love you!* This bed was to die for and felt like a mirage of clouds encompassing me.

We showered and dressed, then plucked up our coats and sat around the kitchen island having a coffee before we left. "You're off early?" Marcus jogged off the stairs, pulling his sweater on. "Did I miss something?"

"I'm meeting Chris at the studio," Brax explained. "I've got some stuff I wanna work through with him before we hit the road. Charlie was awake, so she offered to come with me." *What the fuck? No, I didn't!* He silenced me with a kiss and pleading eyes, then waved without looking up from his mobile phone. "See you in a few hours, M!"

"This better be good," I mumbled as we headed outside.

"I promise it'll be worth it." He reassured me with a cheeky grin once we got in the car. I sucked my teeth, still unimpressed. We arrived at the studio, and he took my hand, leading us inside. I peered in the dimly lit recording booth to see Chris, Nick and some techs occupying it. Brax stuck his head around the corner and waved to them.

"Hey, man! Good to see you." Chris raced out and greeted us. "I was going over that track we discussed with Nick." He turned, pointing to his manager. Nick was in another world, headphones protecting his ears from any outside interference. His foot tapped along to the smooth rhythm only he was privy to. "What brought you down here?" Brax reached into his pocket and waved a folded piece of paper at him. "I came bearing gifts," he said, smiling. My head wobbled between them. Chris leaned back against one soundboard, pursuing the piece of paper. His excited eyes darted feverishly across the page, back and forth. I wondered if he was reading it more than once.

"You wrote this since we spoke?" Chris asked and Brax nodded. *He wrote something?* I knew there was talk of a collaboration, but discussions weren't that advanced. "This is tight!" He sprung to his feet, bumping his fist with Brax. "Can we show Nick? Have you got time now? Could we experiment with it?" His enthusiasm was running feverishly, as evidenced by his rapid-fire questions.

"For sure, that's why I came down." Brax grabbed my hand and led me to the couch at the back, and I sat down next to him. Once Chris headed over to Nick, I asked what was going on.

"Chris invited me to write a rap verse for their new song. We thought we'd see how well our vocals blended, then look at having both bands engineer a track together." Brax shrugged his shoulders and then shuffled into his seat. "So I agreed. It's a mad tune."

"Brax!" My heart swelled with love at his achievement. I knew an international collaboration would be a massive accomplishment for them. "I wanted you here because there's a personal touch," he pressed on. "Just for you." I froze, realising what he'd said. Our eyes locked, and an overwhelming intimacy seeped from the glance he threw me. "Did I just hit you in the feels?" he teased. I blinked rapidly, trying to process what he'd said, but noticed a sense of nervousness wash over him. The shock had only slightly waned when I reached out and took his hand.

"You wrote a song for me?"

"A verse," he corrected. "But, yes, Charlie. It's for you." That's when it hit me. My life was only this beautiful because with his love came reason. In moments like this, I could get lost in his eyes, my thoughts never straying far. Loving someone is the best feeling in the world, and knowing that he wanted to express ours through his words—exposing his heart to the world—was indescribable. His curious voice pierced my thoughts. "Say something."

"Can I read it?" I asked, my pleading eyes meeting him. He dug into his pocket before handing me another piece of paper. His hand quivered, and that slight twitch exposed the depth of his feelings. My opinion meant *that* much.

> She came to me like the flower in the sky,
> The aromatic spring air induced a fever-pitched high.
> Casting a spell with those eyes, so I brought my soul to the moment;
> Was it a love spell, or was this cutie that potent?
> As sweet as the nectar she seeks, she's in the warming summer breeze,
> She's the wings to lift the man and the driver of his victories.
> Her love engulfed me like the waves of a Tsunami,
> Because of all I ever needed, it was always you, Charlie.

Between tear-stained cheeks, I chuckled sheepishly, humbled beyond belief. "Man, I swear even the birds would shut up to hear your laughter," Brax whispered. He reached out, stroking the hair from my cheek, and his intense eyes scrutinised me. "That beautiful melody emerges and fills the air. There's no other sound like it."

"Sorry for laughing. I can't believe you wrote this for me."

"It's the exact reaction I was hoping for."

"You're amazing." I cried, gripping his cheeks, "*and* incredible." Leaning forward, I took his lips delicately on mine, thanking him for his love.

"Are you sure you like it?"

I nodded my head. "I love it."

He took the initiative and rubbed his hand across my stomach, navel, and down my legs, pulling me closer to him. Nick and Chris were in the booth talking, not that he seemed to care, but I appreciated that the room's design slightly obscured us. Seconds later, his mouth devoured me. We took turns letting our tongues twirl, touch, and lick-exploring languidly for as long as we could stand. He pushed his body firmer against me, forcefully probing my mouth, then slipped his hand inside my jacket to cup my breast.

"Brax..." I gently pressed against him, then spoke more sternly. "Brax, stop. Not here."

"I know," he mumbled before his tongue ploughed back into my mouth. I took it without questions, and his hands eagerly rubbed my sensitised skin. We heard the booth creak and turned as Chris and Nick exited. He kissed my nose, squeezing my hip as we separated.

"Hey, Brax," Nick said as they shook hands. "Chris just showed me what you wrote. Outstanding. Truly appreciate it." Brax nodded a silent thank you and he continued. "Did you have some time this morning? I wouldn't mind fetching our sound engineer. See if we can't mix around with it?" He stopped, but then clicked his fingers as he walked towards the door. "Let me get Marcus down here." He raced out of the studio, leaving us stunned.

"He's always like this when an idea strikes," Chris explained. "Would you mind giving us half an hour to prepare everything?"

"It's honestly no problem," Brax assured him. "We don't have anywhere else to be."

"Great! Please make yourselves comfortable while you wait." He waved around the room. "Can I bring you both a drink back? Coffee perhaps?"

"That sounds great. Thanks, man."

The moment the room was empty, we stood to remove our coats, and I turned back to Brax. My eyes quickly scanned the booth, when I realised there weren't any cameras, I moved closer to him. My emotions were coursing through me; the overwhelming desire and love of his lyrics had caused a flood of arousal. My hand pressed on his neck, pulling him down for a deep kiss, I could still taste myself on his lips from earlier. Stepping back, I stared hard into his eyes, and noticed his head twitch. "I thought we agreed we couldn't do this?" His eyebrow raised as he questioned my motives. "You're making it difficult."

His eyes roamed my body, and the provocative sashay of my hips had him smirking. He sat on the oversized leather chair meant for the sound engineer and double checked our surroundings. Leaning back on the control panel, I felt my sweater creep up, exposing a slither of skin. His lust-filled eyes spurred me on, so I bent forward, closer to the soundboard, perpetuating my seduction. Within seconds, his powerful arms wrapped around my stomach, pulling my body upright. His chest rose and fell against my back, and then his face pressed into my neck. While his lips deliciously teased, his hand crept down my torso. I grabbed his wrist and resisted. "Here?"

"Right here, Charlie." The desperation in his voice made my knees wobble. His hand slid inside my waistband, and skilled fingers inched under my panties to glide through my slickness.

"Brax!" A heavy moan whined from my lips as he penetrated me. I lurched forward, gripping the desk to steady myself. He fingered me slowly then quickly, depending on my body's reaction, stopping only momentarily to recheck our surroundings. After making sure the studio was still quiet, he resumed by kneeling and giving my ass cheeks a series of kisses. I whimpered, and he pulled back slightly.

"What is it, baby? Do you need me to show you the love my words can't?" I nodded, still facing away from him, and his fingers started stroking again. My palms stiffened against the panel, and my head hunched forward. He kept moving rhythmically as my hips rocked in sync, then drew me out of the bubble of pleasure when he stood. Turning my head, he greeted me with moistened lips. His stubble rubbed against my chin as he kissed his way up my neck before returning to my mouth.

When our tongues collided, Brax released a raw growl. He yanked me towards him, panting, "Come here." He tried edging my pants down, and for a minute, I panicked when I remembered where we were. I grabbed his hands, trying to push them back. "It's too risky," I whispered with wide eyes.

"We'll be quick," he told me. "I know we have little time, but I'm so worked up." My eyes flicked down to his hard-on. I quickly removed my pants as he sat back in the chair, hastily unfastening his own. Moving closer, I straddled him, and he wasted no time removing my sweater. He pushed my shirt up slightly, exposing my bra-covered breasts. Pulling the cups down, he lapped at them, rubbing, kissing and licking desperately. "Fuck, I love the taste of you," he mumbled into my flesh while continuing his assault. "Every inch." I hurried him along by pulling out Brax's erection. I lined it up, parted my lips, and relaxed onto him. My mouth hung wide, appreciating the pleasure coursing through me. He groaned and offered his arms to steady us. I gasped and looked down as he thrust hard up into me. I rode him wildly, then cried out falling forward onto his chest. His hand connected with my backside, his fingers lingering to grip deep into my flesh. "Hop up, baby. Turn around."

By the time I had hands on the soundboard to steady myself, he was behind me, bending at the knees as he slid back into my moistened centre. He thrust harder, holding my hips while delivering another smack to my ass. Droplets of sweat poured down my spine, and my hair started covering my face. With each thrust, my cheeks crushed against his sweaty pelvis, and the flesh on my backside rippled as he sunk in. His hands wandered from my hips with purpose, gripping my shoulders for more control. The stirring of an orgasm intensified, and his strokes became erratic in time with my quivering muscles. When he rotated his hips, I fluttered over the edge. My nose scrunched through closed eyes as I released a throaty cry of satisfaction. The reverberations continued to shatter me, and my thighs vibrated with each new impact. He came hard inside me, and my whole body spasmed with the ripples of pleasure. A hard orgasm, seeping with love, tingled through me. With a firm clutch on my waist, his chest heaved against my back, desperate to replace the lost oxygen from that explosion. The moment ended when I opened my eyes and remembered where we were. After scrambling for my clothes, we both urgently dressed. I opened the door, looking each way before hurrying down the hallway to the bathrooms. I tidied myself up and returned to the booth where Brax had cleared any evidence of our indiscretion.

"You're so bad." I smirked at him, sitting casually back on the couch. "I love being bad with you," he tormented back with a wink. We sat together, drained and dehydrated. Two bodies soaked in sensory overload, bathing in a cocktail of raw emotion. It was over ten minutes before Nick and Chris returned with their engineer.

Marcus slid in shortly after, cracking his knuckles, alerting us to his eagerness. "Ready when you are."

Chapter Seven

BRAX

My adrenaline pumped like liquid nitrogen as I stood in the booth with Chris, listening to his distinctive vocals. This small token could open many doors for my bandmates, and I wanted that. Their hard work and dedication was paying off.

I regulated my breathing, preparing for my verse, when I caught Marcus' gaze, a slight head nod comforting me in support. He was the most committed and devoted manager we could've asked for. His immense generosity in giving of his time and expertise enabled us to grow and succeed, while also providing invaluable insight into our lives. He had this incredible ability to use rationale and heart to douse the fires that teetered around us.

The words rushed out like a gust of wind, and I opened my eyes, looking for Charlie. I could achieve anything with her by my side. The sensations ebbed and flowed, motivating and inspiring me higher. I felt celestial as the emotional tide expelled and found myself more connected to the music because of its uniquely personal tone. The words were the kind that built majestic mountains from pebbles and stone. The rush of excitement was still pumping through my veins as an eruption of approval from everyone greeted us. "We need to get these bands together," Nick suggested enthusiastically.

Marcus patted him on the shoulder. "Let me set up an appointment."

After shaking hands with Chris, I excused myself, seeing an excited Charlie waiting to the side. Her face radiated as I moved across the room, and when I was close enough, she flung her arms around my neck. "You're such an inspiration to me," she whispered. It tore through me, and tingles rippled under my skin. There were few people whose opinion meant everything, and she was top of the list. "I'm in awe of you."

"T-thank you," I said, stumbling over my words. "That means so much coming from you." She gripped my face and kissed me tenderly. "Let's head out for dinner tonight? I'd love some time alone." Her eyes sparkled and reignited those feelings I'd been experiencing for months—that longing for more. After today, all I wanted was to tell my band the great news and then find my peace in her before we hit the road.

"Do it," Chris answered as he joined us. We both looked at him, amused. "Brett texted an hour ago. He and Chester organised for everyone to have drinks tonight." He shrugged his shoulders, wondering if I knew anything about it. I pulled my phone out and found a similar message. "Of course they did," I added, shaking my head.

"Although he should know better," Chris muttered while tapping out a message on his screen. He glanced up and saw our puzzled looks. "Brett's managing a hernia at the moment. This isn't the tour for him to go wild on."

"And it hasn't even started, yet," Charlie shook her head.

I texted to advise that we were leaving, and Marcus replied he was staying to discuss contracts and coordinate security with Nick. When we returned to the house, I walked inside with an extra bounce in my step. It was the perfect time to share with the boys, right before the tour! *What a way to start.* We hung our coats, headed into the kitchen, and switched on the espresso machine before moving to the bottom of the stairs. "You guys up there?" I hollered and waited to hear. Once they'd acknowledged, I asked, "Can we have a chat?"

"I'll make some coffee so you can fill the boys in," Charlie offered. I thanked her with a kiss and grabbed a seat. When the band assembled in the lounge, Mark turned to me.

"This looks important," he discerned, noticing my serious demeanour, "but also good." He cocked his head, observing closer. I was buzzing, and it was proving difficult to hide.

"Is this why you disappeared earlier?" Liam enquired seconds later. I nodded. "You remember at the airport Marcus and I spoke with you about collaborating?"

"With Glaze?" Chester spelt it out to be sure, then added, "You wanna discuss it further?"

"Yeah, mate. I do." I smiled at my band and took a deep breath before continuing. "Chris allowed me to appear on a new song of theirs."

"You said yes, right?" Shane shot out of his chair, and the other boys hummed a multitude of questions. I waited as Charlie came over with a tray and everyone's drinks.

"I'm going to check on Kendall," she said, pointing upstairs, "and let you boys talk."

"Thanks, Cutie." I took a sip before continuing. "It's a small verse for the song's bridge, but yeah, I did it." They were congratulating me, and I appreciated it, but they were missing the point.

"Hang on." Mark clicked his fingers at me. "You said you did it?" Their heads swivelled as they caught up.

"I showed Chris and Nick the verse this morning, and we experimented with it." They were buzzing and eager to hear more. "It went so well that Marcus and Nick are negotiating a collaboration now." The raucous noise that shattered the lounge room was electrifying.

Shane's jubilant voice greeted me with a fist bump to match. "This is an enormous opportunity, my man."

"I can't wait to see what you engineer on this," I promised him. His cheeks looked ready to burst with elation.

"Now we have a reason to celebrate tonight!" Chester punched the air as he jumped up.

"Yeah, about that..." I clicked my fingers, indicating to sit down.

"I found out today Brett is managing a hernia, so he doesn't need any encouragement. That means *you*." I smirked at Chester. "And second, Charlie and I are going out for dinner."

I was waiting for her to finish in the bathroom when I suggested we go to a quiet pub for a relaxed meal. I'd noticed a few on the drive back.

"Sounds great," she replied happily. I ran upstairs to clear it with security, then let the boys know we would leave shortly.

Twenty minutes later, I walked around to the frosted footpath, helping her out of the car. I held the thick oak wood doors ajar, allowing Charlie inside first. She removed her coat, and my fingers inched across her gorgeous ass, admiring it with a gentle rub. I took her hand in mine, massaging her fingers to warm them, and followed the waitress through to our table. We sat back with wine and beer after ordering meals. The leather booths afforded privacy, which I was thankful for. We sat close, completely engrossed in each other, with my arm lovingly wrapped around her.

"You're more excited about the tour, aren't you?" she asked as we ate our meals. My head turned with a questioning look, so she added. "It buzzed you—telling the boys."

"I was rattling," I chuckled. "Today was…" I struggled to articulate my feelings. She put her cutlery down and turned to face me. I picked up her hand, kissing her soft fingertips. "Everything's finally coming together. When I think about what I went through to get here, I'm thankful I didn't give up during those hard times." I wasn't always an intelligent fighter and didn't take all the right turns along the way. She taught me to be tough, beautiful, strong, thoughtful, and humble. I was no longer just trying to fit in; I was content within my skin.

"Giving up isn't in your DNA, Brax." *True*. She met my gaze and added, "Just look at us." We shared an intimate kiss, my way of thanking her without words, and finished our meals. My thoughts wandered to what the next few weeks could have in store for us. Shaking it off, I patted her thigh, drawing attention.

"Fancy another drink before we head back to the circus?" I smirked. "I would love to." She giggled, then slid closer to me in the booth. "Although I have to ask, are you trying to get me drunk to take advantage?" She turned her body, and her hand grazed my jeans, sliding closer to my groin.

"Always," I whispered, adjusting in my seat. I wrapped my hand around her fingers, dragging them up to rest over my dick. The amusement was comical when I called her bluff.

"Behave yourself. It won't be long before the band's as well known globally as you are back home." I pecked her nose, appreciating her investment in my career. "Let me go grab those drinks," she said. She leaned in and kissed me again, mumbling, "I'll be back."

She returned with our drinks and as she sat down, said, "May I ask you something?" I nodded behind my beer bottle. "What made you decide to write those lyrics? You hate sharing your personal life with the media. That was a pretty bold move." My eyes roamed down to meet hers. The bond of love we had created gave free passage to our souls and reflected the sense of home found together.

"Truthfully, I wasn't thinking about any of that," I admitted. "The only person I was thinking of was you." Charlie's body relaxed and her arms caressed me into a loving embrace. A silent thank you. "Finding inspiration used to be a genuine struggle. I wanted to write, but the words would never flow fluently. Jumbled and combative, a vortex of inner monologue would make it difficult to get out of my head. Then you came along." I remembered when I first met her and started forming our song. "It helped me to write 'Clarity.' Did you know that?"

"Really?" Her shock, while adorable, laced me with amusement. "Why do you still struggle to believe the impact you play in my life?" I brushed back her golden hair, wanting to see her radiance unhindered. When I cupped her cheek, her head rolled into it further. "One day, I hope you can see yourself through my eyes and understand you are so much more than you give yourself credit for."

"I never knew I needed love. It wasn't until you, Brax. You're the key to all of this." I shook my head in disagreement, but she stopped me by putting her finger to my lips. "I'm so glad I stayed that night in your arms back in Stanthorpe. You took my heart in a way no other person is capable of. *I'm* the lucky one. Because, after all this time, you've chosen to remain my lover and best friend. I can't wait to see what we accomplish together."

Without a word, I wrapped my arms around her tightly and pulled her into me. I found the sweetest of passion on her lips as we deeply embraced. Our bodies moulded effortlessly and enticingly. In that kiss, I felt the tangible nature of our weaving souls.

"How about one more drink before we go?" she suggested.

"Sounds good, Cutie." I pulled out my wallet, handing her my card. "Would you mind grabbing them while I use the restroom?"

After finishing, I quickly made my way back through the dimly lit hallway to see if I could help Charlie. As I rounded the corner to the bar, she was still at the counter, ordering our drinks, but I noticed a man had approached. She turned her back when he called her by name, so I waited to see how she would address the familiar stranger.

"Charlotte, is that you?" he asked. Her body became rigid, and he pressed on when no words were forthcoming. "I knew it was." She stepped back as his eyes drank her in. I felt a wave of protectiveness when I noticed his primal intent. "Wow, you've grown, haven't you?" The bartender put the drinks down on the counter, drawing her attention. I moved closer and heard him repeat her name again, his thick London accent piercing the room. He stepped closer and towered over her. He was well over six feet, but not as tall as I was, and appeared regimented—almost military—with a buzz cut of gold hair plastered to his head. Overcompensating muscles made her look smaller in stature. "Aren't you going to talk?" he pressed when she still hadn't spoken up. Stumbling over the words and hands shaking, she finally mumbled without making eye contact. "I-I.. ahh, what are you doing here?" The ice rattled against the glass as she tried to steady her hands while holding our drinks. The onset of panic was visible.

"Ski season." He shrugged casually and pointed to a table occupied by three other men. "I'm here with friends. Why don't you join me?"

When he reached out to touch her arm, she immediately dropped the drinks, trying to retreat. The explosive sound of glass shattering on the tiled floor made my bones rattle, and the entire venue turned to look at the commotion. She spun around, fumbling an apology to the bartender. I finally reached them, placing my hand carefully on her waist so as not to alarm her any further. With glassy eyes, her head spun, and I knew she was in a heightened state of panic. The trembling had taken over her body, spreading like wildfire. Not to mention the death grip she had on me, willing for protection.

"Are you okay? What happened?" I looked between Charlie and the guy that was still lingering. "You're shaking." She opened her mouth, still stunned silent, and just when she went to try again, the guy cut in.

"Excuse me, do you mind? We're having a private conversation." His thick English drawl, while distinguished, had a less than innocent sneer behind it, immediately rubbing me the wrong way. "I do mind," I snarled. Standing taller, I turned directly to him and felt her grip tighten. She inched her body behind me, using it as a shield for protection. "I'm Charlotte's partner, and I don't know exactly what happened here. However, I know my girlfriend well enough to see when she's uncomfortable." I wrapped my arm around her shoulders, pulling her in. A defensive move, just as much for my benefit as it was hers. "Who are you anyway?"

"It's Calvin," Charlie's quivering voice explained. I looked down at her, instantly grabbing her hands when I saw the tremors had intensified. "Brax, can we go, please?" Her eyes swelled with moisture, the tears threatening to take over at any second. She sucked in a deep breath as her body shook.

I'd seen enough. *Never* in my wildest dreams had I imagined I'd be standing in front of the man who'd tormented the woman I loved for so much of her youth. Rage coursed through me, and while my masculine instinct was to knock the porcelain veneers smiling back at me down his throat, now was not the time. She needed me more. I swallowed the anger that felt like a fire seed burning in the pit of my stomach.

"Come on, baby. Let's get you outta here." I focused directly on her as if he didn't exist. It was the only thing stopping me from acting on the scenes of carnage swirling in my mind. The acidic fury battled internally.

I held Charlie in front of me, keeping myself as a shield between her and Calvin, while we collected our coats and made our way to the door. Once we were in the cab's safety, she buried her face in my chest while the tears tore through. It was more than crying; it was the desolate sobbing from a sudden confrontation with one's living fears. Not wanting to startle her, I lowered my voice and promised she was okay. "No one will hurt you, Charlie. Not while I'm here. You have my word. You're safe." She nodded, but still found little strength to form words. "Sweetheart, I need you to tell me everything. As we did with your Dad, you know I'll always stand by you. But you have to let me help."

"What do you mean?" She sobbed back, trying to wipe her face of the distress.

"What did Calvin do to you?" My voice was nurturing and soft, but demanding. While she'd told me of her father's role in her childhood traumas, encouraging her to open up about Calvin had proven difficult.

"Can we get outta here first?" she asked weakly.

It took a while for Charlie to calm down, and rightfully so. She'd been upset before, but this level of anguish was like nothing I'd experienced. There had to be more to the story that she hadn't told me. I waited until she settled before we took off back to the house. For the entire drive, I kept my hand firmly in her lap, squeezing her tiny fingers between mine—a token gesture of comfort.

The ride was silent, and it took a few minutes for her to register when we arrived. I walked around to her side and took her in my arms when she got out. We stood in comfortable silence, her heart racing against mine. Her arms wrapped around me tightly, fear driving her to squeeze harder. I didn't want to push her into talking; I could sense she wasn't ready. All I needed her to know was that she had me, that I had gone nowhere. With a heavy sigh, she pulled back. I stroked her face and wiped her tear-stained cheeks, which had flushed from the bitter cold lashing against us.

"Do you wanna go to bed?" I asked. "I can let the others know you aren't feeling well after dinner." She didn't speak at first, then she slowly shook her head, unsure of what she wanted. "Can we just stay here for a few more minutes?"

"As long as you need." She cuddled back into my chest as I vigorously rubbed her back, trying to warm us both up. I leaned down and kissed the tip of her nose. "I love you."

It seemed to be what she needed to hear as she mumbled into my chest, "I love you too."

Reaching up, her arm wrapped around my neck and brought my head down to hers. I kissed her softly, a gentle caress, raw in emotion, passion, protection, and love. *So much love.* I could see the tears in her eyes, and my thumb tenderly wiped away the strays until the front door opened. She quickly hid her face in my chest, unsure who it was, but sighed in relief upon hearing Marcus' voice.

"I thought I saw a car pull up. Are you two okay?"

"We're fine," I told him. "Just enjoying a few more minutes of quiet before—"

"Chester?" I chuckled and agreed when he cut me off. "Alright. Well, don't stay out here too long. You'll both freeze. Mace has arrived safely, and the other boys are here."

Marcus left the door slightly open for us as he headed inside, and I turned my attention back to the only one that mattered. "You ready? You know I'll support you either way."

"Just give me a minute. I wouldn't mind freshening up, and then I'll come out to see Mace. Play it by ear from there, babe." I nodded and extended my hand.

We headed inside, and she went to our room to tidy up and give herself a few minutes to process what had just happened.

I grabbed a beer from the fridge, then greeted everyone. "There's one of my other favourite girls. Glad you arrived safely." Mace turned when she heard my voice, then came bouncing over to greet me. "Where's my beauty?" she enquired, pulling out of the hug.

I cocked my head with a smirk. "You mean *my* girl?"

"No, I meant *mine*." I laughed and cuddled her tighter. "She'll be out in a second. How was your flight?"

"Painfully long and boring."

"He didn't ask about your relationship with Liam, Mason! He asked about the flight!"

Fucking Chester! We all cracked up as she flipped Monkey the finger, and Liam called him an asshole.

"So, where *is* my favourite girl?" he teased.

Raising my eyebrow, I corrected him. "My girl."

"No, I meant mine."

"No, you didn't," I replied in a monotone. "She's just chucking on some warmer clothes."

"But she loves the cold?"

"I know. Don't ask me to explain female logic." I shrugged, then took a sip of beer.

"I heard that, Brax! All of it." Chester bounded out of his seat towards her. Charlie's immediate reaction was to question, "What did you do now?"

"Me?" He pressed his index finger to his chest.

"You're being nice, sucking up even. It usually spells trouble."

"Sweet Cheeks, can't I just be happy to see you?" I kept a cautious eye when Chester mucked about with Charlie, knowing she'd had a turbulent evening. If nothing else, it was the distraction she needed. He bent down to her eye level, inspecting her closer, before ushering her inside. *What's he up to?* The pair looked thick as thieves whispering with their heads huddled together. With his arm slung around her shoulders, they moved from the lounge to the kitchen. Leaning on the kitchen island, he listened intently. I could only assume she was telling him about the incident with Calvin. I appreciated Chester as one of my closest mates, especially when I saw him open his arms for Charlie bringing her around the counter into a hug.

I afforded them a few moments of privacy before excusing myself and heading in to see if she was alright. I got to the kitchen and leaned against the doorframe, being sure not to interrupt their conversation.

An opportunity arose to speak, and I asked, "you alright?" Chester turned when he heard my voice.

"Sorry, bro, I didn't mean to take her away for so long. I just…" I cut Chester off, holding my hand up. "Mate, it's fine. Thank you."

He nodded in understanding before Charlie explained, "apparently my puffy eyes gave it away." I'd believe it. Chester always was the observant one.

"You all good, Brax?" He tilted his head, forcing eye contact. I gave him a polite nod. "If that were me, I would've buried him."

"Why are you talking in the past tense?" My question told him that the fury was still bubbling.

"Well, the plus side is we leave tomorrow." Charlie nodded between us both.

"Let's just hope we never see him again." I shrugged, stuffing my hands in the pockets of the hoodie. My fists knotted against the fabric as I tried not to let the aggression he evoked consume me.

"Happy to help you take care of it?" he offered. I lifted my head. We had a silent understanding. He could see the internal battle I was facing. I was where I needed to be, making sure Charlie was alright, but damn, if there wasn't a part of me that had thought about returning to find him.

"Thanks, Monkey, but I prefer to keep you out of jail." She gave him another hug. She started poking his ribs as she told him, "you need to find yourself a nice girl already." Her way of changing the conversation.

"I find many nice girls all the time." Our eyes locked, and I smirked.

"Not those kinds, Monkey!" She squeaked, to my amusement.

After Mace and Charlie had a catch-up, she came and sat down in my lap while we got stoned together. It wasn't the best coping mechanism, but it was the only one we knew. Demons from her past ruined what should have been a good night out for us together, and it pissed me off. After a couple of joints, Charlie sat up and told me, "I'm going to bed, babe," before saying, "goodnight" to everyone. I excused myself to join her after agreeing to meet Glaze in the city tomorrow morning at ten. They were heading off also, ensuring Brett got plenty of rest.

We walked to our room and undressed. I pulled on my track pants, ready for bed, and I couldn't help but smile, observing her shuffle over to my suitcase. She picked up the shirt I had just taken off and put it on. It was when I found her the most beautiful. During those times I'd travel for work, or when she wasn't feeling her best, she turned to something of mine for comfort. I realised some time ago that it was her finding safety in the love we had created. *Fuck*, I was one lucky bastard to experience that with her. We laid down, and she rolled into my arms. Her cheek pressed against my chest while her hair splayed down her back, the occasional stray strand tickling the sensitised skin of my stomach. I flicked the television on to the football and slouched back into the pillows, while stroking her silk strands through my fingers. The television had become white noise as I lay quietly in the darkened room with her.

"Brax?" I twisted my body to answer her. She swallowed deeply, mustering what energy she could find. "Do you remember I mentioned we went over to England and Calvin and his parents came to see us before we left?" I nodded, then she said, "I've prayed every day since then, hoping I would never see his face again." My grip tightened, but I stayed silent. They had silenced her for too long. "The phone calls that started when we returned were worse than I could've imagined. But I sat quietly like I was told, hoping it would be over soon."

"Can I ask you something?" I stroked the hair back off her face, and she blinked up at me. Struggling to maintain eye contact, she eventually nodded. "Why's he scare you so much?" I felt her shake again at the mention of Calvin, those past traumas threatening to distort the present. It was a deathly blanket of emptiness as the vortex sucked her back into the nightmare she had long suppressed. "You know you're safe. I'll let nothing happen to you. But I need you to tell me everything; it's time, Charlotte. You've gotta let it go to move forward."

As children, we turn to our fathers for protection, so any feelings of betrayal Charlie had were well justified. I'd always felt this gnawing sensation in the pit of my stomach, as if there was so much more to be said. Yet, repeatedly, Charlie failed to find her voice. Her terror tonight confirmed my suspicions, so I asked, "Why're you scared to tell me the full story?"

"I-It's just," she went to speak. Her mouth closed momentarily before lowering her voice, "I don't want it to change things between us or for you to look at me differently." I moved closer to her on the bed. We lay side by side, heads resting on the pillow, and I reached over to stroke her cheek. Her eyes searched mine, fear with a slight tinge of hope engulfing her face.

"I'm going to marry you one day, Charlotte. Don't mistake those words." I spoke in measured out syllables, "it will happen." I nodded my head to emphasise the point. "It's impossible to imagine my life without you. Something you had no control over, that you were a victim of, will never change how I feel." A weak smile crept across her face; her eyes, full of emotion, mirrored my own.

"You know, I used to be terrified of that word."

That word. Marriage.

One word that held so much weight behind it. I was pretty sure I knew the answer, but had to ask, "and how does it make you feel now?"

"All I can think about is what it'd be like being married to you," she sighed. "To call you my husband... I want that. But only with you." I covered her right cheek in a flurry of soft kisses as my hand gripped her head.

"Good. I want you to be my wife, to spend our lives together, to share everything that comes our way." I softly stroked her cheek, and pleaded, "open up. Let me be here for you. We're better together." Her hand slid up and gripped my wrist. She moved her head back to make eye contact so my body half covered hers.

"It's hard to explain," she said. Blowing out a heavy breath, adding, "sometimes, it's easier if there is a single incident or, as much as I hate to say it, physical abuse. Because those scars are easier to explain and for people to comprehend." She paused and looked over. "Does that make sense?" Her eyes searched mine, hoping for my understanding.

"Of course. But it doesn't diminish what happened to you, either." Charlie had avidly fought against the stigma of being a victim, and I'd never once seen her as anything other than a survivor, a warrior, a force to be reckoned with. She was the phoenix that rose, the enigma we all chased, the spirit no one had a right to control.

"It was the ongoing emotional stress, Brax." I felt her body relax slightly in my arms, contrasting with my hold. "When they arrived, the information his parents wanted to know made little sense to me. Then the phone calls started not long after we returned home, and their intentions were pretty blatant." The raw pain she had suppressed leaked painfully and visibly, though she was quick to shake it off, determined to take this next step in her freedom. "They asked questions about my sexuality and activity because naturally, they expected me to wait for him." I tried to speak, but she rushed on, preventing any of the multiple questions that triggered. "They monitored what I ate, my figure, weight and size, even my intelligence. You name it; they wanted to know everything." It rushed out so rapidly that she had to stop and take a few deep breaths. Years of digression had built into a cyclonic eruption of words. "They didn't allow me to colour or cut my hair without checking first. They scrutinised my clothing and prohibited me from wearing make-up. The choice of friends had to be approved because appearance was everything." The more she opened up, the more the adrenaline increased, causing my heart to hammer against my chest. I bit my tongue, patiently reminding myself I was doing this for *her* benefit, not my own. "I tried to tell Dad what was going on, but he never believed me. Whenever I'd repeat what they'd say, he'd shut the conversation down. I don't know whether he didn't believe me, or he didn't want to admit what was happening." The realisation caught her breath.

She revealed her genuine pain. Her father wasn't there for her.

"Calvin offered a stable life, where I'd be quietly out of sight." She mumbled quietly, "that's how dad would have preferred it." My blood boiled over, and against my better judgement, I interrupted her.

"That's bullshit! We both know it. You're too important to be silenced." Charlie stroked my cheek, and I moved in to kiss her, mumbling against her lips. "You're my equal. You complete me, and I hope one day when people see what I accomplish, they know it's because of you." I kissed her again before putting my head back on the pillow, my hand caressing Charlie's shoulder.

"No, babe, you did the hard work; this is-"

"But you gave me the strength to do it," I cut her off. She went to speak again, and I held my finger to her lips. "You challenge me. Because of you, I want to do better, and be the best version of myself. Why would I settle for less?"

"Wouldn't it be easier than my emotional baggage?" *Really?* I couldn't fathom how she thought of herself as anything but strong and impressive. I wished I knew how to stop their domination of her headspace so that she could live unrestrained.

"I never liked it easy. You know that," I rubbed her arm. "I live with a Liverpool supporter." The crinkles in her nose caused me to smile when she scrunched it. Just as quickly, she flicked me on the ear. "Ouch, Evil Midget!" I rubbed it furiously. "I wouldn't have it any other way," I smirked.

"Lucky save."

"I want you to promise me something." I rolled on top and wrapped one arm underneath her head, stroking her cheek with the other. "Hmm, okay," Charlie mumbled curiously.

"Stop giving people space they don't deserve, especially when they don't know your worth. You're so much more than what you just told me. I know it, our friends know it, and baby, I need you to as well." She softly whispered, "I'll try."

"And I'll help you. You're my girl, no one else's, and I'll always lift you when you need it."

"Literally?" I smiled and answered her with an "always."

"Sometimes I just need reminding. I try not to let it affect my life. It's hard, especially when you're not prepared to be confronted by that person." I understood, but didn't want her dwelling on it any further.

She was exhausted and fell asleep quickly. After the game, I was still wired, so I carefully rolled out of bed, pulled the doona up and gave her a gentle kiss. I grabbed my jumper and coat and headed outside for a smoke. The bitter night chill gripped me as I slid the door open, so I fastened my coat tighter. The boys had the same idea and already sat around the table. Chester looked up and asked, "how's Midget doing?" It was a relief to say, "she's finally asleep. Also, thanks for earlier, mate." The rest of the boys were understandably worried, too. "Cheers, boys. I appreciate how much you care." I sparked up and took a draw before I explained what'd happened. "You remember the shit she went through with her father?"

"Has he started again?" Liam jumped in with a raised eyebrow. "I'm not sure yet," I waved my hand to stop him. "It may just be a coincidence." My reply only seemed to puzzle them further. "We went out for dinner, Charlie ordered some drinks while I went for a piss. When I returned, I noticed a guy speaking to her at the bar. She looked panicked, and when I got closer, the old mate gave me attitude."

"Bet that went down well," Shane quipped, and the others agreed. "Any other day," I brushed it off before continuing. "Except, I immediately noticed Charlie was shaking and knew something was wrong. She couldn't wait to get out of there, once we finally did, she explained. The guy who'd approached her was the one her father wanted Charlie with. His friend's son, Calvin."

"Fuck off," Mark's shock was vocal. "What are the odds?"

"Right?" I waved my hand at him. Who would have expected we'd travel halfway across the world, only to walk into a bar and there he was? "The silver lining is, she finally told me the full story of what they did to her," I murmured.

"Good timing," Liam replied. I showed my confusion when I made eye contact with him. "What we discussed at your housewarming?" he prompted. "It's great you got to clear the air first." His face dropped the second he realised what he'd said; however, the rest of the guys were firing questions left, right and centre by that stage—especially Chester, with his fear of missing out.

"Why the fuck does Hippie Boy know something and I don't?" He spat in disgust.

"You guys can't say anything," I pleaded. They immediately started nodding. "Especially you, Chester." The rest of the boys laughed as he tried to protest his innocence. "I know it's not intentional, but this is serious." My stare made him understand how important this was.

"You know I've always got you when it matters, Brax," he promised. It was true, the trust we had in each other was the foundation of our success.

"I'm ready for more with Charlie," I whispered, and with a crack of my knuckles, added, "I'm gonna ask her to marry me." The guys all started muttering, but Mark's comment struck me.

"I'm surprised you haven't already," he shrugged. Then I looked at the others. They all agreed, which left me refuting, "no way! It would have been too soon."

"Are you taking the piss?" Shane laughed out. "You've been after that girl for as long as I've known you."

"I second that," Liam raised his finger. Mark and Chester followed.

"Why are you waiting?" Chester asked directly, sensing there was more to it.

"Until recently, I didn't even know if it was something she wanted." I explained to them adding, "The thought of marriage terrified her because of her childhood." The realisation washed over their faces. The trauma of having to go through life wondering if you would ever get to choose your own happiness was unimaginable. Yet, she survived it. "We talked it through. She knows it's different, and it's something she wants as well."

"When are you gonna do it, Brax?" Shane pressed for more details.

"Once we get back home."

"You won't last that long." Chester's voice broke over the top. I raised my eyebrow, wondering how he knew that, given he seemed so confident in his position. "You'll blurt it out one night when you're buried deep inside her." He jumped up, humping the air. "Charlie, I can't live without your golden pussy; let me wife it." The others laughed while I sucked my teeth at him.

"You need to get laid or watch some porn," Mark shrugged at his antics.

"Nah, just getting it out of my system. Not another word on the subject for the rest of the tour." He pretended to zip his lips and inclined his head towards me.

"Thanks, man." And I meant it. If ever there was a time I needed my bandmates to have my back, this was it!

We'd met Glaze at the cafe and fuelled up with a big brunch and coffee before they took us on a sightseeing tour around the city. We strolled idly, listening to our Canadian counterparts give us the guided experience. Charlie decided she wanted some photos as we wandered closer to the CN Tower. I stood rubbing my hands, feeling the bitter cold snapping against my skin now we'd stopped moving. After digging through her handbag, she pulled out her Nikon Z 7 to line up the shot. I noticed someone moving toward her and realised it was Calvin. By then, he'd already spoken. Charlie's body *froze*, no longer from the chill in the air but from the fear that rattled her bones.

"Are you still wasting your time on that crazy hobby?" He pointed to the camera she held in front of her. I inched over, and I could see her knuckles draining of colour, paler than the snow that laced the footpath. "Such a childhood dream, with no real ambition, Charlotte."

What the fuck?! How dare he demean her accomplishments, especially when he knew nothing about her! She was the essence of innocence in this fucked up world. The more I learned about her past, the greater my protective need grew. Seeing her intimidated had stretched me like an elastic band, the rage ready to explode. The outcome would be catastrophic. The arrogant motherfucker smirked, knowing the effect he had on Charlie, so I stepped between them.

"C-Calvin, what do you want?" She stumbled over her words. The rest of the group quickly moved after hearing his name. I took her wrist and pulled her back. Mark shocked me when he flared up.

"You've got some balls showing your face near us." He was furious. Honestly, I couldn't ever recall seeing him shaken so much. The physical effects of the trauma had set in, and I felt Charlie's hand tremble. I wrapped my arms around her. I didn't need to worry about Calvin. My boys had him covered, and her well-being was more important.

"I'm sorry, did I speak to... who are you anyway?" Calvin's pompous attitude spat back. "I don't know who you think you are, but I can assure you, if you'd like to ring Richard, he will be happy to explain." Livid when he used Charlie's father against her, I was about to respond when Marcus beat me to it.

"Fuck Richard, and fuck you! What kinda sick bastard grooms and emotionally abuses a teenager?" He spat in fury. The noticeable gasp from Kendall reminded me she wasn't aware of Charlie's past.

"You sick bastard!" She spat at Calvin through utter disdain.

"Fucking predator," Mace raged.

"You need to get your women under control. Disgusting mouths on them, especially in public." Calvin tried berating the girls as if he had any moral high ground here. That did it for me, and I nudged Mark aside as I squared up to him.

"What the fuck did you just say? You never disrespect a woman!" I spoke calmly but with determination as I leered closer to him.

"It's understandable, being so common, that you'd think this is acceptable. I thought you had more decorum, Charlotte."

I moved into his line of vision and reminded the asshole, "her name's Charlie."

He smirked back at me and laughed, "Exactly my point. No class-" A fist flew over my shoulder before he finished speaking, causing me to stumble. I turned back to see Calvin on his ass, gripping his left eye, while Marcus stood over him. Stunned momentarily, he glared back up at my manager and sneered, "You'll regret that."

"You know what? I don't think I will." He replied, rubbing his knuckles. "Asshole," Marcus muttered under his breath, punching the air in frustration as he walked away. Craig, our Head of security, immediately rushed over. No doubt to do some damage control.

"I'll be speaking to Richard about this, Charlotte." Calvin tried one more attempt at exerting control over her. She gripped my wrist tighter, and I reached across, wrapping my arm around her shoulder. "Let's go, Brax." She turned as she spoke, but stopped in her tracks when Calvin had to get in the last word. "Think about your actions before I ring him." Something in her snapped. I felt the shift in her body language, she stood taller, firmer, with a new resolve. When she walked back to him, I didn't know what to expect.

"I suggest *you* shut the fuck up and stop telling me what to do!" Her deathly tone was venomous. "You know *nothing* about me! You make me physically sick, and I will never be your trophy wife." Trying to maintain some dignity, he shook his head, not realising how close Charlie was to breaking point.

"It's such a shame you chose this avenue." Calvin paused before delivering the final blow. "You had so much potential." Her rage swelled inside like a deep water current, breaching the confines of the riverbank that kept it flowing safely. The elastic that held her tightly wound for most of her adult life snapped-in spectacular fashion. The years of being forced into passivity against her will had bubbled over. Anyone standing too close would have suffered first-degree burns from the explosion as she flew at him.

"Potential for what, Calvin?" She spat back. "For you to groom me as a teenager? Because that's what it was! Let's not mince words here." Her face turned bright red; her mind catalogued everything faster than her mouth could convey her frustrations. Desperate for air, a reprieve came when he dared to interrupt. "Charlotte-"

"That's not my name," she bellowed. "Leave me alone! Leave my family and friends alone, and if I ever see you again, I'll tell everyone what you did to me!" I glanced sideways and noticed the entire group glued to the spot, unable to look away. He stared back at her for a minute -in shock or too scared to move- as the realisation hit, he couldn't control her. Using his hand to push up, we continued to stand watch until he slowly turned and walked away. The other band was visibly confused and concerned about what transpired, when I went to explain, it was Nick who extended us a courtesy.

"It's fine, Brax. We got the gist of the story." He looked to Glaze, who agreed somberly. "I'm really sorry that you went through that, Charlie." The sincerity and soft tone comforted her heightened state. "Thank you," she acknowledged with a soft smile.

"Let's head back to the house and get packed." Marcus directed. "We hit the road this afternoon."

"Speaking of the hit." Charlie turned to him to address the biggest problem.

"If any of you did it, the media would be all over it by now." That was all he said before ushering us out of there. A sense of nervousness washed over us both, still unsure.

I wrapped my arms around her tightly once we got back in the car, and buried my face in her neck. Kissing her sweetly, I whispered, "I'm so proud of you. Now, do you see the woman I always knew you could be?" I pulled her in, desperate to show her. It wasn't one of those close-mouthed kisses like you do when you're in eighth grade, and you've never held hands with a girl before. It was full-on... open-mouthed, and almost sexual. I relished her small body melting into mine and the way our lips fit together like puzzle pieces. I played with her hair and with a firm grip, she sunk further into me. We pulled back, that's when we saw Chester; his face so close, he may as well have been in the kiss with us.

"Agh, fuck, Chester! Would you piss off!" Charlie flung the door open after realising he'd turned around to say we were back. His wicked grin had me sucking my teeth. "You just had to wind her up, didn't you?" I blank stared him, except for a slight twitch of my eyebrow.

Chapter Nine

CHARLIE

We'd returned to collect our belongings, I followed Marcus into the kitchen, insisting we needed to speak. Brax knew my concerns, so he lingered behind while the others finished packing. Marcus fussed around, switching the coffee machine on and waving a cup at us both. "Yes, please," we both answered. I pulled out the stool at the island, adjusting the seat to find some comfort. "Marcus, I'm concerned Calvin wasn't making that threat lightly and-"

"I'm sure he wasn't," he cut me off and turned to face us, leaning on the bench. "My responsibility is to avoid negative publicity for the band," he explained, then leaned closer. "Who is Marcus Bradley?" We looked at each other, confused. "I'm just the manager of Abandoned Bygone; I'm not the guitarist, drummer, or even the lead singer." Marcus pointed the teaspoon in his hand at Brax. "If the band had lost their temper, the fallout from it would have been catastrophic."

"Are you saying you took one for the team?" Brax joked, trying to lighten the situation. "Even I have my limits, Brax." Marcus reminded him, then turned to pour our coffees. "And what he did to Charlie is disgusting."

"If Calvin presses charges, doesn't that defeat the entire purpose?"

Brax asked, and he stopped what he was doing for a moment, turning back to us. "It's just as bad if the media puts it together that our manager was involved." He tapped the teaspoon against the palm of his hand, all three of us racking our brains.

"I'll say I did it!" I shot up in my seat. The kitchen was silent momentarily before both of them buckled over, laughing. "What?" I was a little annoyed they weren't taking me seriously, and their humour seemed to intensify. "With what? A step ladder?" Marcus barely muttered as he tried to wipe his reddened face. I glared at Brax, who couldn't get control of himself, my anger increasing rapidly.

"Brax! Would you stop laughing? I'm not joking." I pushed him in a huff.

"Cutie, I love you, but let's be serious for a minute." He turned in his seat to face me. Folding my arms across my chest, I glared back, wondering where he was going with this. "Stating the obvious, Calvin's a lot bigger than you. How would you have reached him?" He waved his hands in front of me, gesturing to the floor, then up above his head.

"He caught me by surprise when I was taking your photo," I explained. "He leaned in to whisper and the sudden intrusion scared me. I flung my arm back and accidentally hit him." I shrugged and saw Marcus and Brax sideways glance and smirks. Realising they wouldn't consider it, I pushed away from the bench, standing up. "If he reports it, and I admit to the assault; there's no way Dad would allow it. I don't think he'd want the Embassy involved in his own daughter's arrest." *How's that for funny?* Brax's eyebrow immediately raised. I turned and walked off to our room, leaving them both to ponder that.

"She's got a point," Marcus had stopped laughing now. I didn't turn around, just continued to our room. While most of Brax and my belongings were ready to go, it never hurt to double-check. Plus, I needed to keep myself busy. I was worried about what Calvin would tell dad. So much so that I was prepared to take the blame at all costs. I appreciated Marcus as a boss and friend, especially after what he did today.

The door creaking open drew me back to the room, and I glanced over my shoulder to see Brax entering. I returned to the suitcase and folded the last of my clothes, putting them away. "You ignoring me?" His whispered breath skimmed across my neck. I stopped what I was doing and turned to face him.

"You didn't even take me seriously, Brax. Your first reaction was to laugh," I huffed back in annoyance. "Sure, it wasn't the best of ideas, but this isn't the greatest situation to be in either!"

"I'm sorry, I truly am. It's a natural reaction, but not to be excused." He threw his cap on the bed and pulled me flush against him. In one swift movement, he pinned me up against the wall. "Can you see it? Can you feel it, Charlie?" My brows knitted in confusion. "You have strength when you believe in yourself. You didn't hesitate to jump to Marcus' defence. That's the woman we notice and love. That's the woman I want you to see." My knees swayed slightly, appreciating his soothing words. "Do you realise you make me need you so much that it physically hurts?" His hand gripped my hair and our lips crushed together. I pulled him closer, wanting to feel his warmth as he ravished my lips. My heart raced, and my skin was on fire. I could feel his hands shaking as he gripped my back. Every muscle in my body screamed for him, but I knew we had to keep moving.

"Mmm, stop." I mumbled between stolen kisses, "What's gotten into you?" He broke the kiss and ran his lips over my jaw and down my neck. I may have told him to stop, but my hands continued to rove over his shirt and jeans, exploring his well-defined physique. His fingers teased and pinched my swollen nipples until I ached for more. "Brax, not now." I half protested, enjoying the attention he was showing me, but conscious we had to leave. "Everyone will be waiting."

"Let them," he replied flatly, nudging my feet further apart. He'd trapped me against the wall, and I could no longer hide my arousal. His hand ran down my back, over my ass, taking extra time to knead the cheeks before sliding back up my spine. He tugged my hair back and teasingly nibbled my lip. I moaned, my nails digging into his shirt-covered shoulders, rewarding me with a deep groan of appreciation. We pulled apart after several minutes of exploring each other. "You're incredible; you know that, right?"

An hour and a half later, we were loading onto the spacious tour bus. Brax took my bags, storing them underneath with the equipment, except for a carry bag with essential toiletries and a change of clothes. I made my way through the row of seats when I felt my phone vibrating in my back pocket and reached into my jeans to yank it out. Staring at the screen, I stopped, seemingly in quicksand, as my feet failed me. I had expected problems from the fallout with Calvin, but I was praying to be spared this call.

"Cutie, what is it?" I looked down at the phone as it rang again, my eyes meeting Brax's and he immediately knew from that one look something was wrong. "Charlie?" He pressed me again.

"It's Dad." I stared down at my phone ringing, I wasn't sure what to do. I knew this call was coming, but I didn't prepare for it. "What did I tell you earlier?" I thought of Brax's comforting words back in the room, and I found the strength I needed with a new resolve. I pressed the answer button and took a big breath before speaking. "Yes, Richard?" I saw everyone's eyes fly open when I said dad's name, but I was too busy listening to the spray coming out the other end of the phone.

"I beg your pardon, Charlotte Maree!" His usual authoritative voice stumbled slightly, a shock I had not heard from him before. "Don't you mean, Dad?"

"That would imply you've been a father and not just a financial aid when I was growing up. So I'll ask you again: what do you want, Richard?" In true fashion, it did not surprise me when the power play came out next, and he tried to tell me to change my tune. "Richard, if you just rang to berate me again, I'm sorry to hurry you along, but I'm rather busy. Perhaps I can entertain you some other time?"

"Charlotte Maree, you'll listen to me, and you'll do- "

"I'm busy," I cut him off. "Unlike you, who seems to have nothing better to do than constantly chastise and belittle your daughter." I rubbed my brow as I waited for whatever it was dad had to say. Brax ushered me through to the bedroom compartment at the rear, affording me the privacy I needed. The rest of the band was naturally curious and concerned, but I still appreciated the privacy they gave me. After shutting the door, I moved into the room. Brax grabbed my hips as he sat on the bed, drawing me close to stand between his legs and taking my spare hand in his. Curiosity painted his face as he tried his best to comfort me.

"All I have ever done is support and guide you to make the right choices." I couldn't believe the words dad had just spoken and almost laughed down the phone. Realising where we were and knowing Brax's tour was about to start, I had neither the patience nor the will to discuss this further with him.

"I have to go, Richard." I couldn't say another word when dad's thundering voice broke the receiver. The fright immediately saw me react physically while pulling the phone from my ear.

"Stop calling me that right this minute!" Brax heard dad's voice raise over the phone, and immediately he went to stand up. I placed my hand carefully on his chest pushing him back into his seat.

"Stop telling me what the fuck to do!" I took a deep breath, full of courage to answer him. "In case you hadn't noticed yet, I'm an adult capable of having my own thoughts and opinions. And I *won't* allow *you* or anyone else to dictate to me!" I had made a point of keeping my voice neutral. I didn't want dad to have the power over my emotions anymore. When I saw Brax looking up and smiling at me, I knew I was going to be alright. I ran my hand through his hair and down to the nape of his neck; my nails stroked his scalp as he leaned forward and kissed my stomach. I barely heard a word dad said as I got lost in my calm.

"I had an interesting phone call from Calvin today." Dad huffed. "Your attitude right now is doing you no favours."

"I'm sure your golden boy had plenty to say." Hearing that, Brax's head shot up, and his eyes widened. I muted the phone momentarily to explain, "Calvin called Dad."

"What has gotten into you?" Dad huffed furiously down the phone.

"You'll show some respect for me or so help me god- "

"You'll what, Richard?" I cut him off. No longer did fear flood my veins, just pure rage. "Standby while your sick friends try to groom a thirteen-year-old for their adult son?"

"Charlotte-"

"No! It's your turn to listen," I demanded. No longer would I be silenced! "What else can you do that you haven't already?" I was so lost in that moment of fury, and the torment my brain was in, that my eyes glazed over. Tension coursed through my muscles, unable to think of anything other than the pain he had allowed. The rational Charlotte known to him was offline, replaced by the primitive Charlie. My ability for nuance and emotional generosity had long left, and I felt my fist firmly planted by my side. Not that my words weren't damaging enough. "You wouldn't even listen to what they asked me on those calls!"

Brax gripped my hip when dad cut me off again, and he saw my frustration. "You know I did everything I could to supervise those calls."

"Well, not good enough, Dickie Boy!" Brax snorted when I used the reference. "That guy you think is so wonderful that you defend to the end of the earth, even over your daughter, is nothing more than a sick and disgusting pervert. And you do not know the pain I endured from him." My face felt hot with rage as I sucked in a few calming breaths. "How does it make you feel, Richard, that your perfect Calvin was asking your thirteen-year-old daughter if she was sexually active yet? Because if she was, that was a problem. Or how about when he tried to get me to give myself my first orgasm at sixteen? Then, abused me because I refused to touch myself!"

"Charlotte, please- "

"No!" Brax was too slow to react, as I screamed back, "You'll listen to me this time! I don't care how uncomfortable it is for you." The frightened girl inside had found her voice, and nothing was going to stop it. "How many times did I beg you to make it stop?"

"Look, perhaps this isn't a good time?" Dad butted in again.

"Why? It was perfect timing when you wanted to talk!" I practically laughed back at him. I was projecting all my fears and anger. He needed to hear this because, for so long, he refused. Fumbling over his words, I realised he still didn't grasp the true extent of what they had done. "How about when Calvin's father, Mathias, got on the phone and told me if Calvin gives me an order, I'll listen? That's a woman's place, and Calvin wants his money's worth. Because that's all you've ever seen me as, Richard! A means to an end. You even tried to bribe Brax to leave me!"

"Charlotte, why didn't you tell me any of this sooner?" *Is he for real?*

"I tried to! You didn't want to listen. You never do. In the end, I gave up." That was difficult for me to admit. The tears soon swelled thick and fast in my eyes. "There's only so much anguish a person can take. Try post-traumatic stress disorder, Richard. I'm sure you've heard of it! But, let's be honest with each other for a minute; you wouldn't have believed me, anyway. Not over your precious Calvin. After all, I was nothing to you; you always wanted a son. Women are to be seen and not heard, right, Richard?" There was a long pause, and I thought he might have finally hung up for a moment.

"Charlotte, you don't honestly believe I knew all this was going on, do you?"

"You know what, Richard? I don't care anymore. Whether you did or you didn't is irrelevant." It was too little, too late. "I begged you repeatedly to make it stop, to the point I was physically ill, and you still did nothing to protect me. That's not a father." Brax made eye contact with me when I said that, the pain I expelled reflected strongly. He felt everything I did, and it reminded me I had love. He was mine. "You can lie to yourself if that helps you sleep at night. However, until you want to make amends for ruining my childhood and try to build some minuscule relationship with me, which, to be honest, I don't even know if that's possible, do me a favour and lose my number."

Dad let out a heavy sigh before I heard his voice come through again. "Charlotte, you're upset right now. You don't mean that. We can talk further when you aren't so emotional."

"So, I'm too emotional right now?" I laughed hysterically. That was the tip of the iceberg. "That's coming from the guy who knows fuck all about me." As I went to end the call, something dawned on me. "Just so we're clear that any future discussion around Calvin is dead in the water, there is something I need you to hear."

"Charlotte?" I ignored him and put my phone on speaker. I then placed it on the bed next to us; making sure the call was still active. Dad needed to hear this! I turned back to Brax and took his face carefully in my hands.

"Brax?"

"Yes, baby?" he answered with confusion. I got down on my knees in front of him and glanced up with loving eyes. "Will you marry me?" His eyes bugged out as I continued to smile, and he asked, "repeat that again?"

"You're the love of my life, my daily reason to keep fighting," I rushed out. "You're my strength, my comfort, my best friend and lover all in one. They say penguins mate for life, and it made me realise… you're not my Batman. You're my penguin. I love you; I'm in love with you… marry me, Brax."

I suddenly found myself unable to speak as the adrenaline pumped through me. My stomach contracted, and a thousand butterflies erupted from their cocoons. An icy shiver ran up my spine and raised the hair on the back of my neck. Without a word, he reached over and hung up the call. His gorgeous eyes stared back, and I felt myself jolt as he stood in front of me, using one of his hands to tug me off the floor. It was an unspoken beckoning. He spun me around, with the momentum, I couldn't stop myself and I tumbled towards him. He nuzzled me up against the wall, pinning me with his body. I inhaled sharply as his lips slid almost nonexistent over my right cheek, tickling the sensitive skin there. He dropped his head and kissed my shoulder lightly while he reached down to grasp my wrists.

"Yes, Charlotte Maree Bancroft, I will marry you."

I adjusted my head to the side as the joy flooded my face. "Yeah?"

"Yes, baby," he repeated. "I'm buying you a ring," I went to argue when he put his finger to my lips and continued. "I don't care what you say." I lunged forward, kissing him deeply. He raised my hands above my head and pressed his erection against me.

"Brax…" I whispered breathlessly. One of his hands dropped from my wrists and disappeared under the edge of my pants. His fingers grazed lightly over the skin on my hip, making my breath catch. His chest rumbled with a smooth chuckle when he discovered only skin farther down. My throat was dry and constricted as one of his fingers gently trailed a line along my lower abdomen. Goosebumps tickled across my body as he silently pressed his lips into my skin. I was dying to talk, but the passion swirling between us drowned me. My eyes flew open when his fingers slipped between my legs. One of his knees slid between mine and forced them apart. I struggled to maintain my balance as I moved my legs wider to accommodate his leg. "Mmm, Brax… Baby, I need to stop before I get too worked up. We're supposed to be talking- "

"Who said we're going to talk?" I pointed toward the phone, but he cut me off. "Right now, I wanna spend a moment with my fiancée."

"Mmm… I love you." His teeth dragged along my neck, weakening my legs the moment he bit into my flesh. His finger withdrew and his hand slid around to cup my ass. Without thinking, I reached for the waist of my pants and pushed them down, kicking them across the floor as my legs rose and wrapped around him. Both of us shifting for better angles, Brax's mouth crushed down on mine, causing my senses to explode in multiple directions. A small grunt of surprise rumbled from his throat as I instinctively ground my hips against him. He released my wrists and used his hips to pin me to the wall, while his hands cupped my breasts. Heat radiated from them, even through the thick cotton of my shirt. I cried a muffled protest as one of his hands withdrew from my chest and pushed between us, while the other slipped to my waist as he moved back slightly. I watched as his fingers played with the snap on his waistband, teasing me with glances of his flesh. Heat flooded me as he slowly pulled down on the zipper; each tooth of the metal popped like gunshots echoing in my ears. I gasped silently as more skin became visible from each agonising pull. It seemed like forever before I was staring at his entire length. A sly smile spread across his face when he saw desperate hunger, the raw desire that was now visible.

He dropped his pants and pressed forward-flesh on flesh-and heat began erupting between my legs. I was being eaten alive when he roughly pressed his mouth over mine. A wild, untamable beast consumed him. Even with my eyes closed, I felt the world tilt, and I struggled to maintain my bearings. Brax shifted his hips down, then back slightly, and I heard myself whimper in pleasure as he *finally* pressed himself into me. My arousal was *so* high that he slid inside with little resistance. He cupped the back of my upper thighs while he shifted them slightly before burying himself completely.

An intense roaring buzzed as he filled me, making me think I would surely burst. He did not move, as if he sensed I needed this. Lowering my arms, I slid them over his cotton-covered shoulders, stopping when I reached his lower back. I grasped the thin fabric and pulled at it. He shivered as my fingers brushed his bare skin, and his hips thrust forward, causing me to gasp and dig my nails in hard. I needed what was soaking from his skin, what his eyes silently promised when he'd stared at me. He shifted slightly and withdrew, dropping his head next to mine. I cried out as his teeth sank into my shoulder, and he thrust again. Within seconds, my lower back was beating against the wall behind me. Teeth grazed my neck as he shifted them higher again, allowing himself deeper access—the need to mate devoured us both mindlessly. A raging beast inside, fighting and tearing for release. My vision exploded into a thousand lights, then plunged into pitch blackness as my body contracted. Muscles deep inside of me clenched tightly around him, and I heard a low groan in my ear.

The world shattered.

My body went rigid as the climax ignited deep inside, a torrent of shockwaves overrunning my system so powerfully that I could barely breathe. I was dimly aware of his continuing movements, the powerful strokes making me feel as if he would pound me into the wall. My head screamed that I could no longer go on, but my body refused to listen. I clawed at the flesh on his lower back, demanding and pushing him to continue. His eyes were darker, his control was slipping. I raised one of my hands from his back to slip through his thick hair and pulled his face roughly towards mine. Our mouths and tongues met in fiery passion, before he slammed me against the wall, his hand pounding the plasterboard for support. Firm, pulsating flesh colliding caused my body to defy my brain, as I crashed over the edge one last time.

"Fuck, Charlie!" He broke the kiss, buried his head back into my shoulder, and thrust one last time upward. A loud pounding in my ears brought me back to myself. I realised it was my heart hammering against my chest rapidly. Swallowing deeply, I struggled to regain my breath and felt Brax mumble into my neck. "What you did today was the most amazing thing I've ever seen. I couldn't be more proud of you, Charlie. It would be my honour to be your husband and love you for the rest of our lives." Brax lifted me off the wall and carried me over to the fold-down bed. He carefully lay back, bringing me on top of him. Our bodies entwined, making out, loving each other, and excited about this next step in our relationship.

My phone started ringing, breaking our trance. After looking at each other, our heads turned to check the phone screen. It was *mum*.

"**H**i Mum," Charlie answered with an edge of concern. She sat on my hips as I lay back on the bed, one hand behind my head, the other giving her breast a cheeky squeeze. Slapping my fingers away before placing the phone on my stomach, she continued, "We're both here. You're on speakerphone."

"Why do you sound so concerned, Pixie?" Carole quizzed.

"Well, I'm sure you know what happened with Dad earlier," she trailed off. With a slight nudge of my elbow, our gaze met, and our souls intertwined without saying a word, expressing every feeling. "I heard you two may have something to tell me?" Carole's question lingered. So strong was the bond between us it felt as if nothing else in this world existed. "We do," she finally replied. Her eyes radiated the happiness we both felt. "And I assume Dad told you?"

Carole's natural amusement flowed while she confirmed, "Of course."

"So, it's that good?"

"With any luck, he'll give himself an aneurysm tonight."

Knees slammed against my hips in shock when she pressed on my stomach and fell forward, laughing. "For fuck's sake, Mum! And I thought I was bad!"

"Well, my love, where'd you think you got it from?" *True.* "Now tell me everything." We spent the next half an hour explaining what happened with Calvin and Richard's phone call. Of course, either's conduct did not surprise her; however, her apology on their behalf went a long way. What interested me most was when she mentioned Richard. Carole explained he hadn't been his typical demanding self since Charlie's dress down. Carole was adamant that something Charlie had said impacted him. He was never this reserved. "So, that's all you have to tell me?"

"I may have asked Brax to marry me, too," she blushed. I reached up and cupped her cheek when I saw that shy tenderness sweep across her face.

"I'm delighted for you both," Carole's elated voice drew me back. "I'm most excited for myself."

"How so, Mum?" Charlie pressed me back as she leaned closer to the phone, resting on my chest.

"If you hurry and get married, I'll have grandchildren in no time." She fell sideways, the sheets rippling between her fingers as she buried her head. Hearing my laughter, Carole cleared her throat. "I won't hold you up. I know you're both busy, but I needed to check in and make sure you were okay, congratulate you, and wish Brax a successful tour."

While she tried to compose herself, I responded. "Thanks, Carole. We'll see you when we get back."

"I love you and we'll check-in when we can," Charlie promised. "Bye, Mum."

"Please do, Pixie."

After hanging up, she flopped onto my chest, hugging me tightly. I rubbed my fingers along her spine before letting out a sigh of resignation. "I suppose we better get up." Charlie lifted her head to me. "No doubt the others will have questions, plus I promised Marcus I would complete the setlist with Shane before we arrived in Winnipeg." I wanted to find some time to speak with Marcus. After what just happened, I was hoping he'd allow us some time off tomorrow night, away from everyone, before the tour started.

After we dressed, I unlocked the door pulling it open and everyone immediately greeted us.

"What?" my eyes roamed between them.

"Fuck off, Brax!" Liam seethed at my delay tactics.

"You all heard that?" I flicked my thumb over my shoulder at the cabin we had just walked out of.

"All of it...." Kendall mumbled discreetly. She locked eyes with Charlie, and her cheeks pulsed a deeper red, realising they heard *everything*.

"Don't you feign ignorance," Mace took up the argument for Liam.

"Charlie and I are getting married." I couldn't hold it in any longer. Our closest friends were delighted, and I pulled Charlie into my side, kissing the top of her head. This tour would be the end of one chapter, and the beginning of the next. The outcome is favourable both personally and professionally.

"Didn't I say you wouldn't last the entire tour?" Chester gloated.

"I didn't ask!" I laughed back in his face. A confused Charlie tugged on my sleeve and I promised, "I'll explain later." She headed off to join the girls. I could only fathom to explain what had happened when Richard called. I turned back to Marcus, giving him and Shane my full attention as we pulled up the options for set lists.

"I don't think "Homegrown" will resonate as well with the audience here," Shane explained his position and why he had cut it. "There are specific references in the lyrics that rely on the audience either having an excellent knowledge of Australia, or they've visited."

"I agree." I clicked my fingers at Shane, then added, "Plus, Chris mentioned they were opening with "Starved." "Imagine Joy" could compliment that?" I asked the two technically minded of the group.

"If you start with "Imagine Joy," then I suggest you finish with "Private Destiny." Marcus had implied that it was a proposal, but he looked assured of his convictions. "That way, you could lead straight in from "Closer Than You Think?" His head inclined towards Shane, who was furiously scribbling it down.

"I like that," Shane pointed his pen towards Marcus. "Thanks, M."

"Alright, I'll email Nick now. The other band is directly ahead of us, and we're staying at the same hotel, so you boys will have plenty of time to align before soundcheck. Please use it wisely." He tapped the desk as he went to stand when I held my hand up.

"Can we have a quick chat?" he agreed, and I looked sideways at Shane. "Would you mind if I got a bit of privacy, mate?"

"Not at all. I'll lock this down with the other boys and confirm the set list." He collected his laptop, then scuttled out of the booth with a firm pat on the shoulder from Marcus.

"Can I ask you a massive favour?"

The look on my face was pathetic, pleading desperately. I hoped he'd give me some leeway when I asked if I could take Charlie away from the others to celebrate. He finally agreed to one night, and a security guard to accompany us. I'd take what I could get! I wanted to head off as soon as possible once we arrived, so I started scrambling to see what I could book.

After nearly a day on the road, we finally pulled into our hotel, filing out as we greeted Glaze. Our rooms were all confirmed, and Marcus soon handed out swipe cards. We entered the elevator, I was eager to get to our suite. I opened the room up, she walked over to our luggage and went to undo the suitcases. I wrapped her hand in mine and pulled it to a stop. "Leave that for now, please. We can sort it out tomorrow."

"Really? You want nothing out of it?" She crouched beside the suitcase, twisting on her feet to face me.

I bent down beside her, tapping her on the nose, "We aren't staying here tonight."

"What are you talking about?"

"I want to spend time with *you*, to celebrate properly before the shows start." Hearing my words caused a flood of emotions, and her eyes welled up. I reached out, wiping a stray tear, and added, "I remembered to clear it with Marcus and security this time." Laughing, she fell forward onto her knees. "I've promised to text and confirm our movements and safety." She hugged me tight, and I heard a muffled 'thank you' against my shirt. "Anything for you." I texted Marcus to tell him we were leaving after packing an overnight bag, then met with security out front. Our ride dropped us at the entrance of Thermëa Spa Resort, the sight instantly captivated Charlie.

"You organised this for us?" her head wobbled between the resort and me as I fetched my wallet to pay the driver.

"Of course, and I'd do it again in a heartbeat."

I took up our bag, headed to check-in, and made our way to the cabin. We used the time to have a hot shower and get dressed for dinner at the restaurant in the main lodge. When she came out, I lost my breath; just like I did every time this woman entered a room.

"You're perfect."

"Thank you." She looked down, fussing with her dress that was already sitting on her curves sleekly. Moving closer, her hands slid over the lapels of my jacket, her eyes roaming my chest, before locking on mine. "You look so handsome, Brax."

Upon arrival, the waiter escorted us to the reserved booth before returning with a bottle of champagne. He uncorked and poured us each a glass, took our meal orders, then excused himself.

Finally, I raised my glass to her. "To you, Charlotte."

"To us, Brax." She smiled and it shone brighter than any star known to man. We tapped our flutes before taking a sip. I placed my drink carefully on the table, taking her hands in mine.

"I promise you, when we're back, I'll find you a ring that compliments your beauty because nothing will ever truly compare to it." She couldn't hold in a sob and reached forward, gripping my cheeks firmly between her hands. The stark difference between her lips sweetly caressing my own was fascinating.

Last night was one of the most unforgettable of my life. We had spent hours celebrating; spending loving moments in the hot springs at the resort, between the sheets, as well as cherishing the time we had alone. Just when I thought things couldn't get better, I woke to the best surprise a man could hope for. I felt something immediately, when I glanced under the sheet and saw Charlie with her mouth around me, I felt like I'd won the lottery. My eyes were wide open now, and I couldn't believe how incredible it felt. She was sucking away, my erection covered in saliva. I could feel her tongue press against the bottom of my shaft, almost as if she was licking it like an icicle. Charlie smiled around me when she noticed I was awake and watching. She crouched up and began talking to me while rubbing me up and down with her hand.

"Morning, baby. I woke up and went to the bathroom when I noticed how erect you were this morning. I figured you didn't get enough last night?" Mischief seeped into her tone, and she kicked her feet playfully. She loved the position she had me in.

"Mmm, maybe I was dreaming about what we did last night?"

"Well, when I saw you were pitching a tent, I figured you were inviting me in to go camping?"

"Ahh-" I groaned as she gripped me tighter. "It's all yours for the taking," I gritted my teeth through my pleasure. She smiled wickedly before going back to sucking, and I couldn't complain. I laid there letting it all soak in. She was like a sex machine, sucking furiously and even deep-throating me several times. She massaged my balls while she blew me, making me squirm. *It felt so good.* Fuck, I loved when she played with my balls! It didn't take long before I climaxed. It never did. "Fuck! Charlie... I'm gonna...." She kept on going, with her vacuum like suction, as I felt her soft hand press on my stomach, inviting me to lie back and enjoy. I let out a big breath, and it wasn't long before I climaxed. With closed eyes, she took it all, sucking the tip, ultimately moving towards me to watch her swallow. That alone instantly left me wanting more. Charlie crawled closer, leaning over my body, her chest pressed to mine as my arms wrapped around her, gently squeezing those luscious buttcheeks. Our mouths connected in a fierce temptation, devouring each other unashamedly. It was all-consuming, lasting just a moment, our lips still clinging together when we broke apart.

We kissed again, our bodies combined, while I rubbed the side of my thumb against her chin. She opened her mouth, accepting my tongue. My nose nestled against hers while we continued, her tongue pushing into my mouth. Her lips were full and soft, the pouty flesh expanding the more we attacked each other. Charlie put her hand on my chest, feeling the hair against her palm as I let go for a second. The kiss grew more passionate with each passing moment that our lips smacked against each other, making me want to grip her waist and pull her closer to me. Her arm wrapped around my neck while I ran one hand up and down her body. She was so fucking sexy, I couldn't get enough of her. The feel of her tongue scorching my own was overwhelming and seductively alluring. She nibbled at my lower lip, just for a moment, before returning to my mouth. Eventually, we pulled apart and smiled at each other.

"I suppose we have to get back to reality?" Charlie asked, brushing the hair from my face. She leaned forward, peppering my face with a few quick pecks, then adding. "Race you to the shower?" I lunged off the bed as she bolted into the bathroom. After getting washed, changed and caffeinated, we packed and checked out, then headed back. The joy we felt was immovable, and our eyes stayed glued together. We were so consumed in our happiness when we walked up to the entrance that I stumbled when Charlie pulled me to a stop.

"This tour is the opening to your global stardom, Brax."

Being loved is a sensation to embrace, and it's true what they say. You'll feel it. It's impossible not to. In the wake of our good news, Charlie's words reminded me of this. She stepped closer, placing her hand on my cheek. My gaze wandered down to meet hers.

"I see how you use your talent to bring radiance and love through music to all around you. Go out there and be the light, Brax."

Chapter Eleven

CHARLIE

Glaze and Abandoned Bygone filed into the cramped radio booth of Kiss Winnipeg station at six that evening. Marcus, Nick, the girls, and I observed and listened through our earpieces from the other side of the soundproof glass. My index finger clicked rapidly, capturing the moment they introduced the boys, the smiles and appreciation painting vivid colours across the lenses. *I need to get these up on their social pages tonight.* They were being interviewed by a local host, Lacey Kensington, during her daily show.

"I see you have brought some guests with you today?" Lacey beamed through her headset as she spoke to Glaze via Chris. "Just for you." His friendly tone suggested a long working relationship between the two. "This is Brax, Chester, Mark, Liam and Shane, or as Australia knows them, Abandoned Bygone." The studio producer queued the cheering and clapping sound effects while the boys waited to thank everyone for having them.

"I have to admit; I listened to some of your tracks after Glaze announced you were touring with them," Lacey admitted.

Brax and the others were eager for her feedback, so he asked. "What did you think?"

"Canada is in for a treat!" Lacey's sound technician faded in the sound, and the first verse of "Horizon" came through:

I'm taking off on a journey. I'm Livin' the dream.

Leaving behind my worries, I'm gonna let 'em be

Time to let go of the pain and nurture some peace of mind

To find a place where I can shine and leave my worries behind.

The sound faded in the booth. The lyrics of "Horizon" had never rung more true. This was a new journey for Abandoned Bygone, one I was certain would create more opportunities.

"We appreciate that," Brax acknowledged. "Especially given your accomplishments in the music charts." He tipped his hand back to Lacey.

She reached across her booth to high-five Brax, clearly impressed. "I see I wasn't the only one who came in prepared." Marcus always stressed to the band that there was never an excuse to go into an interview unprepared in the age of technology. "I have one specific question, though, before we get back to the tour," Lacey continued. They all nodded, as she turned to Chester. "Private Destiny." She held eye contact, but said nothing further. He sat straighter, and instantly the room's ambience changed. He had a healthy sense of pride around the work on that track, and rightly so. For he pursued his passion and raised the bar for the band. "The transition on the bridge going into the final chorus," she stated, and he nodded. "How did you not run off the fret and straight onto the neck?" He cracked up, laughing at her animated face, one that made an obvious point of highlighting her astonishment.

"I hit it a few times, hey, boys?" Leaning forward, he looked across to the others, still humoured. "It took plenty of practice. I won't lie."

"It was an art in the making," she cut in. Her appreciation for his craft was obvious.

"Thank you." He nodded humbly. I peered sideways when I sensed movement. Marcus was rocking on his heels, arms folded across his chest as he scrutinised the interview. Chester wasn't always the easiest to read. He was sporadic, unpredictable and flighty, but Marcus had spent the time cultivating an appreciation for their elevated position in the industry. And his responses to this interview were certainly highlighting that. "You just need to keep plucking the inner fret while hitting the E. Then you can run straight to middle C." His simple explanation had everyone in the room humoured.

"You make it sound so easy," she replied. "The transition to hit the F, though…." With a raised eyebrow, she tilted her head, returning the serve.

"Beginner's luck?" A fresh wave of amusement crashed around the room. Once it settled down, she reverted to the prepared questions, and the bands took turns answering them. There was one particular question that drew my attention more than any other.

"What do you feel is the best song you've ever released, and why?" They all looked at one other before she added, "let's start with Abandoned Bygone. Which song should us Canadians be on the lookout for?" Brax's vision searched across to his bandmates, giving them the opportunity to answer first.

"Collectively, there isn't one," Mark spoke. "Each of us has given a piece of ourselves to our art, but there is always one song you resonate more with." Everyone nodded, including the two managers standing next to me. "Homegrown" will always be special to us. It was one of the first songs we constructed for our debut album and an homage to Australia and what we were fortunate to grow up with. But for me, it's "Private Destiny."

"Why's that, mate?" Brax's head spun as he questioned his guitarist and friend.

"This lifestyle can feel isolated." Mark pressed on, and everyone agreed. "I find sweet relief in letting myself dream of why we do it, and that's where I realise my destiny is. Not the endless darkened nights leaving the studio, or the blistered fingertips that come from one rehearsal. It's that special fan, hoping you can reach them when they need it. I can't heal anyone, but maybe our art can help someone heal themselves?" The selfless pleasure Mark took from the fans didn't surprise me, and I could see that Brax felt the same.

The interview went well, and it was an excellent introduction before the first show the next day. I was keen to get the photos on the band's social media so they could share the natural exuberance captured during the radio chat. We filed out, the cold snap not doing much to chill the vibe buzzing around the group.

The next day, we arrived at the unique venue. The banner immediately drew you to the exclusivity of the performance, reading 'An intimate night with,' followed by the two band names emboldened. Hearing of Abandoned Bygone's success with their Regional Tour venues encouraged Glaze to do something similar. However, their public persona was highly elevated, which made the logistics slightly tricky to navigate. They finally announced this tour after strategic discussions with Marcus and the team at Aushop, who orchestrated it successfully. These small venues pulled the artists back to their roots and had everyone alive with excitement. Things like extensive sound checking, staffing, set lists and the amount of organisation involved in bigger concerts chipped away at the fun.

Brax's joy radiated as they took to the stage. He glided effortlessly with the intimate crowd, reminding me how much he loved live performance. His face was a picture of concentration, devotedly engaged with the music and fellow musicians to make it work. His body flowed fluently as he removed himself from the preconceived notions of pop music and mainstream hip hop.

In between songs, the bands welcomed questions from the audience, allowing the musicians time to catch a breath and grab some water. The room was stifling because of the additional body heat, as well as the warmness put off by the strobes and stage lighting.

"Why do you love performing?" A young girl's voice asked as I bent down to grab my drink. "You travelled all the way here to follow your passion?" The two groups realised she was talking to Abandoned Bygone. I leaned against the wall, folding my arms across my chest, eager to know that answer as well. "Who wouldn't want to play with Glaze?" Shane quickly jumped in. "Am I right?" The entire venue boisterously agreed.

Brax's gaze was distant as he tried to articulate the many emotions that can rush you on stage. "It's an ecstatic frenzy of overwhelming thrills, blissful senses of delirium, and an abundance of gratitude."

"That's why my guy writes the lyrics." Chester waved his thumb at Brax while directing that comment to the audience. Of course, everyone loved it!

"It's the anxious jumping up and down, the nerves and all the pressure-" Shane stopped mid-sentence when Liam chimed in.

"The sweats and shaky fingers," he provided additional examples, Shane agreed. "Feeling like we're about to shit ourselves any second." Everyone laughed when Liam dropped that in.

"The blinding lights that come up on stage, moving in sync with the music, as panicked nausea subsides." The slight twitches and dreamy look on Brax's face hinted he had drifted off to a fond memory of performing. "Seeing the many nameless faces in the audience and knowing that their eyes are all on us." To emphasise the point, he looked sideways at the others. I noticed Chester nod before turning back to the crowd. "The utter love and appreciation, and knowing they blessed us to deal with this life again tomorrow. An unreal dream in our reality." The eruption that filled the room left me scrambling for my camera, desperate to capture one fleeting memory. When Glaze took to the stage to play their smash hit, "Flawless," they gifted the audience with the perfect example of everything the boys had just explained. In those lyrics were their immortality and the reason they were so beloved.

Got my eyes on the prize and I ain't stoppin' now
Gonna make something of myself, yeah I'm showin' them how
Gonna be somebody they remember and never forget
Gonna leave my mark on this world and never regret
This is a brand new beginning. Nothing can keep me down.
I'm ready to take on the world, no more looking around
The sun's on the horizon, I'm taking control
Living the dream, Livin' life like it's whole

Marcus allowed the band to enjoy *one* beverage after their performance before they had to pack up. It was an excellent opportunity to get the perfect photos to open the tour. I moved around the room, excusing myself and happily capturing keepsakes for those asking. Through the lens, I witnessed life in pictures. I saw the nuance of emotion portrayed in high definition. The beauty of Brax's art poured out, one frame after another, and my clicking finger felt like it pulsed in tune with his beating heart. The passion that burned through his eyes was a vivid reminder that music became a guiding light, illuminating the way for Brax. These photos would be their portal to the world, a way to reach all their fans on the human level.

Moving back from my latest shot, I bumped into someone and turned rapidly to apologise. "I'm so..." *Calvin*! My jaw dropped, and I stopped mid-sentence. My eyes quickly blinked as I tried to process if this was really happening. How could he possibly be standing here in front of me? *We left Toronto over a day ago.*

He cleared his throat, and I snapped out of my stupor. "What are you doing here?"

The arrogant smile that spread across his lips had my blood boiling off the stove. "Is that any way to greet an old friend?"

"You might be *old*, Calvin, but we are not friends." I turned on my heel, eager to get away. That's when I felt his fingers around my wrist. My skin instantly crawled, and I tried to shake him off. "Leave me alone, you creep!" I inched closer to his face, giving my arm a firm yank from his grasp.

"I see you grew a spine as you matured." I glared at him, continuing my retreat. "So feisty," he taunted. "No wonder your little band over there loves keeping you close." Despite my brain screaming no, my primal instinct was to attack. It stopped me in my tracks when Nick blocked my path.

"Everything alright here?" He gripped my shoulders in support. Turning back around, he made eye contact with someone across the room and immediately raised his arm to flag them over. Within seconds Brax was stepping aggressively close to Calvin. Angry eyes told me his brain was in a different mode, that he had switched gears from empathy to cold emotional indifference. Never once had he directed this toward me, yet it emerged when he sensed a threat, and so this was part of his full on protective mode. I flung my head sideways as Chester and Mark raced in.

"Why are you bothering Charlie again?" The fierceness in Brax's voice caused me to shiver, and as if sensing it also, Chester and Mark stepped closer. By now, many attendees had turned around to gawk, aware of the unease in the air, and when I saw Marcus hurriedly making his way with security through the crowd, I felt some relief. Sensing a disturbance was imminent, Mark slid between them, wrapping his arm around Calvin's shoulders.

"Mate!" he was over-animated for the benefit of onlookers. "I haven't seen you in years. We've gotta catch up!" He patted him on the shoulder, speaking directly to Calvin with a stern glare. Before Calvin could cause any further disturbance, Chester had appeared on the other side, and with Mark's faithful guidance, they escorted Calvin outside. My mouth gaped like a goldfish as I turned to Brax. He placed two fingers under my chin, pushing my mouth closed. Shaking his head, he looked down at me when I finally spoke.

"This won't end well," I protested.

He put his finger up to my lips. "What I was about to do would have been much worse." He kissed the top of my head, and when he pulled back, his eyes were laser-focused on the door. Holding hands, we went to walk further into the venue when I tugged him to a stop. He patiently waited while I thanked Nick before turning back to speak.

"Can I ask you something?" Hearing my concerned voice, he guided me off to the side of the room. He gripped my hips, using his towering body to shield us from prying eyes. "You don't think Calvin's following us, do you?"

"Nah," he shot back instantly. Yet he wouldn't directly look at me.

"Honestly?" My head bobbled sideways, trying to force eye contact. "Brax?"

"I hope not, Cutie." He shrugged his shoulders and pulled me closer.

I hugged his waist, resting against his broad chest. "I hope not," he sighed heavily. Several minutes later, I opened my eyes, and after adjusting to the glare of the room, I saw Mark and Chester had returned. They were by the main doors, talking with Marcus and security. Instinct had me racing over, eager to know what had happened. *Where was Calvin?*

"**W**hat did you do?" I fired at Chester and Mark while racing over. "Me?" Chester pointed his index finger to his chest. "Nothing! Except stop Brax from laying out that asshole." He turned outside and then back to us.

"Where's Calvin?" I asked directly while Brax caught up.

"He left already." Mark shrugged, with hands stuffed in his pockets, and turned on his heel to leave. "Wait!" I touched his arm. "Are you telling me Calvin left here without a scratch on him?"

"Sure." Mark pursed his bottom lip and nodded. "His ribs may be sore, but not a cut on him," Chester muttered quietly. My head spun toward Monkey. I glared at him, asking, "You didn't?" *My head was reeling.* I was terrified that Marcus and the studio would blow a head gasket if this got out into the media.

"Not me... it was *him*." Chester pointed to Mark, who had slipped away while my attention was on the Monkey of the group.

"No?" Shock widened my eyes and made me disbelieve what I heard. "It's time to get packed up." Marcus clapped his hands on the boy's shoulders, ushering them to get moving.

We filed into the elevator back at the hotel; Brax, the band, and Marcus had to race off to meet Nick and Glaze to debrief from the concert. I'd observed Chester couldn't keep still and had to ask, "What the hell is wrong with you?" The rest of the group nodded, showing they'd noticed it as well. "If this elevator doesn't hurry, I'm gonna shit on the floor." Instinctively, I gagged at his comment.

Brax piped in, "so, you're gonna take that crap to another level?" The snickers in the elevator sounded like a pack of hyenas. "Same shit, different story." Liam chimed. While shaking my head, I nibbled the inside of my lip to stop the smile from spreading. "Fucking hell, you guys. Do you ever stop with that?" Mace asked exactly what I was thinking.

Arriving at our floor finally, I waved Brax off, as I didn't want to intrude or interrupt. After entering the room, I flopped back on our bed and texted the girls to see if they wanted to catch up. The smile spread across my face when Mace's reply lit up the screen - confirming she was all over the wine selection and I needed to order dinner. Twenty minutes later, I greeted them with a hug, as they made our way inside, accompanied by a sizable glass of wine, while we waited for the food delivery.

Since Kendall wasn't used to the tour lifestyle like Mace was, I checked in with her over dinner. It could become overwhelming, and she needed to know she had support from Mace and me. "So, how are you finding the tour so far?"

"How do you do this all the time?"

She raised her eyebrows, leaning forward, hands clasped between her knees. It made me laugh, and I reached across, taking her fingers in mine. "Those fans are full on! Did you see them the moment the band joined the crowd?" Kendall waved her hands at us for any input. "Vultures."

"It's a lot to process initially." I conceded. "I still haven't got used to the fan girl squeals. Earplugs are a godsend." My comment tickled them both, since they knew it to be true. "I know I've seen Shane perform many times now," she took a deep breath, pondering the best way to articulate her feelings. "The tours, however, have a heightened sense of frenzy." Kendall paused again, then added. "Hearing them speak earlier tonight resonated with me. I don't think I could explain it any better than that."

She mindlessly picked at her nails, buying herself some time and composure, when Mace shuffled forward and asked, "Is there more to it?" I nodded in agreement. I knew the signs well and felt obliged to remind her she had a safe space with us. "Kendall," I waited before continuing, needing her full attention. "What can we do to help?"

In times of high stress, I didn't like to be pushed into explaining my emotions or triggers. Instead, I longed for someone to offer support in navigating the complexities I was battling internally. "Sorry," she fussed, waving her hand at us. "I don't mean to be a downer."

"You're not," Mace assured her with a warm smile and an eager ear. "Just before they found out about the tour, Shane asked how I felt about moving to Sydney permanently." We listened quietly, allowing her to relax. "The thought terrified me... it still does, if I'm truthful." She slouched momentarily, second-guessing herself, and a cloudiness cast over her porcelain features. "It's not that we aren't already exclusive, but the thought of living together makes our relationship even more real."

"What scares you about that, babe?" Mace gently glided in. "It's their fans," she hung her head, ashamed to admit it. But I understood what she was trying to say. "Coupled with the fact I'd be moving states and wouldn't have anyone I know around me." Realising what she said, she looked up, horrified, and shook her head. "Except you girls, of course. I'm sorry. I didn't mean for it to sound that harsh." Her words came out rushed as she struggled to explain herself.

"It's okay; I get it. You wouldn't have your parents nearby or the comfort of familiarity." She nodded, appreciating my empathy. "I also understand what you're saying about the fans," I reassured Kendall. "I hope so." She smiled tight-lipped at me.

"It's not just the hysteria of the music. It's deeper than that." I took a stab at expressing a common concern we've all had at some stage. "But," they both immediately looked up, and I pressed on, "the problem isn't really that all these girls wanna bang your boyfriend." I bit the bullet and addressed the elephant in the room. They looked at me, confused by what they heard. "Marcus got it into my head long ago," I explained for context, waving them off. Then I continued, "The problem is *you*. Or me when I went to him with the same issue. I was jealous of those other girls who were suddenly in his life, especially after their stardom increased following the Regional Tour and the shift in our relationship."

"Wait until after this one," Kendall beamed back, the smile tugging her lips lovingly.

"True." I agreed. "See, the knowledge that other girls wanna sleep with Shane doesn't mean that suddenly you have competition or your relationship is in danger. It actually means fuck all, babe." She mumbled, '*does it*,' and I stood firm. "Yes. Because he doesn't wanna sleep with them." And that was the truth of the matter. After everything Natasha had done, Shane would *never* have entered this without total commitment. No one had compared to Kendall. "He doesn't notice them, babes. He only sees you." She smiled at me with eyes full of emotion and squeezed my hand a little tighter.

"It must've been difficult for you after the Regional Tour?" I nodded to Kendall that it was, but I also knew the battle *was* worth it. "I guess that's why you sensed it…." She trailed off.

"We both did," Mace answered. "None of us are that different from each other." She had my attention, noticing the shift in her voice. The personal undertones had softened her, and when I tried to make eye contact, all I saw was a dreamy gaze. I knew she recalled her challenges in this lifestyle. "Even the guys," she continued, shaking it off. "Looking back over the last year, I'd like to think we became a second family. We've had our difficulties, but we've always gotten through them together."

"I think their success depended on it," I mumbled quietly, but the girls heard me. "That's not to say I don't believe they wouldn't have become famous. I think if the guys weren't friends, and the band suddenly made it big and went on tour… they would have been around each other every second of the day without knowing the complexities of individual personalities-"

"Monkey," Mace coughed behind her hand. We both laughed and agreed.

"They could have resented each other. It takes time and effort to be this successful, just as it does with any relationship." Kendall nodded, as her body relaxed on the couch, I pressed on. "The groupies never change, babe. But I have known these guys since the beginning, and they've grown. You light up his world, Kendall."

"Really?" she squeaked, and I smiled warmly at her shock. "Charlie's right," Mace picked up. "Shane adores you. He's always gushing when he returns from visits and can't wait to tell us what you've been up to. He's so in love with you, Kenny."

"Kenny?" she raised her eyebrow with a question to Mace. "Would you prefer Chester to assign you a nickname?" I laughed at Mace's comment. *No one deserves that torture!*

"Do you want to live with him?" She nodded a *'yes'* in response to me, "Then don't let trepidations hold you back from something that could be amazing. Your fear is proof of the love you have, Kendall. It's hard, but you're tougher." She smiled widely, nibbling her lip, attempting to contain it. "What?"

"When you said that, I heard the chorus of 'Private Destiny' in my head."

I am stronger in the bonds of love than I could ever be alone, but were it not for the still dark, lonely nights, my soul would've never grown.

Sometime later, Brax texted he and the boys were back at Marcus' suite and asked if we wanted to join them for a smoke. I wondered why they'd finished so soon, but their faces showed something was wrong once we joined them. I also noticed April and Chris, but not Brett. "What's going on?" Brax's leg was twitching as he cracked his knuckles, and he swallowed hard before meeting my worried eyes. "It's Calvin, isn't it?" I asked, falling onto the couch beside him.

"No, babe." He quickly grabbed my hands to settle my nerves. "It's nothing like that, Midget. You're safe," Mark promised after hearing the exchange. I looked around the space and noticed all the guys with a sense of dread painted across their features. "They rushed Brett to the hospital. We're waiting to hear if he's okay."

"Oh fuck, what happened?" Mace's worry laced her normally even-toned voice.

"He hadn't been feeling well for a few days, as Nick explained he's had a hernia he's been managing." *That's right.* I remember Chris mentioning it at the studio. Brax rubbed his face, shaking his head before he continued. "They think it might have ruptured during the show tonight, so they've transferred him to the hospital to get it checked."

"Will he be alright?" Kendall asked a concerned-looking Shane as she stroked his shoulders.

"We hope so, Nick promised to call once they have any news." Mark stood as he spoke, "does anyone want another beer while I'm up?" We all nodded.

"Are you both alright?" I turned to ask April and Chris. They nodded with weary smiles.

"My balls ache in pain for him, Midget...." Chester added that in the end, hoping to lighten the mood- it worked. Brax threw his head back, laughing, before grabbing his crotch. I appreciated Monkey in situations like this, always helping to calm our nerves.

Everyone broke into their own conversations. I leaned closer to Brax, stroking my nails along the back of his neck. He reached over, rubbing his fingers across my knee. "Did you have a good time with the girls?" I nodded and turned to see Kendall and Shane deep in discussion while enjoying a smoke outside.

"Mace and I wanted to check in with Kendall; it's her first tour, after all...." my gaze wandered back to our friends. "Everything okay?" he nudged me. I pressed my mouth to his ear, dropping my voice to show some discretion. "Shane asked her to move to the city with him." His face radiated with happiness as he turned toward me. "Yeah?" his eyes expanded, and I nodded confirmation. "That's a good thing for them both, especially Shane. Huge." He smiled radiantly.

"Naturally, she had her concerns. It's a big decision. I hope the talk with Mace and I helped."

"Looks like it," he tapped my knee and used his index finger to point to them stealthily. I turned to see Shane and Kendall in a passionate embrace, their bodies pressed tightly together as if starved for one another. "Let's grab a smoke. I need to take the edge off tonight."

He clasped my hand, leading us outside, and, as we sat down, a lightbulb switched. I realised, in the hype of the last few days, I'd forgotten Brax's birthday was coming up. "Fuck, I'm such a shit girlfriend," I muttered while slapping my forehead. "Lucky you're a fiancée then," Brax chimed in proudly. "But also, what'd you do?"

"Don't you act innocent." I pinched the spliff from him having a draw. "You were hoping we'd all forget being so busy with the tour. Your birthday is in ten days." Brax smirked, dropping his head. "Don't remind me. I know I'm getting old." He patted my thigh, and I leaned in, kissing my way up to his neck. "You're only as old as the woman you feel." My lips brushed his earlobe. The warmth of my breath sent goosebumps rippling down his skin, so I took the chance to torment him further. Using my tongue, I licked at him, enjoying the delicious taste. "I wanna do something special for you, Brax. Especially seeing how stressed you are tonight."

"A blow job will help." With a shake of my head as well as an eye roll, a wicked grin spread across my lips as I enquired, "Where are you gonna find a dick to suck at this time of night?"

"Ha! You funny fucker," he snorted. "Don't stress about it, Cutie. I just figured we'd do something once we get back home."

"Maybe something small, you know, in between shows?" I pressed on, not letting it drop. Realising I wouldn't, he agreed, and I grabbed his face, covering it in kisses. Our mouths locked together, and gentle caresses quickly became heated. "Let me take you to bed, baby," he muttered against my lips between kisses. "The night is a writeoff, anyway." I glanced at my watch and noticed the football was kicking off shortly, so I eagerly agreed. He took my hand and led me inside, stopping to pat Shane on the shoulder as I waved goodbye to Kendall.

"Off to bed, mate?" Shane questioned as he and Kendall turned to us.

"Yeah. May as well catch up on the rest while we can." Shane agreed and said they were just a little behind us. "And Marcus will throw us all out soon, anyway."

"You sure he hasn't already? Sounds pretty quiet in there."

We opened the door and stopped dead in our tracks. There was Mark and April in the kitchen, looking very cosy. "Get in, Mark!" Shane's voice burst through, followed by a powerful wolf whistle. The boys were both animated in their amusement, and it instantly reminded me of Stanthorpe, getting caught ourselves, when April buried her face in Mark's chest. "Your timing sucks, assholes." Mark let out a heavy sigh as April's legs unhooked from his hips, and she slid down off the kitchen countertop. "Where've the others gone?" I changed the subject, giving April a way out of the ribbing the boys would no doubt deliver Mark later.

"Mace went to bed when Chris, Liam, and Chester went to the bar for a few drinks. Marcus' just in the bedroom; he had to take a call from AusHop."

We thanked him and said, "we're heading off."

"Yeah, looks like it's time to bounce. Chester said he'll see you later, Brax. He forgot to leave you a smoke." We nodded and waved goodbye to April before sticking our heads around the door to let Marcus know we were leaving.

Once we got back, I made my way into the bedroom with him hot on my heels. His fingers gripped my waist as he gently pushed me back onto the bed. My laughter filled the room just as quickly as he ripped off his shirt. "Someone's eager?" I mused. Brax placed one knee up on the bed, leaning over me. "Always for my sexy, Evil Midget."

"How good is it to see Mark hooking one in?" He cocked his eyebrow at my comment, edging closer. Wrapping his hand under my knee and pulling my leg up over his hip, he pumped his hips into mine before asking, "Do you really wanna talk about Mark while I'm trying to hit a home run?"

"Sorry, my love," I tapped his cheek softly and kissed him. Turning to the bedside table, I picked up the television remote adding, "But you're just gonna have to wait ninety minutes." He grabbed my ankles, pulling me back to face him, and mumbled, "you're taking the piss."

"Braxton, we've set these ground rules before. Do I need to repeat myself?" His face was priceless, and it laced me with amusement.

"No, dear," he muttered, which set me off. He reminded me of a child being chastised and the laughter rippled out of me. "You could've told me that Liverpool was playing. I genuinely thought we would get some sexy time. I couldn't wait to get all up inside you." *Is he playing the guilt trip?*

"You make it sound like I never put out for you."

"When are you going to realise Charlotte Maree? I can't get enough of you." *This fucker is trying to make me feel bad!* "You tricked me and played on my emotions."

"Wanna make a compromise?" I offered him an olive branch.

"No, I wanna fuck!" He sat back on my hips, and I raised to lean on my elbows, waiting for him to answer me correctly. "Fine, I'm listening." I pushed further off the bed, as Brax scooted back to straddle my thighs. My fingers gripped the hem of my shirt, and when I started lifting it over my head, he was keen to help me along. I could sense his breathing increasing with the speed of his desire. Chucking it across the room, I pressed light kisses to his chest as my hands gripped his face.

"How about I let you fuck me while I watch the game?" He froze, and when his whole body stiffened, I pulled back to meet his gaze. His eyes darkened, and that look alone left me wondering if he had just cum in his boxers. It confirmed my thoughts when he rolled off the bed, pulling me by the hips closer to him. "Fuck me," he mumbled against my neck. He unfastened the button of my jeans, moaning, "That may be the hottest thing you've ever said to me."

"I can tell, you look like you're about to poke my eye out." My grip on his heavy cock only emphasised my point. I started grinding against him, while he slid his hand up my spine, tugging my hair to tilt my head toward him.

"I'll poke something; don't you worry about that." Teasingly, I slowly removed the rest of my clothes while he looked me up and down. He seemed mesmerised and never had a man made me feel so comfortable in my skin. "When I'm with you, Charlie, nothing else matters. You consume my every thought and being." His words of love spurred me on, and I shuffled back on the bed, laying on my stomach with the television remote in hand. I turned to the game just in time for kick-off, urging him to ask, "You're kidding, right? You're going back to your game?"

"Come and take what's yours, Brax." He growled noticeably and wasted no time in disposing of the rest of his clothes. He lay on top, his lips caressing my shoulders and back as I enjoyed a pressure-filled kick-off from Liverpool. My team scored just as he reached the bottom of my spine, where it curves to meet the buttocks. I went to jump and realised just as fast that he'd pinned me underneath him. "Yes! What a goal, VVD!" The vibration of his laughter rippled across my skin between stolen kisses. No sooner had he reached my ass cheeks and nipped at the flesh, VVD scored again, fuelling my excitement.

"Come here, please, Cutie," Brax pleaded while sitting up.

"Why?" My confused gaze turned to meet his lust-filled eyes.

"So I can bend you like Beckham." Once his broad head nestled between my warm and swollen lips, I dropped my head in time to see him disappearing inside of me. I moaned out my arousal the deeper he went. He pressed me further into the mattress with a loving hand. My ass was now high in the air, giving him deeper access. We groaned in pleasure, all the while my eyes glued to the television. "Fuck, Charlie. This is the hottest moment of my life." His husky voice sent shivers down my spine. "If someone had told me one day I'd be buried inside of the woman I love, while watching football, I would have called bullshit." I cried out, unable to articulate the indescribable waves of euphoria his words had spurred on. We found a sexy rhythm, almost all the way out, and then slowly and deeply back in when the whistle for halftime blew.

"Oh god, Brax! Fuck me harder, now!" We rode the waves of pleasure from each other with passion and desperation bordering on primal. Between gritted teeth and deep thrusts, Brax groaned, "I swear this is every man's fantasy! I'm so close, Charlie. You ready to take me, baby?"

"Mmm, Brax. I am, keep going," I gasped between breaths while pushing back to meet his brutal pounding. "Right there… Brax…" He started flowing deep inside me, holding himself still as he felt my pleasure squeeze tightly around him. My head flew back, and Brax's lips greeted my neck, sucking the sweat-covered flesh with a delicious tongue lick. We collapsed onto the bed, completely spent, and he rolled off to the side. I moved my hand, as my nails dragged along his lower stomach, leaving a trail of excited frisson in their wake. I rolled over, hearing the whistle begin the second half, and a few seconds later, his skilled fingers teased their way up the back of my thighs. Leaning over, he kissed my spine tenderly.

"I fucking love your legs, Cutie." His comment drew my curiosity, and I turned to him. "They're so soft to touch, and having them wrapped around me has an intensely visceral effect." We lay naked in each other's arms, enjoying the rest of the match and the warm sex glow that surrounded us. After a scary last ten minutes, following our goalkeeper's red card, we had safely secured the win, and I turned from the television.

"Wanna grab a spliff before getting some sleep?"

"It's like you can read my mind," he winked, confirming he did. Chucking some clothes on, we padded through to the kitchenette, fetching a bottle of water and our last smoke. We stepped out onto the balcony, and immediately Chester drew my attention. He was with a mystery redhead on his adjacent room veranda. It took a minute and a furious rub of my eyes to focus in the dark, but they were in a very compromising position. Brax made a noticeable cough behind his hand, drawing his attention. The look on Chester's face found immediate favour with me. "Are we interrupting something, brother?" Chester all but jumped back from the woman. Even in the night, I was sure they both had reddened cheeks.

He spluttered while trying to clear his throat and answer simultaneously, "Agh.. no… yes," he nervously giggled. I had *never* seen him anything less than confident, so I loved every second of this! "Chrissy, meet Brax, my best mate, and singer of Abandoned Bygone. And that's Evil Midget." He and Brax both cracked up laughing, easing the tension.

"Hi, it's nice to meet you both." Her accent was such a playful tune as if she were the star of her own movie. I could see why Chester was so enamoured.

"**P**retty sure you were supposed to drop me off a smoke?" I quizzed, waving my last blunt at him. He grumbled, then stepped back from Chrissy, who he'd pinned up against the railing, and mumbled they would be around in a second.

I welcomed them into our suite a short while later. "I'm Brax, and this is Charlie," I said, introducing Chrissy properly, since he hadn't. Charlie reached forward, shaking her hand before we all headed back outside. "I hope I'm not intruding." Chrissy questioned, realising their sudden arrival may be uninvited. I shook my head to let her know it was fine. "Not at all, although I'm not sure we can say the same about Chester." Charlie turned her mischievous eyes on him.

"I have feelings, you know," he retorted, earning himself a shrug from Charlie. My smirk grew, then he added, "is buttcheeks one word, or should I spread them so you can kiss my ass?" she didn't get the chance to answer him when Chrissy beat her to it. "No one wants to kiss an ass that shits every time it talks," she mumbled, but Charlie and I heard it, causing a chorus of laughter to rupture the quiet night. "Ouch!" Chester gripped his chest, pivoting on the spot to look at Chrissy. "You wouldn't say no to me, baby."

"True, I would probably just laugh instead." *Oh, I like this girl!* She was precisely what Chester needed. She met his puzzled expression with a sly grin, so I threw the poor fucker a lifeline and changed the subject.

"Chrissy, can we have a blunt?" I asked politely. "I wanted to check before lighting up."

"Of course," she agreed with a friendly smile. "I'm the guest here."

"You're welcome to join us," Charlie offered. I was sure she wanted to spend time with her to pry for information. "Grab a chair."

"Here, sit on my lap. We can chat about the first thing that pops up." Chester patted his knee while lowering into the seat.

"Why would I want to talk about your ego?" Chrissy was all over his shit, and even he guffawed, paying credit with a small applause.

"So, how did you end up with this Monkey?" I asked, curiously. Although, I had suspicions about why he'd gone to the bar earlier. Chrissy confirmed it. "He gatecrashed my catch-up with a friend." Shrugging her shoulders, she added, "He refused to leave until I agreed to have a drink with him."

Chester tweaked his nipples. "She couldn't say no to this body."

She was fast on the counter-attack. "There's only so much whining you can put up with from a grown man."

"You couldn't drag your eyes away from this sexiness."

"Consider it my charitable contribution for the day." *This is great!* We were both thoroughly amused seeing Chester meet his match. This battle of wits was enthralling, even as he lay it on thick, she had him bouncing on his toes.

"What's the news I heard about Mark and April earlier?" Chester asked, deflecting attention from his failed attempts. He took a draw of the blunt before offering it to Chrissy, who thanked him.

"What were you told?" Charlie quizzed before disclosing any information.

"Because it's probably true," I piped in. "And Mark didn't have to share this time." Chester's eyes widened in a clear warning to shut the fuck up, realising I was referring to him.

"Did they leave together?" I was about to answer, but he rushed on, "Not that you would have noticed. I came to see you when I got back, but heard you two going to pound town."

"I'm surprised you didn't listen like you normally do," Charlie retorted. Leaning forward, she thanked Chrissy for passing over the blunt.

"What can I say, Midget... Brax moaned 'Oh yeah' so much, I was about to burst through the door like the kool-aid man." *This fucker!* I pegged my cap at him, but Chester dodged it just in time.

"You can fuck off now." I flipped my thumb toward his adjoining veranda. We both laughed, with him ignoring me. The girls had moved their chairs closer to each other and seemed to have struck up their own conversation. Chester drew my attention back, asking, "Wanna have another smoke before calling it a night?" I nodded, and he sparked one up.

"Did you hear if there's any update on Brett?" I was worried, and the anxious wait was taking its toll.

"No, mate." He tilted his head back, exhaling heavily. "Only that Marcus and Nick think we'll have to postpone the next gig." Stress pained his features, and I understood. Until we had an update, the tour was effectively on hold. "I'm sure Nick will contact Marcus as soon as he hears anything."

"I'll message the boys in the morning," I thought out aloud, adding, "We should use the time to get some practice in." Chester passed me the spliff to have a draw and agreed. "No point in dropping the ball when we could still be on schedule, right?"

"It'll be alright, Brax. We worked hard for this, and these Canadians will see what we can do." A smile crept across my face. Chester's optimism was the energy we all needed to remember. Leaning forward, he tapped the screen on his phone, then looked up and lowered his voice. "We'll get heading after this smoke. I don't want Midget fucking up my chance tonight." He threw his eyes toward the two girls as they huddled even closer together.

In mumbled humour, I reminded him, "I'm pretty sure you had your work cut out for you, my guy, even before she spoke to Evil Midget."

"Did you really say that to me?" he asked, his face flat except for dilated eyes. When I shook my head, he added, "I'm pursuing that hard. She's feisty as fuck," he adjusted his trousers, whispering, "I need it." We both laughed, and he stood, turning to Chrissy. "Are you ready to go? It's getting pretty late, and Brax already blew a nut tonight, so he won't be able to stay up much longer."

"Fuck off already, you prick." My apologetic eyes found Charlie while Chester laughed in our faces.

"It was nice to meet you both," Chrissy said. "Thank you for the smoke."

"Hopefully, we'll see you around while we're still in town," Charlie quizzed her as we walked them out. Neither of us moved, watching to see what would happen next, secretly hoping she would send him to bed with blue balls. Chester tapped his swipe card against the door panel and held it open, allowing Chrissy to proceed. Turning back to look at us, he grabbed his crotch and thrust his hips, sending us into a fresh wave of amusement.

After I shut the door and locked it, I turned and found Charlie had strolled through to the kitchenette. She grabbed two bottles of water, asking, "One more smoke and bed?"

"Definitely." She sat on my lap and rolled up, allowing us a moment to unwind. I was mindlessly stroking her leg when she leaned back into me, lighting up for us. "Sorry about the show, babe. I know how much this tour means to you and the boys." Her apologetic eyes met mine, and I moved forward to kiss her on the nose.

"It's just a minor delay, Cutie," I said, trying to keep my voice positive.

"The gig may have to be postponed for a few days, but does that mean we can do something for your birthday with the schedule change?"

I raised my eyebrows in question. "I thought we agreed we'd just have a party when we get back and incorporate it with our engagement?"

"How about just the two of us celebrating on the day?" I smiled lovingly, appreciating her attempts to distract my wandering and concerned mind.

"I'll never complain about spending all my minutes with you."

Happiness swept across her face, engulfing her in a loving glow. "What'd you have in mind?"

"A private dance party," Charlie teased, swinging her legs around to straddle me. She wrapped her arms around my shoulders, nestling her mouth into my neck and kissing up to my ear. I gripped her hips and pulled her closer, burying my head into her hair. My senses flooded with her intoxicating scent until she pulled back to have a draw on the smoke. My intent stare followed the mist of smoke as it swirled around her lips before filling her lungs. I leaned forward to smother her mouth with mine, and Charlie exhaled, letting me receive the combination of expelled air and smoke.

"I'm gonna eat your pussy like it's the last birthday cake I'll ever receive." She shivered, hearing my hunger for her, and moved to kiss me again. My hands slipped under her clothes, fondling the creamy flesh of her buttcheeks and grinding her pelvis into my increased desire. "How about round two?"

"I'm always ready for you," she groaned, spurring on my urgency. After taking the last drag of smoke, I stubbed it out and stood, still holding on to her body. Her legs wrapped around my waist as I carried her to the bed.

Banging on the door woke me the next day, and I reached for my phone to find it just after midday. Tapping Charlie on the backside, I kissed her shoulder and mumbled, "Time to get up, sexy." I shook the sleepy haze from my head as I made my way out to answer the door. Liam spoke first.

"Hey. Chester mentioned you wanted to work on some beats while we could?" I nodded, running my hands down my face, rubbing the sleep from my eyes. "Brett's still in the hospital. Marcus should be over in about half an hour with an update."

"I'm grabbing a coffee," Shane announced, continuing to the kitchenette. "You guys want a cup?" All the boys said '*yes*', Charlie trudged out of the room, still drowsy and raising her hand to one as well.

"Where're the girls?" she asked Shane and Liam, looking at them.

"Mace is on a Google call for work," Liam explained. "It should only take about an hour."

Shane hollered over his shoulder, "Kendall's chilling back in the room, Midget."

"What's he doing?" she pointed to Chester, who was getting his instrument ready. "Fingering his g-string to make sure it's securely over his nut," Mark replied, unfazed, while the rest of us stifled our amusement. "We were going to have a session while we had some downtime." Liam explained once he settled down. She made her way over, offering to give Shane a hand as the rest of us fell back on the couch.

Chester swung his guitar across his lap, and soon the sweet chords of his craft filled the surrounding space. Even with the concern drowning us, there was a divinity to his musical instrument. I watched the way his guitar interacted with the bright sunlight and how the sweet hues sang to us all. It was a portal of sorts for the artists in us, which was why our music was so beloved. Mark once told him that *'the guitar can only meet its true destiny when the player is ready to embrace theirs.'* In those acoustic chords, the instrument had made its way into skillful hands that gave it a soulful caress. The chorus was as playful as Chester was himself. With closed eyes, I could envision the music in colours, painting a vivid path in beautiful chaos. The calm of our music saw my heartbeat steadied with the melody. My voice seeped into the moment, allowing my lullabies to skim the air with him. In singing, I healed myself and those who loved my music. Thus, as I gave to my soul, I offered to theirs, too.

"You know," Mark's voice floated in when the song finished, "I think an acoustic version of "Imagine Joy" and "Private Destiny" would be insane." He shrugged his shoulders as I lifted my head to meet him. "Maybe even an album one day?"

"Our greatest hits in their rawest form," Shane agreed. He and Charlie joined us, passing everyone their drinks. "What time did Marcus say he'd be around?"

"Any time now," Liam answered between sips of his hot drink. "He'll probably wait until he has an update from Nick."

"We should check in with Chris and April to make sure they're alright." I looked between the boys, wondering if anyone had spoken to them yet today.

"She's fine," Mark mumbled, his eyes burning into the coffee. I noticed the other guys smirking, even I smiled.

"Chris went to the hospital with Nick early this morning," Chester confirmed. "I ran into them downstairs when I was seeing Chrissy out."

"I really like her," Charlie chimed in with a massive smile.

"Of course you do, you fucking menace," Chester quipped back.

"It's about time you got a taste of your own medicine, Monkey. When aren't you riding our arses?"

"Well, if I'm such a pain in the ass, Midget, why don't we add some lubricant?" He wiggled his eyebrows at her, so I quickly leaned over and punched him in the arm.

"You prick." He rubbed it furiously, but before he could say anymore, we heard a knock at the door.

"That'll be Marcus," I figured since the boys mentioned it earlier. Charlie had already moved to let him in.

"I'm impressed." Marcus pointed to the guitar resting between Chester and Mark. "You're practising without being told to for once."

Chester tormented him. "You've already got enough grey hairs, M. I don't wanna get the blame for anymore."

"Have you heard from Glaze yet?" Shane quickly asked, and Marcus nodded with a weary smile.

"Brett's in surgery now."

"Fuck," we all mumbled in unison, hen I added, "What does that mean for the tour?"

"We'll be postponing a couple of shows, but he should be fine after resting for a week or two." Marcus took a seat with us and continued. "Nick is confident they'll be able to manage it as long as he does nothing too strenuous."

"Doesn't really sound ideal," Liam mumbled, concern painting his face.

"It's not," Marcus conceded, "but Brett is adamant he's finishing the shows with Glaze, so I need you boys to stay focused." We all promised, and I believed it. This opportunity was significant to each of us, and we had no intention of messing it up. "I've spoken with Nick, and we'll use the time to collaborate with Glaze."

"Really?" I shot forward in my seat, my mouth agape. "You think it's the right time?"

"I want you and Nick working on the lyrics." I eagerly agreed, and he continued. "Shane, I'm going to pull you in with the other three, Chris and myself. We can start engineering the track. We'll be able to record before we leave Canada if we pull our resources."

"You're not joking, are you, Marcus? You really want to move now?" I was still shocked and needed to confirm this was happening so quickly.

"I've spoken with AusHop and Glaze's label under Nick's instructions." My leg started bouncing as he paused for dramatic effect. "Glaze will join us for the Australian Music Awards later this year, where you will release and perform the song live for the first time."

Chapter Fourteen

CHARLIE

Following the news from Marcus, the boys spent the afternoon with their heads buried together, plotting ideas for their collaboration. Both Managers had told the bands to 'take tonight off before it was business as usual tomorrow.' It allowed me to assist with the rescheduling of the next show in Regina, Saskatchewan, and adjusting the rest of the tour. It also gave Glaze and Abandoned Bygone an opportunity to visit Brett to ensure the surgery had gone well.

We arrived at the hospital and checked in at reception late afternoon before being directed to Brett's room. Chester knocked as he stuck his head around the door frame. "I come bearing gifts." This drew Brett's attention, and he broke out into a smile as Monkey waved a blunt from side to side.

"Hey! Come on in." Brett shuffled in the bed, sitting up slightly as we all gathered around the small room, mumbling multiple questions to him. The obvious was how he felt, Brett confirmed, "Good at the minute. I'm still pretty dosed up, so I'll milk that for as long as possible."

"Well, it's the only thing that's gonna get milked at the moment, bro." Of course, that was Chester, and I noticed Brax rub his groin in sympathy.

"Thanks for reminding me, asshole." Brett rubbed his lower stomach, emphasising his discomfort.

"We bought you some proper food. Hopefully, that'll help?" April said while stepping forward and handing Brett the gourmet sandwich and other assortments we'd picked up on the way.

"You're the best, darling." He immediately unwrapped it, the aroma taking hold of his appetite. "I was starving. They feed you like fucking pigeons in here." Everyone could sympathise.

"How did the surgery go?" Brax asked his burning question. I knew he'd been anxious since news broke of the hospitalisation, both about his recovery and the tour.

"Nothing to stress, mate. He said I should be good to go in a week to ten days." Brett assured the group in between bites of his sandwich.

"That's not what he said," Nick mumbled from his seat at the back of the room. We all turned to find out what that comment meant. "He said light activities only after about ten days."

"Yeah, but either way, he cleared me for the tour to continue," Brett countered.

"As long as you don't overdo it," Nick continued. He reminded me of Marcus, and while the tour came with commitments, they always put the health of their artists first. "Any antics from you, and I'll cancel the shows myself." Brett's jaw dropped. I had to bite the inside of my lip when I saw the Managers smirk at each other.

"Goes for you as well, Chester," Marcus added, throwing fuel to the fire.

"What?" he was vocal in his shock. "There's nothing wrong with my health."

"I know," Marcus confirmed. "I just don't want any of your shit." The entire room cracked up laughing.

"Will you really pull the shows, Nick?" Chris asked, needing to know how serious that comment was.

"No," he shook his head, grinning. "Brett needs to make sure he does nothing too strenuous, though, at least for a few weeks."

"We've got him covered," Shane jumped in as Nick barely finished speaking. "Whatever we can do to help, right boys?" He looked around the room and we all nodded.

Meanwhile, Brax moved closer behind me as he whispered, "I suddenly feel very sore for him."

I turned my head slightly, a twinkle in my eye as I enquired, "Are you just saying that so I might take care of you later?"

"Well, I won't say no if you're offering." I dug my elbow into his ribs in response.

We spent a few hours with Brett, keeping him company, then returning to the hotel. Everyone went to their rooms to shower before dinner. I was in the bathroom, warming the water up, when Brax came through and started stripping off. "Really?" He looked perplexed. "I need to wax and wash my hair tonight," I explained.

"Yeah, and I need to wash my balls in case they end up in your mouth later." My head rolled backwards and the laughter that expelled echoed in the confined space. Through continued humour, I mumbled, "fucking hell, Brax. Your head is demented."

"That's because it's constantly banging against your cervix," he shrugged, to my horror.

"Not that head," I squeaked. Not phased at all, he grinned, picked me up, and walked into the shower. After repeatedly slapping his hand away in the hope he'd behave, we finally washed and moved into the lounge room. Brax opened the door so the group could enter when they were ready.

"Baby, Chester just texted and asked if he could invite Chrissy around tonight?"

"Sure, no problem at all. I really like her." Brax texted him back and soon everyone joined us.

"I reckon we should go out tomorrow. No point in sitting around when we have a free night, right?" Chester raised the question, the boys looked at each other, then at Marcus.

"Depends how much work you get done on the new track tomorrow," Marcus threw the ball back in their court.

"Wanna join us, Chrissy?" Chester asked hopefully. After a quick shrug of her shoulders, she agreed, and the relief that washed over his face was new. He really did like this girl. Chester turned to Mark and added, "You should invite April?" tilting his chin towards the front door where she and Chris had just entered.

"Thanks, Chester, but we already have plans." Mark didn't offer any further information.

"Smoke the grass, skip class, and eat some ass, brother." We all laughed when Mark shook his head and said, "Fuck, this is going to be a long night." And he was right.

Now that we knew Brett was okay, the stress the boys had been carrying dissipated. When Marcus left, Chester had gone from loose to completely feral. And for the last half an hour, he'd non-stop tormented the entire group, trying to get someone to take the bait. It finally worked, and I just had to ask, "Why do you have to be a pain in the arse?"

"Think of me like a haemorrhoid." Chester shrugged and then wickedly grinned. "I enjoy annoying assholes." He winked at me as the group laughed. Brax went flying at Chester, but he was on the ball, and jumped out of the way just in time. Mace drew our attention and curiosity when her extended humour burst through.

"Sorry," she mumbled while trying to control herself. "Liam reckons if that's the best pickup line he has, it explains why Monkey's single."

"Go on then, Hippie Boy. Let's hear yours." Chester waved his hand in Liam's direction as he took a seat, sparking up a blunt.

"You first, big mouth." Liam sipped his beer before pointing it at him.

"Do you believe in Karma?" Chester asked Chrissy, turning to her. She nodded a 'yes', before he continued, "Amazing. I know some good 'karma-sutra' positions."

"I need to steal that one," Chris laughed into his beer.

"Do you believe in dragons? Because I'll be dragon my balls across your face tonight." I nearly spat my drink out when Kendall shared hers, and if I thought that was funny, the entire group roared in hysterics when Shane pointed out, "hey! I fucking said that." Brax only stopped laughing long enough to share one a fan tried on him.

"I may not go down in history, but I'll go down on you." He finished, and I caught the eyes of Kendall and Mace. Our unspoken acknowledgement said we all agreed that sounded like something a fan-girl would try.

Liam said, "Pizza is my second favourite thing to eat in bed," and Shane cracked up. "That sounds like Chester's life story." Everyone agreed with him.

"The only reason I would kick you out of bed would be to fuck you on the floor." Kendall glared at Shane, which drew everyone's attention. It was as if she couldn't believe he was being serious. "Just returning the favour, baby," he squeezed her cheeks between his fingers. After a quick kiss, he explained, "you wanna throw me under the bus? I'll bang you on the floor."

"Did you actually say that, Kenny?" Mace's highly amused tone quizzed her. "Yeah, I was trying to be romantic." Even the guys lost it with her answer.

"I'd like to use your thighs as earmuffs." Chrissy's contribution had Chester reeling, and he asked, "is that an offer?" The intense and silent stare between the two that followed highlighted some heavy sexual tension.

"Excuse me, I'm about to masturbate and need a name to go with the face." Liam groaned before expelling a sarcastic laugh when Mace told us that one. "I remember that gimp, too," Liam shook his head, Mace nudged his shoulder with her own.

"It was that nasty fucker at Grunge bar, right?" Chester clicked his fingers as he remembered as well. "He was chewing his face off all night from too many pingers." They both nodded, confirming that's who she was talking about.

Chris jumped in with, "I wish you were soap, so I could feel you all over me," which prompted Chester to rub his own nipples.

April's turn had Brax very tickled. "You know how your hair would look good? In my lap."

"Fuck, I'm definitely using that on Charlie." Brax explained in between his humour. "Is that a fact?" I lifted my eyebrows and twisted in my seat to glare at him. The twinkle in his eye revealed that he was intoxicated and enjoying himself.

Mark continued with, 'What time do you get off? Can I watch?' The boys all laughed, and it was finally my turn.

"I'm a zombie. Can I eat you out?" Brax rubbed my butt before giving it a little tap. "They aren't all bad, though. What was that romantic one I said to you a little while ago?" He had another drink of his beer while I tried to remember when he added, "and you still rolled your eyes at me!" That's when I knew exactly what he was referring to. "If that was your idea of romance, you're lucky. I don't expect it often." The girls chuckled. Curiosity got the better of them, so they asked what it was. "I'd love to kiss those luscious lips. And when I'm finished, I'll smooch your face as well." Poor Mark, who was rocking backwards on his chair when I spoke, went barreling over. Tears rolled down my face, the chaos of the situation finding favourable humour with us all.

Once things settled down, I saw Brax eyeballing Chester, who looked cross faded and drunk as a skunk. "What's wrong, baby?" I moved my chair closer to him, cuddling into his arm and resting my head on his shoulder. Instead of answering me, Brax tilted his head slightly as he shouted to Chester, "Bro! What're you looking at?" His head immediately shot up before rolling back, laughing.

"Tell her boobs to stop staring at me," he whined, running his hands down his face, shaking his head.

Shane smacked his hat off, asking, "What the fuck is wrong with you?"

"I dunno, man. I'm about to pass out."

"I'm not surprised; you look cooked," Brax tilted his chin, noticing his head wobbling.

"I am! You even look hot right now, brother," he laughed as he combed his fingers through his hair.

"Oh, thanks, baby," Brax clicked his teeth, winking back. "I always knew you had a wet spot for me." He blew him a kiss, which Chester reached into the air to catch. I nudged his ribs and smiled at the pair of gronks. Truth be told, Brax looked tanked as well.

After another beer, I stood to go to the bathroom and break the seal when he followed me. "Brax, what are you doing?"

"Coming with you?"

"I'm going to pee," I chuckled, before turning to head inside.

"Okay," he mumbled. I walked inside when I noticed him still tailing me and laughed as I took his hand to help. "Never mind, Chester, you're just as wasted," I murmured as I helped him through the sliding door.

"Lead the way," he pointed through the hotel room. I moved towards the hallway, and his hands wandered to my ass, which I tried to push off. When I finally whined his name, his breath skimmed my neck. He pulled me back into him, and his slurred voice quizzed, "Why do you think I always say you first, Cutie? So I can check your ass out," he pumped his hips into my backside to emphasise his point.

"Brax! Knock it off," I whined, while trying to wiggle from his grasp. *I was desperate for the bathroom!*

"Was your ass forged by Sauron? Because it's precious." Laughing at his own joke gave me time to create space between us, and I pressed him into the hallway walls. Holding his shoulders pinned to the wall, I glared at him, begging, "Just wait here, please."

"Are you sure you don't want an extra hand?" he tormented as I opened the toilet door.

"I'm fine!" I groaned, shutting and locking it.

When I returned, I found him crouching on the floor with his head resting against the wall and eyes closed. Striding forward, I stroked the hair off his forehead, but stopped when Chester and Liam came around the corner, and Monkey bellowed, "Yes, bro! Go muff diving!" He thrust his hips towards a stunned Brax, and I glared at them. I had no time to register a protest when Brax grabbed my waist and yanked me forward to meet his face. He rubbed his cheeks across the front of my jeans, growling feverishly.

"Brax, get up," I cried while tugging his shirt. "You need some water."

"I think you already wet my whistle enough." Liam took the chance to sneak into the toilet while Chester and Brax continued their carry-on.

"Don't tell me I have to babysit both your arses tonight?" I grumbled as they swung their arms around my shoulders. "I thought you had a gorgeous redhead waiting outside for you?"

"Midget," his eyes lit up with recognition. "Have you seen the ass on her? I wanna dive in face first…" he started blowing raspberries into the air.

"Do it, don't be scared, bro," Brax encouraged.

"I'm not scared!"

"Sit down, now," I ordered both boys, pointing to the couch. With rolled eyes, I headed into the kitchenette and retrieved two cold water bottles.

"I'm telling you, Chester, I'm gonna give it to Charlie so hard tonight she'll feel me in her stomach…. from the inside." I heard him carrying on with Chester and sucked my teeth.

"I was going to contact heaven earlier to see if they had an angel for me, but decided I wanted a slut instead." They both sounded like a pair of hyenas to no one else's entertainment but their own.

"Man, Charlie gets so fucking dirty when she's off her head." I went to lunge, and noticed the deplorable state he was in, slouched drunkenly on the couch.

"Brax!" My stunned squeak stopped him only momentarily. *My god, this man and his mouth.* "Baby, it's true! The way you wrap your tongue around-"

"If you ever want that again, you'll shut the fuck up while you still can." I cut him off, throwing the bottled water. He nodded furiously, "And drink." I threw the other one to Chester.

"Okay, baby." When he thought I had turned around, I saw him lean over, trying to whisper. Neither of them knew how to be inconspicuous!

"Yes, Bro! No wonder you hit that ass so much." Chester roared across the room. I turned, pointed to his bottle, and showed he needed to drink as well.

"She loves a good spanking, too."

"For the love of fuck, Brax. If you don't shut up, I'll spank you."

Once Chester finished laughing, he muttered, "I told you so."

"What did you tell me, bro?"

"Remember, after our Regional Tour, what she said about *'kinky'* being hot? I told you to hit it then, did I not?"

"Yeah, Chester, I guess I owe you… for telling me to do something I already thought about daily." Brax barely pushed him, but given his state at the moment, he nearly tumbled off the couch.

"Oi, you pair of gronks. Thanks for fucking leaving without me."

"Sorry," Chester apologised to Liam and asked, "were you waiting for us?"

"Yeah," he retorted sarcastically, I buckled over, laughing. "You realise, Liam, you could have just walked out of the hallway, and you would have found us?" Brax also lost it at my comment and asked if I remembered when "we caught him talking to his reflection in the mirror?"

The three were sitting on the couch in hysterics when Mark came in to find us. However, that soon turned to him, diving across the top of them and yelling, "Mosh Pit!" His comment saw Liam and Shane scramble to join in as well. "Oh, for fuck's sake, seriously, guys? Hope you're babysitting tonight, Charlie?" Mace had made her presence known just as the fuckers started wrestling on the couch and eventually fell on the floor. They ended up sitting around the coffee table, packing another smoke and mumbling with Chris and April about finalising lyrics tomorrow. My eyes flickered in delight when I noticed Chester finally got his own way, and there sat Chrissy firmly in his lap. *I'll give him stick for that tomorrow.*

Soon after, once I was confident they had settled down, I called it quits for the night. "Behave you lot. I'm heading to bed," I waved. "I'm coming," Brax bellowed, then added, "You will be too." Ignoring his suggestive wink, I turned and started walking down the hall.

He jumped up to run after me when I heard an all-mighty crash and swung around in a flash to see what had happened. There, splayed out on the floor, was Brax. The laughter emanating from the group was deafening.

The boys were rolling on the ground, and I saw Chester grab his crotch as he swore he would piss his pants. My confusion bounced back and forth between the girls on the couch, who sounded like a chorus line of chimpanzees. "What the hell just happened?" My confusion bounced rapidly between them. "Is someone going to tell me?"

Kendall managed, in between chuckles, to explain, "He flew up to race after you, missed the hallway, and ran straight into the wall." She spat her last few words out as she pissed herself laughing again.

Chapter Fifteen

BRAX

After shaking off the hangover from hell, not to mention the headache from running into the wall, I was fed and showered, with my full commitment to this collaboration. Chris and I spread out around the dining table. It was large recycled wood upon strong iron legs, each at a jaunty angle as if it was stretching before a pleasant jog. In the grains were flecks of colours that magnified the heat the sun sought to carry. I wondered how many conversations took place here, laughter shared, or how many had smiled and felt relief at this very table. Yet for now, it was my doorway into adventures of words and imagination, the tip toes of each emotion I wrote in pixelated ink. In a good mood, I could paint words that were like fine wine. They were clear water over rocks, a shelter in the storm, food for the soul and every flower in the light. With a tormented mind, though, writing was like making another hole in the bucket that carried my hidden pain. My soul went full raw so that I could go full roar.

Some writers started with careful planning, others began with a feeling or a single sentence and let it grow like crystals on a string. There was no right or wrong, for art wasn't a technical skill, it was an expressive path to resuscitate me. And as I scrunched and tossed one page after another, it reminded me of the words my high school teacher once shared with me—*Your first draft is like a lump of clay ready to be formed and sculpted.* And so I tried again.

A chance encounter, a spark, they say
Felt like the stars aligned for us that day
A moment of fate, a sign from the sky
That it was meant to be just you and I.

I read it once... twice... three times, before scrunching it up. Hearing another crinkling piece of paper, Chris lifted his head, asking, "you alright?" I dropped the pen, taking my cap off and brushing my fingers through my hair while expelling a heavy sigh.

"Everything feels personal now," I exhaled. "I've always hated sharing too much of my life. Yet my head feels trapped in a cloud of self-indulgence." He relaxed back into his seat, stating, "Harness it." My brows knitted, unsure how to do that. "Just because we're in the public eye doesn't mean we have to share everything. But we can use those emotions to reach people at their level of understanding." My biro twirled between my index finger and thumb, concentrating on the advice he was graciously offering. "Let the lyrics fashion below the level of fear, transform them into wings that can fly for so many years, beyond the generations and into the horizons yet unsung." He noticed my confusion, adding, "Lyrics can raise or chain you, Brax." He turned his notepad around, letting me peruse his sprawling words. While I read each line repeatedly, he reminded me, "we channel *true* art through the loving heart, guided by emotions that stir the soul to loving bonds." Stirs the soul... there was only one thing—or should I say, person—who held all the power to do that. I passed him his notepad back as I really thought about every word he said.

And then I wrote, with the emotion that burned, the joys that sang and the tears I never cried before because I didn't think anyone would care. Hours later, ankle deep in littered paper, Charlie returned after spending some time with the girls, just as Chris was packing up to get ready to visit Brett.

"Hey you two," she smiled, waving to Chris and coming over to greet me. "How'd you go?"

"We got through a lot today, right?" I looked at him hopefully, relieved by his assurance.

"Creativity is messy, brother. But we got there," he offered. "A few more tweaks and we will have another hit on our hands." He patted me on the shoulder encouragingly. "I'll catch you later. I promised to take Brett a proper dinner tonight."

"Bye, Chris, send him our regards, please." Charlie said as she moved to the kitchen while I saw him out. "You want a drink, babe, while I'm making?"

"Love one," I joined her, stretching the aches out of my hands from all the writing. "Suppose I better clean this mess up, too." I leaned down, picking one ball of paper up after another.

"That's a lot of frustration there," Charlie joked as she saw the mounting pile on my arm. She knew what this process was like for me, but I can't ever recall it being this bad.

"I couldn't get out of my head at first," I recalled, "but something Chris said finally helped to lift the writer's block." She waited for me to explain. "Everything I was writing felt like I was allowing an invasion of myself." She walked around the bench while waiting for the kettle to boil, helping to pick up the mess. I saw her unscrew a piece of paper and start reading it when I waved my hand at her. "Don't worry about that, babe, it's just a piece of two-dollar scrap paper now."

"The words are without price, though." She looked up at me. Then back down, reading some of my discarded lyrics aloud. "No matter what life brings, we'll be side by side. Some things we don't understand, but time will tell us why. Our story is written, it's our destiny, and I'm ready to share it with just you and me." She looked up to see me cringe, stepping closer as she tossed the piece of paper, attention solely on me. "Everything you say is music to me, no matter the words or topic." Her soft hand brushed my cheek before cradling it. "Because it came from your mind and flowed through you to the pen that would otherwise rest lazily on the table." A tender kiss thanked her for the loving words and I realised she was right.

Writing was the deep expression of so many parts of myself, the conscious me and my dreaming brain weaving new words with healing power.

Forty-eight hours later, they released Brett from the hospital, and after *nine* days, we were back on the road to our next stop, Regina, Saskatchewan. Little missy was hyperactive as hell because my birthday was close and she had something up her sleeve, but wasn't telling me. She was even letting me get loose, which was a surprise given my latest escapade. Tonight we had a gig and, as a thank you for our audience's patience, given the hospitalisation of Brett, we were including a 'meet and greet.'

The trip from Winnipeg to Regina was comfortable as we went straight down the Trans-Canada Highway and arrived a little over seven hours later, getting checked in quickly. We were staying at the Ramada Plaza, as it was one of only a few hotels in the area that could accommodate our requirements.

It pleasantly surprised me when we arrived at our assigned suite. I was even more excited at the idea of getting her half naked and bent over the edge of the indoor pool and spa the hotel boasted upstairs. Because of the downtime we had suffered in Winnipeg, we were on a tight schedule. Marcus and Nick were keen to make up as much time as possible, so that left us just thirty minutes to get changed and ready for tonight's show.

The show went really well and even though we had pushed it out for several days, because of unforeseen circumstances, the crowd were really appreciative that we didn't cancel, still trying.

Both bands had played an awesome show, and we were loading the bus when, out of nowhere, a hail of rocks and chunks of red bricks came raining down on us. We all turned around to see a group of teenagers, chucking stones from a nearby empty lot at any cars or people that went by. Shane turned to me and the other boys as he questioned "Anyone else feel like fucking those little punks up?" Chester jumped straight onboard, having just been hit on the back of the head by a projectile, and Mark followed suit after. Security scrambled to control the situation, as Marcus barked order but when Mace got hit in the arm, causing a laceration, Liam went postal.

"Liam," Marcus shouted. "This is not a good idea! There is a reason we have security."

"That little fuck there," he pointed to where they had raced off, "just hit Mace! You can't see her arm?"

"Wrong guys to draw blood with Marcus, you know that." It bewildered me that he even thought that would work. Chris was straight on our side, offering their help. We put our shit on the bus and went to head over when we all heard Kendall scream and turned to see one of the cinder block pieces they had thrown in a fresh round of attack caught her across the thigh. Now we all saw red.

Shane took off yelling back to Marcus, "Don't you dare try to fucking stop me!" Security was hot on his tail.

"Charlie, help Kendall on the bus, babe, and get that cut covered." I noticed April had already taken Mace under her wing. "None of you leave." I instructed, adding, "And lock the door!" The boys and security had already taken off the moment they saw Kendall get cut, and I followed, catching up to Mark. I turned a few times to make sure the girls were secure.

Heading back into the venue, I saw a kid dash past me, holding a skateboard, with two other little fuckers trailing behind him. We took off, but Marcus, Nick, and security had already got there when I arrived. "Who's got him? Where's the son of a bitch that hit Kendall?

I shook my head at Shane, not sure, having just arrived out the back. "No idea. Two of them raced out here, so we followed."

We ran over to the others when we saw a scuffle, and sure enough, Marcus and Nick had him and his mates cornered. We restrained his friends while we left the little prick that hit Kendall for Shane to sort. He didn't waste any time as he tackled him and pressed him up against the chain-link fence, using his elbow to press his face into the cold steel. When his mates tried to break free to help, we all joined in with security, quick to detain them.

Shane was still laying into the kid that hit Kendall and was now using his own skateboard as a weapon against him. Once Shane had finished, Liam picked up the kid, recognising him as the same one that hit Mace and dumped him upside down into one of those barrel garbage cans that were full of rubbish. Kicking the can over with the teenager inside, Liam booted it one more time, giving his head a good wobble. We turned our attention back to his friends, making sure they got a nice touch up as well. A few minutes into the scuffle, two cops pulled up watching from the safety of their squad car. Eventually they called out, "Alright boys, I think they've had enough now and learned their lesson." One cop shouted as he emerged from his car to drag the frazzled youths away from the melee. The other told us that these kids, ages ranging from eighteen to twenty, were the town's biggest shit stirrers. They had fucked with every visitor that passed through and no one ever did anything about it. "While I'm pleased to see someone finally put an end to their shenanigans and taught them a lesson, I think you all should probably leave and let me get these little punks booked in down the station." They explained to the head of security concerned revellers inside, saw what the boys had done and called it into the station.

Getting back on the bus, I could see the relief on Shane and Liam's faces after inspecting the girls to find they were just superficial scratches. I took the time to check Charlie over making sure she was fine as well. We got settled on the bus and started heading back to the hotel, not before she wrapped her arms around my neck and nuzzled my neck. "That was so hot, Brax."

I chuckled, not wanting to draw attention from the motor-mouth sitting near us as I asked, "why do you always get aroused when I bork up?" She insisted she didn't, but I knew otherwise. Running my hand down her back, I slid it into the waistband of her pants and grabbed a fist full of her gorgeous butt. "Don't lie to me, Evil Midget."

She bit down on my neck teasingly before moaning. "I don't know, but I promise you the moment we get back, you are fucking me in that pool just like you wanted."

Chapter Sixteen

CHARLIE

Marcus and Nick agreed we could have drinks tonight to celebrate Brax turning thirty tomorrow. The usual beverages back at the hotel weren't anything outlandish, and it minimised the attention drawn to the bands from the media. Brax was happy with this, so we piled onto the bus and returned. Everyone decided they wanted to shower and get changed first. Sometimes, it was easy to forget that the stage was boiling during a performance. Combine the lights, pyrotechnics, strobes or lasers, and the stage soon heats. Add in the crazy theatrics these guys do—minus Brett at the moment—and they were quickly sweating like a sinner in church. We got to our room, and I started ordering drinks from the in-house menu. I'd just placed the request through the app when Brax grabbed my waist and picked me up. "What are you doing, you baboon? Go shower." I pinched my nose dramatically and added, "you smell like one too."

"No way, this is all caveman." I laughed as I called him a "horn bag," telling him to "get in the shower before everyone arrives."

"So, you don't wanna join me? I have a surprise for you."

My eyes lit up as I kicked my legs around his waist. "Really? What is it?"

"This baboon bought you a big banana." I slapped him lightly. The man was incorrigible. "Are you saying you want me to change and stop finding you incredibly attractive?"

"Babe, don't be silly. We already had one of those nights this week." Now it was his turn to laugh as he kissed my lips, mumbling against them how much he loved me.

"The moment this tour is over, Cutie, we're planning our wedding." I nodded and said, "yes," he patted my ass before grabbing a firmer hold of it. "Good girl. Now give me another kiss."

"Where?" My playful wink and suggestive lip bite soon had him grinding his groin against me. Before I could blink, he flipped me over his shoulder and raced to the bathroom. "No, Brax, what are you doing?"

"Steaming up the bathroom... in more ways than one."

"I already washed earlier." I tried to wiggle out of his stronghold before changing tactics. "Wait until later, Mister Impatient."

"Baby!" Brax pleaded his case. "It's my birthday."

"No, it's not. It's tomorrow. And if you behave then, yes, you can start it with a bang... me!"

"I'm taking you up on that offer," he groped my ass.

"I knew you would." I finally got away from him, while he washed, I made sure everything was ready for when the others arrived. Sitting down, I rolled up and ordered some Chinese food to be delivered later in the evening.

People slowly made their way through. The entire group was jovial and enjoying ourselves in each other's company, although only with a warning from Marcus first. Monkey had received the strictest of instructions. I listened to Shane and Liam bicker like a married couple. Liam had expressed his shock at how quickly Shane flipped out yesterday. Anyone who knew his history would understand why he was highly protective of Kendall. It intrigued me that Liam hadn't noticed he was precisely the same. So when they started getting heated, I chuckled at Chester, who slapped them each across the cheek. "I'm pretty sure you both carried on like baboons. But let's be honest, we've had worse horror stories on tour than that."

April was quick to agree and asked, "What's the most memorable tour stories your band has had, or even as artists yourself?" I could see the cogs turning, and after a few minutes, she started it off. "Mine was in Scotland when I first started as a naïve little girl. You used to get extra money to play over there because it was dangerous." The boys sat straighter in their chairs, suddenly intrigued to hear where this was going. "However, luckily the Scots took to us early on. We were in this brand-new room with parquet flooring when a fight broke out. I'd seen nothing like it, fifteen hundred people, everybody punching each other… it was like the fucking wild west — People using bottles, glasses flying everywhere." The group eagerly listened on after expressing a few muffled obscenities. "And we were stuck on stage, wondering what the hell to do. Luckily, one of the staff helped us to get our stuff, and said to come back in the morning as they ushered us through a side exit. We didn't argue and left straight away. We returned in the morning, and there were around twenty people on the floor scrubbing blood out of the new floors."

"So you must have felt right at home, then?" Shane joked, and April chuckled. Chester chimed in next, remembering an experience with his past group.

"I stood with the rest of the band at the top of the ramp leading down to the stadium we were playing at," he started out and everyone settled in to listen. "In those last moments before walking out onto the field, something suddenly drenched me with warm, sticky liquid from high above, where some of the rowdy fifty thousand-strong audiences looked down onto the players' access ramp." He animatedly used his hands while explaining the layout of the Rugby Stadium where they had played. "Only, as I began the inaudible first verse on my guitar, did I realise with horror that the liquid I thought was just grog from the crowd being thrown was not. It was fucking piss!" My stomach lurched as the revolt ran down my spine, causing me to gag. "We were on our way onstage, so I had no fucking choice but to play covered in urine." We mentally banked that one to give Chester hell over at another time before Shane took his turn.

"Mine was also with my first band," he pondered, "when I'd just started out. It was an early evening show. If I remember correctly, it was before dinner, so on an empty stomach." Brax's hand gripped the front of his cap, head hanging as he shook it from side to side. "I had a few drinks before the gig. Nothing too exciting, just a rum and coke. The show went well, but before the encore, one of our sponsors brought out a bottle of Mezcal, which usually comes with a worm in the bottom." I wondered if it was like tequila when he addressed that for me. "Most confuse it with tequila, but it's much stronger and can come with a scorpion, too."

"You're shitting me?" My eyes flew open, wondering if he was joking.

"Legit," he confirmed, nodding. "It was some weird fucked up brand that none of us could read. But we were told it was the best to drink," nonchalantly shrugging his shoulders. "So we took a couple of shots. The bottle ended up on stage with us, and during the encore, we passed it around. Shortly after, I had an alcoholic-induced fit... during the last song."

"Shane!" Reflex saw Kendall slapping him across the chest in shock. "Why would you do that?"

"Clearly I didn't know that was going to happen, woman." The boys all snickered, but Kendall was none too amused. "I don't know what happened next, but I came around hours later, a gash on my head from hitting the keyboard on the way down. I couldn't see anything except in multiple weird dimensions, so they chucked me in the bath."

"Can we try this?" Everyone was quick to yell 'no' at Chester for that. Once he sat back down, Brett shared his horror story with us next; and it didn't involve a hernia surgery.

"This was before we took off; we used to do pub gigs, covers of artists, that kind of thing. You can imagine the usual venue: people chatting and drinking, playing pool and dancing." We all nodded, knowing them as the local pubs back home. "So we went on stage and played. Halfway through, some guy, completely off his face, marched up to us, snatched the microphone, told us we were rubbish, and then said the best band that had ever played was Rush. It is a shame they broke up." April's chortle pierced the air, and we looked at her quizzically. "This was hilarious to us, given that Chris was the lead in Rush when he started out."

"Fuck, that's brutal!" We all nodded and agreed with Mace's sentiment before April added, "he was a wanker."

"You've been spending too much time with Evil Midget," Brax muffled into his drink.

We lit up another joint to reminisce, and Chris continued. "They had invited us on tour with Rancid, Canada's biggest breakout, and we went to Australia and New Zealand with them. I noticed one night that something bit me, and by the time I woke up, the spot had travelled up my leg in a line."

"What was it?" Mark's concern interrupted Chris.

"I never found out," he shook his head, "but it turned out to be blood poisoning from the bite. It was the day of the gig, so the doctor had to cut me to drain it, but I still went on stage... in all my leathers. It's called being a pro, so the show has to go on." He laughed, but added sheepishly, "I curse myself now as the pain was excruciating, but I couldn't miss a chance to go on stage with them."

Mark explained his story took place during a festival in Germany. "I got the feeling they couldn't understand a single thing we were saying. Everything on stage went down like a lead balloon, so at the end, I blurted out, 'Thank you for your benign Teutonic countenance.' I'm confident they still didn't get it." Mark rolled his eyes in disgust. "Gigs like that make you want to bash your head against a brick wall. It's less painful."

"The show we did at ANZ Stadium in Sydney." Liam clicked his fingers when he piped up. I noticed the collective head nod from around the table. "It was afterwards that things went to shit. There was total hysteria, and we couldn't get out of the stadium. It was a full-on punch-on between thousands of people, police and security guards." When Brax likened it to "a scene from Braveheart," we all giggled nervously in humour.

"Mine would be that old cougar when we went to Tasmania... getting it on with the kid young enough to be her son." The band imitated vomiting when Brax said that as I asked him, "what had happened?"

"She wasn't unattractive, but it was beyond what you expect. I would've said she was in her late forties, and he had just come of age. By the second set, she was all over him, and the audience had noticed them." Knitted brows told Brax I wasn't following, so he spelt it out clearly. "She sat straddled on his lap as they pashed like their life depended on it." Widened eyes and my tilted head silently asked Brax if he was being serious. "I struggled not to laugh, and when they disappeared outside, I thought, 'thank fuck!' That was until fifteen minutes later when she returned *licking* her lips."

"Ew!" The guys laughed their heads off at the disgust on our faces, Kendall and I shaking our heads furiously, trying to get rid of the image. Catching sight of my mobile screen, I noticed it was a couple of minutes to midnight, so I said I was going to get another drink.

Really, I had a secret surprise for Brax.

As it hit midnight, I flicked the lights off and walked back out, so the guys knew it was time. In unison, we sang happy birthday to Brax as I reached around him, placing his cake on the table. I knew he would get a chuckle out of it. I had chosen a basic vanilla cake and stuck a giant blunt in the middle that I rolled for him. "Happy Thirtieth birthday, baby."

Seeing the crinkles of happiness frame his eyes, his humour breaking free, had me feeling mighty pleased with myself. I stumbled back freely when he grabbed my hip and pulled me onto his lap after his humour distracted me. "Thank you all." Everyone took the turn to come and wish him a "happy birthday." Seeing the friends who had become family wanting to celebrate with him was beautiful. "Thank you all so much. You guys are amazing. But I need you to fuck off now so Charlie can give me my real present." Of course, that found favour with them, as if he had told the funniest joke under the sun. It wasn't until an hour later that I had finally helped him shove Chester, the last person, out of the door, with the promise there would be further partying Saturday night. Brax's impatience had grown the longer it took. And being his birthday, I, too, wanted to do something very sexy, wild and reckless for him.

My virile man was the guy who enjoyed scorching sex, and the more I added to the menu, the more he craved it with an even greater capacity.

I knew he watched me move when we went out; he loved seeing the sway of my hips, and his eyes were always on my ass. I would wiggle it at him exaggeratedly, knowing it tormented him. I would tease Brax unmercifully by shaking my full breasts so they would highly arouse him. Knowing he wanted to reach out to grab me and pull me down onto his lap was such a turn-on, especially when we both had to restrain ourselves because we were out in public. It heightened the arousal, making me ache more for him.

I took his hand and walked Brax into our bedroom, locking the door and telling him to 'wait,' while I put on a very sexy little two-piece lingerie set. I had bought it primarily for tonight; a red lace bra and matching thong attached to a micro mini skirt. I sprayed body spritzer on and brushed my long hair out, standing up and tossing it around to give it a wild look for him. It screamed *wanton* and was so very sexy. Just how I knew he liked it.

It flushed me with anticipation, my breasts almost falling out of the shelf bra, with its bit of faux fur around the edges that lightly tickled when touching my skin. My midriff was bare, and my ass looked good, *I thought*, with the minimal amount of coverage that the thong gave me.

I tossed my head haughtily and then looked at my reflection again, thinking I *truly* wanted to be the wanton and vamp tonight and make him sweat… have him desire me so severely that he'd crawl towards me. Beg me for some action and I'd look down at him and smile in an enticing way… while he gazed up at me….

I turned on the music in the background, a very seductive tune. I looked at myself for a last inspection and pulled my silk stockings up a little higher, liking how my thighs looked in this outfit. My perfume was subtle, yet very sensual. It suited me, my mood and the night of passion I had planned for him.

I stepped into the doorframe of the wardrobe to observe Brax. His shoulders were broad, and his face was half-cast in the night's shadow. I could see his jeans-covered legs and ass and how tightly they fitted. He sensed me in the doorway observing because he moved forward, his eyes perusing me from head to toe, slowly, with a lot of passion in their depths.

Those gorgeous eyes darkened *so* intensely with love that I felt weak. The smile that hovered on his lips was one of pure delight. His arms reached out, and I moved forward, almost jumping into his rugged muscular strength. He grasped me closer, and his erection was so overwhelmingly extensive and pulsating with life. Strong, large hands moved over my ass with loving gentleness, squeezing suddenly and moving his fingers slowly towards my honey pot…. I squealed in delight but forced myself to push them away, as I had other plans. Excitement dampened my panties, and I squeezed my thighs, craving more, but I wanted to perform a little first, just like I promised.

I stood on tiptoes to kiss his lips, and he reacted by biting my bottom one. I moaned as he moved closer again, almost grinding his erection tightly against my pelvis. My answering thrust was virtually my undoing as he grabbed my ass and kneaded my round cheeks. I had to force myself to stop again for the plan to work, so I took his hand and led him over to the settee in the room's corner. I nuzzled him into its plush softness. He looked up with elevated brows and went to grab me when I laughed suddenly jumping back. Moving towards the stereo, I searched Spotify and skipped to 'Too Close' by Next. I turned towards him and moved my body in slow, sexy circles, gyrating my hips in a very beguiling manner. His eyes showed great hunger, and that I had his full attention. I danced sensually with abandon and gracefulness as my hands roamed the curves of my body while I took my clothing off, one piece at a time… starting with my bra, sliding it onto the floor. My round breasts moved in time to the music with a life of their own.

His face had taken on that passionate look he got just before he was ready to explode. He held me captive with a determined gaze, while my mouth made soft kisses as I stared at him. Next came the little micro mini with the attached thong, which left me in only stockings and heels. I went to begin with the shoes, but Brax couldn't take it anymore…. He got up suddenly, and I let out a shriek as he rushed towards me. His fingers gripped under my armpits, lifting me up like a feather before laying me down on the large throw cushions of the bed. I looked up into his eager eyes, almost black with desire. He reached down to kiss me slowly, seductively, taking his time, and I felt my moistness growing. He was sending those unique quivers up and down my spine as he moved his lips away from mine, took his tongue and moved the tip with slow, tortuous licks over my throat. I wanted to cry out and beg him to just take me... but I knew he wouldn't. He'd take his time to make the enjoyment a slow and beautiful process.

His hands moved over me, a symphony of their own, casting their spell upon my body with graceful beauty and soft seduction. Tweaking my nipples until they were stiff peaks, he slowly took each one in his mouth, carefully sucking back and forth until my hips were coming off the bed. I wanted to beg him and end the torture, but he was enjoying himself far too much. He moved with a subtle smoothness down over my stomach and tasted me, sliding further into my soft mound. There was only a small thatch of hair there, and his tongue moved over me until he found the entrance to my moist core. Flicking the tip of his tongue inside, in and out and then thrusting it thoroughly up, I was thrashing around on the bed as I felt that beautiful 'O' just about to begin. Brax sensed it—withdrew his tongue—and moved it over my plump nub. I gasped and cried out, unable to withstand this. I was ready, so very keen... begging him not to stop, as I was enjoying this *too* much.

I wanted him to finish this beautiful intense pleasure. My cries were wild as I called out his name repeatedly. He complied as he moved his tongue over and around me, knowing the sensitive areas that would bring me to a full, wondrous, complete climax. "Brax! Oh fuck... yes, baby!" How wonderful it was as I lay in the final throes of passion. My mouth wanted to reciprocate and suck his delicious cock. His clothes had come off somehow when he brought me to that place of no return. I looked down over his naked body; his erection was magnificent and enormous.

I longed to take him, to give him so much pleasure. I touched him softly, then grasped him with my hand. He moaned as I stroked his shaft with a gentle grip. I loved the feel of his cock. It excited me beyond belief. I rubbed him harder, groaning as he grabbed my hand suddenly to stop me. I felt his pre-cum on the tip of his shaft and knew he was more than ready. Sitting up abruptly, I moved my hands over his hard, smooth body, loving the feel of his rippling muscles.

Everything about Brax was like an elixir, an aphrodisiac of erotic delight. Tonight was *all* about his pleasure. I knew he was close, and I had to be very careful. I kissed his lips hungrily, our mouths devouring each other. We couldn't get enough. It was pure beauty and wild bliss, so very erotic and passionate. My fingers moved over him again as my lips slid downwards, kissing and licking as I proceeded towards his dick. I pressed him backwards, and he growled deep in his throat as I found his hard, perfect erection, licking the tip then moving my mouth over him with wild abandon. I couldn't get enough. Sucking harder, his body moved in thrusts, groaning and yelling out my name. I slowed my pace and moved my mouth with precise movements over him, allowing me to give him what he wanted. I groaned in my throat as his fingers sought and found those delicate areas that made me want to cry out again. "Shit, Charlie! Fuck... yes, baby!"

Moving my mouth over him up and down, I continued until he grasped hold of my head and held me in place as his hard cock pulsated fiercely shooting its load deeply, hitting the back of my throat with its hot, salty thickness. He moaned fiercely, yelling out my name, making me feel triumphant in knowing he had enjoyed it so much. I pulled away reluctantly, always loving the feel of him in my mouth or inside me.

"Come here," Brax reached down to me, beckoning a return of our closeness, enveloping me in his arms. I moved over his body, ensuring my breasts touched every part of his skin. Nuzzling into his neck, I felt the tickly bit of stubble on my lips and enjoyed that bit of roughness. I nipped his earlobe and whispered into his ear... telling him in my sexy voice how much "I adore and love you, your caresses and hardness, every part of you." I moved towards his mouth again and kissed him with all my passion, every fibre of my being. He returned them with intensity and equal desire. I felt his body relax eventually, fatigue taking over, as his eyes fluttered shut. His breathing changed, and I knew he had drifted into a peaceful slumber. I grabbed the soft, warm pile-lined fleece blanket and pulled it over us, as it had become chilly in the room now. The warmth of his body and the blanket made me so cosy that my eyes closed as the slumber took over.

His hands moving over my body woke me some time later, like velvet, along with lovely soft kisses to my neck and breasts. I smiled and stretched like a very supple, sensual kitten. My arms reached over my head, and I heard him laugh as he moved up to my mouth, kissing me into full wakefulness. My nipples became hard, those little pebbles standing up proudly. Brax's wickedly delicious smile made me feel sexy and loved. I knew he wanted me again as my hands found their way to his firm body. I sunk into him and we kissed with a raw, deep, sensual emotion. He would take me this time, and my body was ready for him to work his magic. After all, this was his day, and I was all his.

Chapter Seventeen

BRAX

I t had been two weeks since my party, and we'd carried out six more shows. We were all feeling completely exhausted, the gigs were now crammed back-to-back because of Brett's hospitalisation. It had blown the tour timeframe out, and we were staying on for an additional ten days.

We had also seen Chrissy for the last two weekends, as Chester had paid for her to travel into town with us. Of course, this was the hot topic of discussion, as none of us had seen him so whipped before, and we were definitely using it to our advantage. The boys and I were enjoying a few schooners at the pub tonight, as Charlie had stayed at the hotel. She'd been irritable and tired over the last few days, understandably, with the tight schedule. I knew the feeling well. My brain kept ongoing as if it were on some marathon sprint. I used that energy for creativity until my head was ready to explode and I would crash. The other girls gave the band some time alone when Charlie had pulled out.

"So what's up with Midget, bro?" Chester drew my attention from the now flat beer that stared back at me. "She was in a foul mood by the time we got here."

"Yeah, I know," I sighed. "She said she was tired and needed sleep, so we will go with that." I shrugged my shoulders and reached for my glass, taking a sip.

"You're a wise man for not arguing," Shane whispered behind his drink. He was right. She really had a face of thunder.

"Guess I will find out later. I get it though. The last few days have been hectic." They all nodded. "A good stretch of the bones, and a big sleep usually helps."

"You sure you haven't pissed her off?" I frowned at Marcus' comment as I tried to rack my brain. "Not that I know of."

"She probably is tired then," he eased my concern.

"What's the deal with you and April?" I asked Mark, hoping to change the subject. "If you don't mind me asking."

"We just have a lot in common," he brushed it off casually. "And enjoy each other's company."

"She's a freak, isn't she?" Chester wiggled his eyebrows at him, Mark sucking his teeth in return.

"I just can't picture you being one; you're always so reserved." The rest of us smirked at Marcus' statement, knowing better when Chester pointed out, "Mark's an animal."

"And how the fuck would you know?"

"Chester and Mark banged the same bird a few times, Dad." Liam informed him, "together." We all laughed at their previous exploits, and Marcus smirked, "Agh, spit-roast."

"Like you can talk, you dirty bastard. I believe you were the one who suggested the Eiffel Tower." Chester, of course, laughed at Mark and said, "it was pretty epic."

"And besides, three weekends in a row with Chrissy. What's that about?" Mark flipped it on him.

"Fucking amazing sex! That's what," he didn't shy away from the truth. "That girl is a freak, and goddamn it, she gets me fucking her like crazy."

"Can we swap?" The moment I replied to Chester's comment, every one of them looked up at me in shock and asked, "what the fuck?"

"I dunno, guys, sorry." *Shit!* How the *fuck* could I say that? My voice trailed, like my words were unwilling to take flight, "since my birthday, she's been in a foul mood and not *enthusiastic* if you get me. Maybe she's bored with me. Who knows?"

"Why are you sitting down here whinging?" Chester provoked me, "go upstairs and show her who's boss."

"Do *not* take his advice," Marcus quickly interjected.

"Go back and show her some extra love. She's likely to open up to you more." Liam tried a unique spin.

"You're too domesticated." Chester rolled his eyes, disgusted. "Does Mace carry your balls in her handbag?"

"Do you want us to get the girls to speak to her?" Shane offered, and I shook my head. "Nah, but thanks, mate. Let's see what tomorrow brings."

We had a few more drinks before heading back, not wanting too late of a night. As we got outside, we noticed a bloke stumbling down the road that had been in the pub, sculling drinks faster than we were. He stumbled down the cobbled street, and we saw him swerving into the road and off the path several times. "Thank fuck he left his car behind," Shane whispered as we watched a cop pull up alongside him. We observed from a distance, being the nosey pricks we were.

The cop turned the light on the drunk and asked, "what are you doing wandering down the middle of the road at midnight?"

"I'm on my way to a lecture, officer," the drunk slurred.

"And who in their right mind is running a lecture this evening, sir?"

"My wife." We all buckled over in hysterics, along with the cop, and we offered, "would you like us to drop him home?" and pointed to our maxi ride that just pulled up.

"He's a local. We spend more time at his house than he does." The Police laughed it off and thanked us, anyway.

I entered the hotel room after arriving back, and found it dark and quiet, except for my bedside lamp, which she'd left on for me. After using the bathroom quietly to shower and change, I climbed into bed. I tugged her gently into my arms when she stirred. "Shh, baby. Go back to sleep."

"What time is it?" she purred sleepily.

"Just after midnight." I pressed my lips to her cheek in a soft kiss. "Sleep." Before I knew it, the alarm was disturbing my slumber. Charlie was being silent and sluggish, so I had to ask, "What's wrong, Cutie?"

"Nothing," she brushed me off.

"You're not being yourself, babe." When she said "I'm fine," I was having none of it. "No, you're not."

"Brax! I said it's nothing, for fuck's sake!"

Something in me snapped at that moment. I'd had enough of her foul attitude, and biting my head off was the final straw. "I'm sorry for giving a fuck about your wellbeing, Charlotte." Did she seriously think I was asking just to pester her? *No!* I was worried, especially when I knew she was acting out of character. Slamming the door behind me, I left the suite before a further argument erupted. *I was seriously pissed off!* I needed to go cool off somewhere.

Exiting the hotel, I pulled my coat up tighter, crossing the road towards the park. A spliff and some time to think was exactly what I needed. Sparking up, I soon got lost in my head. I was stunned she'd snapped at me. I didn't know what her problem was, but it was bugging me more than I cared to admit, this being kept at arm's length — moody little bitch when she wants to be. Like fuck, she's just tired. Obviously I've done something. *Have I?* Ugh! I hated that she was hurting, and she wouldn't let me comfort her. But mostly, I needed her to open up to me again.

MARK

A door slamming nearby startled me awake. I jumped out of bed and stuck my head out the door, just in time to see Brax storming off. Scratching my head, before shaking it off the sleepy haze, I heard April ask, "What was that?"

"Brax," I muttered, "he looked furious."

"Go," she added before I could even ask. I leaned over, kissing her plump lips, lingering to enjoy their taste longer than I should have.

"I won't be long," I promised. "Don't get dressed yet. We're not finished." I cupped her face, my tongue sliding between her lips, leaving her a taste of more to come.

"Of course not."

I stumbled around, hurriedly changing, before grabbing my coat, a spliff, and a room swipe card to get back. I went to head out towards him, when I stopped, turned and went to Midget instead. Something had me feeling this was about the conversation we had at the pub last night.

I made my way to their room and knocked on the door. At first, no one answered, so I hit again. I waited a few seconds before Midget swung the door open, tears streaming down her face and ready to scream, probably thinking it was Brax. "What? Did you forget your key when you stormed — Shit! Sorry Mark, I thought it was—"

"Brax?" She nodded and said "yes" quietly. "Can I come in?"

"Of course, he isn't here, though. I need to find out where he went. Sorry, Mark." She rambled, trying to avoid eye contact.

"He walked down that way." I pointed towards the direction I saw Brax storm off to, and she gestured for me to come in. Once inside, she turned to face me. "So what's up, mate?" I looked at her, and I could see the tears threatening to spill again and she tried to look away. Instead of saying anything, I walked over and pulled her into a tight hug. She started sobbing, and I held firmer, letting her cry out her frustrations. After a few minutes, she pulled back and walked to get some tissues. "Sorry."

"Not needed. It's fine." We sat down in the lounge and I softly asked, "Do you wanna talk? Or do you want some time? I checked on you first, but I'll go see Brax after.."

"Thanks, Mark."

"I didn't hear what happened, Charlie, but felt the door slam."

"To be honest, I don't even know," she spoke. I looked at her, puzzled, and asked, "what'd you mean?"

"He wanted to know if I was alright, and I said I was, but he kept pressing, insisting I wasn't myself," she stood up, shaking her hands out while pacing, "and the next minute I just snapped his head off." I passed her another tissue as the tears fell again.

"Are you alright?" I enquired carefully.

"I don't know, Mark.... Maybe. I'm just so goddamn tired at the moment."

"The tours take it out of you, babe. The exhaustion can hit without even realising it."

"Yeah, but it wasn't like this last time," she trailed off, remembering the Regional Tour.

"But you didn't come face to face with Calvin, did you? Have you taken the time to process that?" I provided some examples, just from what I'd observed. "Last time you weren't engaged and surrounded by everyone in your face, you couldn't even have time to enjoy it properly together."

She shrugged her shoulders and replied in a monotone, "I guess."

"You can tell me if I'm overstepping my boundaries, but has Brax done anything to upset or anger you?"

"No, never. He's incredible, even with all my emotional baggage."

"So, maybe it is exhaustion, babe. And that's okay," I nodded to reinforce that. "If you need rest, listen to your body. We all understand, and we've been there at one stage or another."

Charlie sat and processed this for a minute before wiping her eyes. The tears had finally stopped, leaving me to ask, "Are you okay now? If so, I'll check on him." Leaning forward, I took her hand in mine, "but if you need me to stay a little longer, I'm happy to do so."

"Thanks, I feel better already," she smiled softly, and gave my hand a squeeze. "I'm gonna lay down. Please tell Brax to come back when you're finished talking."

"I'll bring him myself, I promise."

"I love you, thanks, Mark. I don't say it enough because everyone else is boisterous, but I'm glad to have you in my life."

"I love you, too. Don't be going all soft on me, Evil Midget, alright?" She laughed and said "alright" as I gave her another hug and kiss on the forehead before heading off to check on Brax.

I moved out of the hotel and looked both ways. Turning left, I saw an extensive park and thought it was probably my best shot. We are all creatures of comfort, and when we need some quiet time, we find a smoke and a calm spot to step away. I walked down and headed across the park when I saw a bench with someone sitting on it. I realised quickly it was Brax, and he eventually heard me and looked up with a face like thunder. "You know, bro, we aren't in Australia any more? It's fucking freezing out here."

"Yeah, I lost the feeling in my ass about twenty minutes ago."

"Lucky I brought you this, then." I pulled out one spliff and handed it over to him as I grabbed a seat.

"Cheers, Mark," he took it with a pat on the shoulder. "What brings you out here, anyway?"

"Funny story, that. I was in bed with April until some prick slammed the door so hard it rattled our walls and woke us up."

"Sorry," he mumbled deplorably.

"I'm not that bothered," I promised. He took his hat off, brushing his fingers through his hair before putting it back and blowing out a heavy breath. "You gonna talk to me? What's going on?" He went to speak, and I added, "Full disclosure. I just spoke to Midget before coming to see you."

"Hopefully, she talked to you," he turned to look at me. "Is she okay?"

"She is now. She's gone to lie down for a bit."

"Thanks." I looked at him to offer more, but he continued to stare aimlessly, blowing out a large breath. "I just don't know, mate. In the last few days, she's gotten worse. She isn't herself, always looks despondent, and when I ask if she wants to do something, she just says she's tired. I felt like I was making love to a corpse the other day."

"Which reminds me, that was a pretty fucked up thing to say last night." I glared at him. "Asking Chester if he wanted to swap." Then punched him hard in the arm.

"Fuck, I know," he shook his head. "I hated myself the minute I said it, believe me. I'm just so frustrated," he huffed. "She won't let me in."

"Good, I'm glad you know, because it pissed me off," we made eye contact. And he could see how disappointed I was with him. Nodding and accepting his mistake, I nudged him with a reminder. "You love Charlie too much to disrespect her like that. Don't do it again."

"You're right, and I won't," he sincerely assured me. "I hate that I can't make her feel better because she won't talk to me."

"She's got exhaustion, Brax."

"Yeah, I get that much."

"No, I mean, after spending the last twenty minutes with her, she's exhausted. Think about it, bro." I gave him a chance before adding some examples. "We travel halfway across the world, jet lagged and supposed to be recovering. Then she runs into Calvin — of all people — and has to relive her childhood trauma. She doesn't get the time to process it because we're back on the road, and then she runs into him again." I took a heavy draw on the smoke, then passed it back to him before continuing. "You two get engaged in the middle of this and have nowhere for privacy. You can't celebrate it properly like you should. She organised something special for your thirtieth, and we added a hectic schedule that was all out of sync because Brett's injury cost us so much time."

I watched as he thought about it for a moment before finally slumping in defeat. "Fuck!" he wailed. "I'm such an asshole. How did I not see it? I should have known the signs."

"Don't beat yourself up about it. It's hard when it comes on suddenly. We've both been in that situation. Just get back.. You don't need to say anything; you just need to be there."

"Thanks, Mark." We got up and hugged before heading towards the hotel while we finished our spliff. Once in the elevator, we returned upstairs and walked down the hallway. The mood was sombre, and I knew he had a lot on his mind.

I went to put my key in the door, when I heard Brax knock lightly on his. I waited to make sure he was alright to get in. After a few minutes, Charlie opened the door and started crying the moment she saw him. Brax didn't say a word, just picked her up and cuddled her into his chest, carrying her inside their room and kicking the door shut.

Chapter Eighteen

CHARLIE

The bands had just finished another show, and packed up before we headed to the hotel. It had been a few days since Brax and I had that argument, and I still felt like something was wrong. Neither of us was addressing there was an issue, either. When Monkey asked "who's coming out tonight?" I declined. It didn't surprise me that Liam and Shane were keen, but when Brax said no, my head turned in shock.

"What!" He glared at Brax, horrified.

"Serious, Chester." *Okay, something is definitely wrong.* It wasn't like him to turn the boys down.

"You can go, babe. I'm heading back for an early night."

"It's fine, Cutie. I'm tired and ready for bed." We said "goodbye" to everyone and made our way back to the hotel. Neither one of us really spoke. He had things on his mind, and so did I. I think we needed to talk, and I wondered if tonight was the right time. We returned and put our stuff down as he turned to me and announced, "I'm just gonna have a shower."

That confirmed it! Something *is* wrong. He would typically ask me if I wanted to join him or just drag me, anyway. I couldn't take it anymore and walked over to him. "What is wrong with you?!" There was an edge of irritation in my voice.

"Nothing," he replied flatly, but didn't look at me.

"Is this about the other day?" I gripped his arm and, with some force, spun him to face me. Brax stared down at me for a few minutes, saying nothing.

Then, he grabbed me by the arms and lifted me onto the desk, causing everything to go flying on to the floor. He eagerly spread my thighs while unzipping his jeans, and it flattered me he could get hard so quickly, given the tension. I was incredibly excited to feel him rip my skirt up, push my panties aside, and plunge his cock into me. My arousal was dripping, and the moist fuck sound amplified as he grabbed onto his stiff cock and thrust into my eagerness repeatedly. He took my ankles, spread my legs and tightened his grasp.... leaving little doubt about who was in control now.

I felt defenceless lying back while he was giving me this punishing fuck, and I whimpered as he drove in and out of my swollen centre. Moaning louder with my increased pleasure, I took his massive cock deep. He lifted my legs and tightened his grasp on my ankles as he ground inside me. I could tell he was enjoying the sight of fucking me while he explored the recesses of my insides with his hardness. But there was something else on his face... guilt, anguish, I didn't know.

My large breasts bounced every time he ploughed into me. My legs were becoming sore, spread wide open and held so high up. His cock was unbelievably hard, and I moved my hips rhythmically to meet him. He was pounding tougher and deeper with every thrust. Our pent-up frustrations meant we hadn't been intimate in the last few days since our argument. "Please, Brax, fuck me harder! Right there, I need you. I love it.... Aww," my words jumbled into a moan. "I love you."

"Fuck Charlie, I needed to hear you say that! I love you, baby... so fucking much." I looked up and saw a small tear leave the corner of his eye and reached up with my thumb. "Brax?"

"Shh, it's okay. I love you." My body was so alive that when he brushed against my clit, I felt an incredible tingling sensation. I felt flushed and tensed up, letting out a long, loud cry as I came. I tightened, causing his aroused groans to intensify. My head moved back, and I closed my eyes, humming with satisfaction, in complete ecstasy. Seeing the look on my face, he started panting in my ear again. With one last thrust, and I honestly thought he would tear me open, he spurted into me and gave his last act of love. I smiled in bliss, feeling the pulsing inside as he collapsed on my body. "I'm so sorry, baby, I really am," he whispered into my neck. "Please forgive me."

"What's wrong? What is it?" I tried to grip his head, forcing eye contact.

"I didn't mean to say any of it, Charlie. I was so angry and acted like an idiot. It's fucking eating me up.." He ruffled his hair frustratedly through his hand.

"Brax, I don't understand? What are you talking about?" I gripped his head firmly, forcing his concentration. Panic was thumping in my bloodstream.

"We had been arguing for two days, then I went out with the guys—"

"Wait! Did you cheat on me?" I cut in, pushing him away from him, but he gripped me tight and glared at me. "What?! No! I *never* would. I couldn't."

"Then what are you saying, Brax? You're scaring me." I relaxed slightly, although his grip on me didn't.

"The guys noticed something was wrong with you, also, and we were talking about it. I made the worst comment of my life and I physically hate myself for it." I looked up and asked "what did you say?" because I needed to understand what was wrong. "Chester was saying how good it is with Chrissy right now, and well…. well…. I asked if he wanted to swap." He dropped his head shamefully, unable to hold my eye contact.

"And," I fumbled, before whispering, "did you mean it?"

"No!" His head flung up, and his eye contact was fierce. "I was tanked and being an asshole, not that it's an excuse," he shook his head, adding, "there is none."

"And so you've barely touched me and been acting weird because of this?"

"Yes," he muttered, just above a breath. "I feel so bad for saying it, and had to tell you, Charlie."

"Honestly, you should." We both remained slouched for a moment on the desk, still wrapped in each other, before I pushed him off and stood, heading to the bedroom.

"Charlie? Say something, please," he pleaded. "Scream at me even. But not nothing, don't walk off." I went into the bedroom and rifled through my suitcase before storming back out. I returned to find him leaning against the desk, hands buried in his head, slumped and defeated.

"It hurts what you said, Brax — a lot."

"I know, and I'll do anything to make it up to you," he stood up a bit. "We're always honest with each other, so I had to tell you. I can't keep anything from you. You mean too much to me."

"And that brings me to my next point," I spoke up before he could say anymore. "I'll get over it. You said something stupid, but you didn't cheat or step out on me."

"I couldn't, Charlie. Despite that, I should have been here when you needed me, not out being a prick." I threw what I was holding at him and watched as he fumbled to catch it. He looked down, twisting it in his hands, before his head snapped up at me in disbelief.

"Well, you have the next eighteen years to make it up to us." I assured him once our eyes met.

"You're pregnant?!" His eyes roamed the test again. Slouching further against the desk, a sense of shock filled the space between us. "This is yours?" He turned it towards me, the two lines still beaming positively. I offered a quick head nod. He looked at it and I watched the moment his brain stuttered. His eyes took in more light than expected. Every part of him went on pause while his thoughts caught up. And then, "We're having a baby?" I nodded, but he stalked closer to me this time. His fingers clasped my chin and titled my head. I got the distinct impression he needed to hear me say it. So when he asked directly, "Charlie, are you pregnant?" I expected it.

"Yes, Brax." I whispered into the thin space between us.

"We're going to have a baby?" I nodded as best I could, with my chin still cradled in his grasp. "Our baby? Yours and mine?" He dropped the test and his muscular arms cradled my waist, pulling me flush against his body. "You're giving me a baby?"

"No, we're having one." I reached up to his fingers now, tenderly stroking my cheek. "We've established that, though. I kinda need you to say something else." He saw the tinge of concern I was trying to hold at bay when our eyes met. He picked me up, holding my body to his, so we were at eye level.

"This is the best gift anyone has ever given me, Charlie. You're having my baby." He smashed his lips to mine, his hold on me primal and fierce. "I'm going to be a Dad," he mumbled against my lips between heated kisses. "And I get to do it all with you." His tongue skimmed my lips before lusciously looping with my own in a dance of love.

"So, you're happy?" I pulled back, staring at each other while I stroked his cheek.

"Happy doesn't even describe it." He barely finished speaking when tears traced a delicate line down his cheek, each stronger than the other.

"Brax?" I wiggled to get out of his grip, but he pulled me in tighter, lifting my legs up around his hips.

"It's okay," he nodded furiously, and the twinkle behind the tears reassured me. "I'm gonna be a fucking Dad!" He screamed and started spinning in a circle. He covered my face in kisses, holding tight as I gripped his neck and chuckled softly into his skin. Placing me on the ground, he stepped back before dropping to the floor. His hand gently caressed my stomach, before soft lips lovingly thanked me. I reached down, taking his hand, drawing attention back up to me. "Thank you, Charlie. This is invaluable to me." He moved forward and kissed my stomach once more. "Hi baby, I'm gonna be your Daddy." I struggled with the lump in my throat, hearing those sweet whispers. "I can't wait to meet you." He stood and continued to hold me. "When did you find out? How?" He shook his head, still in disbelief. Yet the happiness was impossible to fracture and lit his entire being.

"Something just didn't feel right," I explained. "I know it could have easily been exhaustion, too. Except, then I realised I'd missed my contraceptive injection with everything going on." His compassionate eyes told me he understood. Life had been a whirlwind lately. "So I took a test yesterday. Two, in fact," I shrugged and inclined my head towards the test on the ground. "I'm really sorry I forgot to make my appointment," I started apologising rapidly.

"I'm not," he was defiant. "I can't be." Crouching down, he picked the test up, his eyes fixated. "You're having my baby. I could never feel sorrow for that, but I hate that you haven't been feeling well." I melted into him. This man *was* everything. From the moment our relationship started, it had been one hurdle after another, yet his love had never wavered. As if reading my mind, he added, "What do we need? How far along? What can I do to help?"

"Well, the test says four-plus weeks, so it's still early." I shrugged, having never done this before. "I was thinking we could make a doctor's appointment to confirm it, and find out what we need to do between now and returning home."

"Sounds good, Cutie. Anything to keep you both safe." He kissed my lips softly, and I cuddled into his chest. "So you didn't want to go out tonight because of this?" He pondered and I mumbled "yes," against his chest. "We haven't felt right the last few days, and I didn't want to leave you again."

"Thank you." I squeezed him tighter.

"My two beautiful babies." He leaned down, kissing my forehead, and I tilted my chin up. I opened my eyes to be greeted by his breathtaking smile. "We're going to be a family."

"You're going to be incredible with our child." I gushed, feeling a euphoric energy around me.

"I can't wait to hold our baby—" His mobile rang, cutting him off and he retrieved it out of his jeans. "It's Chester." He turned the phone toward me. "Do you mind if I take this? It can wait," he assured me, but I gestured to take the call.

He pulled me back into his hold as he answered, "What's up? I'm a little busy at the minute, mate."

"Did you just yell?" His concerned voice quizzed loud enough for me to hear. They heard it and texted."

"Sorry," he offered, "I didn't realise it was that noisy. I just got too animated playing FIFA."

"Okay, mate."

"Thanks, have a good night." He rushed the call, other things occupying his mind. "I didn't wanna say anything yet," he explained, stuffing the phone back in his pocket. "I wanna enjoy this for us while we have the chance." He bumped my shoulder and gripped me tighter.

"Let's see the doctor before we tell everyone. At least then we know more information ourselves," I suggested, and he agreed. His fingers inched across my chin and tilted my head up to meet his.

"I fucking love you." Every word was deliberate, with the raw emotion pumping through his veins. My nose scrunched, trying to keep the tears at bay. I threw my arms around his neck and whispered it back, kissing his salty skin. "I don't care how or why this happened. You're all I've ever wanted, and now you're giving me the world." Brax scooped me up into his arms and carried me through to our bed. Placing me down gently, he soon climbed beside me, reaching across, dragging his fingertips lazily along my stomach. He leaned in, kissing my lips delicately. My hands traced his ribs and around to his back, pulling him closer, enjoying this moment of happiness and love together. Resting our heads back on the pillows, we stared into one another's eyes, faces mirroring each other's elation. "You know, there's one problem in all this." My mouth dropped, and I propped up on my elbow. He continued casually, "My boy's going to be a United Supporter. You know that, right?" My head rolled back laughing as a relief washed over me.

"You don't even know it's a boy," I shoved him playfully. He countered with "if we have a daughter she would support—" but I cut him off and finished it with, "Liverpool FC Womens."

"Not where I was going with that," he tapped me on the nose. "One thing is for sure, whether it's a boy or girl, no child of ours is supporting Chelsea." He laughed because I said, "The Chavs," at the same time. After several quiet minutes together, he muttered, "You know what your pregnancy means, don't you?" I shook my head — not a clue. "I just became Carole's favourite son-in-law. She wanted this before any of us."

"You're a dickhead," I chuckled. "And you haven't married me yet, Mister."

"Just you wait until we get home," he promised. Grabbing my lips between his fingers, we kissed hard. "I love you," and again, then looked down at my stomach. "And I love you, our little Peanut."

"Yeah, you can't stick with Peanut, Brax," shaking my head I mumbled in amusement. "Not when we have a Monkey in the group."

Chapter Nineteen

BRAX

A few days later, it was still sinking in. She was having *my* baby. While we hadn't planned it, I couldn't be happier. I always hoped one day we would build a family together, and now it was becoming a reality. Charlie and our child were what I lived for now. With two of the last four days on the road between gigs, I could see it was taking a toll on her. Mostly fatigue, but a few times, certain smells or tastes were setting the sickness off. The most potent fragrance... Marcus' cologne. Hilarious, especially since she wasn't whining at me. And don't get me started on the fuel stops. *Seriously?* This woman wants to stick her head out and sniff gasoline because it's "intoxicating." I had to pin her down to prevent her dry humping the bus window.

After finishing another show earlier, we'd packed up and returned to the hotel for a quiet night. We left at four in the morning, and the next stop was huge. Not just for the tour, but also for us. We'd got a doctor's appointment while there. I couldn't wait to hear it confirmed.

I looked down at Charlie, who was already falling asleep on my shoulder. Her head snuggled closer, so I wrapped my arm around her, pulling closer. "Are you okay?"

"Tired," she mumbled.

"Sleep, Cutie. I'll let you know when we're back."

"I got some outstanding photos at tonight's show." She sat straighter. "You wanna see them?"

"Always." She reached forward to grab her camera, turning it on. Shifting onto my lap, she pressed into me and flipped through the film roll. To see myself through my girl's eyes was unreal. The images were breathtaking, and I felt honoured to be loved so deeply by her.

Returning to the hotel, the group said they would catch us shortly, opting to shower and refresh before having a debrief of the show and smoke. Once inside, I picked her up and carried her to our room. "What are you doing?" she smiled.

"Making sure you rest," I placed her on the bed, fussing with the pillows. "When the guys get here, I'll tell them we are going to Marcus' tonight. You're tired, baby, and they are exhausting at the best of times." She laughed although insisted, "I'm fine, Brax."

"Really?"

"Of course, just pull the door shut."

"Message me if you need anything." I went to stand, and she gripped my wrist. "There is something, actually."

"Anything you need.."

"Your lips."

"Mmm, is that so?" a smirk tugged at my lips. I shuffled onto the edge of the bed and leaned over, a hand on either side of Charlie's body, kissing softly. She wrapped her arms around my neck and deepened the kiss, her tongue exploring mine. I undid her jeans, sliding them off, so she was more comfortable for bed.

"Thanks, baby. Go have fun." After shutting our bedroom door, I headed out to the kitchen and opened a beer when the rest of the boys came in.

"Where's Midget?" Liam looked around. "The girls are chilling at ours if she wants to head over."

"Thanks mate, she's already gone to sleep."

"Why?" Chester butted in. "Has she really?" he seemed confused.

"It's usually what people do when they are tired," I went with the obvious.

"Or getting laid," Shane added, and we laughed.

"Why's she always tired?" he wasn't letting it go.

"Shut up, man!" Mark snapped, Shane and Liam laughed. "We've all had exhaustion. Let the fucking girl rest in peace."

"Only the dead rest in peace, dickwad."

"You're a fucking idiot, man," Liam mumbled, shaking his head.

"Is she okay, Brax?" Marcus finally had time to ask. "Does she need a few days off?"

"I'll get her to come talk to you," I replied. "You should see the photos she took tonight, too." I used to divert the conversation.

"Can I go see them?" Chester jumped up, Mark, slapping his hand across his chest and pushing him back on the couch.

"He just told you she was sleeping."

"Calm down, bro," he patted him patronisingly. "She's not your missus, Marky."

"Stop being an asshole, and just go," I pointed to the bedroom. The rest were curious. "She'll tell him to fuck off, anyway." They laughed.

"So that's a yes?"

"Fuck off already, before I change my mind." The knob ran down the hallway like an excited kid, eagerly knocking. Charlie answered and a few seconds later, he slipped inside, shutting the door. I turned back to the group, who were all chatting when Mark asked, "wanna go for a blunt?" Of course!

We headed outside, sliding the glass door shut and taking a seat. After a few draws, Mark looked across the table and said, "It's not exhaustion." At first it caught me off-guard, and I mumbled "what?" in reply. "Common, bro. It's written all over your face."

"What is?"

"Midget's pregnant." I choked on the smoke, having just taken a drag.

"What makes you say that?"

"That ridiculous smile on your face, for starters," he pointed directly at me. "Plus the extra affection, and the rubbing of her stomach," he closed his argument by tipping his blunt towards me. "So how far along is she?"

"You sure you aren't some fucking spy sent in by Chester?" Mark laughed and asked, "So am I right?"

"You're right," his eyes lit up, "just please say nothing yet. We have a doctor's appointment tomorrow afternoon to confirm everything, so we'll know more later."

"You're really stoked about this, aren't you?"

"I honestly couldn't be happier."

"Cheers." He held his bottle up to mine as we tapped them. "I'm thrilled for you." I loved speaking with Mark. He was the most level-headed and talked a lot of sense when you needed to hear it. Eventually, Shane and Liam came out, but I was curious when Chester still hadn't followed.

"Is that Monkey ass prick still in my bedroom?"

"He didn't come out when we were in there." Liam shrugged, so I excused myself to go check.

"He's probably trying to wind her up again, you know." I turned to Shane and said, "That's why I'm going in."

When I opened the door, they were sitting on the bed together, laughing their tits off. My best mate had his arm wrapped around her shoulders, and the pair looked thick as thieves, deep in conversation. The smile was impossible to hold back, and my cheeks ached from happiness.

Charlie looked up and saw me, the love engulfing her face. "Hey baby, I didn't hear you come in?"

"I noticed." I leaned against the frame, crossing my arms over my chest. "What world destruction were you two plotting this time?"

Chester took it upon himself to answer, "the one where you didn't tell me that a little Peanut will be joining Monkey?"

CHARLIE

We'd returned after a long day, and I headed straight to bed. Since finding out nearly a week ago, Brax had been fantastic — caring and attentive. Honestly, I can't ever remember seeing him this happy. Some of his guilt was still lingering over our fight, but I was quick to remind him it takes two to tango, and I was being challenging to deal with. He needed to let it go so we could move forward and enjoy this time. I'd secured a doctor's appointment tomorrow and wanted to be rested and prepared. Laying in bed, watching the Champions League, I heard a light knock at the door. Assuming it was Brax, I yelled, "it's unlocked."

"Midget," Chester smiled as he stuck his head around the frame.

"Hey, Monkey."

"Can I come in?"

"As if you even have to ask." He shut the door, entered the room and dove onto the bed next to me. "So, what are you doing?"

"Football," I pointed to the screen. "Not for long, though. I'm super tired." I shrugged.

"Want me to grab some beers while we watch for a bit?" he pushed up. "Thought I'd keep you company. I've barely spoken to you."

I pushed his shoulder slightly as I asked, "do you feel neglected?"

"Yes, I had to scratch my nuts all by myself." He gripped his crotch for good measure, and I laughed. "So, do you want a beer?"

"Nah, I'm good, babes. But you're welcome to stay as long as you want."

"Why the fuck is this room so cold?" He suddenly shivered. I cracked up laughing, saying, "you sound just like Brax."

"It's freezing outside. Why make your room Antarctica also?" He furiously rubbed his arms for warmth with an appalled look on his face.

"I sleep better in a cold room. I like to snuggle down. It took Brax ages to get used to it as well."

"The only time I'm snuggling is if I'm boning," he smirked and I laughed, "you're an animal."

"Yeah, that's why you call me Monkey."

"Cuddling and enjoying each other's warmth is nice sometimes. Try it." I poked his ribs.

"And how long into this cuddling shit before Brax pokes at your asshole?"

"Shut up," I chuckled.

"Put the heating on."

"No," I stopped him. "Get in the blanket you sook." He dove under, resting against the headboard next to me, then wrapping his arm around my shoulder, pulling me into a hug.

"Are you sure you're okay, Midget?" he nudged my shoulder. "I'm a little worried about ya."

"I really am. The tight schedule because of the delay has just left me feeling so tired."

"I'll grab us a spliff to share, then. You'll be sleeping like a baby," he went to jump up.

"I'm good. I've had enough already today."

"I don't think I've even seen you have one," he pondered while looking directly at me.

I vaguely offered, "Yeah, Brax and I shared a couple."

"But he just said out there the last one he had was at breakfast?"

Fuck! Goddamn it! His eyes sparked, and he started clicking his fingers. "Hold up! You won't drink, or smoke, you're not exhausted — You have a baby baboon growing in your womb." I choked as I told him, "don't be silly."

"Oh, I'm serious right now! I think you forget Midget. We spend pretty much all day, every day together. So did Brax finally get his aim right?" My unfiltered laughter rippled the air. "Stop it," I warned.

"Come on, tell me. He filled your tubes as if you were a cream bun, didn't he?" I kept looking on amused, Chester continued. "I can go chuck a bun in the oven unless you already have that covered?"

I buckled over in hysterics, trying to breathe. "Alright, stop!"

"Tell me, or I'll grab a cheese platter, a spliff and, a beer, sit here until—"

"Alright, you, baboon!" I cut him off. "Yes, I'm pregnant."

"I knew it!" He punched the air, proud of himself. "Also, Brax never mentioned smoking. I just wanted to catch you out." I smacked him with the pillow, knocking him over as I called him a "wanker."

"Is that all you came in for?"

"Midget, I think Brax came in, not me." We both laughed as he asked again, "you're really pregnant?"

"Yeah," I sighed sweetly. "But we need to see a doctor. We're doing that tomorrow, so let us get more information before we say anything, please?"

"You know I'll be the favourite Uncle, right?" He puffed his chest, the grin spreading from ear to ear.

"You better not corrupt my child." I pointed my finger sternly.

"Worry about Brax." We both chuckled, and I begged, "help me."

"Hey, you better give us a baby boy to pass the legacy to."

"Oh sure, no worries. Let me fix that for you right this minute." I rolled my eyes.

"Can I watch?" he lifted the blanket over his head and I slapped him with a laugh.

"I'm so excited for us all." The happiness I felt, knowing the love and family we'd created, who couldn't wait to share in this with us, made the moment even more special. "This little crotch fruit will be the most loved of all."

"Oh my God, Chester!" Horrified, I asked, "what did you just call my child?"

"Baby Monkey?"

"Not you too," I gripped my forehead, shaking it. "Brax has already taken to saying Peanut."

"Well, that's just weird. We have Monkey Nuts already."

I turned to him, exclaiming, "I said the same thing."

"How about Bam Bam, since his father's a Caveman?"

"It's too early to know the sex."

So, of course, he said, "And Pebbles for a girl, then."

"I love your ass, you crazy Monkey."

"We love you, and I'm so happy for you both."

We settled down while still having a hug and were watching the game when I noticed Brax standing in the frame. "Hey baby, I didn't hear you come in?" My face felt like it was going to explode from the euphoria that flooded me.

"I noticed." He leaned against the door frame, then asked, "What world destruction were you two plotting this time?"

Chester took it upon himself to answer, "the one where you didn't tell me that a little Peanut will be joining Monkey?"

Brax broke out laughing as he asked, "really?" and shook his head. "For fuck's sake, I should've known."

"He figured it out, baby." I shrugged; it was the truth.

"Of course he did. I knew there was another reason he wanted to come and see you so badly." He came over, jumped on to the other side of the bed, rubbing his hand on my stomach. After a few minutes, Chester smacked it away. "What the fuck? You little prick." Brax shot up, fist clenched and a face of thunder.

"You stop that right now. Look what you already did to our Midget." Chester challenged him, without turning to look. "Not cool, man. Leave that Peanut alone."

I burst out laughing as Brax immediately highlighted, "it's my fucking child, asshole."

"Our kid Brax," Chester corrected him, adding, "That's the band's baby. Don't be selfish."

"You are off your rocker," he brushed him, slouching back next to me.

"Yes, I am a rocker." *Smartass.* "That kid will have the best family ever, second to none."

"Damn right, they will." Brax twisted and reached across to bump fists with him. Watching their exchange made me realise how truly blessed I was to have them. "Baby, I've something to tell you, too." He drew me back to the conversation.

Chester cut in, "Which one are you talking to?" pointing to my stomach. "Do I need to cover Bam Bam's ears for this?"

"What the fuck is Bam Bam?" He frowned and shook his head.

I giggled, remembering he wasn't here for that conversation. "He said you have to give him a boy to take over the band's legacy, and he's calling our baby Bam Bam because you're a caveman." Brax laughed and asked, "what if it's a girl?"

"Pebbles, of course, for fuck's sake, you want to have a kid with this bimbo, Midget?" Brax threw him a fake smile, then a real punch for good measure.

"What did you wanna say?" I reminded him why he'd come in to begin with.

"Mark knows as well." My eyebrows flew up. "What?"

With a coffee, notepad and pen in hand, I sat back and let the happiness soak right into my bones. I wanted this feeling to still be there when I was old and grey. Closing my eyes, I savoured the moment, but never released my grip on the seemingly inconsequential piece of paper and ink in my hand. For the first time in forever, my body and mind were relaxed. At that moment, there were no expectations, deadlines or schedules to meet. This morning, Charlie and I were heading to the doctors to confirm her pregnancy. And I couldn't wait. But as she slept, inspiration had struck, and I finished the second verse and chorus of our song in collaboration with Glaze.

Home is my perfect haven, a shelter from the storm
The place I go to just be me and not be judged or scorned
I can laugh and cry—this signifies—how comfortable I am
When I'm surrounded by the loving energy of those that I call fam.
Chorus
Home is where I can be myself, no pressures or demands
When I'm free to fly and roam around, and just be who I am,
Surrounded by the hearts and love of family and friends
No matter how far away I am, on home my heart depends.

I'd finished the final touches when I looked up and saw Charlie wandering into the kitchen. My t-shirt that barely covered her gorgeous butt cheeks sashayed as her tiny, stunning legs dragged her through on the quest for liquid energy. The last week had been long, and I could see the toll as she rubbed the back of her neck, waiting for the kettle. My heightened excitement for today hadn't helped in the slightest. We'd discussed it after everyone left last night, and given Mark and Chester were aware, we wanted to share the joy with the rest of my band. Other than that, just our parents and Tina, her best friend. The morning had been slow, and I could tell my impatience was getting on Charlie's nerves. "Do I have to bribe you, Brax? You're driving me insane."

"It'll be good practice for when Peanut comes along," I winked.

"You're an asshole, Brax." She snorted.

"Bribe me then, baby. What you got?" I stepped forward, grabbing her hips, but her fingers splayed across my chest, halting me.

"Hold that thought." She tried to push away.

"Why?" My head wobbled in confusion.

"Because that milk smells rancid." Charlie took off to the bathroom, and I picked the bottle up, checking it. *Five days to go.* Smelt fine to me too. I took a mouthful and didn't see any issue. *Weird.* I went to finish the coffee, and Charlie finally returned.

"Are you alright, Cutie?"

I hugged her and went to kiss her when she started dry reaching… "You drank that—" Before she could finish, her body convulsed and vomit sprayed everywhere. She actually puked on me. *Fuck my life!* Attempting to catch it in her hands only caused further carnage, and I tilted my head to the ceiling, desperately trying not to breathe through my nose while comforting her with a gentle back rub. "I'm so sorry, Brax."

I looked down and saw her body shaking in sobs. "Shh baby, don't cry. Shit happens." I picked her up and walked her into the bathroom, and peeled off her clothes and my shorts. I stepped under the shower and washed it off the both of us as I held her to me, trying to calm Charlie down.

"I'm sorry, but you drank that milk, didn't you?" Charlie managed between deep breaths to calm herself. I nodded. "I need you to brush your teeth."

"Yeah, but Cutie, there was nothing wrong with it. It's fully in date and tasted fine." Her face flooded with devastation. *Fuck!* Wrong thing to say. She burst into tears again, and I realised it was morning sickness. Milk didn't agree with her. "Hey, come on. Let's get cleaned up and go see our Peanut, alright? I'll clean the kitchen while you finish showering and make you a black tea?"

"Thank you."

"I love you, baby mama." Charlie glared at me.

"How fucking long have you been waiting to say that?" Of course, I just grinned and reminded her she was beautiful. I brushed my teeth then gave her a sweet kiss and headed out, leaving her to finish showering. I used the time wisely by reminding her she was beautiful and giving her a sweet kiss. After that, Charlie gave me permission to go have a quick blunt with the guys, and I promised to meet her downstairs in fifteen minutes before leaving.

I headed to Chester's for a smoke and found the other boys there. As I walked in, Liam asked, "where the fuck have you been hiding?"

"Just promised to spend the day with Charlie, so we are heading out in a minute." I brushed it off with the story we'd agreed on. "We should be back to have dinner if you all want to go downstairs together?"

Shane was quick to call me a "rude prick," and say "yes. You can't just blank us all day and think that is acceptable."

"I feel like a side chick, bro." *Of course you do, Chester.*

"Don't you mean side dick, Monkey?" He punched Mark for that before I told him to hurry and spark up. I excused myself seeing the time and made my way downstairs, finding her waiting outside for me.

"Baby, why didn't you wait inside where it was warm?" I looked at the security guards for answers. "They're freezing," I whispered, nodding to them both, rubbing their hands vigorously.

"I hate the heat. You already know that, Brax." *True.* I detested the idea of her waiting out here on her own. We got a car, headed to the doctor's appointment, and filled in all the relevant paperwork. We explained the circumstances of our tour, and they were very understanding. They would arrange copies of the suitable files and paperwork to be sent to our General Practitioner back home and give us a hard copy just in case. The thirty minutes' wait was getting on my nerves now. "Stop twitching, Brax."

"I can't help it."

"You're so impatient," she muttered. *I really am.* I wrapped my arm around her, kissing Charlie's head as she cuddled into my waist. Ten minutes later, we were finally inside and seated. After explaining everything to the doctor, Charlie answered some questions, along with the urine sample results, before the doctor went through her relevant paperwork with us.

"Congratulations Miss Bancroft and Mr Carson, you are pregnant. You're just over seven weeks, Miss Bancroft. Still, as suggested, I would recommend booking an ultrasound test when you can around your schedule. They will give you a better indication of gestation and allow you to see how your baby is growing." We thanked the doctor before she asked if there were any further questions. "I have written some prenatal scripts and recommendations for you and your baby's health."

"Thank you." We shook hands with the doctor and headed out. I honestly couldn't wipe the smile off my face. The doors swung open as I burst through and picked Charlie up, kissing her lips like crazy. "I love you so freaking much!"

"I love you too. Now if you hurry, I'll reward you for being on your best behaviour and apologise for this morning's mishap." Those fuck me eyes she was throwing had my pulse racing.

"You don't have to tell me twice." I quickly flagged down a ride with security soon joining us from their position, and we got back to the hotel.

Once inside, Charlie locked the door and told me to sit on the couch. I watched her remove all her clothing. She was bent at the waist, wearing nothing but her boots. The moment she leaned over, I couldn't help but pull my cock out and start stroking it while fixated. She knew I loved her legs, and seeing this was a visual spectacle for me. Not to mention thinking about what I would do. Oh, the things I would do;

Fuck her? *Duh!* **I'd grab those heavenly hips and slowly slide into her eager centre. She'd already be slick and swollen, waiting to be taken, moaning as my girth gradually impaled her, pushing back encouragingly as her hips ground into me with increased rhythm. Her moans would get louder, enabling me to fuck her harder.**

Or maybe *not* **fuck her. Perhaps, instead, I'd kneel behind her and gently penetrate her with my tongue instead of my cock. Yeah, that's what I would do. Since she's already slick and swollen, I'd savour the delicious taste of her pretty pussy. Her feet were wide enough apart for me to fit there nicely, pressing my eager face to her, luxuriating in the aroma of her arousal. Her scent is like nothing else, sweet but intense, feminine yet raw, drawing me in. I'd tenderly nuzzle her apart as she cooed her appreciation, licking her lips slowly instead of forcing my tongue into her. Yeah, I'd tease her to come to me. As her pleasure progressed, her centre would open, the slickness turning to wetness, titillation to excitement..**

Her back would arch, leading my tongue from her lips deeper inside her tunnel. Sopping *wet.* **No longer would there be any pretence, just unabashed humping, shamelessly riding my mouth and gasping in pleasure. Her back would arch further to drag her clit over my eager tongue.** *No, wait!* **This is my fantasy, not hers.**

She's bent at the waist, wearing nothing but her boots, rubbing lotion into those dreamy legs. I pumped my cock and admired her adorable ass while I conjured up another fantasy of what I would do;

Her ass was quite adorable. Classy and alluring, enchanting, and enthralling. Oh *yes,* **I find it fascinating. It entices me. It** *seduces* **me. My attraction is perhaps not so classy, my reaction more primal. Her ass was lovely, but the thoughts it provoked were lurid. Wild, raunchy** *fantasies.* **As her hands massaged the lotion into her cheeks, my mind wandered into taboo territory. Shit!**

That fantasy almost went too far.

She was just about finished moisturising those lovely legs. What began as a necessary chore to keep her legs silky turned into a risque show of enticing me with the things she knew I loved the most. When she'd finished flaunting her lovely body, she put away the lotion and came over, giving me a deep kiss. While that ending would have been romantic, I had a raging hard dick, and she was still wearing nothing. It was no fantasy this time. Charlie knelt in front of me, in all her naked glory. Warm, soft and beautiful. She looked up and licked her lips. Sometimes this could go slowly and sensuously as she teased the head of my cock languidly with her tongue. Not this time, though; with her face so *very* close to my cock, my urgency was blatant, even vulgar. So she dispensed with the pleasantries and took me in her mouth savagely.

Sucking me *hard*.

I closed my eyes and threw back my head — I swelled, thrusted, and exploded. I didn't just come; it felt like I burst from the distended tip of my raging dick.

It was incredible, and she never missed a drop. All that pent-up energy and excitement released into her lovely mouth, and she just took it. *No,* she didn't just take it; she welcomed and invited it. We relished this time together, and looking at me adoringly; she swallowed. She smiled as I helped her up, then we really kissed. No quick peck on the cheek would do after such an intense moment together. Our lips met with the passion and fire of a few moments ago, but also the memory of our familiar lust and the hope of many more years of it. *I was so in love with this woman.*

"Are you ready to share the news with the rest?" Charlie giggled as I lept off the couch, racing into the shower to wash. And when I returned, I found her ready to go, and sitting on the couch, a million miles away.

"Penny for your thoughts?" I offered, and she looked up, smiling. But there was more. She looked tired. "Are you okay?"

"I'm fine, why?" She fussed with her clothes, "This is okay, isn't it?" She tugged on the sweater and I stopped her.

"I just meant you look tired, baby. Are you sure you feel like going out?" She nodded and stood up. Walking over to me, Charlie wrapped her arms around my waist.

"I'm fine. I think I'm gonna be tired for a long time yet, Brax. It's just something we'll have to get used to." I kissed her forehead. "I feel so bloated and frumpy, though."

"There is nothing," I emphasised that word, "puffy about the beautiful woman standing before me."

"Where is she?" She turned, searching the room. My smirk spread as I rolled my eyes.

"Cheeky shit. Come here," I pulled her closer, grabbing a firm hold on her ass. I leaned down, kissing her stomach, when her fingers gripped the brim of my cap, removing it and throwing it across the room! "Hey, what're you doing, woman?"

"What have I told you about hats in eateries?"

"Fine. You ready to go?" She nodded, and I took her coat off the hook, holding it open so Charlie could slide in.

Taking her hand, we made our way down and outside to walk across to the restaurant. When the others saw us crossing the car park, Shane spoke first.

"Holy shit, I've barely seen you the last few days, woman," the others agreed with him, seeing Charlie shuffle beside me. It was true, it had exhausted her after the cramped schedule and excessive travelling. The girls were still nodding when Charlie assured everyone she was "okay."

"I think I just needed some good sleep." I cringed when Chester opened his mouth to speak, hoping he would remember to be quiet. Thankfully, he just made a joke, "yeah, more like Brax exhausting you," giving Liam a chance to slide in.

"You fucked all day?" He looked genuinely shocked.

"No, you asshole," I laughed. "I promised to spend the day with Charlie so we could unwind and catch up on sleep."

"Bullshit," he coughed behind his hand, earning a nudge from Mace.

"Shut the fuck up, and get inside so we can eat." I patted him on the back, opening the door and ushering everyone inside. I pulled her chair closer to me as we sat down, arm wrapped around the back of her seat, rubbing carefully before leaning in to kiss her shoulder. We placed our orders and had a catch-up reminiscing on a hectic five weeks.

"Three weeks to go," Mark sighed like he'd transmitted my thoughts. We had to extend the original itinerary from leaving next week, following Brett's accident. I loved performing and touring, but with everything else going on, my head was already back home. Planning this next chapter… "I'm looking forward to a long rest once we get back." *You and me, brother.* I eagerly agreed, and Chester laughed at me.

"You'll need it, prick." I glared at Chester once again. With his big mouth, I was just waiting for him to put his foot in it. "Is that right, asshole?" My raised brow challenged him.

"You're thirty now. Almost as old as Marcus." he threw his thumb in our manager's direction.

"And who's next, asshole?" Marcus reminded him of his own immortality. I looked down when Charlie started picking food off my plate and realised she had finished while I was too busy talking.

"You good?" I nudged her with prying fingers. After grabbing another handful of hot chips and popping them into her mouth, she smiled and said, "yes." The waiter came back around for drink refills and everyone looked horrified when Charlie requested a lemonade.

"Come on, girl. We need to have at least a couple of drinks together." Mace pressed, April and Kendall agreed.

"Sorry, girls, no can do." I rescued Charlie with a firm shake of my head. "Soda only for the next seven months."

"Holy shit," Mace spat her drink in shock before hands flew over her shocked mouth.

"Are you…" Kendall's face was splitting with excitement as she pointed between the two of us.

"Brax can drink for two, while I eat for two," Charlie explained, pinching a few more french fries off my plate.

"You're pregnant?" Marcus finally asked directly. The moment we both said "yes", the girls squealed, and instinctively the guys cringed. That squeaky sound sent a chill up my spine. Everyone raced around to congratulate us, and thankfully Chester and Mark didn't let on to their prior knowledge.

"When did you find out?" Mace wondered while hugging Charlie tightly.

"A week ago," she explained as Mace pulled back in shock. "We only got it confirmed today by the Doctor. We told you all straight away, I promise." Mace laughed, calling it a "lucky save."

"So that's why Evil Midget was extra moody?"

"I'll cut you, Monkey?" She turned on him, pointing her finger as the band laughed. I explained to everyone "our appointment was this afternoon," when Marcus enquired "how far along are you?" and Charlie said, "Around seven weeks, so early days. We need to book an ultrasound when we get back to confirm exact dates."

"I'm thrilled for you both. Truly," Marcus hugged her tightly and gave a gentle kiss on the cheek, before turning to shake my hand and pat my back.

"To Peanut!" Chester hollered while raising his glass.

"Who the fuck is Peanut?" Shane's knotted brow turned to Chester. The penny dropped, and he quickly scrambled backwards. "Well, it's the nickname I picked for the baby, you moron." I smirked, and Shane shoved Chester.

"Dude, when you're a fucking Monkey, you can't call their kid Peanut. That's just wrong," Shane shook his head, explaining to Chester.

"Says you. But nobody asked, Shano shit pants."

"Haven't you got a television with Porn Hub to spray over?" He gave it straight back to him. We were all in hysterics as they went at each other. Still, when Chester told him, "don't hate on me because I'm not expected to return the favour," Kendall slapped him faster than he could blink.

"You watch your mouth, asshole. Don't bring me into your shit show." Charlie and Mace giggled as she waved her finger at him, and he threw his hands up in defence. "Wait, I have a question. Does this mean we can all come back and celebrate for you? And our newest addition?"

I smiled at Kendall. I really loved this family of ours, and seeing how happy they were. "It sure does."

After dinner, we went back to our room to celebrate, and as everyone filed in, I stopped Charlie and pulled her aside. Holding her waist, I moved and kissed her nose, feeling her grip on my biceps. "Can I have five minutes before you get settled, babe?"

"You can have all my minutes, Batman."

"We need to make a phone call, Cutie." She raised her head to look at me curiously, but all she saw was my beaming face. "Don't you think we should call Grandma Carole? After all, she wanted this more than anyone?"

Chapter Twenty One

CHARLIE

Womanhood had defined my life, and now that would be motherhood. Feeling a new person grow within and raising them to become an independent person are the greatest privileges and the biggest challenges. They will weave with my other accomplishments to form who I become. Being a parent should be that way. Mum taught me that, not an additional thing or an 'add on,' but a central theme that other passions revolve around. Finding out the news that she was going to be a Grandmother had flooded all those emotions for both of us.

Travel over the last week had been hell, as the morning sickness kicked up a notch. It's the hangover that lingered, but then our love had me quite drunk, so what did I expect? Brax was his normal incredible self, trying to do everything he could to ease my suffering. The rest of the group had also been sympathetic and respectful. On travel nights, they let me have an early one and wouldn't pester too much, except for Monkey Nuts, of course. I'd be disappointed if he changed his ways.

We had three days in Thunder Bay, right near Lake Superior, so it gave me a reprieve. I was getting upset and frustrated with always being tired, which had translated into Brax taking the blame. He'd just smile and remind me, "It's still the best thing that's ever happened to me."

Tonight, I joined the group. Not that we were doing anything too exciting. Dinner and a few drinks downstairs, then we would likely hang out at someone's suite for a bit. I was feeling better and wanted to try while I could, and that suited Brax perfectly fine. He'd gotten so used to it being the two of us, so it was nice to step out together. I had missed this.

"Baby, are you nearly ready?"

"Don't you rush me! I'm trying to make an effort for you instead of just going with my sweatpants and jumper."

"Cutie, you know you could wear nothing at all, and I'd still love every minute." I burst out laughing, shaking my head at the mirror. "It feels so good to hear that," he continued, causing my heart to swell as he joined me in the bathroom, "even though I know it may not be long before the sickness returns." Wrapping arms around my smooth waist, he rested his head on my shoulder as I finished my makeup, his fingertips stroking my stomach. His dark, hungry eyes met mine. "Scrap my last comment. This is a good look for you."

"Stop staring. You're making me feel paranoid."

"Why? You're beautiful. That's exactly what I was thinking." When I raised my eyebrow, Brax explained further. "I can't help but see the minor changes to your body already. Most people wouldn't notice, but I can spot the smallest things because I'm familiar with it. I love the little tells," he kissed my shoulder, "and knowing that's my child."

I brushed some bronzer across my cheeks, trying to bring them to life, and muttered, "Lucky save."

"Never. I meant every word. I think you look amazing." He kissed my cheek and hugged tighter. "And the fact it's my baby makes you even more beautiful."

Turning to face each other, I wrapped my arms around his neck, looking up into his eyes. "You know what, Batman? For the first time, I'm not scared of what comes next. I can't wait to marry you and have our baby together."

"My heart just burst." He sucked in a deep breath. "I know how much the thought of marriage terrified you because of your past, but the fact you want that, with *me*, means I'm the luckiest bastard under the sun. Everything I need is right here," he promised with a nod of his head and a tighter grip. "I love you."

He kissed me softly, but deepening our intimacy didn't take long. Our tongues danced as one, bodies moulded together in unison. Two pieces that perfectly made a whole. I tried to pull away, but he held tighter, tugging me back and kissing me more profoundly than I thought possible. His hands ran up my sides, moving to my chest. When he slightly squeezed, I practically jumped out of his arms.

"What? What's wrong? You love it when I play with them, babe."

He tried to grope again, but I stopped him. "Normally, yes, but that really hurts."

"Aww, are they sore? Want me to kiss them better?"

"Later! Let's get sorted before you get distracted." He laughed and smacked my butt as we went.

"You look beautiful." Brax's eyes lusted over as I stepped out in a wrap around print dress.

"It's about the only thing I can fit into right now. My pants are already getting tight."

"That's because they fit you like a glove. Don't think I don't know you pinch my track pants, especially at dinnertime." He waved his index finger, calling me out.

"But they're so cosy and smell like you."

After grabbing our keys and phones, Brax took up his wallet and we headed to the elevator. We walked across the lobby to everyone else waiting and joined the line to be seated at the restaurant.

Of course, Chester took little time to carry on, especially regarding food. "Don't they know who I am? Why do I have to wait in line? I'm going to starve to death!"

Shane, who seemed to have had enough of his shit on this tour, flew at him again, much to our amusement. "First, they don't know or care who you are, and second, you have enough cushion for the pushin'. You won't starve. Third, stop being an asshole! If Charlie can wait without whining, so can you."

Chester turned around to address him. "Yeah, well, just for the record, Shano… I'm not an asshole. You are. I'm a haemorrhoid. I annoy assholes." He gave Shane the finger and his dumbest, goofiest smile as we all laughed.

"You're a fucking idiot, bro."

Brax had barely finished speaking when I heard a voice behind me that rattled my bones. He noticed it also, and I immediately saw a cloud of rage mist in his vision.

"From what I've seen, most of you are idiots, especially Charlotte. Have you regretted your choices yet? You're clearly letting yourself go."

"Who the fuck are you calling an idiot?" Brax spat, turning to face Calvin. "Because I know you did not just speak to my girl like that!"

The chick hanging all over his arm laughed at his arrogance, clearly highlighting her for the bimbo she was. "Shut up you wannabe, I wear heels bigger than your dick!" she spat out, laughing pathetically.

"That's great, I take shits fresher than your pussy," Chester slammed her.

"You've got a big fucking mouth on you." Liam stepped up and pushed Calvin flying, having heard enough. I couldn't believe his rage. I'd seen him mad, but not like this.

The bint on Calvin's arm decided she would get some courage and interfere, mouthing at Liam, "Shut up and go wash that filthy mop on your head. I believe he was talking to the fattie there, thinking that ill-fitting dress is hiding her bulges."

The chick was shocked when Mace pushed her backwards into one of the potted plants, causing dirt to fly everywhere. I glanced over in horror, noticing Marcus and security furiously trying to minimise the damage.

Chester burst out laughing, as did the other boys, when Mace stood over her and yelled back, "She's pregnant, you arrogant slut, and don't speak to my man!"

Calvin turned to me, a look of disgust on his face. "You're pregnant, Charlotte? To him?" He pointed at Brax next to me.

Brax squared up and grabbed his collar. "What the fuck does that mean?" I, too, was raging, but I knew what Calvin was like. After the last time he tried this, it was just a matter of time before he would come for us again.

"Could be worse." My evil tongue cut through the tension filled space. "I could have been stuck with you if your disgusting parents had their way."

"Don't you dare bring them into this, Charlotte!"

Brax grabbed Calvin's shirt harder, snapping his gaze from me and back to him. "Like you just brought our unborn child into it? With your two-bit ho hanging off your arm? If fucking plastic was your thing, Calvin, you could have saved a small fortune and bought a sex doll instead."

The woman tried to push Brax as she fired back at him. "Fuck, you think you are some big fucking hip hop artist. No one has heard of you here!" Not that it did her any good. Calvin had his full attention.

"Surprised you can hear anything with the way your flaps must waffle in the wind, you dirty old slapper," Chester spat. She turned to Calvin, expecting him to defend her honour, but he couldn't even protect his own.

Mace continued to torment her. "Yeah, Calvin, be the big tough man and do something. Little miss gobby—pun fully intended—needs rescuing now."

Brax, seeming to have had enough, shut everyone up when he noticed security coming over to interject at Marcus' instructions. "Nah, you know what. I've had it with this shit. Give me your phone, please, Cutie." I looked at him with curiosity. "Babe, give me your phone."

"Oh look, a big tough man is going to call the cops, hey?" Calvin turned to his bimbo and laughed.

I was the one to suck my teeth and shake my head this time. "Really? Ironic coming from the guy who hides behind my Father all the time. What does he do for a living, asshole?" I pointed out the obvious. "Who's the little bitch now, Calvin?"

He snarled. "You've got a big mouth on you, Charlotte!"

"I swear to fuck, if you speak to her again, you'll eat your teeth."

I could tell by Brax's face he meant every word. He had his phone to his ear, annoyed I hadn't handed mine over yet, his impatience growing. I didn't know who he was calling, but soon found out.

"Carole, it's Brax. How are you?"

My eyes bugged, and I saw Calvin look on, puzzled, when we realised Brax was talking to my mother. Unfortunately, we couldn't hear what she was saying.

"Is Dickie boy home yet? We have a minor problem, and before I do anything stupid, I need to speak to him. After all, I have to be respectful here." It was apparent mum had asked a few questions as I saw Brax growing impatient. "Nothing, except for this fuck Calvin, insulting your daughter, my fiancée, while his whore called her fat. I think the best part was when they attacked our baby." The vein in his neck pulsed, his jaw ticking with anger and frustration. That seemed to have done the trick as he thanked her and said he would see her when we returned. "Of course, we love you too."

I smiled warmly, but I could see the disgust on Calvin's face. The guys laughed when I gave him the finger, but Marcus' eyes and head shake told me he didn't want a commotion, so I stepped back.

"Richard, it's Braxton. Thank you for your time. I'm well, thank you, sir, and you?"

Okay, what the fuck? How are you? Sir?

Am I the one who fell and knocked my head here? Since when did dad and Brax become best mates? I looked over at Calvin, who was being ear bashed by his lady friend, demanding he defend her honour. His mates had stepped closer, as they threw shady looks back at us.

"I'm sorry to bother you, but we have a bit of a situation, as I understand Carole has spoken to you about me and Charlie?" I guessed he was referring to the fact I was pregnant. "Yes, thank you. We are too. I appreciate your support, Richard."

I wanted to know what was being said, but it frustrated me that I couldn't, so I stepped closer and took his hand. He squeezed back.

"Of course, another day. Anyway, Calvin is here and has insulted Charlie and this time our child."

"And you can't fight your own battles," Calvin commented.

"Shut up, cunt, before I do it for you," Brax fummed. "Sorry, Richard. Yes, with all due respect, I understand you have a personal relationship with this clown and his parents, so I'm ringing you to explain our side of the story before I knock his teeth down his throat."

Brax listened for a few minutes, and the most I could hear was Dad mumbling before he spoke again. "Yes, of course. Hang on a moment." He extended his arm with the phone. "Here cockhead, it's for you." Calvin took it and stepped away.

"Babe, what is going on?" I tugged on his arm, trying to get his attention.

"I was extending a courtesy to your father before I knocked every one of Calvin's teeth out."

Marcus stepped forward, letting his presence be known. "Brax, you really need to calm down, mate. This isn't a good idea for you or the band."

"M, give me a bit more credit, please," he huffed out. "This is my fight, okay? Let me handle it my way. No one is insulting Charlie or my child. There is *no* negotiation here." Brax turned back to Calvin before shouting, "Oi, asshole! You're looking a little flustered there. Wanna get on with it, so I can smash your teeth in already? Or have you suddenly lost your guts?"

Marcus stepped away from the group, furiously tapping away a message and barking orders to security. Calvin finally passed the mobile back and turned to the woman on his arm while Brax tapped something on the screen, holding his phone securely in front of him.

"Well, you've heard it from Charlie's father, too. Now get the fuck outside, Calvin. You're the one who keeps coming at us, continually threatening and intimidating Charlie, and I'm telling you, it stops tonight." Brax stepped closer to him. "So you have two options here. First, I ring Richard back and ask him to tell his team to follow you for the rest of your stay, or we go to the police and have you charged with stalking. As you can see, I've plenty of witnesses." He turned to reference everyone who was watching. "But seeing as I'm feeling nice, I'll give you a third option. We go outside now and sort this like men, toe to toe. Your standard ammo is to attack women because you're a pussy. But you won't have one more conversation with my girl after today."

"Your boys stay out of this," Calvin said, puffing his chest. "It's one-on-one."

"After what you've done, I don't need anybody else to help me put you on your ass." He nodded and agreed, but before walking past, Brax stopped him again. "I'm telling you this once only. After today, any more harassing my family, and I'll fucking bury you."

"You'd need to walk away from this first to do that."

They went to head outside, and I grabbed Brax's arm. "Please don't do this. I don't want you to get in trouble."

"Hold these for me, baby." When I refused, he took my hand. "Please. I love you." When he passed me his wallet, key, and phone, I noticed the call was still active and lifted it to my ear.

"Hello?"

"Charlotte?"

Realising it was dad, I told him, "You need to stop this."

"Charlotte, I know I've done many bad things, and all I can do is spend the rest of my life making up for it. That man there loves you more than anyone ever could, and I know the day your mother and I are no longer here, he will protect both my daughter and my grandchild." I stuttered and my brow furrowed, not understanding what had changed. As if sensing my confusion, Dad continued. "We'll talk more when you get back, but it was my suggestion to stay on the phone as a witness to Calvin agreeing to fight Brax. I recorded it on this end to prevent any backlash."

"You did all that for Brax?"

"I did it for you both. It's a start, but that's all it is. I don't know if you can ever forgive me. Still, I hope someday to have a relationship with my daughter again and, in time, my grandchild."

"Thank you, Dad." I was so overwhelmed it was all I could manage.

"Just leave the call connected, alright? To protect him from repercussions. We can talk more later, if you want to, of course."

"We both would, Dad." *It's all I've ever wanted.* "It's time you got to know him properly. I believe he's earned that right."

"It's time I started making up for my behaviour. I just don't know if I am worthy of your forgiveness. In fact, I know I am not." He sighed heavily. "But I can be the person you need."

"I need you to stop this fight, Dad, please."

"I've tried. He is defending your honour, and for that, he's earned my respect." I sucked in a deep breath. "He will be okay. He knows what to do, and if nothing else we can talk more when you get back, if you want to."

"I would like it if you and Mum came for dinner at our house. We do need to talk, finally, as a family."

"I'd like that too, Charlie."

"You called me Charlie!" It flew out in shock. "You never call me that!"

"I hear from your Mother you prefer it. And it suits you, don't you think?" I smiled and said 'thank you'. "Remember, do not hang up. By now, all your friends' phones should be on record, so you have multiple devices to back up events should the police arrive."

After I was finished talking to dad, I rushed outside to find Brax, still hoping to stop the first punch from being thrown. Before I could get close, Chester wrapped me in a bear hug from behind and carried me in the opposite direction.

"Chester! What are you doing? Put me down."

"No, sorry, Midget. I'm on strict instructions, and you're staying right here with me."

"But Chester! What if Brax gets hurt?"

"He won't. Promise."

My head flung at him. "You can't promise that! You don't know."

"I know two things. First, I've seen him fight before, and he can throw a mean punch. Second, I've never seen him this angry."

I struggled to break Chester's grasp, flailing my arms as I watched Calvin land the first punch. "Brax!"

Chapter Twenty Two

BRAX

Charlie screamed my name, but I had to stay focused on this fucker. He'd definitely make a cheap shot, given the chance. I knew Chester wouldn't leave her side, nor the rest of the group. "Brax! Watch out," she wailed again, but I was looking. What she didn't know was I wanted him to hit me first. The moment he finally did, I burst out laughing.

"Try again, pretty boy." The boys mumbled behind me, this infuriated him further, causing him to swing at me again.

"Chester, stop them!" Charlie pleaded. "Brax, please." *Oh Cutie, if only you knew.* I'd dealt with worse than this fool before. Sure, I'd also taken a flogging for it, but I had also learned. He hit me a second time, and I smirked. His confusion struck, but didn't allow him any time to register as I head-butted the bridge of his nose. He dropped like a sack of potatoes, gripping his face, cries of agony shattering the otherwise quiet carpark.

"Learn to shut your mouth in the future, pretty boy. *Especially* with Charlie!" My adrenaline was thumping, and I flexed my fist, trying to control the rage. "Any fool can see a punch coming. You're lucky I let you get two shots in." I kicked his foot out of my way, asking, "bet you didn't expect that, though?" He blinked rapidly, with widened eyes as I crouched down. "You think you know her, but you don't. She belongs to me. She *is* my soul. And that *Liverpool Kiss* was especially for her." I'd barely stood back up when she threw her arms around me. I glared back at Chester, who was racing after her.

"Brax, you have blood on you!" She tried turning me, inspecting closer to check for any injury. I gripped her upper arms, steadying her, "It's not mine. It's from his nose," I looked over to Calvin. "I'm fine."

"Before you get any ideas of running to the cops, you should know it's all recorded," Kendall explained for Calvin's benefit. "You hit him first, it's all here," she waved her phone at him.

"Come near my family again, and I'll bury you — with a smile on my face." He sat there on the ground, a stunned expression staring back as I took Charlie's hand and led her back to the restaurant. "Come on guys, I think we may need to dial in takeaway tonight. Not sure they will let me in looking like this." I spun around, holding my shirt out for everyone to see. Little splotches of blood covering it from when I connected with his nose.

"You can eat a dick, Brax." Charlie wrenched away from me. The rest snickered behind us at her sudden mood swing. "What the fuck did I do?" I was stunned!

"You promised to take me out for dinner. I got dressed up because, for the first time in ages, I actually felt well enough to do so, and you pull this shit?" She started storming away as I shook my head, not understanding how we got here. *Fuck! I didn't even think when I fought him.*

I raced ahead, grabbing her hips to spin her around. She was chuckling in my face! The seal burst when our eyes connected, and the humour overtook. "What's so funny? Is this some hormones thing going on? Should I be afraid?" Unable to do any more than laugh at my confusion, it took her a few seconds to calm down before she could answer. "No, I was just fucking with you." The look on my face found amusement with her as she lost it again.

"You Evil Midget!" I smacked her ass swiftly. She squealed and jumped, giving me the perfect opportunity to grab her waist, pulling her in tighter. I softly bit her neck and whispered a promise for what would come. "You're going to pay for that later."

This little thing threw me off guard, and she started pushing her hips to mine, gripping my face to whisper, "Good, because I'm so worked up. You're so fucking hot! The way you took control of that whole situation…." biting her lip, she trailed off.

"You love it when I take control, don't you?"

"Mmm, especially if it involves me in our bed."

"Or in the kitchen." Chester chimed in as he walked past us. The rest of the band also wanted to get in on it.

"Don't forget the couch," was Shane's contribution.

"Tour bus," Mark muttered.

"Jealous much?" Charlie shrugged, and the girls laughed.

I hope Chrissy is back soon so he will stop focusing on our sex life again!

"Damn, you two fuck a lot! That's hot to still have so much passion after all this time." Everyone laughed when Charlie blushed at April's comment, but she wasn't entirely wrong in my book. I gave the guys the finger as I took her hand and returned to the room.

I turned to the group and noticed Marcus was missing once we got in. "I'll text him-"

"I wouldn't," Mark cut in.

"Why's that?" I asked.

"I think he understood why you had to do it, but he still wasn't happy," Mark shrugged. "Let him cool off and speak to him later." I nodded and banked it to come back to later.

"So what's for dinner?" Charlie asked me.

"Pizza? It's the easiest." When Charlie shook her head, uninterested, I suggested "Thai" instead, as I knew it was one of her favourites.

"Nah, I don't want Thai." Mace tried "Indian," and that wasn't it. "Chinese?" Kendall quickly got a scrunched nose of disgust from her.

"Fucking pregnant women!" Shane muttered, earning a slap across the arm from Kendall and a kick to the shin from Charlie.

"Shane! You can't say that," Kendall glared at him. Not bothered, he replied, "Just pick already, woman. I want to eat."

"Just eat Kendall, bro." We laughed when Chester raised the apparent solution to him.

"Don't have to tell me twice!" Shane tried grabbing her hips, she jumped back and put her hand up. He wrapped his arm around Charlie's shoulder and brought her into a side hug as she smiled. "You know I love you…. like a sister before you have a hernia, Brax! But please, for fuck's sake, pick some damn food already."

"Ooh, I want a big fat greasy-"

"Cock," Chester cut her off. We fucking lost it. Even Charlie couldn't hold it in.

"KFC Bucket," she finished once we all settled. "With chips and gravy, oh, potato and gravy, and—"

Chester seemed to have a death wish tonight and cut her off again. "You know that is dual carbs, right? Not good for the hips and—"

"Continue that sentence, and I'll cut you." I pulled her into my lap on the couch, opening my phone so food could be ordered. "That's gonna take at least half an hour."

"Sook all you want, I'm not going out. The only thing I'm doing is washing Calvin off me." I mentally kicked myself the moment I said it as the group fell on the floor, laughing. I could feel the vibrations of hysteria ripple through Charlie's tiny body as she fell into me, tears streaming down her reddened face from amusement. "Now you can all eat a dick."

Charlie turned back to my phone, scrolling through the app and ordering practically everything on the menu. "You good now, Cutie?" I tapped her butt, smirking.

"Yeah, sorry. I got a little carried away."

"Do you, baby, it's okay," I kissed her. "Look at these wankers. It'll get eaten," I pointed to the boys. "Hop up for me, beautiful. I need a shower and a change of clothes." I patted her bum and nudged her off so I could get washed.

I got myself washed and chucked some sweatpants on, heading back into our bedroom. Drying my hair off with the towel, I heard a low whistle, "Now, I'm definitely feeling these pregnancy hormones." I turned to find her walking into our room, instantly recognising the lust.

"You better behave, Missy. Your food is on the way."

"I'm suddenly hungry for something else. Mmm—you know I love it when you wear these...." She bit her lip as she ran her hand along the edge of my track pants, sliding her fingers underneath. "And seeing that sexy chest out — this hair I love pulling on — she twisted her fingers through it as my arms wrapped around, gripping her hips. Running her hands up my chest, she tugged on it gently.

"Hmm.... you know you are on a very slippery slope?"

"Let's get wet together, Brax."

"Fuck, you're such a naughty girl." My lips destroyed hers without hesitation, and she kissed me back with the same equal fire and passion. I bent down a bit to grab her beautiful body more, one hand automatically trailing to her ass as the other gripped the back of her neck. Our faces smashed together in a fiery mess as she moaned into my mouth wildly.

I was about to pick her up when I heard—fucking Chester! "Enjoying the show, guys, really! But the food arrived. Never guess what else turned up?"

Charlie's frustration boiled over into sarcasm, much to my amusement. "Oh gee, I don't know. Maybe a cock-blocker called Chester?"

"I never asked you to stop, Midget. Carry on if you like?" This fucker leaned against the door frame. He smirked back at us as if to say go on, then.

"So what else arrived, dickhead?" she huffed.

"Marcus."

"Oh, yay," Charlie retorted sarcastically. "How exciting! I haven't seen him in ages."

"Alright, little miss, smart ass. I won't tell you the part where he rocked up with some tidy as fuck bird on his arm. I'll just tell Brax instead." Of course, that soon sorted her out as she bounced in excitement, and he called her a "gossip girl."

"Says you who ran in here to tell us."

"Damn you and your attitude, Midget! I like it."

"What's not to like?" she blew him a kiss, and I pushed her hand away, tapping her ass in a warning not to encourage him. I pulled her closer, and the little ass rub she gave me got the reaction she was hoping for.

"You guys seriously need to see this Tessa bird." He used his thumb to point outside. "How Marcus pulled that is a Houdini act."

Curiously, we followed Chester and saw Marcus talking to a brunette on the veranda. When he heard us come out, he stepped aside, which gave us a better look.

"Damn, she is tidy!" Charlie whispered, and I glanced at her.

"Am I allowed to say anything?"

"No," she replied flatly.

"How does that work? You can comment, but I can't?"

"Correct. You got me pregnant." I laughed. *Really?* "Pay me all the compliments now before I get huge."

"You're not gonna get huge," I sucked my teeth. "And besides, we can work it off all the way through your pregnancy." I winked at her. I was only playing, but I loved seeing her get worked up.

"Wrong answer, asshole." Chester laughed as she went to storm off to the kitchen, but I snaked my fingers across her hip and pulled her back. I wrapped my arm around Charlie's waist, my hands protectively holding her as I pushed my hips into her backside, kissing her neck delicately.

"Did you just dry hump her ass, bro?" I looked at Chester and said, "yeah, why do you ask?"

"I just wanted to know if you did. That's all." We grabbed a few bottles of water and headed outside.

"Fuck me! What is it? Like minus two degrees out here?" Marcus answered Chester by saying he was "willing to bet it was colder."

"Why are you here, then?" I questioned.

"Because he's fixing to get sweaty," Chester joked. "And you are, pretty lady?" He turned to the woman.

Marcus shot him a severe looking warning, "Cool it," he glared. "This is Tessa."

"Hi, all," she smiled warmly. "Marcus had just been telling me a few things about everyone."

"Well, let me tell you some about him…." I discreetly elbowed Chester in the side, trying to give a hint to knock it off, while Marcus told him, "piss off inside with the rest of the kids."

"Fine. I see how it is. I'll just pack my bags and head straight for the highway…."

"You've got a better chance on the bus."

He was shocked, and vocal, "I have feelings."

"So you keep saying and I'm yet to see them," he shrugged.

"See, this is the real Marcus." Chester looked at her and pointed to him before heading inside. I felt obliged to speak, "I would apologise for him, but truth be told, that's him at his least offensive."

"He's an acquired taste," Charlie explained.

"Like arsenic," Marcus laughed. We quickly chatted with them before giving them some privacy by heading back inside. He was clearly into her, and given how well he handled our relationship, we decided not to bust his balls over it tonight. There was plenty of time in private to do so later.

I grabbed another beer from the fridge and some dinner before heading to the lounge room with the rest. I sat down and went to pull Charlie into my lap as usual when she turned to me. "What are you doing?" She shook her head when I highlighted, "I was helping her sit down."

"You know soon, I won't be able to sit on your lap anymore?"

"So, this is where it starts? I wondered how long before you looked for excuses." I pulled her onto my lap, and she fell back, wrapping her arms around my neck. "This is all for you, alright? There will never be a time I don't want to hold you."

"I could get used to this extra pampering."

"Does it make you feel something?" I wiggled my eyebrows at her.

"Yes, even more in love with you." I kissed Charlie deeply and patted her gorgeous butt as she hummed against my lips.

"I have a surprise for you tomorrow before the show." She jumped in excitement and asked, "What is it?"

"It wouldn't be a surprise then, fool," I chuckled. We sat around and watched the others chatting and relaxing, and soon she was nodding to sleep. That was until we saw Liam launch himself across Shane at Chester, tackling him.

"Alright man, sorry," he burst out laughing as they rolled around on the floor.

"I heard what you said, asshole," Liam spat while locking him in a head-lock.

"Truce?" Chester cackled.

"Fuck off." Liam locked his arms tighter. "Here, Mace. Get him."

"What the fuck is going on?" I had to ask when she ran over, sucking her finger and sticking it in his ear.

"He asked Mace to lean further forward, then he would have the perfect view."

"What is wrong with you?" Mark asked gobsmacked.

"Do you need to watch some porn again, buddy?" Kendall asked patronisingly, roughing his hair up.

"Nope, I'm good. Chrissy arrives tomorrow." He tugged his shirt down, smiling as he took back his seat.

"Mate! Three weekends in a row. What's going on there?" I had to ask. It wasn't like him—at all.

"That little redhead's got you sweating, huh?" Mark added in.

"I enjoy talking to her," he tried to explain.

"You told me the other day that you don't even do cuddling unless it leads to boning, Chester." Charlie continued, "stop lying." By now, we were all laughing at his expense.

"You like talking to us also, but you never take us off to your room to talk in private." Shane's comment tickled us all.

"Aww, has our little Monkey got his nuts in a twist?"

"Nah, Midget, I am yours."

"Fuck off, asshole." I threw my hat at him, but he ducked it quickly.

"So, have you told her you get a hard-on just thinking about her?" Liam asked, stone-faced.

"I'm not a total animal, mate." A beat dropped before we all laughed in his face, saying, "yes you are."

"Yeah, I didn't even believe it myself." He stared over my shoulder, then pointed, "But, if you think I'm the one that can't control myself, turn around." We all spun and looked outside to see Marcus with his tongue buried halfway down Tessa's throat, just as Chester yelled. "Yew, Dad! Get it!"

Chapter Twenty Three

BRAX

It was now the weekend, and as I lay in bed, I realised we only had one show tonight to do and then one more week before heading home. For the first time, I was excited to be finished with a tour and return to life. I wrapped my beautiful blonde Cutie around me, and as I stared down at her, the flood of emotion ripped through me causing a sharp intake of breath. I was excited to get home, plan all the things we wanted... announce our engagement, baby, then plan our wedding and the birth. Fuck, I hoped Charlie wanted to know what we were having. No way could I wait for months. We need to book our first scan in with the hospital... fuck, I couldn't wait for that! To see our baby growing inside her... honestly, it was a dream come true. And then, a month later, we had the music awards to attend, and they had asked us to perform this year. I couldn't wait to unveil our song with Glaze.

So much was still to happen before the year was out, yet I couldn't wait to tackle it head-on and begin our lives. I was over the tour because my mind was on us for once. That never happened because the music was my everything. Something niggled inside, a need to get my girl home, share the news with our friends and family. My god, I couldn't wait to marry her! I was most excited because today, I finally got to have some time out before the show tonight. This was much needed after such a crammed schedule. And I knew how much she wanted to see a hockey game, so that's exactly what we were doing. I even scheduled a tour of the stadium before the game, so we could go on the ice. I snapped out of my daydream and checked the time, knowing we were on a schedule. If I let her sleep too long, we'd miss out. I rolled towards Charlie and kissed her neck and cheeks, softly running my fingers up her ribcage. "Fuck off, I'm sleeping."

I chuckled into her skin as I kissed it softly and mumbled, "good morning. I love you."

"Why!" she whined. "Why do you always do that, Brax?" Throwing the blankets back in a huff, she stared at the ceiling.

"Make you feel guilty for being an asshole in the morning?" She mumbled "yes," as I pecked at her soft skin again. "Because now you will stop being one and kiss me."

"You wish, fool." I laughed as I rolled over on top of her and came down closer.

"Morning, my babies." Our lips met briefly before I slid down her body and kissed her stomach. Charlie stroked her slender fingers through my hair and smiled sweetly. "Now get up."

"You're still drunk if you think I'm doing anything other than going back to sleep."

"Guess you don't get your surprise, then. Suit yourself." I shrugged my shoulders nonchalantly as I rolled off the bed and headed to the door. When I walked down the hallway to the kitchen, I heard her shout she was coming! "Nah, baby, it's good. I understand you want to stay in bed. I can take Chester with me."

"Well, where are we going?" I shrugged, ignoring her. She wasn't interested in anything other than sleep. "You're such a wanker. I know what you're doing, Brax."

"It made you get up, though, didn't it?" She said "yes" as she came up behind me, face pressed to my back as she wrapped her arms around my waist. "You're such a good girl, baby. Look at you."

"Fuck off, Brax! I'm not a dog." She laughed as her hands wandered up to my chest, brushing over my muscles and exploring every curve while we waited for the kettle to boil. I picked her fingers up and lifted them to my lips, giving them a gentle kiss.

"I wish you woke up earlier this morning."

Her head lifted off my back as she asked, "Are we going to be late?"

"No, but we don't have time for you to sort this out." I slid her hands down my chest, gripping them tight, past my stomach to the front of my boxers. Charlie started cackling the moment she realised, and the vibrations that rippled through her body were heavenly.

"You're so bad. If the surprise is as exciting as you're making it out to be, I will thank you kindly for it tonight." I turned around, smiling from ear to ear, and passed her a cup of tea. I sipped my coffee, the smirk more predominant as she asked, "why are you smiling?"

"The surprise is so good. You will do some nasty things for me later."

"Is that so? Are you confident?"

"I am!" I leaned in, pulling her closer and pushing my tongue through her lips for a deep kiss. After a few minutes, she pulled back quickly, dropped her cup on the bench, and ran off to the bathroom. I couldn't help but yell, "Really?" I followed and soon found her bent over the toilet bowl. Then it hit me like a ton of bricks. "Shit! The milk in my coffee?" She tried nodding as she gripped the toilet, and I walked over to hold her hair. Squatting behind her, I stroked her back, trying to provide some comfort. "I'm so sorry. I'll try to remember in the future." Guilt etched my tone.

Charlie eventually settled and sat back. "It's okay. Hopefully, it will pass soon."

"Come on, let's get you washed up so we can leave."

"Could you just—"

"Brush my teeth first?" I cut in. She nodded, apologising. It didn't matter. I just wanted to know she was alright. I turned the shower on as she got undressed, and then brushed my teeth. After a quick wash, we dried and dressed when she stuck her head out of the bathroom. She seriously looked fucking adorable right now, a curious look, eyes wide like a deer in headlights. "Umm, since you haven't told me where we are going, I don't know if what I'm wearing is alright?" I looked over the white woollen sweater she had chosen with black leather pants and boots and told her, "grab a warm coat. It's cold outside today, and we will move around." Nodding, she grabbed her jacket, and I texted Marcus to remind him we were out for the day.

"Don't forget to check in regularly with security. We have one car stationed outside the stadium at all times."

"Thanks, M." I typed back, then pocketed my phone. We headed down and got into the taxi, as it set off, I turned to Charlie. "Do you trust me?"

"No." We both laughed before I threw her a deadpan stare. "That's why I'm having your child and marrying you."

"Smart-ass." I didn't continue, so she asked, "why do you want to know?

"When we get closer, I'm putting my hands over your eyes to surprise you."

"Is this just an excuse to touch me?"

"Yes. Is it working?" I looked sideways with smouldering eyes, begging her silently to fuck me. When we were only a few minutes out, I wrapped my arm around her neck and brought it to her face. I placed both my palms over her eyes and leaned in to whisper that "we're nearly there." She nodded and reached across, stroking my leg with her delicate hand. Once the car pulled up, I told her to turn towards the window and removed my hands.

"Brax! A hockey game!" she squealed and threw her arms around my neck, whispering thanks and love. I couldn't help but get caught up in the excitement, I grabbed her soft cheeks and smothered her face in kisses. Her happiness was spilling over, I had to laugh at her antics. She looked like a shaken bottle of coke about to explode with contained exuberance.

"Come on, Cutie, let's go in."

We headed inside and did our tour first. She gripped my hand like a bewildered school kid, overstimulated and mesmerised. While I wasn't a massive hockey fan, I enjoyed most sports. However, her excitement was enough to make anyone value the place. We headed to our seats, when she threw herself at me, knocking me flying. I had to grip the arm of the chair to stop from falling over.

"These seats are incredible. Today was amazing. You are definitely getting all the kinky shit you want tonight." She quickly fired at me.

"You're insane," I laughed in her ear as she gripped me in the biggest hug I could remember.

"I love you. Thank you so much, Batman. This is a dream come true." I put my arm around her shoulders as we sat waiting for the game to start. We had seats near the goals, so Charlie didn't stay cuddled into me for long, getting involved in the game and screaming like a maniac. I listened as she explained the ins and outs to me as I observed her rants in amusement. Getting into the game didn't take long because her enthusiasm was contagious.

Afterwards, we got in the car and headed back to the hotel while Charlie checked out her photos, I asked if she got any good ones? "I wish I had my camera, but this one is good." She turned her phone to show me one player pressed to the glass behind the net in front of our seats. "I can't thank you enough." We shared a tender moment in the back of the car before we arrived back, she took my hand, leading the way to our room. We could hear the racket from the other guys in their room and she turned, holding her finger up to be quiet as we tried to sneak past quietly, wanting to enjoy a few more moments before we had everyone cramming in our space.

I sat down on the settee, kicking my shoes off, and chucked my jacket over the back. Charlie did the same then came over, to straddle my lap. She ran her hands up my chest as I gripped her hips. Her fingers made their way up to my neck, leaning forward, she kissed behind my ear gently, and moved across my cheek. I gripped her hips tighter, pulling her closer when our mouths finally met, and her tongue passed between my lips to capture mine. I slid down on the couch further, pulling her hips up to feel her rubbing against my growing cock as our kiss heated. My hands were now making their way up inside her shirt as she ground softly against my pelvis. "Mmm, fuck, I want you, baby."

"Then take me." She gripped my face tighter as we kissed, but not nearly long enough.

"You want to hear something super funny?" Charlie shot up, squealing, her frustration boiling over into expletives directed at Chester for his interruption. We looked over and saw him leaning on the edge of the couch, all the other guys standing at the door, ready to burst out laughing.

"Fuck! Just let yourself in next time." I groaned and adjusted my pants. *My cock was aching!*

She asked "why do you always do this?" he just smirked at her, raised his eyebrow and said "it's amusing. So, as I was saying. Would you like to know what the funniest thing is?" I waved my hand at him to hurry. "That's a pull-out couch, right?"

"Yeah, and your point is?" I asked, recognising she was in no mood to deal with his antics.

"Fucking while pregnant on a pull-out couch." He burst out laughing. "The irony of it!" As everyone chuckled, I wasn't sure if it was more directed at him or the fact Charlie called him a "fucking idiot."

After Chester finally got over how hilarious he thought he was, everyone piled out and made their way to the venue for tonight's show. Charlie headed to the back of the bus to get her equipment when I snuck up and smacked her on the ass hard. "Don't you dare lift that!"

"Oh, but is it okay for you to slap me?" She glared back.

"Really, Charlie?" My eyes rolled at her exaggeration. "I don't slap, baby; I spank. And I have it on good authority that you love it."

"I enjoy spanking the Monkey. See, we have something in common, Midget." She laughed at Chester and said, "we really don't." When I went to speak, she turned and pointed, "Stop now, while you still can."

"Why wouldn't I be able to?"

"Because I will strangle you, Brax."

"You wouldn't. You would miss this dick too much." I thrust my hips towards her as I grabbed my junk, and she pushed me away.

"What the hell has gotten into you tonight? You have this show to do. Go away and stop being a pest." I walked behind her again and rubbed

Charlie's ass as I bent down and kissed her neck. She was quick to slap my hands away. "Ugh! I hate Pre-show Brax. You're so obnoxious. You're like a child the night before Christmas."

"Well, I don't know about Santa, but I know of someone who will come tonight." He winked at me as Chester and he laughed and high-five.

"Go, now! The pair of you."

"Love you, baby." Distracting her with gentle kisses on the cheek, I picked her bags up, anyway.

"Love you, baby," Chester copied and went to lean in and kiss her. The swift impact of me giving him a jab to the biceps made him wince. "Fuck!" Shaking his arm out, he grumbled, "Alright, sorry." He dragged the word out dramatically while eyeballing me. Turning back to Charlie, "Love you, Sweet Cheeks." He tried to move in again, and she laughed when I whacked him a second time. "What the hell, man! Quit hitting me. I have to use those arms tonight."

"Well, you should have thought about how you'd play the guitar before carrying on."

"I wasn't talking about going on stage. I mean when I wank later." Her body instinctively cringed, Charlie muttered he 'was a fucking animal,' much to Chester's amusement. He reached for her, slinging his arm around her shoulder as they side hugged. When he reached over and started rubbing her stomach, I smiled. "Hey, Peanut. You're like the mini version of me," he leaned closer, whispering to Charlie's stomach. "I'm Monkey Nuts."

"My kid will not be the mini version of you, Chester. The laws are stricter now than when we were children." I reminded him.

"Are you saying I would have been in Juve if I was younger now?" he glared at me.

"Or a madhouse." I had to add that, I couldn't help myself. We arrived inside and Charlie wished the bands a good show as she pulled her photography equipment free from their cases.

From stage left, I had the privilege of watching Glaze illuminate the arena in their spectacular and unique style. The crowd was a river of people, everyone moving in the same direction. There were only joyful faces throughout the venue, each here for the music to fill them chock full of adrenaline pumping happiness. They moved not like pebbles in a jar, but like water molecules flowing smoothly past one another, friends staying together with fingers entwined. When the boys and I took to the stage, from the crowd came a sudden rising of energy, a joy that the long wait was over. The supporters were an encore for my heart, a rainbow of people arcing through the blackened arena. The international reception had been overwhelming!

I'd just taken a seat in the green room when Charlie walked up to me. It was like an instant ray of sunshine and I felt my smile beaming back at her. I pushed my chair out and gestured for her to sit on my lap. "You alright?" She nodded and said she was "fine," as I kissed her cheek and she enquired back. "As long as you are okay, I'm good." I tapped her nose. "Do you want to go stand outside? Get some fresh air?" It occurred to me just how smokey and cramped this space was and Charlie and our baby's health was of the utmost importance to me.

"Sure, let's go for a little walk before we have to pack up." She took my hand, standing up. I turned to the guys, my index and thumb in each corner of my mouth, before my high-pitched whistle silenced everyone.

"We'll be back in ten minutes," they all nodded. "I'm just taking Charlie out to get some fresh air. It's pretty smoky here." I waved my hand in front of my face to emphasise the point. They acknowledged, and we headed out, walking down the side of the building. I finally pulled her to a stop and leaned against the fence, our hands still clasped together as she moved into me. She wrapped her arms around my waist and rested her head on my chest. "Not long to go, then we'll be back home," my lips caressed her temple, "and you can relax as much as you need to."

"This has been great, but I can't lie; I'm looking forward to that."

"Can I ask you something?" Charlie chuckled into my chest as we huddled together and she whispered "no," to my amusement. "Does it seem like going home is when it really begins? I mean, our lives together?"

"Yes, I feel exactly that." Her head shot up, revealing her loving eyes to me. "I can't wait to get off this tour because I know once we're back, that is when everything begins."

"We get to see our baby for the first time." The smile she gave me hearing that was the most radiant I had ever known. It melted my heart.

"I love that you went to that first." Her soft fingers brushed the hair back off my face before resting at the nape of my neck, tenderly stroking my skin.

"I love that you are carrying my baby." I kissed her nose, my heart swelling when it scrunched. "And that right there," I tapped gently. "It's so fucking adorable." I continued with, "we can announce our engagement properly to our friends and family."

"Then plan our wedding." When she said that, I felt like my entire world was finally spinning as one. The years I had spent longing for this woman, wondering if it would happen, and now my universe rotated around her axis. "I can't wait to meet our little Peanut," she sighed.

"So we're really going with that?" My shoulder playfully nudged.

"Well, what else is there? We don't know what we're having?"

"Do you want to find out?" I was desperate to know, so when she said "yes," I exhaled heavily. "Thank fuck!" she laughed. "We're finding out the first chance we get." I pretended to wipe the sweat off my brow, heightening her amusement.

"Well, that makes sense. You have worse patience than I do." *Cheeky fucker.*

"The music awards will be here before we know it." Her eyes lit up, as she cut in.

"I can't wait to hear the song!" I smirked, knowing how desperate she had been to read what Chris and I had written. Not this time. It was… personal. For everything she had given me, it was my turn to give back. I was keeping it a surprise until awards night. "This is an incredible achievement in your career," her proud voice brought me back.

"I just can't wait to have my life with you finally begin properly." I reached down and stroked her face.

"You know what I love about you the most, Brax?"

"This dick?" I grabbed my crotch, and she burst out laughing.

"Fucking hell," she muttered. Looking up, her sparkling eyes met mine, and she reached out, her soft fingers brushing against the shadow growth on my jaw. "You always act the most grown-up and sensible one of the group, trying to keep everyone in line, looking for more opportunities to grow. Then I get to go home with you at night and see the beautiful, loving man that you are. And, I know you adore our friends and family just as much as I do. But in moments like this, when it's our child you're putting first, it's a piece *just* for me. It's a part I've always been missing that you reserved just for us." A lump formed in my throat. "I can't even describe how much I love you." Charlie pushed up on her tiptoes, kissing my lips. "You can do better, since you're the wordsmith of the family."

"I think you said it perfectly." I gave her a kiss back, adding, "thank you." Just as Charlie rested her head back on my chest, I teased, "You can give me a blow job if you wanna show how much you appreciate this." I took her wrist in my grasp and started trailing her hand down my stomach.

"Ugh, Brax," she groaned as I laughed. "Why do you get so horny on performance days?"

"It's all the extra adrenaline rushing to my dick," I pumped her with my hips. We stood outside for a few more minutes and held each other with the dull sound of the music in the distance and the crowd screaming. We headed back as the second half of the show began. I gave Charlie plenty of photo opportunities, both during and after the show. As we returned to the bus following the performances, I wondered what kind of mayhem would erupt tonight because everyone seemed extra buzzed. It confirmed my instinct right when Chester jumped off the bottom step of the bus, racing over to the Bottlo.

Chapter Twenty Four

CHESTER

The show was lit, but the best part was that we were about to get more so! Everyone was here tonight, so there were no holds barred. "You all have to drink double to have Midget's share."

"Thanks, man. I appreciate you reminding me I can't drink." She smirked sarcastically.

"You're welcome. But fear not, I have many wonderful things in store for you, dear Midget."

She looked at Brax as she pointed her thumb towards me. "Is this guy for real?" The drinks flowed heavily and quickly, although I noticed Brax was taking his time. I guessed to be considerate of Midget, so I followed when I saw her go inside.

"Question, please?" With a frown, she asked, "what's that?" not looking up, but I waited until she turned her head. "Can I get him cooked tonight?" I inclined my chin towards where he was sitting.

"Brax?" When I said "yes," she questioned "why are you asking for my permission?"

"Because he's drinking like a bitch, obviously trying to be considerate for you, which is why I wanted to ask first." She grinned and said "do it," so

I held my hand up to high five. "Yes! Pregnant Midget of Tour is the best!"

"Do not call me that ever again." Her deadly blank stare pierced.

"Roger." We headed back out, and I waited as everyone passed the beers around before I pulled the shots out. "I have an announcement to make!"

Mark muttered from the corner, "You fingered your own butthole one time at school camp?" Everyone cracked up laughing at my expense before Brax took his shot.

"You masturbate more than you admit to?"

"Suck my dick, assholes!" After they stopped ribbing me, Brax told me to go on with this announcement. "Everyone sits around the table. Shots too."

"No shots for me tonight, bro." he immediately protested, raising his beer bottle and tapping the side of it.

"Already cleared it with the Pregnant Midget Wife, so you're good to go…" Brax's brows flew up, unsure if he heard me right. Then an idea came. "Ooh, we could make a reality show based around it. Pregnant Midget Wives of Tour."

Marcus cracked up laughing. Tessa, who was with him again, highlighted it "sounded like the making of porn," with Nick's wife Jewels agreeing. Chrissy said "exactly what I was thinking," and I saw Brax giving Charlie the side eye and a smirk before he spoke.

"I mean, I'm not opposed to making a sex tape if that's what you want, baby?" She glared at him and mouthed a firm 'no!'

"So now we've established that you can't hide behind the excuse of your Pregnant Midget Wife, it's t—"

"Would you stop fucking calling me that, Chester!" Charlie butted in, frustrated with me.

Ignoring her, but first throwing a wicked smile, I yelled to everyone it was time for "more shots!" We all clinked them together, except for poor Midget, and took the tumbler of drink. I saw Brax give her a kiss afterwards and whisper something. "Detach your balls from the Midget, and man up. You, pussy whipped spandex-wearing baboon, motherfucker."

Charlie cracked up laughing and asked, "what the hell was that?!" I winked at her. "Just a collection of your finest, Midget."

"So why did we all have to sit here, asshole?" Shane asked, reminding me that I had gathered them for a reason. I excused myself, promising to return as I raced inside to collect it and threw it on the table, yelling in surprise - "The Bible!"

Charlie immediately said "no." However, we cracked up when Brax slid his hand across her mouth and nodded "yes." Of course, the rest of the boys ultimately agreed as well. "Chester, I'm not playing the bible sober!"

"Well, look at that. She gets knocked up and automatically turns into a pussy."

I knew that would work, as she reached across the table and snatched it from me. "Give me that damn bible, you fucking baboon."

In the excitement of riling her up, we'd forgotten we had people here who didn't know about it. So, when Tessa asked, "what is that?" I felt obliged to explain.

"So the bible is our collection of the best... dares or twenty questions we have played over the years. We have added any deemed worthy to collate and form the bible." Chrissy asked, "how bad?"

"It will make you question our sanity and why we date them," Kendall gave as an example.

"Hey!" Shane glared at her, horrified.

"So Charlie, you can go first since you're Pregnant Midget of Tour and can't drink."

"I swear to fuck you say that one more time, and I will give you Pregnant Midget Crazy!"

Ignoring her threat, I asked if she was "picking truth or dare?" So when she chose the "truth," I said, "pregnancy made her dull."

"Eat a dick!"

"Ok, are you a dirty talker in bed? If so, how dirty?"

"Fuck off, Monkey! I'm not answering that question, especially for you." The guys laughed, and Brax immediately asked, "is that even in there or did you just make it up?" Luckily, Mark remembered.

"No, it's there. Remember, Shane had to answer it when we were in Townsville? It was the same night as the Hagrid incident." Liam agreed, as did the rest when Mark explained, before Midget spoke up again.

"Yeah, I don't give a shit. I'm still not giving Chester that bit of information!"

"And I respect you even more for it, baby." Brax hugged her tighter. Marcus was the one that called him out for his bullshit. It was apparent he didn't want me to know the answer to that, either. "I know. I don't deny it."

"So what's your final answer, Midget? Are you refusing?"

"I decline! What's the dare?"

I looked up and smirked at her because this was even better. "Suppose you were a dirty talker in bed. Give us a demonstration on Brax of what you would be prepared to say or do."

The moment I said it, Brax threw his head back laughing, and she slapped him across the chest while Kendall reminded me, "I might be dead after this stunt."

Chrissy pointed out "the truth didn't seem so bad after all compared to that," the girls agreed.

"You're so full of shit! That's not conveniently on the same page!"

Brax patted her butt as he explained it was. "We did them like that on purpose. I should have remembered. If you tried the pussy avenue of truth, the dare that counteracted the truth was much worse." We heard her say "fuck," into his chest as she thought about it momentarily.

"I hate you so much, Monkey. My child must find a new favourite Uncle because it can't be you!"

"That cuts deep, Midget! Well, as thick as your little arms will let you go." She threw her empty water bottle at me. I ducked just in time as everyone laughed when she said, "you'll pay for this."

"It will be worth it."

She turned on Brax's lap and straddled him. His fingers gripped her hips possessively as the Pregnant Midget of Tour moved in, grabbing his face and seeming to whisper to him. I watched my boy's fingers grip her tighter, and when I saw her hips swivel slightly on his lap, I knew whatever she just said had the effect Midget was searching for.

"Hey! We're waiting." Charlie lifted her head, still gripping Brax tightly as his hands tried to push her hips back down, asking me what the problem was. "Start speaking." When she said "I am," I pointed out the obvious. "We can't hear you." Charlie ignored me and moved into Brax again, he suddenly wrapped his arms around her waist, pulling her in tight and giving her a big kiss. When she moved away, she looked over, smirking. "So, are you going to do this dare or not?"

She sat there still grinning as she rubbed her hands up and down Brax's neck and into his hair as he pressed her body to him, head nearly buried in her tits. "She already did, Bro."

Shane and I both highlighted we didn't hear shit, and this little thing finally spoke. "Who said you had to?" She cut me off when I started reminding her what the dare said. "I know what it said, Chester. You read, and I quote…. "Suppose you were a dirty talker in bed. Give us a demonstration on Brax of what you would be prepared to say or do." When she had finished, I told her, "do it then."

"You said Brax. And he heard it. You never said you had to, as well."

The girls all laughed, congratulating this Evil Midget on getting one over me. Still, I wasn't letting her beat me again. "How do I prove you completed it if I didn't hear you?"

So what did she do? She stood up, pointed to Brax's raging dick, and turned to me, smirking. "I think that's sufficient proof, don't you?"

"Fucking hell, Charlie!" We all cracked up and gave him shit over it. My poor guy tried to grab her to sit back down to cover himself up. She definitely got us good with that one.

We went around, and it got to Shane, who had drawn Marcus. Dad had gone with the truth. "What's the wildest fantasy you ever had…. that has come true."

When I shouted, "how kinky are you, Dad?" I saw the girls cringe. Marcus was too busy focusing on Shane.

"You little fucking prick!" Shane laughed in his face until Marcus reminded him, "you have a contract negotiation coming up."

"Yeah, you'll still need to answer that." Brax appeared to have caught on as well.

I saw the girl's jaws drop with what came next, but the rest of us buckled over, laughing. "You're a real cunt, Shane." Chris quickly pointed out that this had to be good for Marcus to be wound up. That was when he finally shook his head and explained. "I fucked someone backstage while you played a few years ago. She was so loud I needed the sound from your gig to disguise it. She was still going when you finished, so I ended up gagging her and, well…. let's just say she was into it more than I was because shit got wild from there." Charlie's shock was verbal as we boys listened amused, and Shane told him to "keep going."

"Fine! She was a dirty bitch, and it was great. I held her arms behind her back, her panties stuffed in her mouth while I gripped her hair for leverage. Smashing that, I saw two stagehands walking past. They noticed us and stopped dead. I didn't tell her and kept going while I knew they were watching."

"Woah! You kinky fucker, Daddy!" He punched me quicker than I could blink, but it just made me laugh even harder. Liam said, "I'm in awe," and he, too, copped a punch from Mace.

Brax was the next one to go, and when he drew me, I saw Charlie give him a look. I knew that evil glare of hers. "Agh, no, you fuckers. Pregnant Midget of Tour doesn't get to pick. It is not her turn."

Brax looked up at me. "You scared?" Of course, I said I wasn't. "Good, so truth or dare?" I picked the dare, watched as he looked down, and glanced up. Midget had a quick peek, and he seemed to point to the one she wanted. I saw her smirk, and when he winked, I knew something terrible was coming. "Take Chrissy inside and put a porn on. No pre-story attached for wasting time. You then have to act exactly like them for two minutes."

"Show time, asshole!" Midget laughed in my face as she flipped me the bird.

Chapter Twenty Five

BRAX

S o here we all were in the lounge room, roaring in laughter as a porno of Shane's choosing played in front of us. Chester had Chrissy's hands on the coffee table, holding her up by her thighs in a wheelbarrow, pretending to bang her brains out. Half of us were hysterical, coughing up a lung, while the poor girls had their legs crossed, praying they didn't pee themselves. It was the funniest shit I'd seen in ages, and of course, it was this crazy bastard doing it. When Charlie returned from a dash to the bathroom, the relief on her face was comical. I'm sure she thought she might have peed her pants there for a minute. "Close call?"

She said, "too close for comfort." After several minutes, he stopped, and it took some time before we calmed down after that escapade.

We recovered enough to continue when Mark drew Shane. If I thought tonight couldn't get any better, I was wrong. "Order a sex toy of the group's choosing online, in your name, for delivery."

"It's always the silent ones you have to watch. They are ninja assassins." Laughing, we agreed with Marcus, as he shook his head at Mark. We had a look and then discussed and agreed on what toy he should order, then decided Kendall could be the one to deliver the news.

"Thanks a lot, assholes," she muttered, not amused.

Shane asked, "how bad is it?" she turned the tablet to show him. "It's a ribbed butt plug."

"You realise I'm using it on you, right?" The boys burst out laughing at the look of horror on Kendall's and the girl's faces.

"You dirty fuck! I didn't pick it; Monkey Nuts did!"

"Babe, I won't order that and let it go to waste." She sucked her teeth at him, and we watched, amused. He pulled out his card and ordered it for delivery. He then took his turn and ended up with April, who chose dare. "Send Mark a video of you doing a blowjob on a banana."

The girls wished her good luck. I cracked up when Mark, as placid as anything, asked, "why only the banana?" She headed inside with her phone, and a few minutes later, his phone lit up with a Snapchat alert. We watched as he opened it, and the moment the video started, we knew she'd finished the dare. She came back out and grabbed the bible, choosing Mace.

"Dare." Mace never was one to punk out. April flicked it open to a page and then chuckled before showing Charlie. She burst out laughing, nodding to say "yes," I wondered what had her so tickled.

"I love you, Mace, but this is *perfect* for you." She prefaced before April read it out.

"Read an erotic story out loud." Mace grabbed her heart, asking if it was because she had "a voice for the radio."

"Yes, now pick one." Chester cracked up as he high-five Liam's enthusiasm. We got our phones out and found a story we agreed on before handing it over to her. She sat on Liam's lap, and I buckled over, laughing when I saw his face.

"You look as happy as a pig in shit right now, bro." When he said "he was," Charlie put her hand across my mouth, telling me to "shh" so Mace could start. "Someone's keen?"

"Shut up, asshole. I can't help it." I laughed at my Cutie, tapping her on the butt when she wiggled in my lap. Mace took the phone and looked down to begin.

"We were in my car driving back from dinner, late on a summer's night. You were wearing a short skirt, and I couldn't help but get distracted by your bare legs raised as you reclined the seat in its farthest setting. When you placed your feet on the dash, I glanced at your toes and loved the dark red nail varnish. The next time I looked over, you had a naughty smile."

"You slid your hand under your skirt and played with yourself. You pulled off your knickers and threw them over the gearstick. Concentrating on the road was difficult when all I wanted to do was watch you, but I looked back at the road. Then some moments later, I felt your fingers on my lips, then inside my mouth. Greedily, I sucked the juices from your fingers." I felt the atmosphere in the group had changed, having become charged. It was becoming apparent that this might be the last dare of the night, and everyone would be eager for some privacy following this reading. I knew it was accurate as I felt Charlie push her butt back into my groin. Not that it bothered me. I could already feel the dull ache rising.

"I felt you rubbing my crotch with your other hand. Moments later, your fingers unzipped my shorts and freed my now hard cock. You took me in your mouth, and it felt fucking amazing. I couldn't concentrate on the road any longer, so I pulled over into a small layby. You started licking up and down either side of my hard shaft, over the head and around the rim. I almost came there and then once you started to deep throat. My cock was warm and wet from your hot mouth, sucking me. I pulled you up and pushed you back in your seat, spread your legs, with those sexy feet pressed up against the front window. It was hot thinking how any passing cars could see you playing with yourself in the passenger seat. You'd pulled off your top and now squeezed your pert nipples whilst playing with your pussy. I pushed my seat back, so I reclined it, then took down my shorts and pants before pulling you over and atop me. Your hands found the steering wheel, then pushed up against the front window once I'd entered you from behind."

I couldn't help but squirm under Midget's butt, thinking about how badly I wished I was taking her from behind. Watching her shoulder blades squeeze together as I slid into her, her hands gripping our sheets as her knuckles turned white, and she threw her head back. God, it got me every time. *It was poetic.* I shook my head as Mace cleared her throat and continued.

"You moaned as you pulled your pussy along my length. I spanked your ass and sat back further so you could lean into me. I played with your tits, kissing your neck and pulling your hair as you leaned back, grinding deeper. You rubbed your clit as I pushed myself up, making you lean forward so the top of your head almost touched the front window. Your tits pressed against the dashboard. I increased my thrusts while smacking your ass hard, and you…" There was an audible groan as the buzzer went off to show time. Everyone looked flustered and charged. "Well, that was interesting." *You're not wrong, Mace!*

Following a long… awkward silence… Everyone avoided eye contact because we were all thinking the same thing…. "We are going to bed!"

I broke down laughing when Liam spoke. "Thank fuck! Someone said it."

We said "goodbye" to everyone as they headed out, and once the last two left, I shut the door and locked it. I stalked over to my girl, picked her up, and carried her into our bedroom. I placed her on the bed and came over the top, my knee next to her leg and holding weight on my arms. "So how do you want it, beautiful? Rough? Or sensual?"

CHARLIE

Silence filled the room at his question before he kissed me. His arms were muscular and held firm as my lips parted and accepted his tongue. His fullness pressed against my stomach, and my hands danced across the back of his neck. I floated from lightheadedness, lustful, knowing that the man who had fucked me so many times before would soon be inside me again. His hands moved to undress me. Eagerly, I tugged at his zipper. I groped inside his trousers and pulled his hardness out. He moaned into my lips when my encircled fingers stroked him. My mouth slid to his ear, whispering, "I need to suck your dick," before I dropped to my knees. Holding him with both hands, I licked the mushroom-shaped head, tasting his pre-cum's saltiness before taking him in.

His hands gripped my head as I let him slide in and out of my hot, wet mouth. Using my tongue along the shaft freed my fingers to push his pants further down. Glancing up, I saw him eyeing me as I tried to take him. His lips curled upward as he reached forward, stroking my bulging cheeks. I felt his head press along the back of my throat and into it, making my eyes roll with delight. "You look beautiful," he groaned. "Such a good girl, Charlotte." His balls struck my chin as I swallowed him down. Then deep thrusts back and forth as his cock penetrated my throat. The room's atmosphere was intense and filled with frustration after Mace's reading. I knew neither of us would last long. It got me thinking I would have him cum in my mouth; with his need not so urgent, he would fuck me long afterwards. He had other ideas and pushed me off him. With his cock waving about in front of his sculpted body, he finished undressing me, kissing and licking my body as it came into view. I heard an intense sucking of air when he reached my naked centre. "So fucking sexy."

He extended his arm, stroking his hand over the small patch of hair. I smiled back, spreading my legs further open. He laid me on the bed, then licked between my legs, that tongue of his thicker and more robust than I had felt in a long time as his fingers pulled me open. I squirmed on the bed when his mouth found my clit as he filled me with a thick finger. He climbed up and twisted his body over the top of mine. His hard cock was at my lips again, and I opened, accepting. He seemed satisfied with his fingers probing me, even though I couldn't take him deep with me underneath. I was sure he was examining me, as his fingers opened and pulled between the long laps of his hungry tongue. I slid my fingers up his legs, one hand cupping his balls. With a guttural groan, he sat upright and pulled me sideways. Now I was better positioned to suck and lick, which is what he desired. He rocked back and forth into my mouth until I shoved him onto his back. Between his spread legs, I fisted his cock, licking at the head as I pumped. Then I took him deep, one long insertion, ensuring he could see it all. I pulled back with a long string of pre-cum and saliva stretching from my lips to his hardness. He swallowed again as I rubbed his cock along my lips. My gaze held his, and I purred, "Do you like it when I suck you, Brax?"

I throated him once again while I waited for his answer. "Ugh... uh-uh... yes, baby." My hand pumped his cock, and my tongue darted to tease his tip while holding his intense stare. "And you just love coming into my mouth, don't you?" He groaned and mumbled "yes" to me.

"You enjoy watching me do it, don't you?" His hand gripped my head and forced himself back in. His hips jerked upwards, fucking my face. I couldn't speak as he gripped me. I used my tongue as best I could on his shaft while my hand squeezed his balls. Teasing a finger under them on that brief stretch of flesh between his balls and backside, it rewarded me with a long blast of his saltiness into my mouth. I swallowed it as best I could until his hand released me. Then I wrapped my lips around the head and sucked my way up. Not content with ending the night there, I kept going until I had him hard and ready for me again.

He fucked me with unexpected fierceness. His cock was thick and filling. On top of me first, then laying sideways with my leg pulled up, whispering, "tell me how much you love my cock, Charlie." He bit down on my shoulder blade and continued to taunt my desire. "How does it feel when I cum down your throat?" Before I could respond, he was up off the bed and rubbing his dick in my face, painting it with our combined wetness. Then his mouth was on me, licking and kissing, cleaning me of the moisture.

"Damit, Brax, you're so fucking wild tonight. You're making me ache for you."

"You did this. Fuck, you turn me on so much." He pawed at my skin roughly, lifting me from the bed. Holding me up to his body, my legs wrapped around his hips as he lowered me onto him. My fingers gripped his neck for support as I fucked him. My body moved up and down, his rigid shaft sinking deep inside, taking him harder and faster with each bounce. He walked me around the room, letting me fuck him, enjoying me take control. We kissed, swapping tongues and spit as I fucked him with a ferocity neither of us had experienced. He ended up with my back resting on the door to the room... now it was his turn. He banged me against the timber with his thrusts. My mouth left his, and I bit and sucked on his earlobe and neck.

"Brax?" My voice was low, deep, and full of lust in his ear. "I love feeling you inside me. How does it feel to fuck me?" He didn't answer, only pounded me harder into the door, grunting wildly. "Or maybe you prefer when I bounce down on, meeting each thrust... just like this." I used his shoulders for leverage between words. "Fuck me, Brax!" I rolled my head forward and sucked down his neck hard until I felt his skin crack underneath my lips.

"Fuck! Charlie... Agh, you dirty..." I did it again, cutting off his words. He groaned, and I felt his hot nectar shoot up inside me. One... two... three... four... he spasmed over and again. Still joined, his lips found mine, and carried me back to the bed, laying us down together.

Later, as we embraced again, it was slower and not rushed, with me riding him. He played with my breasts and smiled up. After receiving my pleasure not once but twice, I realised this was about me, meaning he let me set the pace. I took my time to enjoy while showing how much I loved this time together. "You look amazing sitting there, riding me." His words of encouragement spurred my passion. "Gripping my chest as your head rolls back, exposing your beautiful neck to me. You're so sexy, Charlie. I can't get enough of you."

When I reached my orgasm, he'd recovered his desire to join me. Laying on top of him, panting and sweating, with him pushed inside me, he gripped me tight, driving in and out. "Mmm, where do you want me?" I pleaded with him, feeling the telling signs of his impending pleasure.

"Right here, Charlie. Just let me hold you like this...." He thrust faster, and his grip on me turned carnal. "Ugh, you feel so good, baby girl." I wrapped my arms around his back and hooked them under his shoulders, gripping them as I lifted my head to his face.

"Look at me, Brax," I whispered against his throat. His eyes flew open, catching mine as he pushed in and exploded.

"Fuck! Yes, Charlie… ugh." he held me, pushed down tight, as we calmed down and got our breaths back. Our room fell silent as we lay wrapped in each other, beginning to fall asleep.

We froze, shooting upright when we heard Chester's groans of pleasure. "Aww, you're such a good girl, Chrissy." We looked at each other and laughed, knowing we'd definitely use that against him tomorrow.

Chapter Twenty Six

CHESTER

Last night was massive, and when I woke up this morning, I was too scared to wake because I knew the hangover would be fierce. I slowly peeled one eye open, praying I had shut the curtains last night.

Thank fuck!

Blowing out a huge breath, I stared at the ceiling, trying to find the courage to sit up, because the moment I did, I would hug the porcelain bowl. Staggering out to the kitchen, I grabbed some pain relief and water, quickly swigging it. A piss and clean teeth later, I was walking back into my bedroom when my jaw dropped. There was Chrissy, buck naked, sitting cross-legged on the bed. My brain stuttered. She was the *only* one who had that effect on me. "It's about time you got back," she spoke first. "Take your clothes off and come over here and fuck me."

What? She stood off the bed, hands on her hips, waiting for me to take her. "Chrissy?" I questioned, raising an eyebrow at this opposite of her usual demeanour.

"Didn't you tell me last night I need to be more aggressive and take what I want? So here I am. I need your thick cock inside me. And I'm going to have it." She jerked her head toward the bed. "Get your clothes off and on that bed, ready to fuck. I want you now, Chester." My mind was reeling. Not that I had a problem with the thought of a naked woman in my hotel room.... hell, it's one of my favourite concepts. But sweet little Chrissy, telling *me* what to do — drove me wild.

Mesmerised, my hands fumbled with my pants and worked on shedding them. But my mind struggled with the ethics of the situation. Sweet little Chrissy, who had let me bang the fuck out of her every which way to Sunday and took it all, was now telling me what to do? She lay back on the bed, her legs spread, knees up, and that glorious pussy open for business. The glistening lips, creamy thighs, and the smouldering look on her face all evaporated any moral misgivings I might have had. And I would have her—now. "Eat me, Chester. I wanna feel your tongue inside me."

Fuck! She was a goddess. My biggest fantasy was coming to life. I couldn't help but drop to my knees and start lapping at her swollen lips. "Mmm, you animal Chester... yes, lick me, eat me... cover your face in me."

I placed my hands on her knees, spreading them further, and redoubled my efforts on her moist slit. I lapped and clawed at her clit, licked her all up, and she threw her head back, moaning wildly in pleasure. My tongue danced around while her body shivered and shook underneath me. Finally, she struggled up. "Enough, I want you to fuck me. I need you to take me like the animal you are." She shimmied up the bed a bit, still on her back, with her pussy near the edge. I came close, my cock raging. "Give it to me hard, Chester." I eagerly nodded while grabbing a condom out of my wallet, and rolling it on.

Her hands massaged my dick, stroking it to maximum hardness. Then she guided it to her dripping hole. Standing on the floor by the bed, I pressed forward and swung my hips. She kept up her dirty-talking diatribe throughout, which got to me, rendering me mute. The awe of the filth coming out of her pretty mouth. After a time, she pulled herself up and got onto her hands and knees. "Keep fucking me, baby." She implored, her ass wiggling with wanton need. "Shut me up, Chester. Fuck me like the little slut you want me to be."

"Fuck, Chrissy!" She pressed her ass and her swollen lips back towards my waiting cock, which I pushed into her. "Aww, yes!" she cried as I pressed my cock into her core once more, feeling my hips ram against her ass cheeks as I penetrated her from behind, over and again. Her tight, gripping hole felt beautiful, and I could sense my balls working overtime on a giant load. I pounded and rammed as she moaned an obscene amount of profanities with each thrust. Her sounds told me she loved the ramming I was giving her.

Knowing how much she enjoyed it, I grabbed a fistful of her hair and pulled her head back and even as my cock continued to pound her mercilessly; I felt the need arise. I smacked her beautiful round ass hard and fast. Her body fell forward, and I used her hair to pull her back into me. Slapping it again, I gripped her throat and moaned into her ear, "Is this what you wanted?"

"Yes," she panted, her hand reaching down, and I could feel her finger slide into her pussy alongside my dick. She slid it back and forth with me, further stimulating us while her thumb tickled her nub. Even though I was the one fucking her, I felt, somehow, that she was the one holding all the power in this sex romp. Obviously, she was the one calling the shots and doing all the dirty talking for my benefit. I needed to match her to gain back a bit of power. Most of my blood and willpower were on my hard-working dick, but I engaged a bit of my brain and planned my next move.

I pulled out of her suddenly. She turned around, mouth open to admonish me. "On your knees, now," I commanded, pointing to the floor as I ripped the condom off. "That filthy mouth of yours needs my cock stuffed in it." Her eyes widened with delight, scrambling to the floor before me and looking up.

"Fuck my face, Chester." I had to admit, she was much better at this naughty patter than I expected. It was causing my dick to ache more, watching her match my usual filthy nature. She was also a mighty good cock-sucker and soon had me aching with pleasure. Her lips slurped, and her hands jacked my shaft. Soon she had a middle finger tickling the skin just behind my balls, increasing my stimulation further.

I felt the tingle that signalled an imminent orgasm. She sensed it and took her mouth off me, looking into my eyes with a gaze like a steel hammer. "Cum on me, Chester."

"*Fuck!*" she grasped at my shaft with both hands, jacking up and down and twisting them in opposite directions. It's not a manoeuvre that I can withstand for long, and soon I felt myself rising to the occasion. When I heard her goad me again, I looked down and saw her face, her eyes begging me for it. "Ugh, I'm gonna give it to you, alright, and you want it, don't you?" I gripped her cheeks between my fingers, squeezing her lips together, then kissing them. Standing back up, "Tell me again."

"I wanna watch you cum on me, Chester."

I stroked her face as she sucked on me like candy. "Yeah? You want me to cum on your pretty little face?" When she said "please," I knew I was done. "Ahh, here it comes, baby…. take it like a good girl…. be Chester's good girl." I groaned as the waves of orgasm shook me. It felt like a gallon escaped my cock, splattering her in the face. She held my spasming rod, aimed at her tongue, as I watched her lap it up. My knees buckled at the sight. When the flow slowed, she wiped the remaining from her lips and tongue and looked up at me as I panted heavily, holding her eye contact. I brushed my thumb across her lips and smiled. "You're such a good girl, baby," I pushed it into her mouth, watching her suck my juice off. "Come here."

I picked her up and smashed my lips to hers, carrying her back to the bed. As I placed her down on the soft quilt, that mother fucker next door yells out, "Aww, who's a good girl, baby?" Brax hadn't even finished his sentence when the fucking Evil Midget from hell cracked up laughing.

Fuck!

BRAX

We were in hysterics by the time Chester finished this morning. The tears rolled down my face in humour and I realised there was the most innocent kind of mischief in our giggling, so when it went quiet next door, I just couldn't help myself. "Aww, who's a good girl, baby?"

The moment we heard Chester say "fuck," we lost it again. Rolling on the bed, amused, mimicking the many things we had just heard coming out of his mouth while he banged Chrissy. Then I realised. When I tried to draw Charlie's attention, she answered me between giggles. "Umm, I had a thought—"

"Look at you go, baby. I'm so proud of you." I smirked back, "smartass," and swatted her ass cheeks.

"You realise if we heard them, then the same goes for last night.." Charlie's jaw dropped, and I put two fingers under her chin, lifting it up.

"No!" She seemed to think about it before a light switched on. "He would have said something if he did. He couldn't hear us over himself." I laughed and acknowledged "valid point." Kissing her, I couldn't deny there was only so much of that you could listen to before it became like watching porn and being a precursor. I tried pushing my tongue into her mouth. She pressed on my shoulders and turned her head away, motioning for me to lean in. Whispering, "If you want to fuck me, take me in the shower, so big ears in the next room doesn't listen." I didn't even answer. I picked her up and carried her through to our bathroom, shut the door, put my Spotify on — loud, and ran the shower, stepping in with her.

We spent the morning relaxing before getting on the road again for the next show. Thanks to Chester, we had woken early enough for me to watch Manchester United play and get the win. Of course, I was even happier to see Rashford score again. Charlie played along and gained interest for my benefit, but I knew it was all for laughs unless we played each other. Then shit got *real*. It was nice to see her happy for me. Either that, or she hoped I would leave her to watch the Liverpool game in peace later tonight. After the game, we chilled with some Fifa as we both fanged for a game. I turned to her and asked her, "what's the bet?" this had become our thing.

"If I win, you give me a massage when we get on the bus, and if I lose, you give me a massage on the bus anyway because you love me."

"Nude?"

"Negative, Ghost Rider."

"Denied."

"Partially?" she backtracked.

"Elaborate."

"Lingerie?" she raised her eyebrow.

"Negotiable."

"Do you want to risk Chester coming in and I'm nude?"

"Fine, agreed! Lingerie massage. Now, what do I really get?"

"My love and appreciation?" She scrunched her nose at me for being cheeky, but it was that look I found most sexy. It got me *every* fucking time.

"Loser! I get my hands on you either way." She laughed as she called me "naughty," and we gave each other a quick kiss before getting into the game. Of course, because we're both such competitive assholes, it ended up being a best-of-five, and it tied us into the last round. There were ten minutes to go when the guys all walked in.

Liam yelled across the room. I told him to shut the fuck up. "Give me ten minutes. I have to beat this Evil Midget thing."

I could hear Marcus suck his teeth as he said, "I'm going on the veranda for a smoke."

"Fuck off already, Dad!" We all laughed at Charlie, not before my attention was back on the television.

We continued our game, and the little miss won. And the worst part was, I wanted to beat her this time. "You suck balls, Midget!"

"And you love it," she poked her tongue. "It makes sense why you support Manchester United."

I took the bait and quizzed her. "Why?"

"You both love going down in the box." Charlie jumped up and grabbed my head and humped it with her cute little pussy before going to get down off the couch as the guys roared with laughter. I let her get down before I grabbed her by the waist and pulled her back onto my lap.

"What the fuck was that, you maniac? Did you just dry-hump my face?"

I laughed as she said, "what of it? You dry-hump my ass all the time." We joined the others outside, standing off to the side so Charlie had some fresh air. We noticed Chester was avoiding us, and the moment an opportunity rose, Charlie dove in. "Monkey, could you pass me that chair, please?" Without question, he shuffled it from around the table and brought it over.

"Aww, who's a good girl?" she patted him on the cheek and I fell over sideways. My mischievous soul is childish. I grant you that. But it keeps me feeling more alive, and I needed that laugh more than ever.

"You're a fucking menace," he groaned.

"Takes one to know one." That set me off again, and I was laughing so hard it only sped up my high. I was buzzing, and he was getting more frustrated by the minute. He launched himself at me, rolling around laughing on the veranda. The rest didn't have a clue what was going on — looking at us, stunned.

"What's the deal?" Liam asked, and I turned to see him next to Charlie.

"It wasn't Chester who heard *everything* last night," she chuckled. "This time we heard *all* of him."

Mark shrugged. "I already knew what he was like." I laughed wildly again. We got up and cooled off, and when Charlie headed inside, I snuck in a quick cone with the boys.

"Alright, all, if you need anything, grab it from the cafe downstairs, now. We won't be stopping for a few hours," we nodded, "that means you, Chester." Monkey went to backchat him, although Kendall threw her arm around his shoulder and dragged him off to the confectionery stand.

"Baby, we are already sweet enough." He winked at her, while Shane just shook his head, smirking, opting to let the prick get on with it this time. I saw Charlie walking around aimlessly, deciding what to pick while I reminded myself it wasn't her fault. It will be fine once she has the baby.

Just smile and agree, Brax.

"Baby, why don't I just get one of each, so if you want it, you have it there." I pointed to the bag of crisps and lollies in each of her hands.

"Brax! Do you even realise how fat I will get if I eat all that?" She looked horrified. "I will eat it if it's there."

Ok, not that suggestion, then. "Come on, babe, stop stressing. I promised you I would work it off you in no time." I winked at her and wiggled my eyebrows as she giggled. "You're so bad. Let's just take these and go." She decided on a bag of jellybeans and an iced tea. We headed to the counter, ready to pay. Taking my wallet out, I noticed Charlie grip the counter. I placed my hand on her back asking "are you okay?" while she shook her head.

Before she could stop it, she vomited all over the counter. I tried to grab some napkins and throw them over the top while the store clerk passed Chester a bin bag for me to put them in. I held her hair back with my other hand while still wiping, and when she settled down, I moved closer. "Take your time," I whispered while she sucked in some breaths. I looked up at the store clerk. "I apologise. My partner's pregnant. If you have some disinfectant spray and wipes, I will finish cleaning this up and any costs incurred."

They were very understanding, and when she stepped away to get some cleaning clothes and spray, I saw the cause of the problem. The coffee machine behind the counter where they had been steaming the milk. "I think I am alright now," she mumbled, grabbing a tissue and wiping her mouth.

The clerk returned, and Charlie apologised while helping to tidy up. Chester was holding the bag open for the napkins and I saw him put his arm around Charlie's shoulders.

"You good now, Midget?"

"I'm okay." She gave him a quick hug back.

"You know you are part of a very elite club, right?"

"What?"

"Only one other in this group has vomited on a countertop." She tried to argue she was "not in his group, and you were drunk. It's different."

"Doesn't matter, baby, you and me. We have our own little club now." I couldn't help when he called her baby, and I gave him a quick jab to the arm. "Aww fuck, alright man! Sweet Cheeks."

"Aww, who's a good girl, baby?" We all burst out laughing, much to the clerk's confusion.

Chapter Twenty Seven

BRAX

One show to go, and one more stop — it couldn't come soon enough. The morning sickness — also why do they call it that when it lasts all day — and the hormones were making travel extremely difficult for Charlie at the moment. The most random shit was triggering her. Twice already, we had to stop and buy fresheners for the bus because Marcus' cologne had her throwing up. I finally had her settled and laying down asleep with an ice pack for her headache, and a bucket next to the bed. I walked out, closing the door to ensure we didn't wake her, and parked my ass in the seat at the table next to Shane.

"How's Linda Blair back there?" Chester asked, and I warned him, "don't let her hear you say that."

"I'm an idiot, mate, but I don't have a death wish."

Liam pointed out, "Sometimes you do, bro."

"Has she stopped being sick?" Kendall asked, worried.

"For now, although she told me to say you stink, Marcus. And you need a new cologne." Everyone laughed.

"Tell that Evil Midget I hope she chokes on her words."

To be fair—like most of us—Liam had no experience with pregnancy and curiously asked, "Is this like an all the time thing? Because it's kinda gross. Just saying.." he shrugged. "If that is babies, then they are gross." Mace squealed at him, horrified.

"Bro, don't even right now. I'm dead. Between Marcus causing her to vomit and her meltdown over toast this morning—"

"What meltdown?" I glared at Shane, explaining, "We only had two pieces of bread left, and Charlie burned them when she tried to make toast. She was dealing with some hardcore hormones or shit at that exact moment. I don't know."

Now it was my turn to get slapped as the girls turned on me, and Mace pointed out, "She's going to nut you before the end of this pregnancy if you keep explaining shit like that."

"Anyway," I smirked and continued, "she kept saying, 'I can't do anything right! How will I raise a baby when I can't cook toast?' I tried to comfort her, told her it wasn't a big deal, and of course, ran downstairs to the cafe to get her fucking toast."

"Aww, you're such a good girl, baby." Chester used his own words on me.

"Then, not once but twice, I've gone to kiss her, forgetting I've had milk in my coffee, and she vomited all over me. *Twice!*" Mark cracked up, so I called him a "wanker. Just remember, Milk is an absolute no-go at the moment."

"Would have helped before we went into the cafe," Chester highlighted.

"And don't bring that up again, either," I begged him. "She's still upset over it."

"Say no more." I reached across and fist-bumped into Chester, appreciating he knew when to rein it in this time. We sat and chilled out for a while, and I had a cone before heading back to check on her.

She was still asleep, so I lay down and hugged her. "I'm awake, baby. I was just laying here because I still had that annoying headache."

"Can I get you anything?"

"An orgasm." I nearly choked, not expecting her to say that, and I ended up coughing as she turned to look at me, confused.

"Sorry, I didn't expect that."

"So, that's a no?" I sat up on my elbows and questioned, "are you being serious?"

"Well, apparently, it helps with a headache. Plus, not gonna lie.. in the last week or so, my orgasms have been incredible. It's hard to explain, but everything feels much more sensitive."

"Mmm, is that so?" I don't know why I even left her to explain when there was no doubt I would give her what she needed. It wasn't long before I buried my face between her thighs, eating my favourite meal. Sometime later, as I flopped back on the bed next to her, I looked over and saw tears falling. "Baby, what's wrong?" Immediately panicking, I did something wrong. I rolled over and grabbed her into my arms, pulling her close as I looked down. I stroked the tears from her eyes as she blinked back at me with more love than I could ever have expected to see.

"I'm sorry baby, that was just so…. ugh, my orgasms have been so intense lately that I couldn't help it. It was just so much stimulation I started crying…" She scrunched her nose, suddenly shy, and then I threw my head back, roaring with laughter as I fell on the pillow. "Brax! Are you laughing at me?"

"No, baby, just the situation. I gave you an orgasm so good, you wept." She slapped me across the chest as I grabbed her hand and rubbed my stubble on her chest as she burst out laughing.

"Fuck off, you baboon. You can get back down there and sort me out again."

"Really?"

"Do I look like I am joking?"

"Damn! I think I'm gonna love pregnant Charlie."

"Brax, go now before I change my mind!"

"Yes, Cutie." I dove back down as I was told, not before tickling the inside of her thighs with the stubble on my cheeks while she giggled.

"You will luck out if you carry on, mister. There's a fine line down there at the moment. Choose wisely." After giving what she needed, we sorted ourselves out and returned to sit with everyone. I was at the table and pulled her onto my lap, resting my head on her shoulder as I rubbed her stomach.

"Hey, Midget, can I ask you something?"

"Depends what it is, Monkey?"

"Well, I was curious, you know? I was reading about what we can expect to put up with from Pregnant Midget of Tour."

"Chester!" she squealed.

"She's gonna batter you soon, mate," Liam pointed out.

"Nah, hear me out. So anyway, they were saying common things in early pregnancy."

Charlie was getting exasperated and huffed, "Get to the point, Chester." I tapped her butt, as I knew her frustration was growing.

"Is it true you wanna bang all the time? Asking for a friend." He winked at me, trying to make out like I had asked him to do it. "Don't drag me into this, you asshole."

"I'm not answering that, Chester. You can fuck off!"

"I was just trying to figure out if you were faking it then or if my boy was that good. That's all." I grabbed her hips as she went to thump him again. "Ugh, Chester! I swear, one of these days, I will strangle you."

"Don't do that, Sweet Cheeks," my fist flexed, "Ha! I remembered Brax!" he shouted when he noticed it. "You can't hit me." Liam and the rest laughed before he added. "Just spank the monkey instead."

"Ugh, Chester!" Charlie squealed. I punched him just because I could.

"Haha, you're a fucking baboon, bro!"

CHARLIE

They'd just finished the last show of the tour, and even though it was only half the length of the Regional Tour, I think this one had truly mentally fucked us. In such a short time, so much had happened that we were yet to process. We'd not long returned to the hotel, and the guys were all sitting outside with a beer and spliff, toasting to the completion of the tour. They were carrying on like they would never see each other again. Sure, we flew out quickly, but that was because of the extension of the tour and Marcus had said the boys had commitments to get back to immediately.

Glaze would be out in a month anyway for the music awards, where the bands were unveiling their new song together. We had invited them to come as well for Brax's thirtieth, our engagement and the news of the baby at a party we were organising for everyone important to us.

AusHop was happy to arrange accommodation so they could stay a couple of weeks and we could show them around, perhaps even perform the song in other media events. I was trying to see these bookings Marcus had mentioned so I could give them tentative dates, but each time I refreshed the calendar, nothing was coming up.

"Why do we have a calendar booking system if you don't use it?" I looked at Marcus.

"What?"

"You heard me. You reckon we had bookings come in, yet nothing is here. I don't understand? How am I supposed to arrange the party and let Glaze know if I can't confirm Brax's movements?"

"Cutie, does that have to be done tonight? Leave it until tomorrow." Brax quickly realised his mistake by interfering when I replied. "No, and your name is not Marcus."

Mark laughed, "stay in your lane next time, bro," and Brax just nodded, saluting me.

"Marcus, when are the bookings?" He still wouldn't answer, because he was too busy attempting to communicate in silence with Brax. I stood up, annoyed I wasn't getting a response, and I heard Kendall say, "You're in the shit now."

They both jumped like they had just gotten busted. "Why do you always assume the worst, Cutie?"

"Brax, you can not keep a straight face when hiding something. What did you two do?" His face looked guilty as sin, and I didn't have the patience to play games with him.

"I'm tapping out now, mate. This is on you." Marcus said to Brax as he stepped away from the table while Chester chuckled.

I cut Brax off when he called Marcus an "asshole," and asked him again, "what is going on?" hands firmly on my hips as I glared up.

"Bro, you are in trouble. Next, she is going to drop the baboon."

I turned to point at Shane when he had finished. "Next, I will drop you, Shane, if you don't quit it."

"Hormone Midget is great. Can we keep this one too?" Before he could blink, I slapped Liam upside down as the rest laughed. Meanwhile, I was still staring at Brax, who was hoping I would forget that I'd asked him a question. He finally got up, walked over to me, almost laughing at my hissy fit, picking up with his arms wrapped under my bum cheeks.

"Put me down, you baboon. I know you're up to something." The prick just cackled. "Quit laughing! I won't stop asking until you tell me." He walked inside, waving to the girls as they laughed, and marched me up to our room, throwing me softly on the bed. He kicked the door shut and leaned over the top of me.

"You know, you are a pain in my ass, right?"

"Yes, I do, and you love me."

"You're impossible sometimes."

"I'm not," I huffed. "I asked you a question, and you kept avoiding me, Brax."

He patronisingly tapped me on the nose as I slapped his hand away, much to his amusement. "Because, little miss, I was trying to surprise you. I can never keep things a secret because you have to know everything!" I laughed in his face. That was true. "You and I are leaving early and heading home tomorrow. The rest of the band is leaving on a different flight."

"But why?"

"Charlotte Maree Bancroft, what did I tell you?" Now I couldn't help but giggle again at how frustrated he looked. I knew I was a little shit sometimes and couldn't help it.

"I'm sorry. I love you." He laughed and said I was an "asshole," so I thought I better check.

"Not a haemorrhoid like Chester?"

"No baby, not a haemorrhoid." He went to hug me, then realised what I'd said and started tickling me. "You little shit, you just called me an asshole." He eventually stopped fondling and cuddled into me as I kissed him quickly. "We have a stopover on the way back home, babe. That's all I'm telling you. I just thought a break and taking the trip slowly might be good for you in case you got sick."

"I love you. Thank you."

"Now, will you quit being a brat for the night?"

"Promise," I smiled. "I might go to bed anyway soon. I'm pretty tired."

"Alright, baby. Set the alarms for me, please. We must be ready by eight to get to the airport on time. It's a few hours' drive, but I have sorted a car for us to make it quicker." Of course he had. "The guys will take most of our gear home. You just need clothes for a couple of days....*fuck*!"

"Brax!" He told me to hang on as I watched his brain ticking over.

"Okay, you won't need much because I just realised I'm a dumb shit, and in Canada, you pack cold for. This place is hot, so we'll have to take what we can and buy some new clothes when we get there."

"Or go naked?" I suggested.

"Yeah, do that idea! I like that."

"Let me get a water bottle and say goodnight before I sleep." Brax led me back out, and I said "goodbye" to everyone and hugged the other band, promising to let them know when the party was so they could arrange flights. I hugged our little group and vowed to see them at home in a few days or whenever Brax would let us return. I told Kendall, "I expect to see you in the city soon," and she winked at me.

Brax ensured I had set the alarms and tucked me into bed, which he did most nights. It was too cute for words, honestly. It didn't take me long to sleep that night. The prospect of finally going home made it all the better. I couldn't wait to see mum or Tina and tell them everything. I was also excited to see where Brax and my life went next and finally meet our baby.

In such a deep sleep, I didn't hear Brax come in last night. I woke to the alarms going off, and he groaned about it being too early. "Baby, you are the one that booked this, so why are you complaining?"

"I just want to stay in bed."

"Well, I don't know where we're going or what you've planned, but can't we just do that tomorrow instead? The two of us and no interruptions?"

He seemed to ponder this for a minute and then jumped up. "You're right. That's better because you have no excuse to put clothes on either."

"Sex pest kind of morning?"

"Always with you." He put his hand out, and I took it. We had a quick shower before getting dressed and grabbing a cuppa. Unfortunately, milk was still not cutting it, so we sat across from each other until he had finished coffee, and I had my black tea. I couldn't help but smile when I saw Brax eat a mint chewing gum for my benefit.

"You are too cute sometimes. You know that, right?" He looked at me and asked, "what did I do?" I pointed out the chewing gum in his mouth.

"Oh, you thought that was for your benefit? No, it stops me from getting puked on if I kiss you." Even though I called him a "wanker," I still giggled before he said "just messing with you."

"Eat a dick."

"You eat mine." I shook my head as he kissed me, and we picked up our cups. We double checked to make sure we had everything before leaving. We stored the gear we weren't taking on the bus last night, so we only had a little to handle. Quickly sliding a note under Marcus' door, to let them know we had got away safely, we promised to message them when we landed.

Brax grabbed our bags and helped the driver get them into the car before opening the door for me. Once he put his seat belt on, I put mine on in the middle and cuddled him. I reached up to his cheek and cupped it in my hand as I turned Brax's face to look at me when the car left. "Thank you for this, Brax. It's just what I needed without even knowing."

"Me too." He kissed my forehead before moving back.

"So you know how you love me, and I'm giving you the greatest gift?"

"A baby?" he smiled.

"No, you asshole — me!" Brax laughed as he hugged me tighter, I smirked up at him.

"What do you want?"

"Where are we going?" He looked at me for a few minutes, with creased brows, deciding whether to tell me before he kissed me deeply and moved back.

"Bali for four days. A private villa, just you and I, no outside world or distractions, just rest and relaxation."

"Sounds perfect, but you already had me when you said just you and I." He leaned down and kissed me again as we got lost in each other.

Chapter Twenty Eight

SHANE

We had another day left in Canada before flying home. Brax and Charlie had left earlier. He wanted a break before returning home so she could get some rest. While I lay here with Kendall asleep, wrapped around me, I stroked her back and thought about how this probably had been our craziest tour to date. Sure, most of the usual antics were missing. Still, in terms of the impact and gravity of everything that happened, it would stay with us. If I really thought about it, something life-changing had happened to each of us on this tour, and there would never be another one like it.

Being with Kendall full time over the last few weeks made me realise how much I loved her. She'd been a rock for me. Before her, I was a kid, really, trying to play in a man's world. Sure, I could joke with myself and pretend that wasn't the case, and I don't regret any of it. It brought me to where I am now. I was just really fucking grateful to be laying here, a better man for having done it all.

When I asked Kendall to move in with me, I knew the gravity of the situation, primarily for her, having to pack her entire life up. But I was also aware it was something I needed. Because if the truth be told, and she had said "no," I would have gone to her in a heartbeat. I had honestly believed music was my life, but then I met her.

So while I would be such a lucky fucker to be in a band for the rest of my life, the true blessing would be to spend it with her.. "Hmm, can you quit it? You're waking me up." I smiled as she tried to wiggle her shoulder blades to push my hand away. Of course, I couldn't help but do it more.

"Maybe I want you awake."

"Mmm, and why's that?"

"Because I have something to tell you."

I chuckled when Kendall said, "boring. You could have led with 'I want to be inside you,' then I might have woken up." I slid my arm out from under her and moved down the bed, so my head was level with hers, reaching over and dragging my nails down her spine. "You won't quit, will you?"

"No." She opened her eyes, turning to face me, and I remembered exactly why I was doing this. "I love you." It caught her off guard, not expecting that, and her head flew off the pillow as she gazed at me in shock. "You look beautiful right now, too, might I add." I leaned forward, kissing her pouty lips.

"Did you just say that—"

"What? I love you?" She nodded her head repeatedly at me, causing me to laugh. "I did, beautiful. I love you."

"Shane? Are you sure? Don't you fuck with me right now!"

I laughed hard, her shock finding favour with me. How could she not know? "Baby, I swear I'm not fucking with you."

"And you're not just saying this because you want me to move in with you?" She sat fully up now, facing me square on as I leaned up on my elbow. "I already decided yes."

"No, Kendall, I'm saying this because I love you."

"I love you too, Shane." Of course, my baby was wide awake after that as we spent the morning between the sheets showing each other how much this meant. We quickly got up and chucked some clothes on when we heard my phone go with a message to say Liam and everyone were heading over.

Soon, they were all crowded out on our balcony. "So why the fuck does our place get trashed now that Brax and Charlie are gone?"

"Because you or Liam are going to be the next ones to go domestic, and you weren't there to vote, so you lost." Chester answered me.

Kendall asked, "what the hell does 'go domestic' mean, Monkey?"

"You know, like Pregnant Wives of Tour." We cracked up when he repeated it. I laughed more at the look the girls were giving him before Mace spoke. "You guys realise a lot is going to change?"

"No, it won't." Again, the girls argued with Chester, who was standing firm. "Nah, you're tripping. Of course, some things will, but the core of our group… *never*. We'll still be family, except we'll all be making our own crotch fruits around it so we can retire at forty — Sit smoking cones, let the kids carry on the tradition, and make us a buck."

Mace shook her head, chortling before telling Chester, "You're fucked, but you're also an evil genius."

"Shit, even I could get on board with that idea." I laughed when Kendall added her two cents and suddenly wondered what it would be like to see her carrying our child. I guess that is precisely how Brax is feeling now.

Mark expressed, "I'm so happy for them both," and we all agreed.

"It's the best thing that could have happened to them." Liam was right. They were made up.

"Those two need each other like I need wet pussy." Seeming at a loss for any other words to describe Chester anymore, Mace muttered, "See? Fucked in the head…."

"You realise, guys, we'll never have a tour like this one again?" Mark pointed out what I had just been thinking earlier in bed.

"Won't lie, mate, thank fuck for that. A lot of shit has gone down this time." Chester was right. There really had been, and in such a short period.

I explained I had just been thinking this earlier. "This tour has been life changing for us all." They all thought about it for a moment. "Look at Charlie and Brax. First, did anyone expect she would be the one to ask him to marry her?" They all shook their heads, Mace adding, "she was never getting married," and I clicked my finger and pointed at her. "Right?" I nodded. "Then she finally confronted her father, and now they are having a baby. They just became a family, and that's all Brax ever wanted. He declared it was the music, maybe it was at some point, but it is all about her now."

"You're right," Liam agreed.

"Now, look at you two," I turned to him. "You finally told her what you should have done years ago, man, and now you're back together where you belong. All that's left is the ring."

"It's coming." Mace's eyes flew open as she questioned him, but Liam just winked, took her hand and kissed it.

"Mark, you can lie all you want, but April has caught your eye. You never stick around or spend as much time as you do with her."

"It's not that I don't stick around, bro. It's just I never found anyone I wanted to. I like to keep my circle tight, you know that." I understood Mark because we were all the same. We had to be in this industry, as there were leeches everywhere.

"And full respect, mate. I'm just glad you let someone in, finally." Mark and I fist-bumped across the table before I turned to the pest of the group. "And you, you fucking Monkey's bollocks."

"Nah, man, I ain't changed."

"So, how often have you paid to ensure you find time to continue seeing a girl?" He threw his hat at me, shrugging it off and mumbled, "whatever."

"Don't give me that. You catching her again before we fly out?"

"Yeah, of course, a man has needs."

"Are you saying you suddenly lack options?" I pressed him.

"Fuck no!"

"So the need you have is one only Chrissy can fill?" He stumbled and choked on his answer briefly before telling me to "shut up," as I smirked at him. "Admit it."

"I admit nothing." Mark called him a "fucking gimp," and said, "we already know," I burst out laughing. "You know nothing."

"I do." We all turned on Liam as he spoke, with Chester calling him a bullshitter. "I know. I heard you talking to her when you saw her off last time."

Chester launched at him as they started wrestling and called Liam a "mother fucker."

"Shut up, prick! You listen to everyone else. Admit it, or I can speak for you."

"Fine, you hippie punk rocker wannabe." I cracked up. It frustrated him that we'd hit the nail on the head. "That little redhead has gotten under my skin. She's so fucking innocent, but the bad things I can make her do. She drives me fucking wild." Liam laughed as he highlighted, "you caught feelings."

"Yeah, alright, Hippie Boy. Guilty."

"It's a good thing for you. You needed someone who could pull you in line." Chester, still not amused, turned on me when I spoke and asked, "what about you then?"

"Me? Kendall and I are moving in together," I announced proudly, "and I love her."

"You gave her your balls to keep in your handbag?"

I snickered as I replied. "Yeah, Chester, I gave her my balls."

Chapter Twenty Nine

BRAX

I was glad we had stopped for a break before returning. Between the turbulence, the travel sickness and the morning sickness, the flight to Bali was hell for her, and what made it worse was there was nothing I could do to help. I had taken no sleeping pills this time—like I usually do on extended travel—because I wanted to ensure I could be there if she needed me. And she really did.

After a long and exhausting flight, we finally arrived and made our way off the plane, stopping duty-free to pick up some essentials for tomorrow—clothing and swimmers—before heading to our private villa I'd hired for a few days. It allowed us time to have the rest and solitude we needed. As the car pulled up, I got everything inside without waking Charlie, I went back out and undid her seat belt to pick her up as she stirred awake. "It's okay. I can walk."

"I've got you." I thanked the driver and shut the door as I carried her inside, taking her through and putting her in bed.

"What time is it?" She waved her hand in front of her face to get relief from the heat as I turned the air conditioning on and told her it was six thirty in the evening. "Ugh, why is it so fucking hot still?"

"Calm your farm. I just switched the cooling on. Give it a moment."

"Aww, you're such a good girl, baby." I laughed as I swatted at her butt, noting she must be doing better. "I am. Now that we've stopped moving, the vertigo has finally gone." I lay down on the bed next to her, cuddling, wrapping my arm around her shoulders, brushing her hair back off her face.

"How about we get some dinner delivered, and we can just go to bed, babe?" I brushed the hair back from her forehead. "You look exhausted."

"Thanks. Did you just say I look like shit?"

"Don't even go there, miss attitude. I said you look exhausted because you do. And truth be told, I probably look no better. So let's eat and get some sleep, like we both need."

"Yes, boss." I moved my arm down to pat her on the butt. I rolled over to see what I could order around here from the various menus scattered on the table, finally deciding on a local place that delivered, ordering a bit of everything on the starter menu so she could pick as she pleased. While I ordered, she headed in for a shower, I kicked my shoes off, flicking the television on. By the time she got back, the food had arrived, and we curled up under the blankets eating dinner in bed, watching a movie. "Do we really have to leave in four days?" I looked down at her on my chest and asked, "you don't want to?"

"It's so quiet here."

"Yeah, I don't know what that is anymore." I moved all the empty food packaging to the bin and grabbed a bottle of water—nobody wants Bali belly—before turning the light off and hopping into bed. We weren't far into the movie when I noticed she was asleep, so I turned the television off, pulling her closer and enjoying the quiet night. I lay there, content in the darkness, rubbing my hand up and down her stomach, thinking how lucky I was to have everything I wanted right here.

We were up and down all night because of her upset stomach, so it surprised me to wake up the following day, and she wasn't in bed. I shot up, my eyes rapidly searching her out. My beautiful goddess was sitting on our patio, near the pool, with a platter brought to us by housekeeping. "Can I wake up to that sight every morning?" Hearing my voice, she smiled softly as I rolled over to face her, taking it all in. Luscious blonde locks tied in a messy bun atop her head as she sat with her two feet tucked next to her. A two-piece soft yellow bikini that cut perfectly along her round butt, not enough that I didn't feel comfortable with others looking at her, but plenty to let my imagination run wild, knowing what it hid underneath. A silver tray sat on the side of the pool with fresh fruit and juices, croissants and pastries, but they paled in comparison to her deliciousness. Her cute little button nose turned up as her lips parted, and we eyed each other up. "I can't wait to marry you, Charlie." She smiled warmly at me and stood before walking to the bed. She started removing her swimmers, so by the time she got to me, she was standing there in her natural beauty. I reached out and stroked her stomach while I looked up into her eyes and saw my expression masked on her face. "You feeling better this morning?"

I stroked her again, lower, then she gently took my wrist and pushed my hand down where she wanted it. She held my wrist between her legs while I let my fingers caress her. Trembling thighs vibrated against my hand, and her eyes closed momentarily. "Look at me, baby. Show me what you need."

"I need you, Brax."

"Then take me. Seize what you want." One thing I had always made a point of doing was to build her confidence. I longed for her to see how truly impressive she was. As I looked at my beautiful girl, I could sometimes see the years of emotional abuse inflicted by Calvin had taken a toll on her self-belief. For someone so confident in many aspects of her life, I tried to help her find it in herself every day. I watched as she stood timidly, waiting for me to take her. And believe me, I longed to. But I needed her to see she had just as much right.

I want her to take me.

"Please Brax."

"Please, what, Charlie?"

"I need you." Confusion washed over her face, wondering why I hadn't given her what she wanted. I sat up and pulled her onto the bed carefully. Her eyes searched mine, hoping that I was about to give her what she needed.

"Baby, I am yours, alone. If you want me, take what you own. I promise, there will never be a time I refuse you anything I have." When she pinned me on the bed a few seconds later and explored every inch of my skin until we were both aching from the rush of euphoria through our bodies, I understood we'd finally become whole and she now saw herself through my eyes. As I lay back on that bed, watching my love pleasuring us both, soon to be my wife and mother of my child, I couldn't think of anything else other than her.

CHARLIE

We had been back home for three days, and while the break on the way back had been just what I needed, being in my bed was heaven. The first few days, we had kept free, so we could recover from jet lag without pushing, get some groceries in the house and freshen up our home after being locked up for weeks.

Today we had our first scan to confirm the baby and check dates, as well as see our child for the first time. Following that, we'd arranged a first family dinner at our place this weekend. I say first family dinner because all four parents would be together—my father included. We'd spoken about it after he helped us in Canada, attempting a genuine effort to repair the damage of the past. In return, we took steps to reconcile.

I woke up early this morning as I was excited about our appointment. Once we saw our baby, this would become very much real, plus I had a lot of questions I wanted to ask. I mostly felt scared. I hadn't spoken to Brax about it yet, because I didn't want to worry him while he was on the tour. We had been drinking and smoking so heavily during those first few weeks before I found out, and well, if the dates they have told me so far are correct, I was pregnant. It scared me. I could have already done some harm to our baby because we weren't expecting this, and I was being my usual reckless self.

I had finished up my boring ass cup of black decaf and headed into our room to see he was still asleep, so I went into our ensuite for a shower. Lost in my head, it wasn't until he said, "morning, Cutie," that I realised he'd come in.

"Morning—Woah, what are you doing, Brax?" He turned and looked at me, confused, as I stared at him.

"Agh, taking a piss?"

"No. We're not one of those couples."

"Baby, I always have a piss when I wake up. It's not my fault you were already in the shower."

"Luckily, we bought a house with more than one toilet. Go use them." He finished, and being a total shit stirrer, flushed the toilet. "You asshole!"

"I couldn't have been a total prick," he laughed, opening the shower door and stepping in, grabbing my hips while he attacked my mouth. When he pulled back, he added, "I could have pissed in the shower."

I playfully slapped him. "You sound more like Chester every day."

"Seriously? You want to talk about Chester while we're naked?"

"I do not."

"I didn't think so." Of course, even after his little 'pisscapade', he got his own way and had his morning wood taken care of. Dressed, I was sorting out my hair and make-up in the bathroom when Brax reemerged with his coffee. He stood in the doorway, leaning against the frame with his ankles crossed, sipping it while looking me up and down. I pointed at him through the mirror, directing his attention to the cup in his hand.

"Don't think of coming near me with that until you brush your teeth."

"Don't worry, I'm happy watching." He smirked, bringing the mug to his mouth while wiggling his eyebrows and letting them drift back down to my backside.

"Go away, you pervert." He chuckled and told me, "stop picking on me. I'm excited about today." I stopped with the eyeshadow I was applying to look at his cheeky face. "Don't you try to pull the cute card on me, mister!"

"Aww, you think I'm cute?" I shook my head as he took his empty cup back into the kitchen, then came in and grabbed his toothbrush, giving his teeth a clean. While he did that, I moved into our room and slipped a comfy gold sundress on for the day. It was perfect as it wasn't tight and gave me the space to breathe. Grabbing my bag from the lounge, I was packing it when he came out and stood there, smiling at me.

I glanced up before chuckling. "What? You look like one of those clowns on the sideshow alley."

"Thanks, Evil one. I was just about to say you look breathtaking." I smiled back at him, blushing, "thank you. "

"Let me take a photo, please?"

"Umm…. alright, you weirdo."

"Because I'd like a picture of you? Shut up, fool." I giggled, and he held his phone up. Being the cheeky shit I am, I turned my head away at the last minute. "Don't care, I still love it. I got what I wanted."

"And what's that?" He turned his phone around, and all I was looking at was a photo of me standing in my dress, glimpsing to the side.

"Look at your cute, tiny bump. I notice it sometimes, depending on what you wear."

"Are you saying I'm getting fat already?" I couldn't help it. I had to tease him. It was a coping mechanism for us both.

"No! Don't you dare bait me, woman! I know your body because I worship it, so even the slightest changes I'm picking up on. And frankly, it's beautiful."

"Nice save."

He laughed and breathed, "Phew! So you actually bought that shit?"

My eyes flew open, and he was cracking up. "Wanker!" We grabbed our stuff, headed out to the car, and made our way to our appointment.

Getting checked in, we completed the relevant paperwork and handed over the files they had given us in Canada. I explained the situation to the receptionist, and she was lovely, ensuring she had received the electronic files and noted everything. We sat, and I completed the forms they provided me before returning to the wait. "And don't start being impatient like last time, alright?"

"Keep me occupied then, Cutie."

"Well, I didn't think I had a child yet, so I didn't put any treats in my bag today."

"Savage!" We settled back, and thankfully, the wait was not long, and they took us into a private consultation room.

"Good morning, I'm Doctor Anu. It's lovely to meet you both, and congratulations." I introduced myself and Brax to the doctor. "Please take a seat. I have looked over your file briefly. Thank you for having that sent over. So I understand this will be your first scan, correct?"

"Yes. We found out when we were overseas working. We had the pregnancy confirmed, but as we travelled a lot, it was easier to wait until we got back to organise a scan."

"Great, how about we pop you up here and have a look, then we can talk some more afterwards? We'll go through everything and address the questions you have, okay?" Following the doctor over to the examination table, I took the gown she handed me. "I'll close this curtain to give you some privacy while you change." Thanking her, I waited until she walked out and closed it before slipping my dress off and into the gown. I heard the doctor talking to Brax while they waited. "So, this is your first child?"

"Yeah, not planned, but we couldn't be happier. It was the best surprise either of us could have asked for."

I saw the smirk climb across Brax's lips as he tried desperately to stop himself from laughing when I pulled the curtain back. I knew exactly what had him so tickled, too. These gowns were ridiculous; they were dragging along the floor. "Don't you do it, Brax!" The doctor looked between us and saw him on the verge of hysteria. He couldn't hold it anymore and started chuckling. "Will you excuse my French for a moment, Doctor Anu?" She nodded. "My partner is an asshole and likes to take the piss every chance he gets. It's comical to him that I'm so short, and this gown is so...." I pulled it out, staring down, "ridiculous."

"Oh, he doesn't realise Arsenic comes in a small bottle and only requires a drop to make you very sick?" Brax's eyes flew open as he stared at the doctor. I was the one laughing now.

"Ok, we don't need to look at any other doctors. I'm keeping this one, Brax." I smiled at him widely, and he shook his head, amused.

"Right, well, hop up here for me, and I'll put this sheet across for your privacy. Can you roll your gown up, then?" I agreed, following her instructions. "Braxton, you are welcome to come and stand by Charlotte's side, so you can see better if you like?" The doctor explained the process to us and got out what she called a transducer, which I understood was like a portable x-ray machine. She spent some time scanning it over my abdomen as I looked up at him, watching the doctor intently, though we didn't know what she was doing. Seeing the excitement in his eyes was adorable, and I stroked his arm to get his attention. He looked down and took my hand, smiling, then mouthing "I love you," and squeezing my hand. After a while, Doctor Anu turned to us, seeming to have everything she sought.

"Well, congratulations to you both. I have checked everything, and gestation is a healthy eleven weeks. The baby is looking strong and growing well. I'll print you some images to take home, and I would like to book a follow-up appointment for around eighteen to twenty weeks. We will carry out some in-utero tests. All very normal, just to scan that baby is still growing well and we can determine the sex of your child if you would like to know."

"Thank you. We will make the appointment before we leave today."

Doctor Anu nodded and asked us to excuse her momentarily. "I will print these images and let you get changed. Then we can run through a few more things, and I can address questions should you have any."

We thanked her as she headed out, and I hopped off the bed, untying the gown. "Out," I pointed to the curtain.

"Baby, I just saw all up in your womb, and that doesn't bother you? Yet, seeing your underwear, you think will?"

"Yes." I glared back at him as he laughed.

"Yeah, you're right," He admitted and kissed me quickly. He stepped out and went and sat back down, where I soon joined him.

When she returned, she handed up an envelope with the photos. I let Brax take it as I listened to Doctor Anu explain further. "I have written a few prescriptions and recommendations for yours and the baby's health. There is also some information on what to expect, although please do your own research. Let me know if you have questions. Most of it is general information around lethargy, headaches, morning sickness—"

"Oh, we know that one well." Doctor Anu smiled warmly when he said that and advised, "I suspected, but didn't want to jinx Charlotte."

"No problems there. We're old friends," I joked. "Milk is not my friend at the moment. There have been a few events in the morning where someone has drunk milk and came too close. He found out how much it disagrees with me."

"Well, Braxton, it will please you to know if Charlotte is lucky that should settle down and disappear within the next few weeks." I saw her face drop when I said, "I can't wait to have milk again."

"Your taste buds and smell may still not favour that. The symptoms just won't be as strong, so be mindful." I nodded, eagerly listening. "Do you have questions before I stop taking all your time?"

He started shaking his head, but I spoke up, "Actually, Doctor Anu, I wanted to discuss something." I saw him look at me questioningly. "I had a few concerns."

"Every mother-to-be does, dear, which is why I'm here to help ease those worries."

"Thank you. See, the thing is, my partner is a musician, and I work for the recording label he's signed to. We travel a lot with work, and without insulting your intelligence, there is a certain culture associated with being young and in the music industry." She nodded in understanding. "We were on tour when we found out, and based on the fact you have told me we're eleven weeks, it means I fell pregnant before we left. I guess I'm just worried...." I trailed off.

"About the tour?" She pondered.

"Yes," I sighed, and he reached over, taking my hand in his. "We were drinking heavily at intervals, but we were also smoking a lot of marijuana. It's a coping mechanism, although I'm not proud to admit that as I know there are better things out there I could do, but I had a lot of emotional trauma growing up, so I turned to it to calm my anxieties," I felt the need to explain. "I'm scared that those bad habits will have affected our baby?"

"And you stopped as soon as you found out?"

"Yes, Doctor, I haven't touched either."

"Charlotte, everything I saw today, your baby, is fine and healthy," she spoke reassuringly. "The moment you found out, you took every precaution you could. I'm confident you'll have a healthy pregnancy. But we will continue to check and monitor both you and the baby, address any concerns, too, so please voice them to me."

"Thank you, and the travel won't be a problem?"

"It's fine for the moment. However, I wouldn't recommend travelling after the thirty-fifth week of gestation."

"Thank you. Brax, did you have questions?"

"No. Thank you."

"Well, it was lovely to meet you both. We'll see more of each other over the coming months, and I look forward to assisting you with the safe arrival of your baby."

"Thank you, Doctor Anu," he expressed, extending his hand while standing. I followed and thanked her again as she shook my hand and congratulated us. We booked a follow up appointment as we were leaving and got one in my nineteenth week, which thrilled Brax, who was keen to know the sex. Heading back to the car, I went to open my door when he leaned on it and took my hip. "Hi," he smiled brilliantly at me.

"Hey yourself." I wrapped my arms around his neck.

"How are you feeling?"

"Perfect," I smiled up.

"Me too." He kissed my nose, then asked, "Why didn't you tell me you had some concerns?"

"No point in us both being stressed," I explained. "I just made a note of what I wanted to check today."

Brax pulled me closer and tilted my chin to meet his gaze. "That is what I am here for, to help carry your burdens. You both," he rubbed my stomach tenderly, "are my world."

Chapter Thirty

BRAX

The week flew by as we returned to our routine after the tour, sorting the house and getting ready for dinner tonight—with the parents! I was nervous, meeting Richard face-to-face for the first time, but tried to hide it when I saw how excited Charlie was to share scan pics with her mum and mine. Even though I offered to have food catered so she didn't exhaust herself, she insisted on cooking, and I knew better than to argue with her. I never won.

I set the outdoor dining table as instructed and headed to the kitchen. "Right, where do you want me?" I knew she would want to get washed before everyone arrived.

Not missing a beat, or turning around, she replied, "On your knees."

"Yes, ma'am." I grabbed her hips and pulled her into me.

"No, no.... we don't have the time. I was just mucking around." She struggled to get me off.

"You can't do that to a man, Charlie," I huffed, stepping back with arms across my chest. "That's not cool. It causes blue balls. You know that, right?"

"That is not something you've ever had to complain about."

I stayed silent instead of agreeing. "Okay, so what do you need me to do?"

"Watch the food so it doesn't burn."

"Agh, baby." I scratched the back of my neck. "You remember what my fridge and freezer used to look like before you moved in, right?"

"*Shit*! That's true. Frozen meals and off milk...." she trailed off, thinking. "I'm just going to turn it down low." *Smart idea.* "In about half an hour, turn the lamb and potatoes over, then the rest I can do when I get back." I opened the door to the oven and peeked. Immediately, the aroma of roast meat filled my nostrils—I was in heaven.

"Fuck me! What *is* that smell?" I stuck my head in further, taking a deeper breath. "Damn, that's good."

"It's a mint sauce, babe. I soaked the lamb in it first before putting it in the oven."

When I started picking at it, she quickly slapped my fingers out. "Can I wife you?"

"Sure."

After a quick kiss, she ran to our room, so I stacked the dishwasher and tidied the kitchen to make myself useful. I flipped the roast and spuds as instructed, then sat down watching the football, waiting for her to come back. And when she returned, I smiled like a sideshow alley clown.

"What?" she looked down, checking her outfit.

"I can see your bump!" She rolled her eyes, waving her hand to brush me off. "It's so cute. Come here, please?"

"It's barely noticeable," she whined. "Are you going to be like this for the next six months?"

I didn't miss a beat. "Yes."

"I'm moving out."

"Hey! You take that back!" I raced up, grabbing her before she could hurry back to the kitchen. I reached down and softly stroked her little bump. Her hands wrapped over the top of mine while looking deeply at me. "Seeing you carrying my child is nothing I could ever explain—because it is *everything*. I never want to miss a step of this, alright?" We both nodded. "I wish there were enough words to describe how much you both mean to me."

"I love you," she whispered, teary-eyed. My lips glided over hers before bending down to kiss our precious cargo, cocooned safely in Charlie. I covered her stomach in kisses to the sound of her giggles until we heard the door go. "I'll get it, baby."

"Thank you." When she slapped my ass, I turned back immediately, pointing my finger in a warning, "Don't you start."

"I haven't," she smirked. "I'm just getting warmed up."

"Tease!" I hollered, racing through the lounge, before opening the door. There stood Carole and Richard.

She hugged me tightly. "Hello, my darling."

"Hi! It's so good to see you again."

She stood back, holding my arms. "You're looking good, my precious. The tour went well?"

"We finally caught up on sleep." I smiled. "The trip was great. We have so much to tell you." *And not just about the tour!* "Hi Richard, I'm Braxton." I turned as he stood awkwardly to the side, extending my hand. He was a powerful man, the energy seeped in every mannerism and demeanour. Towering at six foot, with a full white beard showing his age, which I guessed to be late fifties-early sixties.

He took my hand in a firm, yet friendly grip, as he said, "Hello, Braxton. Thank you for inviting me into your home." Taking my hand back, I wiped it on my jeans, hoping my palm wasn't too sweaty with nerves.

Nodding politely at each other, I invited them both in. "Please, come on through. Charlie is finishing preparing dinner."

They stepped in, and I watched Richard taking it all in since it was his first time at our home. "This is a really nice house you and my daughter have, Braxton."

"We love it." I offered politely.

"I already told you that," Carole whispered, but I heard it.

"I know," he acknowledged his wife with a half smile. I understood the trials all too well regarding the Bancroft women—headstrong and fierce.

"Cutie, your parents are here," I announced once we got to the dining.

"Coming." We stood in silence, waiting for her to join us. I kept sneaking a glance, hoping to catch a read on what he was thinking.

"Pixie, there you are!" Carole raced forward when she saw Charlie. "Come here." They embraced lovingly before she stepped back, taking in her daughter. "You look beautiful, baby."

"You always say that, Mum," she giggled. "I missed you."

"I missed you, too. So much."

Turning to find Richard standing uncomfortably beside me, she whispered, "Hi, Dad."

"Hi, Charlie. Thanks for inviting me." He grinned softly, and some of her anxiety washed away as she smiled back.

"We appreciate you coming." She walked over, and after some hesitation, carefully cuddled him. I was so proud of her. Given everything they had been through, I knew that was a massive step. I choked up a bit when he returned her embrace.

"You look good." *No, she looks radiant.*

"I feel it."

"And congratulations to you both," he said, turning around to meet my gaze, smiling timidly. "This is from us, for both the engagement and the baby." He reached out with an envelope, and Charlie took it, saying, "You didn't need to get us anything. You being here is enough."

I kissed Carole on the cheek and shook Richard's hand again. When Charlie opened it, we saw a prepaid package to help with setup costs for the nursery, valid for twelve months. I looked at them both and exclaimed, "This is too much!"

"Please, we insist." She looked at her husband, who agreed. "I don't know what to say," Charlie struggled as tears swelled in her eyes.

"Thank you will be sufficient," her father insisted sincerely.

It blew me away and I wrapped my arm around Charlie's waist, gently squeezing. "Thanks, Mum and Dad. We appreciate it so much." Carole hugged and kissed her softly on the forehead.

"Could I get either of you a drink? Come and sit down. Please make yourself at home." I ushered them through.

"Thank you. We bought this for dinner," he announced, handing over a shopping bag. "I wasn't sure which you and your parents preferred, or what meal was on the menu, so we bought one of each." I opened the bag and found a red, white, rosé and champagne. *Where's the port?*

"That's great, Richard. Thank you."

"Yeah, great for you, not so much for me." Charlie elbowed me in the ribs.

"They can wait until you can enjoy them, too."

She laughed. "Unless Chester comes around."

"How is that ratbag? Carole asked, causing me to laugh.

"Still crazy." I shrugged. The doorbell went again, so I excused myself, knowing it to be my parents. I jogged through, an excited step, swinging the door open with a grin. "Miss me?" I threw them my biggest grin, and we all laughed.

"No." Mum shook her head. "We just came to see that beautiful girl of yours. Where is she?" Dad chuckled.

I raised my eyebrows. "Is that right?"

"I have a lot to thank her for," she explained. "Ever since she took you off my hands, I constantly have a fridge full of food."

"And I can find a beer when I want one."

"So you want in on it also, Dad?" I welcomed my parents in, slinging my arm around his shoulders, patting them as we headed downstairs. Carole, Richard and Charlie were sitting in the rumpus room.

"There she is!"

When Charlie heard my mum's voice, she quickly got up and kissed her. Just like I did, mum noticed her bump and made a beeline for it.

Dad leaned over her to give Charlie a peck on the cheek and congratulate us. "Congratulations, Sweetheart. I'm so happy for you both."

"Thank you, we're very excited." When she looked at me, I wrapped my arm around her, smiling back and agreeing. "How about you all sit at the table, and I will dish up?" She pointed to the table she'd tasked me with setting up.

"How about Carole and I help you, darling? Then we can hear the bits we want to know without the men complaining?"

"I'll bring the wine." Carole jumped up.

Mum clapped her hands. "It's like we have telepathy."

The girls entered the kitchen as my father, Richard, and I moved to the dining room. "This is an impressive home, Braxton. It's quite deceiving from the front, isn't it?" Richard turned to the front of the house, then back.

"That's what we loved," I explained. "It affords us the privacy we want and makes it easier to work from home. We are having one room downstairs converted into a studio with soundproofing and insulation, so I can be around to help Charlie once the baby arrives."

"That's very good of you," he said. "Thank you for looking after my daughter."

Before I could answer Richard, dad spoke up. "We should thank your Daughter." Amused, I glared at him. "I often wondered if this boy would ever grow up. I'm proud of what they have achieved together."

"I agree, Karl." Richard turned to my dad. "You've impressed me a lot. I see you two complement each other well." I looked at him, surprised. His face, though, told me he meant every word with all sincerity.

"Thank you, Richard."

The girls returned laden with dishes, Charlie placed the roast in the middle for me to carve. Before we ate, we raised a toast, which my dad spoke of first.

"Congratulations to you both on your engagement. We look forward to you having a loving and happy life together, the same as Maggie has afforded me." I smiled as I saw him reach over and take mum's hand.

"And congratulations on your first child together. May you enjoy the love and comfort of finally having a home that a child brings." Carole smiled at Richard. I knew from that act I could trust his genuine intentions towards our future. We tapped our glasses, and Charlie looked sideways at me as she sipped her lemonade.

I kissed her softly and whispered, "I promise. Just one, babe."

"Until Chester gets here." My eyes widened. "I heard you on the phone this morning in the bathroom, planning for the boys to come over after dinner. You know, just in case you needed to cut loose." She grinned and winked.

"Lucky, I wasn't trying to hide it."

We started eating and spent the time catching up. It was surreal. After everything that had happened, I never thought I would see the day all four parents would sit here with us, celebrating our baby and pending wedding. If I had any doubt about the sincerity, it was all squashed when we saw our parents' faces as Charlie showed them the scan photos.

She sat back in her chair, watching our parents discussing the images, and when I saw a tear falling down her cheek, I wiped it with my thumb. "Happy tears, baby?"

She nodded to me. "Happy tears, Batman."

I whispered to her, reminding her of my love, my left hand sliding into my pocket. When I started to stand up, Charlie turned to me. There in front of our parents, I carefully lowered to my knee, showing her the ring I had finally found to compliment her beauty.

Once our parents left, I texted the guys to see if they were keen for a beer. Of course, I checked with Charlie, as there wasn't any football on, and she was more rested, it was fine. I tidied up the mess in the kitchen and was coming out when I heard, "Fuck face!"

"Wanker!" I shouted back to Chester.

"Hey, Midget," Shane said while walking out to the lounge-room.

"Woah, is that a joey in your pouch, or do you want me to put one there?" Chester shot finger-guns at her. Before she could react, I slid across the floor, crashing into and knocking him on his ass. We were wrestling on the ground when she walked over and threw a tea towel on our heads.

"Hey, Sweet Cheeks! You miss me?" He looked up, blowing her kisses.

"You mean you left? I thought you lived here?" The boys snickered.

"Look, I know you want me to move in, but we discussed this. Brax doesn't know how to share." He imitated whispering, but let's be honest, the guy wouldn't know how to be quiet if his life depended on it. I dug my elbow in hard as we started fighting again.

"I'll be back," Charlie announced. "Just wanna get changed. Cold beer and wine in the fridge. You know where the rest is."

"Thanks Baby Mumma."

"Fuck off, Brax."

"Thank you, Pregnant Midget of Tour."

"Eat a dick, Chester."

We grabbed a drink, heading outside, and she soon joined us, taking a seat on my lap. "Feel better now?" I pointed to my sweatpants she had put on.

"Much better." I rubbed her stomach and kissed her shoulder.

"The awards are in three weeks, right?" Chester enquired.

"Yeah, bro."

"When are we booking your party so everyone can come over?"

After a beat, something dawned on me. "Why are you so excited for everyone to come over? Who are you looking forward to seeing?"

He tried shrugging it off. "Everyone."

"Nope, I see it." Charlie pressed him. "You're inviting Chrissy, aren't you?"

"Shut up, Midget!"

"The fact you just went bright red tells me I'm correct."

He was indignant. "You know nothing."

"Okay, how about I ring, Chrissy?" she teased, pulling her phone out.

"Fine, you fucking menace!" He finally fessed up. "I'm inviting Chrissy."

"Aww, our boy's growing up," I tormented him.

"Who's a big boy now?" Liam patronised.

"You wanna see big, Hippie Boy?" The idiot stood up and undid his pants as we all laughed. Once everyone calmed down, I answered his original question.

"How about in two weeks? The weekend before the awards?" I suggested. "It would work better for us, as we have our next scan a few weeks after." Everyone seemed happy with the plan, so we locked it in.

The following two weeks flew by, with the return of our daily routines and adjusting to all the changes. It pleased me that Charlie's morning sickness had slowed and eased, although milk was still a no-go zone. The night of our engagement party had finally arrived and as we got ready, I looked over at her, struggling to fathom how I got so lucky. This woman was everything I needed and so much more.

I'd chosen a crisp navy suit, with a black shirt and tie underneath to compliment the dress she'd told me she was wearing.

"You look incredible, baby." She kissed my cheek, stopping to help with my tie, while moving from the ensuite to the robe to dress. "I'm so impressed."

"Why?" I looked down at what looked like any other suit to me.

"I didn't have to tell you to remove your hat." I cracked up laughing. "You look incredible." She walked around me, dragging her fingers across my ass, giving it a firm squeeze. "I didn't know we had cake in the house?" My head rolled back, eyes creased from the humour that took over. "Do we really have to go?"

"Yes," I warned. I was so excited about tonight. "Now, get dressed!" I smacked her backside hard, sending her off.

"Fine, but just so you know, you can leave that on for me later. I'll just sit in your lap."

"What the fuck, Midget?" I laughed.

"It's an impressive look."

"I'll take your word for it." I winked. "See you downstairs in a minute. Just gonna have a quick cone while I wait."

"Okay, I won't be long."

Racing downstairs, I headed out the back and had a smoke, mentally preparing myself for tonight, before grabbing a beer from the kitchen. I'd barely opened it, leaning on the bench as I messaged the boys.

"That pesky girlfriend messaging you again?"

The smile on my face instantly turned to lust as I looked up. *Holy fuck!*

Charlie blushed, dropping her head and twisting a strand of hair around her fingers, while intense passion drummed through my veins. She was wearing a strappy dark blue lace dress with a pale grey slip underneath and a v-cut neck. Her hair was down in loose waves with minimal makeup, opting to let her natural beauty shine. I dropped my phone on the bench, stalking towards her.

"What's wrong?" She looked worried.

Once close enough, my hand wrapped around the back of her neck, the other gracing the small of her back. Her lips felt like an inferno raging across my mouth, immediately granting me access the moment my tongue nudged for entry. It was the type of kiss you could get lost in, knowing you finally found heaven. She melted into me, so I held her tighter, bending her backwards while she gripped my neck for support.

Bringing her back up, a spontaneous declaration rolled out. "You're a goddess. I've seen nothing more beautiful in my life." I sweetly kissed her again, still holding her pressed to me. Carefully, I moved my hands down to her stomach, stroking it. "I love you both." One quick kiss on the nose and I extended my arm to her. "Shall we?" She took it as I grabbed my phone and keys, adding, "I can't wait to show you off."

"You organised all this for me?" Charlie squealed, hand over her mouth as we walked towards the room hosting our family and friends for the night.

"I had plenty of help," I explained humbly. "I just wanted tonight to be perfect for you."

"Either way, it is…. you are here." As we walked into the room, she harshly pulled me to a stop, gripping my arm like her life depended on it.

"What's wrong?" I froze, seeing the fear swirling in her eyes.

She pointed, and my head turned. "Calvin's parents are here."

"Are you fucking serious?" I roared.

Chapter Thirty One

BRAX

We were walking into what should have been one of the best nights of our lives. Instead, she was gripping me for dear life, terrified beyond belief, freaking out because Calvin's parents were here. Coupled with the fact I was raging at her father, who I felt had clearly played me, I wanted to take my fiancée and head home where I could hold her and keep her safe, but the primal side of me needed to fight for her honour. I could see the anguish plastering her features, disappointment I, too, was feeling, so I wrapped my arms around her, turning to face each other.

"What do *you* want to do?" I softly asked. "Say the word, no hesitation. I'm right beside you. If you want to turn around and go home, we can do that. Or do you want me to go in and sort it out? Then we can celebrate our engagement and baby like you deserve?"

She looked up at me and gripped my arms that were holding her tight. "We deserve this Brax, not just me. I want to celebrate *us*."

"There's my girl." I brushed my thumb across her lip, fingers cupping her chin. "Then let's go," I announced with an encouraging kiss. I took her hand and led her into the room as everyone cheered and clapped. I pulled Charlie close, politely acknowledging everyone. We headed off to our left because our closest friends were there, not just because it was in the opposite direction from Calvin's parents. When we headed over, it surprised me to see Carole and Dick—*shit*, Richard! I need to get out of the habit of calling him that—standing behind our group of friends and not with Calvin's parents. *Odd.*

I shook it off, not giving them more attention than they deserved. Tonight did not concern them. It was about Charlie. This was *her* night, and she would get the one she always dreamed of.

Our group hugged and kissed us, while Chester pissed around with Charlie, her giggles flowing freely. "Chrissy, it is great to see you again. Welcome to Australia." I hugged her. "I'm only sorry you got given a backpacker's guide by Chester and not the luxury you deserve." She laughed and thanked me. "How long are you out for?"

"A couple of weeks. Let's see how it goes." We both smiled, knowing that meant *see how long before Chester's antics drove her up the wall.*

"I'll be back in a second." I rubbed her arm. "Just going to say hello to my manager." I noticed Marcus standing towards the back, trying to look inconspicuous—Tessa beside him. "You kept this quiet, Dad?" I put it straight on him.

"Don't you Dad me, asshole." He patted my shoulder. "You're also in your thirties and will be a Dad soon!" I couldn't argue, as we both smiled and hugged.

"Good to see you again, Tessa. Thank you for coming."

"Thank you for having me, and congratulations again. Where's Charlie?"

I pointed over my shoulder. "Monkey Nuts barrelled her up already."

"Of course," she said, smiling. We all had a chat before I headed over to say hello to Nick and his wife, Chris, Brett and April. Finally, I got through and thanked Tina, Charlie's best friend, and her partner, Alex, for coming.

After a brief conversation, I returned to my girl. She seemed to have calmed down at Chester's ongoing antics. "Alright, get the fuck off her already, man." I shoulder-barged him out of the way and stood beside

Charlie, wrapping my arm around her. "Not cool, bro."

"Be careful, baby. We just established that Chester's on Shark Week."

"Aww, you back with all the feels since seeing Chrissy again?" She went bright red immediately. "Shit, sorry! I wasn't trying to embarrass you, just him." I gave her a side hug, she told me it was fine. "But seriously, just know it's only aimed at him because I will do it often."

"This is a payback thing, right?" Chrissy jested back.

"Correct," Charlie and I said at the same time.

We excused ourselves to make our way around to the rest of our guests, spending a reasonable amount of time so they knew how much we appreciated them. After we finished with my parents, we approached Richard and Carole. I took a moment to prepare myself mentally as I squeezed Charlie's hip.

"There's my baby. Finally." Carole opened her arms wide for her daughter.

Charlie answered for us. "Saved the best for last, Mum."

"Smooth," I murmured.

Richard extended his hand as he spoke. "Congratulations again, to both of you."

"Thanks for coming." It was the most I could afford because I wanted to punch his teeth down his throat for inviting Calvin's parents. Instead, I'd promised Charlie to give her the night she deserved. While talking with them, we heard an older woman speak from behind us.

"Carole and Richard! There you are," her sing-song voice interrupted. I turned to see Calvin's parents standing on top of us. "Oh, Charlotte and... well, I don't know you." She gave me a filthy stare.

"Good, let's keep it that way." I took Charlie's hand and walked away, but Richard's voice stopped us in our tracks.

"What the hell are you and Mathias doing, Lyn?"

She nudged me. "Did you hear that?"

"I was just about to say the same thing to you." We stood there huddled off to the side, making it appear we were talking amongst ourselves. "Stay quiet and we'll listen from here."

"Rather rude you would ask us that, Richard, considering we invested a lot into that girl." That girl? *My* fucking girl! "Instead, we find you here, watching her frolic with someone else after terminating our agreement."

"Holy shit!" Charlie exclaimed, forcing me to place my hand over her mouth in a shushing motion. The shock that her father was fighting her corner for once was overwhelming.

"First, I did *not* invite you, because you're not welcome," he said, quietly but harshly. "Second, my Daughter is not goods for sale and, in all honesty, your Son never deserved her. I was wrong, and I'm admitting that here in the presence of my wife." Charlie wasn't the only one shocked now. "Third, you treat my Daughter with such disdain again, and you'll soon remember what I'm capable of. Do I make myself clear?"

Lyn tried to respond, but he didn't give her the chance. "Listen, Richard—"

"No. I'm here to celebrate our Daughter's engagement to a man who I wholeheartedly believe deserves her hand in marriage. I can't stress enough how proud I am to see her find a man she adores and loves just as much. And, when Charlotte gives birth to my first grandchild in a few months, I will be the supportive and proud father she always deserved." Richard took a deep breath and stepped closer, his voice somehow more menacing. "Now, I'll kindly ask you both to leave. Don't call my family, do not visit, or come near us ever again. This is over!" Stunned, they failed to move. "Go, or I'll happily remove you myself."

They scampered, shaking their heads, engaging in a heated discussion. Once they'd left the reception, we moved back towards her parents. Richard saw us first, and his neck flushed before regimentally straightening up.

"Charlie...." he fumbled, "look, I know—" Before he could finish what he was saying, she let go of my hand and lunged forward. She tightly wrapped her arms around him burying her head into his chest. It took him a few moments to get over the initial shock before he hugged her back. Carole wiped a tear while reaching out to hold my hand.

"Thank you, Dad."

He lifted her head between his hands. "Thank you for teaching me to be a better man and, hopefully, Father." They embraced again, and after a few minutes, she returned, taking my hand. I extended the other to Richard, who took it warmly.

"You have my blessing."

"It means a lot." More than words could convey.

"Go, you two. You have speeches to make and an important announcement so I can celebrate my first grandchild."

"Okay, Mum. Just for you." Charlie chuckled as Carole shooed us along.

I smiled and took her hand as we headed towards the middle of the room. Chester chucked me a microphone before he wolf-whistled to quieten the room. Once silent and with everyone looking at us, I turned the mic on, holding her tightly as she placed her hand on my chest.

"First, we're thrilled and honoured to share this night with you. Standing together in front of all the extraordinary people in our lives to announce our engagement makes our private dreams public and real. Thank you for being here, for your love and well wishes."

Everyone applauded as I waited for it to quieten down again. "Charlie has made what I previously condemned as trite meaningful. With her by my side, I understand love makes the world go round, and all you need is love." A collective moan of agreement filtered through the space. "Whether I will understand the importance of themed colours for the reception decor and bridesmaid dresses remains to be seen." It humoured everyone, especially the men.

"Just worry about the lingerie colour theme, bro!"

"Chester!" The entire reception roared in laughter as Charlie squealed at him.

"However, like the best of men, my Father and many of you here who've gone before me, I'll endure it because I know what I want, and that's calling Charlie my Wife." Everyone clapped again and sipped their drinks, except for Charlie, so I gave her a sweet kiss. I turned the mic off for a moment at my side. "You ready to make this night everything you wanted it to be?"

"I'm ready for everything that comes our way. With you, Brax, I can't go wrong."

Turning the mic back on, I announced, "While I still have your attention, if you would like to take out the envelopes you received on arrival and open them up. You will find inside invitations for the wedding, date, and venue all to be confirmed. We have also included a little bonus for everyone here tonight."

I put the mic down by my side, switching it off as everyone opened their envelopes. One of my relatives shouted, "Oh my God, you're having a baby!" The entire room roared with cheers and clapping. We smiled at all our loved ones as they found a copy of our scan photo inside their envelopes.

We had an incredible evening surrounded by everyone who mattered the most to us. The moment we got home, I excused myself. "Wait here. I have a surprise for you, okay?" Charlie nodded.

I raced through to our room, setting everything before returning to take her hand. The soft music played as we entered, candles scattered for mood lighting, as well as her favourite flowers and a beautifully boxed gift from me.

"Thank you." She smiled with appreciation. Pulling the ribbon, while carefully opening the box, she finally lifted the elegant, white lace nightdress. It was perfect for my taste, and I knew she would look incredible in it.

She headed for the bathroom to change into her new outfit as I undressed. I stood there, amazed at her beauty, wearing just a pair of boxers when she returned to the room. The two of us walked to each other and embraced, kissing passionately, running our hands over the other's bodies. I led her to the bed, laying her down gently, never separating.

Rolling in each other's, pashing wildly, exploring hands, I finally broke the kiss and descended her neck until reaching the top of the new nightdress. Carefully, I pulled a strap off her shoulder, lowering that side, exposing one of her breasts. My lips feathered across, then sucked delicately on her nipple. I reached to the other, massaging teasingly between two fingers, pulling her nipple to its fullest. Her hands threaded through my hair, letting out a soft moan as I continued the assault on her chest.

I kissed my way down her stomach, pulling the lace up, shifting to the beginning of her legs, when I noticed she wasn't wearing any panties. A tiny strip of hair came into view, and it fueled my hunger.

I took in the sight before me. The most beautiful woman in the world lay utterly naked, carrying my child, just waiting for my loving touch. I began kissing my way up her legs, not missing an inch. As I made my way to her sweet spot, she carefully spread her legs, inviting me in with her sweet aroma. I ran my tongue over her, tasting her juices and listening to moans getting louder and more frequent. She was close to climax, so I pulled her clit into my mouth and sucked, rolling it around with my tongue. Before long, she was grabbing my hair, pulling me closer. She loudly cried, releasing herself into my mouth as her body trembled, her thighs clenching around my head, much to my delight.

Moving back up, I slid in for a kiss, but she pushed me back, rolling over and making her way down my body. She reached for the top of my boxers, sliding her fingers inside, firmly stroking my already throbbing cock. Never releasing her grip, her other hand pushed my bottoms down, before she brought her mouth to the head and placed soft kisses down along the shaft.

"Aww," I groaned as my cock slid perfectly inside Charlie's warm mouth, watching as each inch disappeared inside. Deep throating me repeatedly, my moans became faster as well as louder the longer she took me, encouraging a fastened pace. With one hand teasing my balls, the other started jacking me off in rhythm with her sucking. After a few deep and powerful sucks, I was shooting down her lovely throat, every drop received before a gentle flurry of kisses lashed my still throbbing dick.

We lay in each other's arms, kissing and gently caressing each other. Within minutes, my cock was back up, ready for action. I climbed on top of her and stroked myself against the opening of her waiting pussy.

She grabbed my hips, helping me to slide deep inside. I leaned down and began kissing her, drifting in and out of her. I never quickened my pace, taking things nice and slow, not wanting this to be just another night of sex but a long night of making love. My slow pace drove her wild as a second orgasm swept through her body. Not wanting tonight to end, she took up my rhythm, gently rocking back and forth. When she rolled me over to ride me, I kneaded her breasts, slickly rubbing her clit as she raised up and down.

After hours of lovemaking, I could feel my second orgasm of the night building. I raised myself into a sitting position with her straddling and riding my cock. We engaged in passionate kissing as my orgasm took over my body. I fired deep as another climax ran through her body.

We embraced tightly, collapsing on the bed. We lay there for a few minutes, holding each other, before I slid down Charlie's body. With my loving hands encapsulating her stomach, she turned to face me as I placed a flurry of love across her skin. I wrapped my arm around her hip, closing my eyes, feeling my whole world still.

Chapter Thirty Two

CHARLIE

The last week had been insanely busy but fantastic all the same. We had prepared for the awards tonight and caught up with everyone from Canada. The bands had spent a lot of time in the studio as they were getting ready to debut their new song together tonight. They kept the project so secretive that I could only hear it once they finished it and performed it tonight. I'd tried to get clues from Brax, but he had none of it.

Of course, that didn't stop me, so when I rolled over in bed this morning and saw him still asleep, I had the perfect chance to try my luck again. He lay on his back. I rolled into his side and slid my leg over his thigh. Instinctively, his hand came up to my leg, rubbing it as I brushed mine across his stomach. It didn't take long before he rolled his head towards me, kissing my forehead. "I know what you're trying to do." I pretended I was still asleep and played the game with him. The aim was to trick him into telling me.

"Mmm, what's that baby?" He picked his arm up and wrapped it around me, pulling me closer and lifting my leg further up, his grip stronger as his thumb brushed across my skin. I ran my hand over his chest, to his neck and gripped it carefully. Of course, I was fishing for information on the song, but I also loved these moments with him. It is what I lived for, our little bubble. When he whispered again, "you're not fooling anyone," I tilted my head slightly, with eyes closed and asked, "What am I doing?"

"You're trying to butter me up to get information." *Game time!*

Sitting up, I glared at him. "Do you really think that little of me? I try to hold the man I love and get accused of using you or softening you up for my agenda?"

"What? I didn't say you were using me. I specifically said, buttering me up," he fast protested.

"So because I want to hold you, I'm buttering you up?"

"Cutie," was all he offered as he tilted his head sideways, eyebrows raised.

I sucked my teeth at him. "Eat a dick, Brax."

I went to turn to get out of bed and the moment I swung my legs off the mattress; he pulled me back down and started laughing his head off. Burying his face in my neck, he kissed up to my ear as I gripped his face. "You know what gives you away?"

"What?" I stared back, humoured.

"Your eyes. You look so damn cheeky. It's even more obvious when you are up to something, and it doesn't matter how hard you try. You can't hide it, Charlotte."

"Well, fuck you. You could have told me sooner. I would have used different tactics at my disposal," I huffed.

"And how does that benefit me?" We both chuckled as I reached my arm up behind him and stroked the back of his head. "How's both of my babies this morning?"

Brax ran his hand down my front and rested it on my stomach. "Would you believe we're hungry?"

"You know, I think I would." Moving closer for a kiss, he tapped my backside, signalling it was time to get up.

"So what do you want for breakfast?" he asked, opening the fridge. I sat at the kitchen bench watching him and couldn't stop my mouth before it came out. "You."

"Oh, okay, so you want cream this morning? I guess your taste buds are coming back."

"So wrong." After some breakfast, we got showered and dressed, even though we had kept today pretty quiet since we didn't want to be rushed later. We headed off and did our grocery shopping before collecting his suit for the night. Fuelling up with lunch on the way home, we had a lay down before tonight, primarily for my benefit, so I would actually make it through the awards without falling asleep on him.

"What are you wearing tonight?" he hollered as I was in the bathroom, blow-drying my hair. "You never told me."

"Clothes," I shrugged cheekily.

"Ha, you're so funny." he threw me a sarcastic smirk.

"Pants," I explained, "so I can wear flat shoes for comfort. No one will know under these trousers."

"True, plus heels are redundant on you anyway, babe." I turned the blow dryer around in his face as he laughed into it. He jumped in the shower while I sorted my hair, peering at him in the mirror. *Fucking pregnancy hormones!* They made me want to sit on his dick every chance I got. "I know that look, Charlie!" Oh, and he was all too aware of it.

"Shut up! I can't help it."

"I'll sort it out later for you."

"Yes, you will."

Once ready, I headed down to meet Brax. He looked up when he heard me coming down the hallway.

"You look incredible, baby."

"You look very handsome yourself. I'm a lucky lady." I grabbed the lapels of his navy suit jacket and pulled him down into a deep kiss. When we moved back, I smiled at his sparkling lips before taking my thumb and wiping the gloss away.

"I don't mind. I like the reminder that these lips belong to you."

"Cute." He took my hand, while I grabbed my clutch on the way out.

He locked the door before coming over to hug me as we waited. "So, are you excited about your new song release tonight? What's it called again?"

"Nice try!"

"You can't blame me for wanting to know, Brax!"

"I don't, but I'm still not telling you." The car arrived shortly afterwards, taking us to the venue. Brax texted the guys on the way and they agreed to meet us out the front together.

Once we pulled up, he immediately found Chester and Chrissy waiting with Liam and Mace. "Hey, beautiful!" Mace gave me a big hug as she whispered. "I was going to say hey little mumma, but I remembered you guys haven't announced that publicly, and there is media everywhere."

"Speaking of which, you have one behind you, babe. Have fun." I poked my tongue and giggled at Mace's disgusted face.

"You're ditching me, aren't you?"

"Correct." She rolled her eyes. "You know how I feel about them. I love you, though." I threw her a cheeky wave.

"You're lucky I love you too." I laughed as poor Mace got barrelled up and questioned about her return to the city and the seriousness of her and Liam's relationship. I felt for her, but Liam quickly headed over to pull her away. Brax came up to take my hand as I was watching their interaction.

"The others have just arrived. We're ready to head in when you are, Cutie."

Chester came up on my left, wrapping his arms around my shoulders. "Midget, you look extra short tonight."

"Monkey," I smiled, "Go fuck yourself." Of course, Brax laughed even when Chester kissed my cheek and said, "love you, Sweet Cheeks." I hugged Monkey, soon the other guys joined us, and we headed inside. As we went through, we had the usual calls to stop for photos. I couldn't help but admire how handsome Brax looked as he went through the motions. He revealed his freshly shaven chiselled jaw, and he arranged his hair back off his face without a cap for once! The navy suit with a crisp white shirt underneath sat perfectly on him, especially across his tight backside.

It was my turn to go through, as much as I hated this part of the night. There was a reason I hid behind the lens. I wore a white pair of wide-cut trousers that sat high-waisted. Accentuated with three gold buttons down either pocket, completed by a gold v-neck cut shirt that had glitter thread through. The pants sat above my developing bump, comforting me, and my hair was down in loose curls. As I stood for the photo, I tried an old hack Tina had told me of—putting one leg forward and pushing my backside out—hoping to minimise how prominent the bump had become.

I watched the others doing their bit and made my way over to Brax, whose gaze was piercing into the photographer who took our photos. He was in discussion with another reporter, both looking at his camera. "What's up, babe?"

"Just being nosey, Cutie. Wondering what those reporters are up to and why they keep looking over at us."

"Don't worry about it, Brax. Who cares? Leave them to it." He smiled down and nodded to go. He took my hand and walked away when we heard another female entertainment reporter calling out to us.

"Brax! Would you and Charlie have time for a quick chat?" He looked at me for approval, which I nodded, given she had been respectful and asked rather than just screaming in our faces. We headed over and she thanked us both for our time. "First, congratulations on your very successful tour of Canada. The media and coverage we saw from it was probably the best campaign we've seen in our music industry in a long time."

"Thank you, but that credit goes to Charlie and our Manager Marcus."

"Incredible job, Charlie," she turned to me. "You must be very proud of Brax."

"Thank you. I couldn't be prouder of Abandoned Bygone's achievements." I loved him dearly, but I felt obliged to remind the reporter there were five members in the band.

"And we all know you are releasing your long-awaited single tonight?"

"That's right, I'm excited for you all to hear it." He offered politely.

"Rumours are rife that Canadian sensations, Glaze, could appear on the track?"

"Well, we'll find out tonight, won't we?" I smiled at his perfect, yet evasive, answer.

"I know you don't normally like personal questions, Brax...." she hesitated for a moment, "but it is a little hard to go past this beautiful ring on Charlie's finger. It's positively stunning." She was right, it was. "Would you mind if I asked?" We both knew what she was alluding to.

Brax looked at me, and the stupid grin I couldn't contain spread as my nose scrunched up. When I nodded, he knew it was fine. Whatever he did, I was all in. "It is stunning. I thought so too."

"So we're correct in assuming you've asked Charlie to marry you?"

"No assumption. Charlie and I are engaged." Other reporters heard Brax answer that and quickly turned and moved closer with their microphones.

"Congratulations, I know it will thrill our viewers to hear that. You two are definitely one of the fan's favourite couples." He laughed and said, "I'm not sure how to answer that one," as he scratched the back of his neck. "Well, I believe one fan wrote, and I quote…." She pulled it up on her iPad and read, "Ugh…. These guys are couple goals. Could they be any more adorable together? Where can I find that?"

I felt myself going bright red and tried to hide my face in his chest. He kissed the top of my head and squeezed my waist. Just as we were about to excuse ourselves, we heard another reporter in the back yelling out, "Charlie, while you both are being so candid, I can't ignore the photo taken of you tonight. Can we ask if you indulged a bit during your recent tour, or if you both have another announcement tonight?"

I glared towards where the voice came from and saw the reporter Brax was watching earlier. He pointed to my stomach and then used his hands to imitate a pregnant stomach. Brax's grip on my waist loosened as he stepped closer, asking in an angry tone, "What did you just say to her?"

BRAX

Was this guy for real? I stepped up, livid that he thought he had any right to speak to Charlie, or any other woman like that. It stopped me when I felt Charlie grip my arm tighter.

"You are everything that is wrong with this industry. Healthy people don't need to put others down to make themselves feel important. And that's exactly what you're doing right now, trying to cause a sensation at my expense to fuel your agenda. Whether I've put on weight, as you tried to imply, or I'm pregnant remains none of your business," I heard murmurs of agreement amongst the crowd. "Your behaviour would intimidate only a weak woman. Once upon a time, that was me, until this amazing man," Charlie pointed to me, built me up to be everything I am today. Taking your bait is something he has taught me better than to do," it was then I noticed the rest of our friends, watching on, nodding in agreement. "So while you continue to speculate, I'm going inside with my fiancée, to celebrate his successes because it's all about Abandoned Bygone tonight. Certainly not you!"

She took my hand and started walking away as we heard Chester say, "Sucks to be you, man. She just made you look like a first-grade asshole while live on television." We walked through with the rest of our guys and stopped to take the time to speak to people we knew and hadn't seen in a while before we finally made it to our table.

"Cutie, want to make a deal with me tonight?"

"Depends what it is first."

"I'll have your share of the drinks, and you can have my dessert."

She chuckled, leaning in, then whispered, "I was on the dessert menu tonight."

"Fuck," I adjusted myself, feeling a throbbing in my groin.

"How about you get through your performance, and we can go from there?"

"In case you write yourself off later and I forget to say it, I'm really proud of you, Baby Daddy."

I threw my head back, laughing. "Yes! You finally said it."

"And I won't ever be repeating it," she promised.

"We'll see," I winked.

"Go kill it, like I know you will."

"Love you, Cutie. This one's for you." I kissed her as I stood up, and the guys and I headed backstage to meet Glaze, who they'd snuck in for optics, and prepare for our performance. We left the girls waiting in anticipation of what was to come. I don't know about the rest, but I hadn't told Charlie.

I wanted it to be a surprise for her.

Thirty minutes later we walked out onto a blackened stage, a hush falling as everyone waited. The boys started strumming in, as Liam took his drums, Chris and I stepped up to the mics.

The lights came up, and when everyone saw we had collaborated as per the media rumours, the function room erupted into a standing ovation, my vocals soon caressing them.

> *I'm coming home, back where I belong*
> *I always find such peace and comfort, in my home sweet home*
> *Where I can lay my head down and simply find the rest I need*
> *From the weary days and long hard roads, I've been walking in my dreams.*

Finishing the first verse, my eyes sought and locked onto Charlie's as Chris took up the chorus;

> *Home is where I can be myself, no pressures or demands*
> *When I'm free to fly and roam around, and just be who I am,*
> *Surrounded by the hearts and love of family and friends*
> *No matter how far away I am, home is where I'll always end.*

Charlie and my eyes stayed fixed on each other. I wrote every word only for her. The emotions raged through my veins—an expression of how she made me feel. When I noticed the swell of tears in her eyes, I knew she felt it, too.

> *Home is my perfect haven, a shelter from the storm*
> *The place I go to just be me, and not be judged or scorned,*
> *I can laugh and cry, this signifies how comfortable I feel*
> *Where the walls are filled with memories that remind me this is real.*

I mouthed to Charlie I loved her as Chris took up the chorus again, giving me the chance to fix my in-ear and clear my throat as I clicked the mic back on for the last verse;

> *Home is love and laughter, it's the fire in my blood*

Where I get such determination, to thrive at what I love
It gives me confidence, emotion, the motivation to succeed
Home, it flows right through my veins, it's the colour that I bleed.

Chris closed the song out with one final chorus, accompanied by an incredible swell of the guitars. At the end of the performance, the entire audience stood up and started cheering and shouting as the presenters came on stage and pulled us in for an interview. The two bands came over as Chris and I grabbed our mics and stood with the boys and April.

"Damn, guys! What did everyone think of that?" The crowd roared again as we saw a swarm of bodies cheering and clapping. "Can we expect more of this?"

"Absolutely." Chris was fast to jump in, myself and the boys eager as well.

"Plus, there is the appearance on our album Brax wrote a bridge for," April added for the audience.

"Not to forget the new album launches early next year," Mark said. "And we saw something different from you on this latest tour," the announcers cut back in. "We've become used to seeing you boys run amok, and we live vicariously through you."

"We had some of our usual antics, but this tour was a turning point for each of us, professionally and personally." I explained.

"And the personal, would you be referring to the news we heard confirmed earlier this evening?"

I smiled down at her in the audience, "Well, yes, Charlie and I are getting married, but I wasn't just referring to me."

"Do tell us more, we're excited to hear, right guys?" He waved to the audience, encouraging their cheers.

"For starters, Mark and Chester have some incredible women in their lives now." Chester punched me this time, laughing, as the audience joined him. "And no, I'm not telling you anymore than that." They all booed. "And Shane and his long-term partner have moved in together."

"Amazing," they cut in. "Congratulations to you and Charlie, your beautiful fiancée in the crowd. The lights flicked over to Charlie and the rest of the girls. "And I assume those beautiful women are your partners, and oh, hello, Mace, there you are gorgeous!"

Mace waved back and blew him a kiss. "Thank you. We have a lot to look forward to."

"That sounds interesting, Brax. Anything you want to share?"

I looked at Charlie and saw her smiling at me softly, and after the reporter spoke to her earlier, we wanted to make the announcement on our terms. She nodded to me and mouthed "yes."

"Apart from the upcoming album and now planning our wedding, Charlie and I are expecting our first child."

Everyone applauded us, and I saw a few people turn to Charlie and congratulate her. "Fantastic news, for you all. It thrilled us you could be here tonight to perform and look forward to the new album."

"Thank you," we waved to the crowd.

"And let's give a huge Aussie salute to Glaze for making the trip out here to spoil us all."

We thanked them and waved, heading off stage. The band joined the girls back at the table after nearly an hour had passed and pulled my chair out next to Charlie before she hugged me tightly. "That song was incredible, babe. I'm so proud of you all. Your talent is phenomenal."

"I have a good muse. She inspires me every day."

"Really? Anyone, I know?"

"Nah, better to keep you two apart. It would be explosive." She raised her eyebrow and nudged me playfully. "Whenever I feel lost, I find myself in you."

I kissed her softly, rubbing my hand down her back as she cupped my cheeks. "Can we get the mingling part out of the way so we can get home for the second dessert, please?"

"The best idea you have ever had, my love."

Chester leaned in then, interrupting us. "Did I hear that right? Do you two want to leave so you can fuck already?"

"Fuck off, Monkey," she flipped him the bird. "Yes."

Chapter Thirty Three

BRAX

The moment we got home, our kiss lasted for a long time, but seemed too short. Charlie's lips parted, and the tip of my tongue found hers, nuzzled gently together, then entwined as we enjoyed the touch and flavour of each other. She drew away when I stroked the back of my hand from her waist up to her breast and then to her nipple, which I could feel hard underneath her top. I flicked it gently with my finger and heard her soft gasp. She took my hand and led me through to our bedroom. "So you like my body when I'm pregnant?"

"I like it very much." I pulled her towards me, kissing her deeply and urgently, before lashing my tongue against the skin of her throat and down towards her breasts. Her gorgeous, swollen breasts.

"Do you like my boobs? Not too big for you?" She pulled her top and pants off, revealing a white lace bra and matching panties. She was mind-blowingly beautiful, and her blossoming stomach made her look stunning. I hardened instantly—a rock would pale in comparison—and I could feel myself tingle with the excitement of pleasure spreading through my body. I ran my fingertips over her left breast. Her nipple was long and hard, pointing up towards my mouth.

"Let me help you," I said, putting both arms around her so my hands could reach the bra clasp, unsnapping it with a practised hand. She caught it onto the top of her little stomach, throwing the garment across the room. Charlie leaned back at an angle, still sitting on the edge of the bed so that I could get to her breasts easier. I sucked them, causing her to pant as she stared at the ceiling with a delirious look.

"Mmm, bite it," she whined desperately.

"Are you sure?" I croaked.

"Please, Brax." A heavy breath escaped as I bit down gently, twisting the other between my thumb and finger before nibbling harder. She moaned louder the moment I did. I loved her breasts, but that was not where I wanted to be. I stood up and quickly removed my clothes. She leaned forward and stroked me from the base up to the tip. It was like a stream of electric current. My cock became more extensive and rigid than I had ever known it. It felt like an iron bar wrapped up in velvet. I wanted to plunge into her, but I needed to slow down. Her needs had to be met first.

Crouching down at the end of the bed, with her swollen stomach above me, I pushed my lips against her centre, licking from the bottom to the top, on first one side, then the other. My tongue slipped between her lips and tasted her sweet wetness, intoxicated by her aroma. I licked at first gently, then more firmly, moving in waves towards her little button. My tongue found her proud and erect clit and attended to it lovingly with the tip of my tongue. I felt her orgasm build and kept licking, bringing my forefinger up and pushing it inside. Charlie came with an explosion, the orgasm making her shake and writhe. I sat back and waited for her to recover. She stared at me deliriously. "Brax! That was incredible."

"Kneel on the bed with your back to me, baby." She complied immediately, without comment. Stroking my hands down her back, I lingered on her gorgeous backside before climbing onto the bed behind her. I reached underneath, running my hands carefully around her stomach and then more firmly over her breasts, lingering on her nipples, pinching them cruelly as she whimpered. I raised my right hand to her ass and stroked her from behind. My fingers ran up to her butt and then back down again, and she let out a begging cry in my arms.

"Brax, I need you." I lined up the head, hard and aching for her, to her lips and with a backward and forward motion, I penetrated, pausing when the tip had slipped inside her. It was warm and welcoming, the touch between us tingled, threatening to break into an inferno. "Aww, that's so good, Brax. You feel amazing." I pushed in further with a thrusting motion until I was deep inside her void. I stopped and stroked her back and hair as she pressed into me.

I pumped in and out of Charlie again, slowly but insistently, with a regular rhythm, adjusting the angle until it was just right, with me fitting tightly and comfortably inside her. I continued sliding in and out with deliberate, purposeful strokes as if I intended to carry on for an hour, for the rest of the night…. forever. Her stomach seemed to sway beneath her, and she thrust back, gasping with pleasure.

We carried on for what seemed an eternity. I felt very close to her, as though it wasn't just her body I was loving, but her soul. After an age, her breath quickened, and I sensed her orgasm building. I allowed mine to increase in harmony. She came writhing and screaming beneath me as I felt myself tingle inside her tight walls, squirting into her depths with a long, drawn-out gush.

I withdrew; Charlie rested her face on her arms as I stood on the floor behind her. She sighed and turned to look at me with those enormous, sparkling eyes. "God, Brax! I just can't get enough of you at the moment. I want more already."

I chuckled and tapped her ass lightly, still stuck proudly in the air on display for me. "Give me half an hour, and you can have as much as you want."

"I'm holding you to that."

"You can hold much more," I promised. "But if I give you more dick tonight, you must do something for me." She chuckled and asked, "like that, is it?"

"It is. You're not allowed to get angry at me."

I watched as she shot up in bed, turning to face me. "What did you do now?"

"I might have invited everyone for a sesh tomorrow night."

"Is that all?" I smirked, not expecting that reaction. "I already knew you would. You can't help yourself."

I cracked up laughing, asking, "are you serious?"

"What?"

"You want my dick that bad tonight that you'll bite your tongue?"

Chuckling, she replied, "yes."

"Who's the bad one now?"

"Are you saying no?" She tormented me by spreading her legs wide across the bed, giving me a full view of all glory. *Fuck the half an hour!* I lunged at her, ready to devour that sexy body again. When my arms wrapped around her and pulled her back up flat against my chest, I gripped her jaw and assaulted her collarbone towards her neck. "Aww god, Brax, I love you."

"I love you, my sexy Evil Midget."

CHARLIE

After a fantastic night at the awards, Brax and I had spent most of it wrapped around each other. It didn't matter how many times we went at it, my body screamed for more. *I was a fiend for him.* He was still asleep when my bladder woke me, so I got up without disturbing him. I froze in horror as I finished. "Brax…" I yelled, immediately repeating, "Brax!" I was almost hysterical. The fear was coursing through my veins, my body shaking uncontrollably.

He came racing through, hair dishevelled and wiping the sleep out of his eyes. "Charlie, what's wrong, babe?" he rubbed his eyes, then opened them, asking, "Did you call me in to see you pissing? Is this payback?"

I looked up at him, and he saw the horror on my face as I spoke. "Brax,

I'm bleeding."

"What? Where? What did you do to yourself?" he fumbled, not following what I was saying.

"No, I went to the toilet and am bleeding." It took him a moment before he realised what I meant.

"Babe, do you need me to help you get changed?" his calm disposition clicked in, soothing my raging anxiety. "Let's get up to the hospital, alright?" He supported me, and I put a pad on just in case as we dressed and headed to the hospital. "Are you alright? You're not in pain?"

"I feel alright, but bleeding can't be normal, right?" I asked, worried.

"Cutie, try not to stress. I'm sure everything's fine. Let's get you checked, alright?"

"I'm scared, Brax." He briefly turned his head from the road and saw the tears flooding my cheeks. He reached across into my lap, taking my hand, bringing it up to his lips and kissing my fingers delicately.

"Baby, I know, but it is alright. I'm right here. I've got you, okay?"

"What if something is wrong?" I couldn't stop the tears as I tried to sniffle them.

"Charlie, I need you to stop thinking like that," he spoke firmer, trying to shake me out of my haze. "Everything's going to be fine. The Doctor will check you, and they'll make sure our little Peanut and you are both safe." I took his hand in both of mine as he squeezed them tightly. We arrived at the hospital a short drive later and headed into the Emergency. We explained the circumstances of our visit before being taken back to an examination room.

The nurse returned a short while later and advised Dr. Anu was on shift and would be down shortly. She passed me a gown to change into, so I was ready once she arrived.

I had changed and sat down on the end of the bed, waiting as Brax watched me from the wall he'd been leaning against. I felt like a hurricane of pain hit me full on, my soul bleeding an ocean through my eyes. That was the enormity of my sobs. He raced over, standing between my legs, gripping me close to his chest, letting the emotional tidal wave expel. "Let it out, baby. I've got you. I'm not going anywhere."

"I'm so scared, Brax."

"Me too, baby...." he admitted softly. "But we have each other, and we'll be fine. Our baby is strong like us and will be alright too."

"God, I hope so!" I sobbed into Brax's chest for what felt like hours as he held me and stroked my back soothingly. Eventually, Dr Anu entered, and we both looked up to greet her.

"Oh, no! That's not a face I want to see from either of you," she spoke sympathetically. "The registry nurse has filled me in. Let's see what's happening, okay, and you tell me your side of the story, Charlotte, while I have a look. Is that alright?"

I nodded as I lay back, Dr. Anu ensured I was comfortable. "I woke up this morning and went to the bathroom, and as I wiped myself, I noticed I had heavy spotting."

Dr. Anu turned to Brax as she spoke. "I apologise, Brax, but I need to ask these questions." He nodded, understanding the more she knew, the better it was for us. "Was it darker than you would normally experience during your menstrual cycle?"

I thought about it for a moment and honestly had taken little notice. Truthfully, I just freaked out. Before I could stop, I started crying again as I tried to speak through my tears. "I don't know, I couldn't think.... I just panicked."

"It's alright. How about I do the examination, and if I have any further questions, I can let you know?" I nodded and lay back properly again as he came and stood by my head. He rested his arm around the top of the bed and stroked my cheek while holding my other hand in his. "I need to do an internal examination first, then we will get the transducer and have a look there as well."

I acknowledged as best I could while she sat at the end of the table to begin her examination. The lights on the ceiling were too bright for my eyes compared to the darkening gloom I could feel in the pit of my stomach. They blinded me causing me to wince into a blacker place as I felt her begin. Too much time elapsed as the tears flowed while he tried everything to provide me with some comfort. When I saw her sit back and remove her gloves, my heart stopped, my breath hitched, and I waited, desperately for an answer.

"Well, the good news is everything looks fine from the internal examination. I believe what you are experiencing is just pregnancy spotting. It's quite common," she assured me, smiling, "but I still need you to take it easier over the next few weeks. Were you doing anything before noticing the spotting?"

"No, I had just woken up and gone straight to the bathroom."

"Anything in the last few days? Strenuous activities lately?" she prompted. I suddenly looked at Brax and he realised simultaneously as Dr. Anu asked us what it was.

"Umm...."

"It's fine, babe. I'm pretty sure the Doctor has heard much worse." She looked at us, confused. "I'm just going to be blunt here," he offered.

"Please, do."

"We had a lot of sex last night."

Her shoulders relaxed, and a small smile crept across her lips. "Ahh, alright. Now that makes sense. Spotting and often bleeding after intercourse is usually a normal symptom of pregnancy," she began. "It's fairly common for women to experience this during their pregnancies, after sex, and sometimes for no reason. That was why I asked if you had noticed colouring, as these can show what's going on." I tried focusing, but my brain was still a clouded mess. "While unsettling to see this after sex, it doesn't mean that intercourse hurts the baby or that you must halt your sexual relations. Vaginal bleeding occurs in fifteen to twenty-five percent of pregnancies, usually in the first or second trimester."

"So what does that mean for me?"

"Chances are, Charlotte, bleeding after sex means your pregnancy is progressing normally. At your stage, I'm confident that this just resulted from natural changes to your cervix to accommodate your baby. During a pregnancy, the cervix goes through remodelling to prepare for the birth. This causes it to change shape, open up, shed cells, and become tender.

You probably won't feel it, but your body could be extra vulnerable to your partner's thrusting, which can lead to bleeding."

Brax spoke up before she could continue. "So we should try not—"

"No, I'm not saying that," she stopped him. "It's just something to keep in mind. In fact, sex during pregnancy is very healthy for you both. Now, how about we look and listen to your baby?"

"Please, I just need to see for myself." Brax agreed.

"Well, the good news is the baby is nearly four months or sixteen weeks, so we should be able to get some perfect images for you today." I looked at him, and he smiled, squeezing my hand. He moved down and kissed me softly before squatting next to me, his arm wrapped around my head again. Dr. Anu placed the sheet over my lower half and rolled the gown. After several minutes of moving around and checking the monitor, she smiled at us. "Baby is growing nicely. Perfect little parcel you have there."

"I always say it about her bump and get shut down. Why are you permitted to say it?" I nudged Brax playfully with my elbow.

"Because I'm coming from a medical standpoint." I couldn't help but chuckle as Dr Anu winked at me, squeezed some more jell out, rubbing it around with the transducer. After a few minutes, she hit a button, and we heard our baby's heartbeat fill the room. I burst into tears of relief while he held me closer and kissed my cheek sweetly.

"Shh, see, everything's fine, Cutie."

"He's right, Charlotte. That is a powerful heartbeat." Brax kissed me again as I gripped his head and buried my face in his neck, trying to calm myself. "And here she is. Your daughter wants to say hello."

My head flew towards the screen as I continued to grip him. His gaze was intent, transfixed, as we watched the screen, life swirling around us in slow motion.. "Sorry, you said...."

"You both mentioned at your last visit you wanted to know the sex of your baby when you could find out. Well, there she is. There is your daughter."

I looked at the screen as the tears fell more from a place of love this time. Brax froze, mesmerised by our baby.... his little girl. Tears rapidly appeared, so I reached out and ran my fingers, a feather touch, down his cheek, whispering his name. He looked at me before his head shot back to the screen. "That's our daughter. That's my little Pebbles?"

Chapter Thirty Four

BRAX

uck! I am going to have a daughter! This was huge, and I was absolutely elated. Sure, every man wants a son to carry on the name and be the next generation of the family, but deep down, I had been hoping I would have my princess. The copious amounts of times I had thought about it, there was something so endearing as to think I would have a daughter who could look just like her mother. Fuck, I would be a lucky guy! I was still on cloud nine when we got home, sitting down on the couch, lost in my head, picturing how my daughter would look, wondering if she would have her mother's blonde hair or my light brown. God, I hope she had her mother's eyes. I got lost in those, they sucked me in hook, line and sinker the first time I saw her.

It shook me out of my thoughts when I felt Charlie kiss my neck as she leaned over the back of the couch and wrapped her arms around my shoulders. I reached up to pick her hands off my chest, clasped them in mine and brought them to my mouth, kissing them. "You've been quiet, Batman?"

"Sorry, Cutie, I was thinking." She nuzzled closer and asked what about. "Just today, babe."

"And? How do you feel? You have said little since we left the hospital."

She squeezed my hands and asked, "Are you disappointed? Would you have preferred a son?"

I pulled to the side, pivoting in my seat to face her. My hand came up to grip her neck. "No!" The shock in my voice made it break slightly. "Not at all. I'm the complete opposite. My cheeks feel like they want to burst with happiness." The abundance of emotion spilling out caused me to blush. "I was sitting here thinking about what our daughter would look like," I daydreamed. "I hope she has your eyes."

"But I love yours."

"Too late, Charlie. I called dibs first."

She slapped me on the chest as she chuckled. "You can't call firsts, babe. It doesn't work like that."

"Too late, I already did." The moment I saw her nose scrunch with a smile, I moved forward and nipped softly at the tip.

"I love you. You wanna know what I was thinking about on the way home?"

"Always," I beamed, and I could see the crinkles under her eyes appear, the puffy aftermath of her earlier tears prominent.

"I was picturing what it would be like to see you with our daughter. You've always been the protector of our little family. She'll be so lucky to have you as a father."

"God, I love you." I reached up, wrapping my hand around her neck tighter, pulling her face closer to me as we explored each other's mouths, our tongues dancing delightfully. I caressed her skin and pulled her closer to me, destroying her mouth as I tried to get as far inside her as possible. My tongue tasted every crevice of her beautiful mouth, sucking, licking, and tasting, followed by some soft nibbling before diving back in. We were both panting as I opened my eyes when we finally slowed the kiss down. The same reflection of love greeted me. "So, wanna get naked?"

She pushed me backwards on the couch and stormed off as I cracked up laughing. "We literally just got back from the hospital, you asshole!"

"So I guess what you're saying is too soon?"

"Eat a dick, Brax!" She flipped me off over her shoulder.

"Aww baby love, you know I'm just messing with you. I love my feisty Midget!"

"I know, and you're also aware of how horny I've been lately, so I stand by my asshole comment." When I continued guffawing, she gave me the finger again.

She returned with a cup of tea and placed it on the coffee table, sitting beside me, so I grabbed one cushion and put it on my lap as she lay down. I reached out and rubbed her stomach softly, while watching the cricket on television and saw her look up at me and back at the television. I knew she wanted me to turn it off. "Nope, it's not happening!"

"Fine! I'll just have a nap then."

"It will do you a world of good. Especially before everyone arrives later this afternoon."

"Yeah, you're right." I leaned over and kissed her on the forehead, slouching further onto the couch as she settled in and drifted asleep. I watched the game and browsed through my phone when an idea hit me. A fucking *great* idea! Hopefully, she would be okay with it—I was pretty confident she would be, so I just did it, anyway.

I was lucky, too, as only one place had them, but it was on the other side of town, so I rang them and organised a courier to pick it up and drop it off the same day. I had no issue paying the extra freight charges. It would be worth it, as this was perfect for us.

An hour and a half later, I heard a car pulling up and shortly after; the doorbell went. "Mmm, Brax, is everyone here already? Why didn't you wake me?"

"No baby, just a delivery."

"What delivery?"

"You'll see in a second." I slipped her head off my lap and got to the door, signing for the delivery and sorting payment before thanking them and shutting the door back up. I brought the box back in and sat down next to Charlie.

"Well, what is it?"

I passed it over, saying, "Open it, baby." I watched as she unsealed the parcel and pulled the package out before looking inside. She peeked inside and immediately realised. An amused smile crept across her face, but I saw her eyes twinkling, telling me she loved the idea.

"For the reveal?" The shine in her eyes magnified and was the most beautiful sight in the world.

"Yes. What do you think?"

"It's perfect!" she squealed in excitement.

"I thought so too. Want to help me get it ready for tonight before we change?"

"Of course!" We set it up and headed to our room to get changed. Coming back down, we put some nibbles and finger food out, ready for everyone, and got the drinks out in the cooler box. We heard the doorbell, so I shouted, "we didn't lock it," as we finished taking the last of them out.

"Yo! The party is here!" Chester is always first, terrified of missing out.

"Through here, Fuckface," I hollered.

"Okay, Midget fucker!" We heard Chrissy giggle when Charlie yelled back at him, "Watch your mouth!"

"Sorry, Sweet Cheeks!" Chester with Chrissy headed in, greeting us. The others hadn't arrived yet, so Chester and I went out the back for a few cones while I filled him in about what happened this morning. "Fuck! That's rough. Thank God everything is okay, bro."

"Thought you didn't believe in God?" I couldn't help but joke with him.

"Well, if ever there was a time, this is it."

"Thanks, man."

Once our friends all arrived, we asked them to grab a seat in the lounge, waiting for them to settle. "So we have a little gift for you all."

Chester fist-pumped the air, the rest all laughing. "Fuck yeah! Because you love us."

"Sit down and shut up, Fuckface." He jumped up, carrying on more in defiance. "Or when you have finished, we can continue." I sat, waiting.

"Yeah, Chester, stay in your lane and stop ruining it for everyone else." Everyone laughed when April turned on Chester, eager to know the gift.

He sat dutifully, winking at her.

Charlie went down one side of the coffee table, while I went on the other. "So here is a joint from us, and we hope you all have a good night."

"Fuck yeah, now that's how you greet your guests!" Of course, Liam would be the most excited to have a blunt ready for him. Charlie held the box between us as we picked them out and passed them around, ensuring everyone had received one before we closed it.

We were just settling back in our seats when Mace animatedly jumped up. "Woah! Stop!"

"Woman! Why are you yelling?" I smirked at Liam, knowing his frustrations. I had one of those girls, too, that squealed when she got over-excited.

"Are you baboons shitting me right now?!" Charlie broke out in hysteria at hearing Mace call everyone baboons, while also having to cross her legs, so she didn't pee her pants.

"Holy shit! I will be right back," she turned to head down the hallway."

As Charlie shuffled towards the bathroom, Mace yelled again. "Stop!"

"Mace, I love you, but I'm not joining the Pissy Pants club."

"Two minutes or I'm coming in to get you." Charlie hurried off, and when she returned, the relief on her face was clear. Chester asked, "how'd you go in there?" Mace turned on him. "Monkey Nuts, stop! And you two!" She turned and pointed to us as we stared back with wide grins. "Why are all the blunts pink or purple? Do you two know something we don't?"

We laughed but didn't offer an explanation when Shane piped up. "Holy shit, Mace! You badass detective bitch!"

Chester jumped up on the couch, standing up on it, with sneakers, much to Charlie's disgust, as he yelled over everyone. "Are you telling me I'm getting a niece?"

Her initial anger before he spoke subsided as we both looked at each other, smiling before Charlie answered, "Yes. We found out this morning after an unscheduled hospital visit." I nodded in agreement with Charlie.

She'd barely finished speaking when Chester shouted again, "Fuck yeah! I shotgun Godfather!"

"Bud, you can't just shotgun, my daughter."

"Fuck off, Brax, I just did!"

"Chester, this is a child we are talking about, not a toy." I saw Charlie staring at him, wondering if he would realise.

"I'm not listening to your negativity either, Pregnant Midget of Tour."

Liam and Shane buckled over laughing before Shane added, "Fuck, that kills me every time he says it."

"Fine, then I'm naming my goddaughter."

"You wanker. I know what you did there." He laughed in my face and started begging for permission to name my child!

"Fuck no, Monkey!" We both looked at Charlie. "My daughter would have a stripper's name if you had your way. Something ridiculous like Candy, Cherry or Champagne. *Horrific.*"

The girls laughed before Chester beckoned to them to be quiet. "You Evil Midget, I might think it's nice."

"Nothing nice ever comes from you thinking, Chester." I watched him grab our Midget, pulling her in for a hug while whispering something. Her head shot up, meeting his gaze, eyes twinkling as a grin spread across her face broadly. Hmm, these two.... there was a uniqueness to their relationship, thick as thieves that you couldn't tell chalk from cheese.

He said something else, and then they laughed before he let her go. As he stepped back, I punched him in the arm. "What the fuck, you prick?"

"I've told you before, don't touch her."

"I didn't!" he protested his innocence. "I touched Pebbles! That's her incubator now, not Brax's playground." This fucking idiot had everyone tickled, especially when I lunged at him, tackling him to the ground as we put each other in a headlock.

Mark asked the rest, "Does anyone else feel like his constant taunts tonight are reminiscent of the night he found out Brax and Charlie were together?"

Liam immediately said "yes," before Shane explained for the benefit of Chris, Brett and April, "he spent twenty-four hours using every excuse to reference them fucking."

We finally stood up and grabbed some drinks, the guys took their blunts, heading outside. "Brax, you didn't grab yourself one?"

She went to take one out for me when I put my hand over hers. "I'm not having one, beautiful. I will just have a joint."

"What? Why?" Her confusion was adorable.

I stepped closer, snaking my arm around her waist. "I want to wait and have mine with you when our baby girl is born."

"Do you realise, every time you say something like that, I fall more in love with you?" she spoke tenderly, brushing her hand across my cheek.

"Then I will need to do it habitually for a lifetime."

"Kiss me." I leaned down, taking her lips gently as we made love to each other's mouths before pulling away.

"So what did Chester say?" I figured I would try my luck while she was loving on me.

Charlie giggled, "He told me what name he wants us to use for baby Pebbles."

"Yeah? And what's that?" Her index finger beckoned me closer, while she lent in to whisper it… I pulled back, her questioning eyes greeting me as my smirk spread.

"You know, I don't hate it."

"Me either," she almost giggled in excitement.

"It's so cute and feminine. I just hate agreeing with that pain in the ass."

"You know, I don't hate it myself," she chuckled. We joined the others outside, with me pulling her onto my lap. I was feeling more protective of them both after this morning's scare.

"So I have to ask, what happened this morning?"

"What do you mean, bro?" I was deep in my thoughts, leaving me with no clue what Chester was talking about.

"You mentioned inside you had a scare?"

This fucker just smirked at me. "You're an asshole," I ground out, unable to lunge at him with Charlie on my lap.

He burst out laughing hysterically in his chair as the rest sat there confused, before Liam asked, "What happened?"

"Yeah, Brax and Pregnant Midget of Tour, why did you have to go to the hospital?"

She sat up in my lap, shooting him a look that killed him ten times over already. "Eat a dick, Chester!" He blew her a kiss, Charlie flipping him the bird as she turned to the concerned others. "It was nothing in the end, guys. I had a little scare. Everything is perfectly fine and normal. I was just worried, as it's my first time and didn't know what to expect." The girl's sympathy and understanding were obvious and comforted her.

Shane asked, "what was it?" Charlie hid her face, mumbling, "Oh god, please don't ask."

"You nosey fucks, you don't need to know every aspect of their lives." I chuckled at Mace's observation.

"I just want to know what caused it?" Chester shrugged.

"Shut the fuck up, Monkey," Charlie spoke deliberately and slowly, pronouncing every syllable.

Mark sat forward, studying Charlie before he spoke. "Nah, Midget is bright red. Whatever this is, it's good. Now I wanna know," he pondered.

"I can tell you." Chester said, while she quickly squealed at him to "shut up."

"You're a dead man if you do, bro. You know the payback will be brutal. Choose wisely, fucker."

He laughed in my face and turned to Mark. "Remember the first night we found out they were together? What did I say they were doing?"

Mark thought about it for a minute before replying, "Fucking?"

"Ladies and gentlemen, we have a winner." Quicker than he could register, Charlie scrambled out of my lap, and I was fast to follow. While she put her hand over his mouth to stop him from saying any more, I grabbed the back of his chair, pulling it towards the pool.

He reddened with humour as he mumbled behind her hand when he realised the direction we were travelling. "Now," I told her and she stepped aside while I put all my weight behind it, swinging his seat around and tipping him into the pool.

It was everyone else's turn to roar, laughing as he swam back to the surface. That being said, it took two minutes before he started cackling. Once he dragged his wet ass out of the pool, he raced at Charlie and wrapped her in a bear hug as she tried to slap him. "You wanker, you started this!"

"I know, and I'm going to finish it too!"

"I swear you're impossible." He hugged her tighter again as she flicked his ear. When he grabbed it, she took the chance to get away and headed inside to change out of her now-wet clothes. I shouted, "better grab Dickhead some dry clothes out of my cupboard, baby."

She wandered back a short time later and chucked them at him.

"Thanks, but I need a towel."

"Well, you didn't ask for one." I chuckled at her sassy ass as I tapped it.

"Pregnant Midget of Tour, can I have a towel, please?"

"Nah, mate, I'm not your slave."

"You just want me naked instead. I get it." He dropped his pants without a care in the world to her horrified face, the rest of the boys expecting nothing less from that maniac.

Chapter Thirty Five

CHARLIE

It had been a long weekend. The gang practically lived in our house, too. Sometimes I felt terrible because I didn't have the energy to be as hospitable as I used to be. Brax struggled also, with me reeling him in a few times as his annoyance rose. He's the type of guy who would open his door to anyone. Still, he also went through times of solitude, where he needed to be locked in his recording studio we had installed downstairs. I would find him writing or putting together recent work. He liked his privacy, especially when we weren't on tour, and he could just be Braxton, not the artist. Chester also picked up on it and finally encouraged everyone to give us a break after last night, and I was pleased to have the house to ourselves. Honestly, it felt good to have some peace.

I'd taken a nap and woke mid-morning around ten thirty, surprised to see Brax still hadn't been to sleep. When Chester ushered everyone out a few hours ago, I figured he'd have his head straight down, since he didn't sleep last night.

Getting up and stretching, I went to the lounge room, looking around to no avail, before moving through to the kitchen and switching the kettle on. While I waited, I made my way downstairs, certain where to find him.

And sure enough, as I quietly opened the door, I found him fast asleep in his studio. His giant frame sprawled across the red leather sofa, baseball cap on, hand across his eyes, blocking out the light, too exhausted to move. I opened the door and headed over to the couch, sitting on the side of it near his waist, wrapping one arm across him, before leaning closer, kissing his neck and cheek with feather-light, soft, loving caresses.

After a few minutes, his hand gripped my arm and his head turned to me. "Hmm, stop it. I'm practically a married man."

"What if I don't want to? I missed you last night." I whispered into his neck as I continued to pepper him with kisses.

"Sorry, babe, after everyone finally left, I came here to pen an idea. I must have crashed when I'd finished."

"Why don't you have a coffee, then go back to bed for a few hours? I have the kettle on now if you want me to go make you one?"

"Nah, I'd prefer you to lie with me, babe." He opened his arms up, inviting me to move in beside him. I rested my head on his shoulder while he rubbed my back. He twisted his body towards me slightly and started stroking my stomach. "How did my girl sleep?"

"Good baby, I feel fine today."

"Just ensure you don't overdo it, please."

"You know, you could always persuade me to stay lying down if you're really that worried?" Brax opened one eye and glared at me, his gorgeous smile plastered across his face as he asked, "how would you like me to do that?"

"Are you saying you can't think of anything?"

He sat up suddenly, giving me a blank stare, asking, "you want a foot rub, don't you?"

"That's so sweet of you to offer." I winked with a smile.

"What do I get?"

"I won't brag too much when Liverpool wins later." His head rolled back in laughter as he put his flat palm across my face. "I wondered how long it would be before you brought that up."

"You better not have invited anyone over tonight, Brax? It's our teams!"

"No one is coming over tonight, I promise. It is just us." *Thank fuck.* "We can go to bed early and then get up for the game. Although let's just watch it in bed."

"Sounds perfect. I have to work on some of your new marketing today for Marcus. What are your plans?"

"I want to jot down some new lyrics for the upcoming album. We're aiming to have the songs penned down before we go to Melbourne next week."

We spent the day working, Chester and Chrissy coming around mid-afternoon. As they often did, Chester and Brax had been working on some lyrics together. He wanted to see if Monkey could finish the one he was only partially happy with.

The last thing I remembered was sending some campaigns off to Marcus that he wanted to review for the new album before crashing on the couch. The next thing I knew, I was waking to something wet in my ear, nearly jumping out of my skin. "What the fuck?" My head flung around. "Chester! Did you just stick your tongue in my ear?" After smirking, he licked his lips. "You're disgusting."

"You slept through my entire visit! No way in hell was I allowing that shit."

"I needed a nap," I explained. "We have a big game tonight."

"Oh, that's right, it is a potential divorce night here, right?"

"Correct. I shotgun Pebbles in the divorce settlement," Brax jumped in, answering before I could.

"You are not shotgunning our child as well, Brax!"

"Chester did," he shrugged.

I rolled my eyes at them both and turned to Chrissy. "Did you both want to stay for dinner since it's that time already? Saves you worrying about it when you get back?"

"That would be lovely. Can I help you with it while these two sort their lives out, or something productive?" I chuckled to Chrissy and said, "sure," as I got up from the couch and kissed Brax. I told the boys, "we'll give you a shout when dinner is ready," before we headed off to put it together.

After a nice dinner with Chester and Chrissy, we sat outside talking with them for a while. The boys had a blunt before seeing them off around seven-thirty. Brax locked up before joining me in bed. As he got in and cuddled behind me, I felt him rub his nose up my neck and kiss me softly. "I missed this last night. I never sleep as well as I do with you beside me."

"I'm right here, now," he kissed me again, wrapping his arms tighter, a firm hold that had me sinking into him.

When our alarms went off at three in the morning for the game, I felt like I'd just fallen asleep. I rolled over, opening my eyes, to find him smiling lovingly. "Morning baby, you look delicious," he whispered before sliding closer and pressing his lips to mine.

Our tongues danced and teased one another, kissing deeply, enjoying the bitter and sweet confection that was his taste. When we pulled apart, our desire was obvious in how our breathing had become haggard. I moaned when his hand swept up my thigh, across my hip, to my ribcage. My hands did not remain idle. I used the tops of my fingers to caress the muscle cords that lay under his back's smooth skin. I tickled his ribs, and he rewarded me with a quick bite to one of my shoulders, causing me to chuckle. He slid over me and pressed his hips against mine, holding his weight on his arms to not put pressure on my stomach. The evidence of his arousal was easy to feel. I wiggled against it, coaxing the head to lie just on the upper edge of my centre.

"Like that?" I whispered, sliding my hand between our warm flesh.

"Just a bit…." He answered back, a smirk that told me how much more he liked it. I wrapped my fingers around his shaft, stroking him. I toyed with his rigid tool, his hips moving slowly, then changing at a mere whim. Rolling back the skin, I teased the head, then jerked his shaft with a firm, gently pumping action. "Careful, baby, two can play that game. I know what you're doing."

"Mmm, what am I doing, baby?"

"You're trying to get into my head before the game starts." *Too funny!* We knew each other so well now. "Don't think for a second if you continue,

I won't bend you over and fuck you while I watch the game. We both know it wouldn't be the first time."

"You cheeky asshole. I love you." I gripped his face and pulled it down, kissing him quickly while tapping his ass.

"Morning, beautiful. Thanks for the wake-up call. You can finish me after the game." He jumped off me, pulling his track pants up, grinning, "With your mouth."

I grabbed his pillow and threw it at him as he jumped out of the way. "You shithead!"

"I'll get you a cup of tea, babe?" he questioned. "I'm just going to make coffee."

"Thanks Sexy."

"Stop it, Evil Scouse Midget." He wasn't gone that long before returning with our drinks, settling in to see the teams take the pitch.

"You know you're going to lose, right?"

"I'll laugh my head off when we pummel Loserpool."

"There will be no pummeling on your end tonight."

He turned, looking at me, shocked for a moment. "Really? Not even after the game?"

Less than fifteen minutes into the game, I bounced on the bed as Virgil Van Dijk buried it to give Liverpool the lead. He bear hugged me across the chest, "My daughter doesn't need to be involved in your shitty behaviour." I laughed in his face and told him, "spoken like a true Manc."

The game continued, and since we already had the lead, it didn't take long for the dirty tactics to come out from the Mancs. "Can't beat us, so trying to cripple instead?" I bit my lip and tried not to giggle as I turned and glared at Brax.

"You're lucky it is halftime, and I need another coffee, or I would bend you over for that." I shrugged my shoulders and asked, "yeah, and?"

"Spank the crap out of your sassy ass."

"And that's punishment?"

"Sit down, woman, before you can't for a week!" He headed out to get another drink, and when he returned to bed, I tried to cuddle in front of him. "One word, missy, and you're out of here."

"Don't you missy me. Just because you are losing."

"Forty-five minutes to go, sugar tits." I smacked his hand when he tried to pinch my nipple. "You're still going to lose."

"You need to find the net to make that happen."

The second half started making him agitated as they tried vainly to chase us. "God, you Scousers shit me, whinging that you're so hard done by and have all the refs in your pockets."

"Two names, Brax. Howard Webb and Lee Mason!"

"Never heard of them."

I cracked up laughing at this lying brat. "So full of it. You know you always got your way with them. Not my fault your team fell from grace."

"I'll give you fell." He lunged at me and started tickling me, knowing all too well it would set my bladder off. "Take it back, Charlotte Maree."

"Never!" I said that as he went to tickle me again, but I caught Mo Salah line up the net over his shoulder and bury it for the second goal. "Goal!" His head turned toward the television, before he threw his hands in the air, frustrated.

"Fuck this. I'm done!"

"At Ninety-three minutes, you aren't winning." He snatched the remote and flicked the television off as I cackled at him, sulking. "Who's the sore loser now, Manc?"

"I'm losing nothing. But you're about to gain an entire load." He brought my hands above my head as he straddled my hips. "Of me!"

BRAX

Liverpool winning still had me pissed two days later, Evil Midget winding me up was worse. I was even more annoyed that I had to face the possibility that they would win the league this year, and my cutie would never let me live it down. Being sixteen points clear at the top of the table was leaving a fucking sour taste in my mouth. *Fuck them, Scousers!* It was now Wednesday, and I was packing to head to the Gold Coast for a few days to sort these tracks down with the boys, as well as recording our newest music video.

"Hey, Brax?"

I left our room and stuck my head in the lounge before replying. "What's up, Cutie?" She pointed to the television, and I looked up to see them still going on about Loserpool. "You're dead to me, Evil Midget, and I'm taking our daughter with me."

"Love you too."

"Then come and prove it before I have to get my flight," I challenged her. "Okay."

"Really? Did that just work?"

"Who knows?" she teased back. "Can I wear my Liverpool shirt at the same time?"

I rolled my eyes at her. "Don't worry, I've had blue balls for over two days. I'll survive without that imagery. Thanks anyway." She cracked up laughing, that wicked cackle I loved so much that it made her sound as cheeky as ever. I returned to packing, and after a few minutes, she walked into the room. She pressed against my back, her hand sliding around my waist and down to my shorts. She undid the button and tugged the zipper. "Can I help you?"

"No. I'm going to help myself."

I exhaled heavily as she wrapped her fingers around my stiffening dick. "Agh…. Mmm, goddamn it, Charlie." I turned and kissed her deeply while her hand stayed firmly locked around me. Pulling out of the kiss, I watched as she lowered to her knees, that sexy ass popping out for my benefit as she leaned forward and pulled my shorts down. Her nails dragged up my thighs and gripped my boxers, pulling them down. I had to look away from her eyes for a minute before the heat of the moment got the better of me. She began kissing and licking the plump head, laving the underside with relish. "Aww.. yes baby… that's my girl."

I slid my fingers through her hair and guided her mouth gently, grinding my hips in a motion that had her moaning on me wildly. She took the hint and closed her mouth around me, taking as much down her throat as possible. She hummed against me when I strengthened my grip on her hair, just enough to make her needy for more. "Good girl, baby… such a pretty little mouth you have, Charlie." She looked up at me through her lashes, the bulge in the side of her cheek becoming more prevalent, and my blood rushed faster, the grip on her hair tightening. "You're so sexy, baby…."

I kept up the words of encouragement as she glided her lips over me, sucking furiously, like a woman possessed. I seemed to be made for her mouth and she was relentless. She was wholly absorbed in sucking, licking, kissing and stroking me. "Fuck! Charlie, lift your ass up, baby. I need to play with that sweet pussy."

She spread her knees as much as she could on the floor, and I leaned over her as she pushed her ass in the air, not letting go of the grip her mouth had on my cock. I slid my hand inside her pants, letting it run over her ass cheeks, stroking and pinching lightly, pushing my fingers further into her abyss as I rotated my hips in time with her sucking.

I began fucking her mouth earnestly, tugging on her pussy lips and fingering her clit in rhythm. Soon she was moaning around me, so I slid two fingers in and began a slow circular motion over her nub with my thumb. She pulled in a thrusting rhythm that had me moaning wildly and sucked me deep while massaging the underside of the head with her flat tongue. "Damn it, baby girl, take me, please. I want you to taste me."

I held her head over my rocketing cock as I filled her mouth. She swallowed as fast as she could, but the force of my orgasm sent some trickling back down my shaft. After the last thrust, she began licking the rest of my swollen cock, massaging my balls and thighs. I reached down, picking her up, trying to work my hand back down her pants. "Mmm, no, baby. I just wanted to give you a treat to go away with. You can have me when you get back."

"Such a tease! You know I can't get enough of you. I'm aware it's only two nights, but I'll still miss you."

"You're going to be so busy the time will fly without even realising it."

"I hope so." I checked my watch and realised I needed to get showered and go. "Baby, I'm just gonna grab a shower. Can you drive me to the airport? I get a bit more time with you then."

"Of course."

Soon we were on the road to the airport when I had to ask for my peace of mind, "You remember how to separate the alarms when you go to bed, so the other zones are secured, right, Cutie?"

"I do. We'll be fine," she assured me.

"I just need to be sure you'll be okay while I'm away."

"We will, baby, I promise." I reached over and put my hand on her thigh, stroking it with my thumb as she drove towards the airport. After an hour of battling into Sydney traffic, we finally got there, and I saw the boys waiting out the front for me. "Have a safe flight, Brax. I love you, and I'll pick you up on Friday, alright?"

"Thanks, Cutie. I love you too. I'll text you when we land, but I'll wait to call you until I return to the hotel tonight. At least then I have some privacy." She smiled, and I leaned over, kissing her deeply as my hand stroked her belly. "Now, both my girls behave until I get home." She said no promises as I leaned down and kissed her stomach. "Be good for mummy Pebbles."

She smiled and waved as I got out and grabbed my luggage, blowing her one more kiss before joining the boys. She waved, driving off and Chester asked, "Is she missing you already?"

Before I could answer, Mark spoke up. "Nah, I reckon he's the one that didn't wanna go. He can't handle being apart from Midget."

"Shut up, Dickhead." They laughed and said, "it's true."

Security assisted us through the airport, which was appreciated as we saw people whispering and pointing when they recognised us. Chester elbowed me in the side, drawing my attention. "Have you guys even set a date for the wedding yet?"

"Not yet, bud. I don't want to stress her anymore at the moment. And she will overdo it." He agreed. We knew what she was like.

"True. Stressed Midget brings out Evil Midget," he joked.

"Evil midget is a by-product of your behaviour, man."

We got on the flight and settled, but as it was only an hour, it wasn't long before we were descending. As we landed and exited the plane, I quickly texted Charlie," Hi baby, we're here. Heading straight to the studio for a few hours before going to the hotel. I'll call you tonight when I get in. I love you."

"Your girls' love and miss you already, baby." I had barely locked my phone when her reply came through, and I noticed a photo attached as I looked at my screen. Sliding it open, I found a picture of her standing in front of our mirror with her shirt rolled up and that beautiful bump I love so much on display.

"Damn, I love this! Thanks, beautiful." I locked my mobile and put it back in my pocket as we headed to our uber and went to the studio.

We arrived, greeted everyone, including the producers, who notified us they wanted to lock down the recording and video for our new song today with the guys from Canada. We said hello to everyone and chatted with them while we waited for the studio to complete the set-up. Not long after, the producer came over and started introducing the casting selections.

"Right, I want to start by fully recording the vocals today. We can shoot the film clip first thing tomorrow morning then. Your media team has given me the concept for the video, and the casting has been done, so I would like you to meet everyone ready for tomorrow morning." The Producer addressed the room. He pointed to a team of actors, and models selected for the film clip, who all waved. I noticed one girl looked at us a lot as she pushed her chest out, and I internally rolled my eyes when the Producer brought her forward for introductions. Honey blonde hair and a decent figure, but trying way too hard and stinking of desperation. "This is Melissa. She will be playing the main lead in the clip."

"Hi, boys." She said in her sickly fake voice and waved at me. I smiled and nodded politely.

"Now that's done, everyone head to the dressing rooms, get your stuff sorted and let's record in an hour?" We all agreed and headed off, stopping to grab a drink on the way through and having a quick chat with the stagehands.

"Geez, I'm surprised she didn't drop her pants there and then for you, bro," Chester said as he came over to grab a drink and slapped me on the shoulder.

"Right! I had to force myself not to eye-roll. Desperate hoes."

"You're practically a married man, so you can't stand it," Mark told Liam to shut up when he said that, as he wasn't far behind me.

We headed off to our changing rooms, and as I opened my door to go in and put my stuff down, I saw Melissa in there waiting. I instantly felt the rage grow, especially when I saw what she was wearing.

Standing before me was this desperate slag, wearing only a yellow pair of panties with the Batman logo over her vag and a matching crop top. "So I hear your nickname is Batman, Brax? Is that right?"

"What the fuck are you doing?"

Chapter Thirty Six

BRAX

The moment I opened my door and saw that bitch, I was about to lose my shit. The first fucking trip without Charlie and some wannabe hoe pulled this crap! "So, do you like it?"

I ignored her and continued to stand on the other side of the door… when suddenly an idea came to me. I pulled my phone out and hit FaceTime. Thankfully, it didn't take too long for her to answer, and the black screen filled with her beautiful blue eyes within seconds, that cute little button nose turned up at the end and those stunning pink lips that tasted heavenly on mine. Her blonde hair was down, long and luscious, just like the rest of her. "Damn, there's a sight for sore eyes. Hi, beautiful." I blew a kiss as I had the camera on me before I turned it around on this slag in front of me. "Charlie, check this crap out. Tried to come to my dressing room, and this thing is supposed to be the professional I'm working with on the film clip."

Melissa's face dropped when she realised what I'd done and that Charlie could see everything. "Your first trip on your own in ages, and you have thirsty hoes like this to deal with? You've still got it, babe."

"Pathetic, right? I almost vomited in my mouth. Why would any self-respecting woman think a guy would find this appealing? No one can make a whore a housewife."

"Actually, it's funny." My eyebrows shot up. "What was the endgame? Considering our engagement and child has been all over the news, she still tried this? Maybe she wanted to use you to make a name for herself, babe?"

"Maybe," I shrugged, "but I don't know why she thinks I would settle for a cheap knockoff when I have the Versace waiting at home for me."

"Aww, smooth, babe. Turn the camera back around. I would much rather look at you than that. With any luck, she will get the hint and leave while she still has some dignity."

"I'm not sure she had to begin with if she thought this was a good idea."

"Good point, handsome. I took a screenshot of her while you had the camera up. I'll send it to Marcus to sort out."

"Thanks Cutie. Make sure they fire her, please."

"Of course, my love. Do you want me to stay on the phone until she gets the hint and leaves?"

"Please, babe, I don't trust her not to pull any more shit, or lie that something happened." I completely ignored Melissa as she stood there embarrassed, her cheeks bright red and shuffling her weight unevenly over her legs. I sat on the couch and continued talking to Charlie as I looked back at her beautiful face on the screen. "So, how're my girls?"

"Missing you, papa bear."

"Aww... let's see my little Pebbles."

She turned the camera to her belly and pulled her shirt for me. "See, you have missed nothing in the few hours you've been gone." She rearranged her shirt back down before asking, "has she left?"

"She's rushing out the door as we speak." I watched until the door shut and she exited.

"I'm sorry you had to go through that, baby."

"It's not your fault, but you can make me feel better. Put that camera back down, but a little lower this time." I wiggled my eyebrows.

"Behave, it's two days," she chuckled.

Chester swung the door open, quickly realising I was on the phone to Charlie. "You two face fucking already?" She rolled her eyes at me on the screen. "Hey, Pregnant Midget of Tour, are you dressed? Is it safe to come in? Or not dressed? Because that works too."

The other guys walked in seconds later, hearing the end of that and shouted "hello," to Charlie as she smiled and said, "That might be my cue to let you go, babe. You good now the guys are there?"

"Yeah, thanks for the save, baby."

Shane quickly shouted out, "What save?"

"I'll let Brax explain," she said. "Behave, kids. Love you all. Love you more, Brax."

As they shouted back, Chester had to get the last word in. "Look after my Pebbles for me, Pregnant Midget of Tour."

"That's my child, asshole!" I could see Charlie was still humoured as she hung up when Chester corrected me to say the "band's child." I texted her to let her know I would call her when I returned to the hotel tonight. Tossing my phone on the couch next to me, I sat back and took my cap off momentarily, running my hands through my hair as I exhaled heavily. "Who has a blunt?"

Mark chucked me one as they all sat down, and Liam held up the light before asking, "What's wrong, man? You look pissed."

"I am Liam. Hang on, I will show you." I grabbed my phone and texted Charlie, asking her to send me the screenshot she'd taken so I could show the guys. A minute later, when it came through, I opened it, turned the phone and showed them. Chester immediately buckled over, laughing his head off. "Shut up, asshole. It's not funny."

"It kind of is."

"Is it Shane? Would you find it amusing if it happened to you? Better still, would Kendall?"

"Point taken, man," he said apologetically. "I just meant these thirsty hoes will try anything."

"I swear, I wish Charlie was here."

Mark cracked up laughing as I turned to look at him. "So she could crucify her like Claire on the regional tour?"

"Fuck yeah! That shit was hot!" Chester smirked.

"I want to tell you to fuck off right now, but I also want to agree with that comment." He laughed and decided not to take it any further, realising I gave him a free pass from another punch.

"So what did Midget do? Blow a head gasket?"

I told Liam, "not this time. In fact, she did the opposite and laughed." The guys didn't seem to believe me at first and asked if I was being serious. "Absolutely.... right before she called her a thirsty hoe." They all cracked up as we knew that was definitely the Evil Midget in her. "She took a screenshot and sent it to Marcus. I want her fired. I'm not working with that slut."

"Makes you wonder when slags like her will realise they might be good for an hour, but even then, it's not worth it."

I looked at Chester and smirked at his comment. "Is that the voice of experience? Say, Lizzie, for example?"

"Exactly her! No one has time for a bunny boiler on their hands."

"I just don't want a cheap knockoff, Chester, not when I have the real thing at home." It was that simple.

"You don't have to explain, bro. We fully get it. I mean, shit, look at us a couple of years ago. When we first got together. We hit the jackpot, none of us thought we ever would, and half of it comes down to those girls." I fist-bumped Shane when he finished. He knew the score.

"Except Chrissy. She pulled the short straw with that loose cannon."

"Fuck off. She loves my Monkey Nuts. Who wouldn't!"

Shane turned to Chester and asked him, "what's the deal there anyway, mate?" None of us had ever really seen the guy caught up like this.

"Hard to explain, but what I do know is I look forward to seeing her. I want her around me. Can you explain what it was with Kendall? Or Mace or Charlie?"

"Nah, man, sometimes you just know it's right," I told Chester as I patted his back. We finished a blunt and returned to the studio, ready to record. I was thankful there was no sign of Melissa, but I made a note to follow up on it later with Charlie or Marcus. We concentrated on getting into the booth with Chris to lock down these vocals. After about a dozen takes, I was thankful when the producer called it for the night. My throat was raw as hell, and I could feel the pain stinging the back of my tonsils every time I swallowed. It was also getting late, and I had promised to call Charlie... no, I wanted to speak to her.

The guys and I packed up as fast as possible and said we would see everyone in the morning. We got an uber to the hotel, and I saw a message from Marcus confirming we had fired Melissa. A replacement would be ready for filming tomorrow, but we'd have to push it back to the afternoon.

Once we arrived, I asked the guys to give me half an hour before coming around. I wanted to speak to my girl, which they understood as they also had calls of their own. I fell on the bed in my hotel room and checked the time. It was ten, and I hoped I would catch her still awake, but I wasn't sure. After five rings, I heard her sleepy voice. "I tell you my fiancé is out of town, and you leave it this late to call me?"

"Sorry, I guess you were expecting your other boyfriend?"

"Absolutely! I figured you would have some thirsty hoe waiting in your hotel?"

I cracked up laughing as I begged her, "don't remind me."

Once I stopped chuckling, Charlie asked, "how did the rest of the day go?"

"Superb. We got all the vocals and instrumentals down. It's just filming the video clip tomorrow and Friday morning. Then home!"

"You need some honey. Your throat sounds sore." It was. "Did Marcus contact you and tell you we have fired her?"

"Yes, babe, thank you for sorting that."

"We're a team." She reminded me. "I'll always be your biggest fan."

"I know, it's why I love you, my Robin."

"So... what are you doing?" Her voice was laced with a cheeky seduction.

"Just laying on the bed. Are you tucked up for the night?"

"Yeah, but your daughter stole your pillow."

"You mean her mother has?"

"Same, same. I like it smells of you when you're not here."

"So that means you are wearing my favourite outfit as well."

Curiously, she asked, "and which one might that be?"

"You in a cute pair of panties and one of my t-shirts. I seriously love that shit." Charlie and I got lost in our conversation when I heard a knock at the door. "Hang on, baby, someone's at the door."

She mumbled, "Chester," I laughed and said, "more than likely." I headed into the lounge and checked the door, and sure enough, it was the guys' back, so I let them all in. "Alright, beautiful, I'm going to let my two babies get some sleep and have a blunt with the guys before I do the same. Love you. Please make sure the alarms are on."

"Already set it, locked and checked the doors, Brax. I'll be fine. Remember, I lived alone for a long time before you."

"I know, but now you're mine to keep safe, just like our Pebbles. Speak to you in the morning." We hung up, and the boys and I moved out to smoke. I told them that Melissa had been fired, and we all seemed more at ease with the fact that any potential trouble had been eliminated.

After a couple of blunts, we called it a night and headed to bed. Waking up to my alarm the following day, I turned it off, grabbed my phone, and got out of bed to fetch a coffee. I saw a message from Marcus confirming that he had hired the replacement for the film clip and they would be available by lunchtime today while I was waiting for the kettle to boil.

I called Charlie to let her know. "Hi, you've called Charlie. I'm sorry I can't take your call right now, but if you leave your name, number and a brief message, I'll call you back as soon as possible. Thank you."

"Hey, Cutie! Guessing you're already busy at work, just wanted to ring and say good morning. Marcus left me a voicemail. I'll fill you in when you call back. Love you!" I grabbed my coffee and a blunt and went and sat on the veranda, waking up before it was time to get ready.

A little over an hour later, when the boys and I met out the front to get our ride down to the studio, I had just got in when my phone buzzed with a text from Charlie. "Sorry I missed your call, I've been in and out of meetings since seven this morning. Have an amazing day, but I already know you will." I smiled, loving how even her messages could instantly change my mood.

We arrived at the studio, and it surprised me to see Marcus as we walked in. "What the fuck are you doing here?" I asked, slightly amused at the sudden visit.

"Hey mate! I figured I should show my face after the shit you put up with yesterday. Sorry about that."

"Not your fault, M. Thanks for handling it, though."

"Well, let's just hope the replacement I found is much more professional."

"Probably not if Marcus picked her," Chester joked.

"Could have been worse if you had a say." We heard Marcus' phone ring, and he excused himself to take it. We put our stuff down and grabbed a drink while we waited briefly. "Sorry about that, boys. It was Melissa's replacement, letting me know she had arrived. I'll be right back so I can introduce you all."

"No worries, mate." Marcus headed out, and we all sat and grabbed a drink as we waited. I heard the door go behind me and saw the guys look up. The shock on their faces was immediate. I flung my head around in my seat, and when I saw who was with Marcus, I flew out of my chair.

"Charlie! What are you doing here? Why didn't you tell me you were coming?"

I raced over to her and threw my arms around her waist. I bent my knees to kiss her, as she reached out and touched my cheek. "Hi babe, we missed you."

"Fuck, am I glad to see you. M was just getting that hoe's replacement, so at least with you here, I know there won't be any more problems. So where is she, anyway?"

"Right here, mate." Charlie looked at me, smiled, and waved.

"You are going to do the film clip with me?"

"Sure. I mean, if you want me to?"

CHARLIE

After Brax video-called me yesterday, I immediately got off the phone, called Marcus and let him know what had happened. I sent him the screenshot, and it reminded me of one of the many things I loved about this group.... we all had each other's backs without question. Marcus was just as pissed as I was the moment he received it.

He called Melissa's agent to notify them of what had transpired and fired her, while I rang around to find a replacement. After about half a dozen phone calls, he came into my office, confirming the agency blacklisting from any future work with us, and advised them to get her off the set immediately. I told him of the troubles I was having to find a replacement. The specific requirements meant they needed additional time to scout their talent pool.

We toyed with switching to a brunette to accommodate the filming schedule, but M was insistent there was a specific aesthetic the bands wanted to achieve. I spent another hour making calls. While a couple of candidates were emailed over, we wanted something else.

I was going through another email of potential models when Marcus spoke up. "I have an idea. Hear me out before you freak out."

I looked up over my laptop as I spoke. "Okay... this sounds ominous."

"I think I know the perfect replacement we can use."

"Great!" I sat taller, asking, "who?"

"You!" My eyes immediately flew open as I squealed at him. "Think about it for a minute. It makes perfect sense." I sat back in my chair, allowing him to explain himself. "The video is an intimate scene to match the song. Who else is he going to feel more comfortable with, depicting intimacy? He wouldn't even have to act, and let's be honest, we both know he is a shit actor... lucky he's gifted lyrically."

I had to giggle when he said that. "I suppose that much is true."

"The realism of the video would be out of this world. You fit the part perfectly. Obviously, since we all know Brax wrote it about you."

"I can't act, Marcus, or take direction to save my life. That is why I hide behind a camera."

"But that's just it, isn't it? You wouldn't have to act, either of you!"

"I don't know about this. It's something we would have to check with Brax first."

"I really don't think we do. In fact, I think it would be the best possible outcome for him. And look, if it isn't, I will take the blame for it. It's on me. Just go home, pack your stuff, and get on the plane with me in the morning. I'll sort flights and everything else now." I insisted I needed to call and let Brax know. "Trust me, Midget, this is one surprise he will love."

"Alright, but if it backfires, it's on you."

"Agreed." Marcus got up and left to make the arrangements.

So there I was, standing before Brax, who had just been told I was Melissa's replacement. His face was utterly void, expressionless. I could not understand how he felt about this, and I was positive that was his intent. "Well?"

He took my hand and turned to speak to everyone. "We will be right back. I need to speak to Charlie alone."

Chester chuckled out loud as he spoke. "Bullshit, you are going to speak. I bet you end up fucking. Let's go have a blunt while we wait." He started dragging me off, I turned to Marcus, glaring at him and pointed my finger. I warned him if this backfired, I would strangle him and then some. He shrugged his shoulders, and I was about ready to lunge at him.

We walked down to his dressing room and pulled me inside, shutting the door. He stepped closer and pinned me against the door with his hands pressed on either side, just above my shoulders. He looked down as I glanced up to meet his intense stare. "Hi, Brax."

"Why didn't you tell me?"

I fumbled under his scrutiny. "Agh.... Marcus thought you might appreciate the surprise." I shrugged my shoulders, trying to deflect.

"Marcus? Is that right?"

"Yes. It was his idea." I searched his eyes, desperate for a read on his feelings, but this shithead always had been good at playing the bluff. He pressed closer to me, leaning on his elbows now, pushing his hips closer, while continuing to scrutinise me.

"And what did you think about this idea?"

"I… umm, I thought…" He moved closer, brushing his nose against my neck as I reached up and gripped his forearms.

"You thought?" I felt his warm breath brush across my skin when he spoke, a shiver starting in the base of my spine and running up to explode in a combustion of tingles at the bottom of my neck.

"I thought he had a valid argument."

"A valid argument, hey?" I could hear the humour in his voice as he mumbled his reply into my skin. "Do you want to know what I think?" He gently bit my earlobe, the shiver causing my knees to buckle.

"Yes." I whispered as I leaned my head into him slightly.

"I think I will be so worked up after a day of filming with you, come tonight, I will seduce you, Charlie, and you'll love every minute." He captured my lips, arms encircling me while pulling my body into him and our tongues danced together. I ran my nails through his hair, gripping him tightly around the neck as he held me with equal force. He moved out of our kiss as I slid off my tiptoes and tapped my nose. "Let's go make some magic."

He took my hand and led me out of the changing room, and just as Chester said, we found it empty. Heading out the front, we saw them all sitting across from the building and walked the road to join them. "Woah! That was quick."

Brax pushed Chester into his chair as he replied. "Shut up, idiot. If I started, we wouldn't get any filming done today. She can wait until tonight."

"Oh, I can wait, can I?" I turned and gave him a questioning look.

"Yes! Just like you and Marcus concocted this and made me wait."

I told him, "shut up," when Mark laughed and asked, "did that leave a burn mark?"

"Does this mean you two will dry hump in front of us all day, just for a change?" Charlie quickly slapped Chester as he laughed and grabbed her around the neck, pulling her into a hug.

We headed back into the studio and we took everyone to the wardrobe to get ready, which didn't take long, so we were soon out recording.

I sat on the end of the bed as the director signalled action, and Charlie walked towards me. I realised just how fucking lucky I was to have all the things I loved the most right here at this moment. Her fingers brushed against my skin, wrapped around my neck, and pushed me back onto the bed. *I had goosebumps.*

It would have been so easy to get lost with her at that moment, as I do with every intimacy we share. But as much as it was more in vain than anything else, I had to remind myself we were here to film for the clip. There was only so much of my private life I will share with the entire world.

We got a good half of the video filmed today before they cut. Charlie and I headed back to get changed into our clothes before returning to join everyone. "Guys, come here! You need to see this." Marcus was hovering over one monitor, checking out the footage from today. "I love this print from the pool scene."

He had the photographer freeze and pull it up so we could see. They completely submerged us in the Infinity Pool, the ocean backdrop and cliffs illuminated in the green lights of the shoot and nothing more than the night sky. Brax was before me, dressed in a grey t-shirt, staring dead at the screen. I had my hand on his neck, nails gripped to his skin as my face hid in his neck.

As I took it in, Brax was the one to speak first. "Almost as good as my fiancée's work."

Marcus laughed as I told him, "that was smooth."

"I try." We finished watching the rest of the filming they had completed, and Brax wrapped his arms around my waist, kissing my cheek. I could feel the smile on his lips and knew he was enjoying this as much as I was.

Once it finished, Marcus and the videographer were talking when Brax spun me to face him. "Come on then. Time to get back to the hotel for a shower and change clothes before we go out."

"Why? What's going on?"

"I'm taking you out to seduce you. I thought I already made that clear?"

Chapter Thirty Seven

BRAX

We spent the afternoon filming the video clip for our new song with the guys from Canada, and most of that involved having my beautiful girl wrapped around me. If someone had asked if I would be in a place where everything I loved was in one spot, I would have told them that's the dream, right? But today, it became a reality. The music, which had been the biggest part of my life for as long as I could remember, the only woman I've truly loved standing side by side with me doing it, and to top that off, she was carrying my child. What a lucky son of a bitch.

Once finished, I told her we were heading back to the hotel, showering, and then I was taking her out to spoil her for the night. I desperately wanted to spend time alone, but I also wanted to talk about some things.

While Charlie was finishing getting ready, I told her to text me when she wanted to leave so I could meet her out the front so I could have a smoke with the boys first.

I had Chester barking at me when I arrived. "Can I ask you a question?" Without looking sideways, I said, "depends what it is?"

"The shoot today… Was it just me who noticed how much these are filling out?" I watched him indicate to his chest that Charlie's breasts changed with her pregnancy.

"You Fuckhead! You really think I would have this conversation with you?"

"The way she's going, she'll be a walking advertisement for Devondale farmers soon." The others laughed as I put him in a headlock and told him to "stop now."

"You wanted that shit immortalised in the clip so you can look back on it. I know how you work. Spank bank material!"

"What the fuck are you going on about?" I locked my arm tighter.

"It's the same with the night before the regional tour. You put her in your bed so you got her, and now you're filming, so you can look back on it in years to come." I turned the headlock on him as he laughed harder at me and jabbed me in the ribs.

"You're fucked in the heat." I agreed when Mark said that and pushed Chester away from me when I felt my phone vibrate.

"Unlucky asshole, Charlie just texted. I'm going now." I locked my phone, stuffing it in my pants again, while saying goodbye to everyone.

"Or is that coming?"

"Fuck off, Chester!" I flipped him off over my shoulder as they laughed, heading back down the road. When I saw her out the front, I couldn't help but drop my eyes immediately. I knew we were not trying to get pregnant, but I couldn't lie, this was the best thing that ever happened. And I loved every minute. Whatever it was, I had changed since seeing the transformations in her body, carrying my baby, which had led to me thinking more about marrying her. We hadn't locked it in, or discussed it since getting engaged, although if it was up to me, I would have done it yesterday. I was *so* ready.

I reached for Charlie, wrapping one arm around her back, the other gripping into her hair, while my lips greeted hers with love. The sweetheart-cut black dress clung to her feminine features and wrapped around to gather on her hip, now exposing our precious cargo. "Hi, beautiful."

"Hi yourself." She looked up and smiled at me as her fingers crept across my neck.

"You look breathtaking."

"Thanks, baby, but take this, you smell like weed." She passed me a piece of chewing gum and a small bottle of aftershave she had put in her bag.

"Really?" I did a quick sniff check of my breath and clothes.

"I smell everything at the moment. Believe me." I smirked, unable to help myself, asking, "So, can you smell my arousal?"

Laughing hard, she told me to, "stop it. You promised to feed me and seduce me. I don't see any seducing yet…"

"Baby, let's be honest. Your idea of seducing is when I throw you over my shoulder." I reached forward, cupping her cheek in my hand, my thumb softly brushing her lip. "You're right though, I will romance you a little tonight."

"Just a little?"

"Well, I still know you love your Caveman. You can have him when we get back."

"By the way, you look delicious. I'm pretty sure I forgot to say that."

"Stop it! Don't turn the tables or we are not going anywhere."

"No, it wasn't like that," she insisted. "I just wanted to remind you how much I appreciate you."

"You ready to go?" I smiled. Wrapping my arm around her waist, we headed to the valet who organised a ride for us.

Pulling into the restaurant ten minutes later, I walked around to help her out, when she looked up, seeing the restaurant's name, she rewarded me with that chuckle I love so much. "Are you serious?" Nodding, I laughed back as she giggled even harder. "Sea-duction! Nice play on the word, babe."

"It was pretty good, right? Well, that's the seduction part done. Can we go back to the hotel now?"

"You crack me up. Come feed me first?" She pulled me by the arm towards the restaurant, heading in to be seated by our waitress. After we placed our orders and waited for them to come out, Charlie reached across and took my hand. "Thank you for this. It is nice to go out. Just the two of us."

"It is, babe, but I also wanted to thank you for what you did today. Doing that clip with you by my side meant the world to me."

"Me too, Brax."

"I also wanted to talk to you about something, so I needed to get away from the boys tonight."

"Sure, what's up?" The waitress brought out our meals, and I stopped and waited for her to leave before I continued speaking. We both got stuck into our food and discussed why I bought her here.

"How's your meal, babe?" I started, nerves filtering in about the conversation I was raising. "Sorry, I didn't think it through well when I saw the name. You aren't supposed to have a lot of seafood."

"Babe, it's fine. This is lovely. Here, try some?" She put a generous portion on her fork, leaned across the table, and held it out for me. As I went to take it, I moved forward, and she pulled the utensil away from me a little. I smirked as I leaned in again, this time letting me take the food. I wrapped my lips around it, sucking it into my mouth as I stared deep into her eyes.

Not leaning back yet, I chewed the food and swallowed it before I grabbed the top of her dress and pulled her into me. I kissed Charlie's mouth deeply, my mouth engulfing hers as I tasted my beautiful girl all over my lips. "Mmm, it was good, not nearly as tasty as you."

"You're so bad," she said. Then, "So tell me, what did you want to talk about?" I reached out, taking her hand. "I want to talk about our wedding."

"Okay, what about it?"

"When do you want to get married, Charlie? Because if it was me, we would already be." My heart was pounding in my chest, but I pressed on. "I want it to be perfect for you and everything you ever dreamed of for our wedding. We only get one shot at this because, I promise you, neither of us will do that day again. Unless, of course, we decide to renew our vowels later on."

She looked over at me, and I saw the love in her eyes, the emotions pooling as tears in her twinkling eyes. My hand snapped up, catching a tear as it trickled over and down her cheek. "So, when do you want to marry me, Charlie?"

CHARLIE

When did I want to get married? I saw the blush creeping up his neck as he waited… then it clicked. I had a chance to get a little payback over the 'Sea-deduction' joke. "Agh, I'm not sure how to say this…" I trailed off, looking down so he couldn't see the smile I was trying to bite back.

"What is it? You can tell me anything, except if you try to break up with me. Then don't tell me that."

"Aww babe, no! Never," I shot back. I couldn't have him thinking that. "It's just that… I don't know about the marriage thing anymore."

Brax's eyes nearly shot out of his head as he sat forward. "What? You want to call off our engagement?" he squeaked. "Well… no-"

"Charlie! What are you talking about?" he cut in.

"It's just, do we really need to get married? It changes nothing, right? We're wonderful the way we are?"

"Charlie, I want us to be a proper…." Before he could finish, I started cackling, unable to hold it back any longer. "Dammit! You Evil Midget! This was payback, wasn't it?"

"Think of it as 'Sea-duction' baby."

"You're so wicked!" He reached across the table, grabbed my arm, and pulled me closer to him. Brax deliberately kissed me deeply before whispering, "Sleep with one eye open tonight."

I chuckled again before he asked if I would stop joking now? "Sure, how about we fix the bill up and go for a walk along the beach? It is only eight o'clock. We can talk while we get some fresh air?"

"Sounds perfect. I have a spliff in my pocket with my name on it."

"Of course you do." We stood up, as I took his hand, I said, "Thank you for dinner. It was perfect." We fixed the bill, and Brax held the door open for me as I stepped out, with him following behind. He took my hand, checked for cars and crossed the road to walk down to the beach. Once we got to the sand, we took our shoes off and carried them, walking down along the shoreline and heading left toward our hotel. "With everything that's gone on, I wish we were already married, Brax."

We kept strolling as he squeezed my hand and looked sideways. "Really?"

"It would have been nice before Pebbles was here. But it doesn't change anything."

"You know that little girl of ours is going to be spoiled rotten."

"She's going to have the most amazing family, just like we do."

"The last tour was insane, wasn't it? Or was it just me that never thought we would all come back and finally have jumped off the bus?" I agreed with him, I never thought I would see that day. "Are you disappointed we fell pregnant before we got the chance to marry?"

"Not even a little. It would have been nice. But now, when I picture our wedding, I picture our little girl there, too."

"You want to wait until she has arrived?"

"I want to do what is right for us, babe. It isn't just about me." I brought his hand up to my lips, planting a kiss. "As you said earlier, we aren't doing this again. This, to me, is life. And I don't want to live without you, Brax."

"I think I would love to look back one day and be able to show our daughter photos of her at our wedding. If she looks like her mother, she will steal the show, just like you always do whenever you enter a room." I stopped and turned, he reached his hand up, brushing my hair back and cupping my cheek. "You are everything, you know that, right?"

"I remember the first day I looked into your eyes, my universe flipped upside down, and I still get that moment with you every day. I know I'm an asshole occasionally, but I want to be your asshole." He laughed at that.

"You were the only girl who could make me pause, FIFA." Now it was my turn because it was one of the most loving things he could say to me.

"Or you can stand talking to after the Mancs lose."

"Don't push your luck, woman. Technically, we won this morning." He started trying to tickle me when I said all they won was "a one-way ticket out of the Mickey Mouse cup."

"Hey! The league cup, thank you very much."

"Actually, it's the Carabao cup now. I mean, really, copying Red Bull races much?"

"You're impossible sometimes. I bet you were all smiles when Liverpool won it in 2012."

"And that's why I love you," I smiled. "You're the only one who puts up with my impossible."

"No-one else can match my banter."

"Are we going to dement our child with our fucked up heads, Brax?" He wrapped his arms around my waist and pulled me closer. I hugged his neck as he laughed, "It's highly likely beautiful. If Chester doesn't do it first."

"You know, I feel he will get so protective of her."

"What? Like a Rottweiler protecting its pup?" My jaw dropped as I slapped Brax across the chest, and he threw his head back, letting out a hearty chuckle.

"You did not imply he is a guard dog, Brax, or our child is a puppy?"

"Does the shoe fit?" he threw it back.

"Personally, I think he's more of a British Bulldog." We strolled hand in hand, a comfortable silence and love surrounding us. The sand was the most gentle hue of gold, almost earthen and muted, the humble star of the scene. I love the beach, the driftwood that comes upon the buoyant waves as tiny rescue boats, then there was the seaweed, that flora of those salty waves, as deeply green as any high summer foliage. My favourite, though, of everything that was here upon the softly rolling dunes, was the tall, handsome man next to me that whispered so sweetly into the gusting breeze.

"Do I tell you enough how much I love you?" he quizzed. "Because I really fucking do.."

"You give me everything, because you complete me." He hugged me briefly when he shot back up and said, "I've got an idea."

"And what's that?"

"Dance with me in the moonlight?" I looked around, a silent question, and he sensed it. "Yes, right here under the moonlight."

"But we don't have any music?"

"Hi, I'm a recording artist." He waved at me mockingly while I rolled my eyes, shaking my head.

"But you never just sing to me. You only ever get me to read what you have written."

"Well, it seems like the perfect time to change that. And I want to." I smiled and said "okay," as he pulled me closer to him, one arm wrapped around my waist as the other gripped my hand in his. "So we will plan our wedding after Pebbles' arrival?"

"I'd love that, Brax." He whispered "me too," as we held each other tight, my head buried in his neck as he started swaying us, singing soft lullabies to his audience of one. His voice, the ocean crashing behind us, spellbound me. I felt like the riptide could come and collect us both, washing us away for an eternity together. He continued to sing into my ear as our bodies moved slowly together, our arms holding on to one another as if nothing else mattered.

When he felt me shiver from the cool ocean air, he took his jacket off and put it around my shoulders, wrapping me in his arms as we returned to our hotel. We got to our suite and sat in bed, settling in for the night. I switched the television on while he was in the bathroom changing, and asked, "What do you feel like, Batman?"

He shouted "comedy" back, so I flicked through the channels. As I was doing so, I saw the replay of the game this morning, which highlighted that United had been knocked out of the cup. When he came and joined me in bed, going straight to his phone, I put it on. He heard the commentators, looked up before glaring at me. "You fucking comedian, Charlotte."

"What?" I could hardly contain my amusement, especially since he had gone straight to my full name.

"This is your idea of comedy?" he snarled in question, clicking his tongue. With blushing cheeks, my body vibrated in humour. "You think you're so funny, don't you?"

"Aww, baby."

"No, Midget! Don't you try to sweet talk me!" he held his flat hand to my face, and I playfully shoved it out the way, saying "I wasn't. I was calling you a sook, after all that whining."

"Hey!" he launched off the bed, pinning me to it as he started tickling me like crazy.

"If I pee on you, it's your own fault!"

Chapter Thirty Eight

BRAX

It had been three months since we shot that film clip together, and tomorrow night was the launch of the video. I was nervous as fuck, as this video meant more to me than I had done before. The day had bounced, and we were out for a walk in our neighbourhood. Each afternoon when I got home, we strolled down to the park and playground, stretching our legs properly in the fresh air before heading home.

Charlie felt it was helping reduce the swelling around the ankles, plus, it was a good time for us to clear our heads and just be together. I stood mesmerised as the sun reflected off her golden hair, casting light over the goddess she was. I realised our baby girl must have been moving when she peered down, gripping her stomach and that smile magnified. I couldn't miss a moment like this and pulled my phone out, taking a photo as Charlie cradled her bump. At seven months pregnant, she was looking breathtaking. "Hey! No phones allowed during this time. You know the rules, Brax!"

"I swear I didn't text or message anyone, not social media either. All I did was take a photo of my girls." Her hands reached her hips as she told me to prove it. I turned my phone to display the picture in all its glory.

"Ugh… delete it. I look like a beached whale." She waved me off when I told her, "don't go there." She accused me of being biassed. "No. I'm in love, and I adore every change going on. You've never looked more beautiful." I shrugged when she laughed at me and said, "you're criminally smooth sometimes."

"Well, what do you want me to do? Throw you over my shoulder and drag you to our room to work it off?"

"You dick!"

"You want it. I know you do."

"The only way that thing will get wet once Pebbles comes is if you are in the shower."

"Don't make threats like that, Charlotte Maree. I will draw up a prenup with very specific…." I stepped closer, took her hips in my hand, squeezing her flesh between my fingers as I pulled her closer. "Very detailed….." I moved in and kissed her neck, feeling her hands grip the top of my arms tight. "Highly graphic sexual favours in the clauses." I bit her earlobe before sucking it between my lips to soothe the sting.

"Asshole." I laughed as she pulled back from me. I knew pregnancy had heightened her sex drive, and I loved utilising every minute.

"Come on, Robin, let's get home. I'm starving! Also, don't forget I've got Melbourne tomorrow night with the boys for the video launch and live performance."

She said, "I remember. I'm looking forward to peace." She was referring to Chester…. I knew it. He had been painful ever since Chrissy went back to Canada, nothing short of agonisingly frustrating. "I've never known a grown man to whine so much, Brax." She had yet to hear half of it. He was ten times more menacing at the studio. "I think what has made it worse is that Marcus took the five weeks' leave and returned with Tessa."

"Yeah, but he knew this launch was coming up, beautiful. It's unfortunate, and I feel for the guy, but come on. Chrissy has only been gone for two weeks."

"It's kind of cute, though, let's be honest." I just stared at her and smirked. "Hey! Don't be a wanker. You lasted a night on the Gold Coast."

"Not valid, Charlie. You came with Marcus as a surprise."

"Shh, you're just nitpicking now."

"Get your ass up that hill, woman."

"Carry me?" She tried batting her eyelashes as I chuckled.

"Fuck no." She slapped me playfully across the chest as I took her hand in mine, strolling back up the road, watching the sunset over the hill as we got closer to our home. Reaching the top, we saw Liam and Shane's cars out the front, causing her to stop dead, glaring at me. "Woah! I know that look. This isn't on me. I didn't know they would be here when we got back."

"You would want to hope not, because I was definitely going to put out for you tonight since you are heading out-of-town tomorrow."

"Fuck yes! I wanted you…. hang on! What do you mean you were going to? You still will be Charlotte."

"Well, that depends now, doesn't it? Since we have a house full."

"No, I won't have it. You put the idea in my head, and now it's full of visions." I noticed her look down before her eyes shot back up at me and widened.

"Brax!" She pushed me away teasingly, not before I grabbed her wrist and turned her into me. I flushed her back against my chest, wrapping my arms around her waist and started shuffling us down the hill. "I know what you are trying to do."

"Yes. I'm rubbing my hard-on against your ass."

"You're impossible." I saw everyone in front of us waiting at the door impatiently, and I prayed to god they said nothing to land me in it. Of course, I invited them over, but now I knew I would get laid… I wished I hadn't. We reached the bottom driveway, and that big-mouth asshole went and threw me in a shit pile.

"You're a wanker! You invite us over, then leave us waiting outside in this heat?" Once Chester finished speaking, she grabbed my hands, taking them off her as she pushed away and turned to meet my gaze. I noticed her foot tap, so did everyone else, and they knew this was a sign she'd caught me out. "Oh, I know that look. You didn't tell Charlie we were coming over, did you?" she turned to smirk at Mace before plastering a grin on her face and patting my cheek before walking off to the front door.

"Technically, I didn't lie! I wasn't aware they would be here when we got back." I yelled after Charlie as Chester cracked up, highlighting I was in the deep end. "Yeah, thanks to your big mouth! Now I'll have blue balls tonight, asshole."

"Well, I'm fine." Charlie said, smirking ear to ear.

"If you're happy and know it, it's your meds." The others snickered at Chester, except I had to hold it together; otherwise, I had no way out of this. Charlie gave him the finger and headed inside as we all followed. I went into the kitchen to grab a beer before sitting down when Mace said, "can we order some food? I'm starving."

"I can cook, if you-"

"Sit down and relax, woman." Kendall cut Charlie off. "We'll get takeaway." Doing as she was told, she eased onto the couch and I darted over, diving in next to her. Picking her tiny legs up, I placed them across my lap and started rubbing the bottom of her feet, knowing how sore they'd been getting by the end of the day.

Mark threw one cushion at me, calling me a "suck hole" as I gave him the finger. "Oh, that's exactly what he's doing, Mark. I'll use it for my benefit, though. I'm not above doing that." Mark reached across the table to high-five Charlie as I pushed him back in his seat.

Once the food arrived, the girls were dishing it out when Chester went and grabbed the chopping bowl. "Pass me the bong, please, so I can hit it like a thick ass."

"Chester! You sick fuck!" Shane burst out laughing when Kendall was the first to express her disgust, and not Charlie this time.

"He's a wrong'un," Charlie muttered, with Chester returning serve… "Says the woman eating hard bread in her salad."

"What the hell is wrong with Croutons?" she snapped back.

"Oh gee, let me think, Midget… guy who's about to invent croutons, eating his salad, thinking… damn, I wish my salad hurt to eat." Shane agreed with him and said "he's right, think about it."

Kendall patted him on the shoulder. "Don't hurt yourself thinking too hard, babes." We all cracked up, "just be pretty. You're good at that, boo."

We had something to eat and the boys and I punched a few cones before chilling. Pleasantly stoned, I had my cutie's legs over my lap as I rubbed her feet with one hand. My other had wandered up to her stomach, moving across the top as I felt our baby girl kick about occasionally.

"Hey, I just had a thought," Liam chimed with Mace adding, "that's a first." He looked high as a kite, and smirked. "If a toy from Toy Story died, the kids wouldn't know, right? But the other toys would have to watch the children playing with their corpses." I lost it, nearly dropping Charlie's legs when Mark said, "You just outdid the cheerios one, my brother." This guy was grade A entertainment and never failed to humour me.

I saw Charlie look around and suddenly ask where Chester was, realising it was too quiet without his input. "He's been gone for a while now." Kendall pointed out. "Probably taking a dump after he ate all that food." She slapped Shane as Charlie squealed.

"That's disgusting! At least Chester uses the toilet, unlike you, shit pants." When he leaned forward and called her "Evil Midget," while giving her the middle finger, even Charlie laughed. "Alright, let me go see what he's up to." She went to get up, but I insisted she stay and I would look. "I need the bathroom, Brax. Your daughter's laying on my bladder."

"Want me to get up in your womb instead?"

"Brax!" She slapped my cap off, and I watched her hand come down, grabbing it and pulling her to me for a kiss. I saw the guys trying to choke back a laugh as I helped her up, watching her rub her hips slightly while walking off. Within seconds, her humour filtered from inside like a chorus line... I leaned forward, staring through the bi-folds door to find he had upturned her entire bag of croutons into the mayonnaise to prove a point that no one likes hard salad.

At around Eleven that night, it suddenly dawned on me why Charlie was still up and hadn't gone to bed yet. It was also around the time I decided everyone needed to leave my house. "Okay, I'm ready for bed."

"Yeah, you're a funny fucker." I looked at Chester seriously and told him to "go home" again. "Fucking rude, bro."

"Actually, I'm keen to head, anyway. I'm so fucking tired today." Mace turned to Liam asking, "are you serious? You spent five hours sitting around on the PlayStation."

"You prick! I was playing too, and you didn't mention it when we spoke?" Liam apologised to Shane.

"That's great. Now go home." Chester laughed at me and asked, "you trying to bury a load before we leave tomorrow?"

"I don't care what you think. Go home."

Charlie giggled and slapped me. "Brax! Stop being so rude." I glared at her, and she just smirked right back at me. I let my hand rub her stomach and roam slightly lower, hinting at her to behave.

"Why are you in such a hurry to fuck us off?" I didn't even look at Chester as I answered him. Obviously, I went with the excuse that "football's on tonight," since it was Saturday. Charlie looked at me, about to say something, before I gave her the eye. She knew damn well that Liverpool didn't play for another hour, and Manchester's game was after. She'd clicked on precisely what I was doing. "Well, that's boring and actually makes sense."

"I told you before, Chester. Unlike you, we don't just fuck. We actually do other things together."

"Whatever! I can't deal with your domesticated ass, bro. Grown-up Brax is a buzzkill. Come on, Mark, let's get fucked up and drink all Shane and Kendall's liquor."

"You watch your mouth, Chester! And if you two are coming back to our house, you stay down at the other end. I'm going to bed like a n\ormal person does at this hour."

We hugged everyone and saw them out, watching as they drove off before I shut the door and locked the house. I turned around and saw Charlie back on the couch. "What do you think you are doing?"

"I'm just going to wait until the game, babe. No point in going to bed for an hour." I cocked my head slightly as I replied to her. "Really? No point, none whatsoever?" When she said "nothing she could think of," I stepped closer. "Do you want to know what I think?"

"What's that?"

"You're beautiful; in my eyes, you're more exquisite because of our baby. Something about going through this with you has made you even sexier, more feminine and right now, I'm going to make love to you." I walked over and kissed her, my tongue entered her mouth, and my hands slowly massaged her back, then her full breasts. She returned my kisses, her tongue entered my mouth as she surrendered. Suddenly, her juices flowed, she wanted sex, I could feel the shift in her demeanour. As she relaxed and gave in, I knew I could do anything I wanted. She studied me closely, showing me nothing but pure unbridled love. I was all fingers and thumbs as I unbuttoned the front of her dress. Opening her bra, I stepped back to admire her body.

She was breathtaking, ripe with her pregnancy. Her bodily odours sent wonderful messages to my brain. I sucked one ample nipple into my mouth, running my tongue around lapping her milky skin until she moaned wildly. Since we got pregnant, her breasts had become so sensitive it drove her wild when I played with them, especially my mouth. My mind was full of wonder, when I felt her hand press the back of my head, "more, Brax. That feels amazing," she whispered. I happily obliged her, running my hands down over her backside; my fingers teasing her gorgeous butt.

"I'm going to fuck you," I whispered into her neck, "I'm gonna to take my time, and have you in every way imaginable until you tell me you can't take any more." I took her hand and led her through to our bedroom before I laid her on the bed, kissing down from her heavy breasts, licking her ripened stomach, tonguing her belly button, then moving on until my tongue circled her centre. She moaned and grabbed the hair on the back of my head, grinding her pussy hard into my mouth. I slipped my tongue in, then out of her wet, warm hole, my hands stroking her ass cheeks. Her clit seemed to expand, and I took it in my teeth, nipping, then sucking as she struggled and bucked. Her moans of pleasure became louder. "That's so good, Brax!" She screamed out loud, startling me, not that we hadn't always had a healthy sex life, but pregnancy, I found, was next level. Everything I did seemed tenfold, she reacted more than I had ever known her to. She grabbed my face and pushed it into her, grinding and rotating her hips around... my face lathered in her pleasure. I couldn't get enough.

I sat back with a hand wrapped around my thickened cock. "Kiss it, baby, please. Let me feel your mouth." She lifted her head and wrapped her lips around my head, sucking down on it... hard. "Fuck... Shit, Charlie!" It was too much, and overstimulated me. "No... get off." I pulled back as she tried to continue. "Turn around now, or I won't last."

She rolled over on her knees, pointing her beautiful ass in the air. I leaned on her back, raw and animalistic, fucking her vigorously, using my two hands to massage the mounds on her chest. A low moan of delight escaped from her lips, causing me to roll her over, to suck and bite her nipples. I slipped out, still lapping on her ample tits. I just couldn't get enough. "Come here, Cutie. Sit on my lap. I wanna play with them." She hovered over me, wriggling down on my erection. With her bouncing on my lap, I got what I wanted as my hands found their way to her chest. "Baby... I can't get enough. You drive me wild!"

"I know, Brax, me too." She threw her head back as she gripped my neck, grinding on my lap. Her long blonde locks swayed as she rode me, my hands went down to her hips, fingers splayed as the woman I loved took my cock and claimed it as hers.

My emotions flooded a river rapidly in my veins, she was everything, and she was all mine. I rolled her onto her back spreading her legs wider as I pulled her to the edge of the bed. "Brax, stop teasing." I stood up and slid back inside as she arched her back off the mattress. "Yes!" Her legs came up on my shoulders as I grabbed hold of them, and she pushed into me with each thrust. She had to feel me building to climax, just as I could with her. I cried out as my strokes became erratic. "Fuck... Charlie!"

"I know, Brax. Cum with me, please." I stilled, spilling inside, feeling her clamp around me. As I gradually lost my stiffness and went limp, she let me slide out, and I fell on the bed alongside her. She cradled me to her breasts, I couldn't help but give her still-hardened nipple a little bite. She dragged her nails down my spine, causing goosebumps across my skin, when I noticed her left hand move across to the bedside table, picking up the television remote. I knew she was checking how long before the kick-off.

I looked up at the screen, my thoughts confirmed, as I saw the pre-show fifteen minutes before kick-off. "So what will you do if Southampton beats you and breaks your forty-one-game undefeated streak tonight?"

"Shut up, Brax! Why would you say that after I just let you fuck me? I hope Wolves destroy you later and show Ole up for the fraud he is!" I laughed as she smacked me over the head with her pillow.

Chapter Thirty Nine

CHESTER

We had just gotten to the airport to catch our flight to Melbourne, and Brax was being a pain in the ass, so I felt obliged to give him shit. "Shouldn't you be happy at the moment?"

"Why would I be a cheerful man?"

"Well, you kicked us out last night so Charlie could juggle your nuts with her mouth." The rest of the boys laughed as Brax said, "I told you why I was having an early night."

"Yeah, to watch football. Coincidentally, I checked, and Liverpool didn't kick off for at least an hour after you threw us out, and Manchester played afterwards."

A stunned Mark asked, "Did you actually look that shit up, man, just to call him out?"

"Nah, I saw mates who follow it rambling on in my newsfeed on Instagram this morning." Brax laughed and patted my back. "So, why are you miserable since you got to bang your Evil Midget and watch football?"

Before Brax could answer, Shane did for him. "The Mancs dropped points again, and Midget's team is now twenty-two points clear on top of the league."

Brax turned to Shane and told him, "shut up, asshole." I laughed, highlighting, "she won't let you live that down."

"I know! Which is why I should be happy about leaving town right-"

"But, you're whipped." I cut him off.

"Can we just get on this fucking plane already? I'm not sitting next to you either and listening to this crap all flight. If I wanted to be nagged, I would have stayed home."

"Yeah, well, if I had my way, I'd be in Canada right this minute, balls deep in Chrissy's-"

"Mouth," Shane said, the others smirked.

"Hey! You shut up, or I will bring Kendall into this."

A short flight later, including a quick feed and cat nap, we got into the terminal at Melbourne Tullamarine, and I was straight on the phone to my guy organising to meet us at Docklands for a smoke. The other guys appreciated it, as we had a big night with the performance later and the unveiling of the new music video. I knew my boy would be keen as fuck once that time came.

We organised a ride to the hotel, and I pulled my phone out to check any messages while we were in the air. I saw Chrissy had texted me, and I quickly let her know we'd landed and to see what time she would be home so I could call her. When we went to Canada, I expected to run our usual riots, return, and carry on as normal. It was a smaller tour for us compared to what we were used to. Instead, I returned without my testicles... which had been tucked in that gorgeous redhead's handbag since I met her. I know the boys would always see me as the proverbial playboy, but the moment I met Chrissy, there was something about her I didn't want to let go of. Not that I would ever admit it to Brax, but it suddenly made sense to me exactly what he saw in Charlie and why he was whipped from the onset. And I wouldn't tell him because I'd never live it down. I knew all the shit I had given them over the years, so they were both waiting for that perfect shot to get back at me. Fuck handing them ammo on a silver platter.

We pulled up at the hotel and got all our shit out of the car before checking in. We quickly dumped our bags, allowing us to freshen up and check in with our girls. Afterwards, we would meet back up to grab a smoke and a few drinks before heading to the studios for tonight's live show.

Flopping on the bed, I pulled my phone out, seeing that Chrissy had replied and said she was home. I couldn't wait to call her, before I even second-guessed, I'd hit the green button. The international connection tone rang through my brain, crackling as I eagerly waited. A short while later, that sexy tone graced me. "Hi, Mister."

"Hey, beautiful. I missed that voice."

"So I noticed you couldn't wait to call?"

"I really couldn't, not gonna lie. I kinda miss you already."

"Kind of, hey?"

"Don't bust my balls, baby. Just lick them." I heard her giggle and couldn't help but smile, knowing I had done that.

"You always flip a beautiful moment, right? What will I do with you?"

"Love me?" *Shit!* Before I could filter my mouth, it had come out, and I heard the line go quiet, both unsure what to say next. *Fuck, Chester! Why!* "Is… that what you want?" she whispered. *Damn it! Yes! No! I mean, yes! If it won't scare you off! Jesus fuck, if the guys could hear me right now, they would take the full on piss.* It drew me out of my head when I heard Chrissy repeat my name. "Sorry baby, I'm here." Of course, she wasn't letting it go and said, "you didn't answer." I fumbled over my words for a few seconds before she rescued me. "Tell me, please… what did you mean?"

"I meant that…." I took a deep breath, wiping my sweaty palms, then added, "yeah, Chrissy, I'd love to know what we have is something special, something we both want, because I haven't stopped thinking about you since you left. Baby, you've consumed my head from the moment I met you." *Holy Shit! Now I knew exactly how Brax felt!*

I should feel like an asshole for all the shit I gave him over it, but I didn't. I would do it all over again, because what's a friend if you can't roast each other? "Thank you for sharing that with me, Chester."

"Are you shitting me, woman?" I shot up off the bed, flabbergasted. "I just poured my heart out, and…" Before I could finish my rant, she burst out in a fit of giggles, and I realised she was fucking with me like I did all the time. "You little tease! Not cool."

"Sorry, but it was funny. And in answer to you, Chester, you are special to me as well. I want to keep what we have. And I miss you just as much."

"Just as fucking well. I was thinking I was the bitch in the relationship."

"Oh, you are…." She giggled again. I wanted to dispute it, but could I really?

"Wait until you come back, or I come over there. You'll be my dirty little girl again in no time, and then we'll see who plays what role in this relationship."

"Calm yourself down. You don't have time to spank the monkey. Haven't you got a live show soon? Don't tell me I have been waiting to see you for nothing?"

"Really? You stayed up to watch me?" My heart felt like it could burst out of my chest. "Fuck, you're adorable. You know that, right?" We talked for a few more minutes before I had to say goodbye and get ready to meet the guys.

Once I got to Brax's suite, I saw the rest of them waiting. "Mrs. Palmer, get you off to the sound of Chrissy's voice, bro?"

"No more than Midget playing poker while you listen." The others were amused until Shane said, "terrible. I'd never say that about Kendall." That earned a solid "bullshit" from us in unison. I quickly added his "nut sacks," when Brax asked if "licking sherbet ran a bell."

"I'm enjoying this, guys," Liam said, taking a draw on his blunt. "I miss Mace, but how long's it been since we just had this," he circled his finger, "us boys?"

I agreed with Liam's sentiment. It felt like a lifetime. "It is good, bro, but it sucks without the girls here."

"Yeah, I feel that, brother." I leaned over, and Mark and I fist-pumped. If anyone understood how I felt, he'd prefer to be back in Canada with April. We quickly shared a few spliffs before travelling to the studios. Upon arrival, we ran in and got fitted ready for television with the stage crap they make us wear… mics, earpieces, you name it. Then came the pep talks from the producers, like we had never done this shit before. We finally sat, and the interview went well before they unveiled the video clip. I looked at my boy as it was playing on the screen for the first time. I saw in his eyes the same feeling I had just hours before talking to Chrissy. It was also the realisation I needed that while music would always play a massive part in my life, that girl owned more of me.

We answered a few more questions before heading off to the back of the stage, where they removed the mics for us and all the cords. "Aww, look at you being all loved up. Mentioning your girl on national television. Our little Monkey is growing up, guys." I pushed Brax away and told the prick to "shut up."

"Midget will be such a proud mummy watching you on television back home. Just wait until she sees big boy Chester."

"I'll give you huge, you smart ass." I put Brax in a headlock as we mucked around, wrestling with each other, when Brax stepped back. The next minute, we had both fallen over, going down the first two steps and then rolling off the side of the stage. I was still laughing as I stood up, but that quickly changed when I heard Brax's scream of agony and saw him rolling around on the ground to the side of me. "Brax! Bro… are you alright?" I scrambled over to him and knelt beside Brax, trying to stop him from rolling. He gripped his lower leg, and when I looked down, I knew this shit was terrible. "Liam! Call an ambulance now! Guys, get out the front and show them where to go. *Hurry!*" The boys looked, saw what I was staring at, and quickly raced off. "Brax, just hold still, alright. We are getting you help."

"Fuck…" he wailed. "Agh, Chester!" I could see the pain he was feeling ripping him apart. The veins on his neck popped as he desperately tried to suck in air, a reddened face with gritted teeth, to the point I wouldn't have been surprised if they snapped. I wanted to comfort him and promised help was on the way. "Chester! Make it stop, please, make it stop."

He struggled to breathe through the pain, as panic washed over him. I did the one thing I knew would calm Brax and fast. Pulling out my phone,

I dialled as my hands shook, his screams ripping down my bones. "Midget! Brax-" I stopped, struggling to breathe. "He's injured badly. We're getting an ambulance for him, but he's going into shock. I need you to talk to him. Keep him calm, please. I'm sorry, I know. I-"

"Agh, Fuck! Chester, please!" his screams for help cut off. When she heard Brax scream, the questions disappeared as she told me to put him on the phone. I tried to hand it to him as he rolled in agony.

"Brax, take the phone. It's Midget." He rolled on his side as I placed the phone over his ear. "Charlie, make it stop. Please, baby," he sobbed.

"Shhh, babe, I'm right here," she soothed, the pain and tears obvious in her voice. "Monkey is getting you help, alright. Just listen to my voice while you wait... I need you to focus on breathing, babe."

His wails into the phone saw my throat tighten and constrict... fuck! What had I done? I choked up myself, trying to grasp the severity of the situation. "Baby, please make it stop. I need you, Charlie. Argh!"

"Brax!" she spoke firmly. "Listen to me, baby, please. I'm right here. You can hear my voice, can't you? I'm with you, Brax, I promise."

"Charlie... please," he cried. The tears fell down my cheeks as I struggled for air in my lungs. *Fuck! Hearing him sob like this was killing me! I can't imagine how Charlie is feeling.*

"Shhh, it's okay, baby, I know. I promise, help is on the way."

Chapter Forty

CHARLIE

My heart was aching, hearing Brax in so much pain, but I had to remind myself I didn't have the luxury of breaking on him. He needed me more than ever, and I wouldn't let him down. "Baby, you still with me?" He groaned then replied, "I'm here... *Fucking* hell! I want to rip my leg off. It hurts so bad..."

"How will you kick Pebbles up the backside when she mucks up, then?" I heard him sob in pain again as he tried not to laugh. Chester yelled out that the paramedics were running down now. "See baby, not too much longer. Just hold on for a few more minutes, alright?"

"Charlie! Don't leave, please don't leave me..." he panicked.

"Baby, I won't! I promise I am right here with you, but I will talk to Monkey briefly while they check you out. That's all, Brax." Hysteria flared again, with him begging me not to, and I had to try blinking back quickly, the tears forming. "The medics just need to check you out, I promise I won't go anywhere. In fact, I'm looking at flights right now. I'm coming to you, Brax."

I heard him scream in pain again before Chester's voice came over the speaker. "Midget, you still there?"

"I'm here! Chester, what happened to him? What's wrong?" I choked up, desperately trying to stay in control, which was difficult with minimal information.

"Babe, I'm so fucking sorry. You don't know how sorry I am!"

"Sorry? What do you mean, sorry?" I couldn't make sense of Chester now either, as he sobbed on the phone. "Chester, it's alright, but I need you to calm down and stay strong until I can get there. I love you, Monkey, and I'm worried about you both. I need you to tell me what is going on?"

"I love you too, Midget. I just... fuck! What have I done?"

Before I could answer him, Brax shouted, "Don't tell Charlie you love her, you prick!" I cried back a laugh, hearing his voice, the pain was clear. I asked Chester if he was alright when I heard Brax go quiet, and he said, "they've given him the green whistler while they assess him."

"You need to tell me what happened. I'm trying to book flights here. How bad is it?" Chester asked if I had seen the interview, and of course, I had.

"Well, he was giving me shit about Chrissy all day. Anyway, we were mucking around like we normally do..." I questioned, by mucking around, did he mean "fighting like they always do?"

"Yeah, wrestling, whatever you want to call it. We slipped off the stage and went down the first flight of stairs. When I got up, I heard Brax's screams and saw his ankle..."

Chester panicked again, and I heard his heavy breathing on the phone. "Monkey, stop! Blaming yourself for an accident isn't helping either of you right now. But for the love of god, I need you to tell me what is wrong with him!"

"We fucked his ankle up, Charlie."

"It's broken?"

"Badly, babe. The paramedics are stabilising him, saying he needs to go to the hospital for surgery." I made him promise to ride with Brax and not let him go alone. "I won't. Just get here, please. He needs you."

"Let me know where they are taking him. I can get a flight in an hour and a half, so he will probably be in surgery when I arrive."

"Call me back as soon as you have it booked. I'll make sure the guys organise a car to pick you up. I'm getting in the ambulance with him now. Hold on, and I will ask where they are taking him." I waited while I heard Chester talking to the paramedics before he returned on the phone. "Charlie, they are taking him to St Vincent's on Grey Street." I told him, "I'll meet you there and please keep in touch," as he hung up. When Chester started saying goodbye, I could hear Brax yelling out to him not to let me go. Before I realised it, I crumbled on the couch in tears. Listening to him in so much pain and being unable to do anything had broken me. But I didn't have the luxury of collapsing. I needed to be strong for him. He was all that mattered right now.

I allowed myself a few minutes to get past the initial shock before pulling my shit together and getting packed. I ordered a car for the airport. On the way, I sent a quick message to Marcus to let him know, even though he was away. He would kill me if I didn't tell him, and then I messaged both of Brax's parents and mine. After checking in for my flight I rang the girls to let them know, and Mace said she would race to the office tomorrow and get my spare house key from the office. I appreciated her keeping an eye out while we were gone. I also promised to update her and the other girls once I had more information.

While waiting at my boarding gate, I tried calling Chester several times and didn't get an answer. So I dialled Mark's phone instead, since he was usually the most responsible out of the lot. "Midget, are you alright?"

"Chester wasn't answering and promised to tell me what was happening. Are they alright?"

"Him and Shane have just gone to get a drink. He left his phone here. Brax is in surgery." I loved that Mark always tried to smooth things over. I didn't have the heart to tell him I'd been trying for an hour.

"What is it, Mark? What are they saying? I'm boarding my flight soon." He said it wasn't as bad as initially thought, but they still had to pin his ankle.

"Send me your flight details before you leave, and I'll look it up online and make sure someone is waiting for you when you arrive." I thanked Mark. "See you soon. Call me if you need anything, alright?"

"I will, and you too. I'll be there as fast as I can. Love you all."

"We love you too, Midget. Just be safe, alright?" I hung up and boarded my plane.

It was one of the shortest flight routes in Australia and was still the longest trip of my life. I had never felt such cabin fever, and the moment we landed, I was practically racing through the terminal to get out. Well, as fast as a pregnant midget can move. I came through the terminal to find a sign with my name being held up by the driver Mark organised, I texted him to let him know I was on my way. I tried to call Chester again as I was worried that he wasn't answering and that he, too, had been more injured than he let on. The worst part about Melbourne? The long drive from Tullamarine Airport! By the time we arrived at the hospital, my patience was non-existent. I paid the driver and thanked him, as I was getting my bag out of the car, I heard Liam and Shane shout out to me.

The boys raced over and grabbed my bag as we hugged, and I asked, "how's Brax?"

Liam explained, "he's alright. He's back on the ward. The surgery went fine. He's going to be okay, babe."

I burst into tears of relief, Shane grabbed and hugged me. "Shh, it's okay, babe, he's fine. We promise. Come on, let's take you to see him?" Liam carried my bag as Shane kept his arm around my shoulder, helping me inside the elevator and to Brax's room.

We walked down the corridor, and I asked, "has the surgery worked?" and Liam nodded. "Yeah, it only took a little over an hour, then recovery. Like I said, he's not long been back on the ward. They had to put two pins in his ankle, but he'll be fine, babe."

"Here we are." Shane opened the door for me and held it as I walked inside. When I saw Brax and Chester, I was ready to strangle them.

"Braxton?" I saw them both quickly spin around with Chester still sucking on Brax's gas mask, pumping pain relief through it. The pair of these fuckers were both high as a kite!

"Cutie! You came!" Brax sighed, then Chester added, "Hey, it's Pregnant Midget of Tour!"

414

"Are you pair of fucker's high right now? While I was trying to call you!" When Chester moved toward me, I held my hand up to stop him. "You're the reason the gene pool needs a fucking lifeguard!" If I had it in me, I probably would have shanked them both with my nail file right now. Instead, I glared at the two of them before taking my bag off Liam and wheeling it out of the room behind me. "Baby Mumma?" I heard Brax holler after me, and that confirmed I had made the right decision. I was nuclear, although thankful he was okay.

"Mate, I'd shut the fuck up if I were you." I agreed with Mark, but he knew these two clowns wouldn't listen. I moved through the corridor, stopping intermittently, unsure where to go, knowing I just needed to get out of there. A door slammed behind me, causing me to speed up in case it was Chester. "Charlie! Wait up, please." I stopped and turned around to see Mark running after me. "Here, take this." I looked at his extended hand and caught him holding Brax's room key with the hotel details. "Go get settled. Let me sort this pair out, and I'll return to the hotel then find you, alright?"

"Thanks, Mark."

"I'm really sorry, Midget. I tried to tell them it wasn't a good idea, but by that stage, he was already fried from the surgery."

"You don't need to explain, Mark. I know what those baboons are like together. This isn't your fault, and I appreciate you keeping me updated." I gripped Mark's arm as I leaned up, he bent down to help, giving him a kiss, as I wrapped my arm around his neck, hugging him tight.

"Go get yourself and Pebbles sorted. I'll settle this lot, grab a pizza to share, and head back to see you."

"Sounds good, Mark." Thankfully, there was a taxi rank right out the front of the hospital, so I was soon on my way to the hotel.

I arrived at Crown, heading to reception and explained what had happened. Thankfully, they were accommodating, having recognised me, assisting me in the right direction towards the room. Once I got inside, I put my bag down and lay back on the bed. My hips were killing me from all the travel and those ridiculously uncomfortable plane seats. On top of all that, I get to the hospital and find them off their guts! "Agh, little fucking pricks!" I screamed out of pure frustration before crying out of relief that he was alright. "Fucking hormones! Ok, Pebbles, don't give Mummy a hard time, please. Your Dad's doing plenty enough of that for both of you." I rubbed my stomach gently as I got my frustrations out before shaking it off and pulling my shit together. I got into the shower and changed, ready for bed. I was tired and hungry, so I hoped it didn't take Mark long to sort those twats out.

When I came back out, I saw three missed calls from Brax, which led me to believe the guys had left, and it had suddenly dawned on him just how pissed I was. Not ready to call back, I sent a text message instead. "What do you want, Braxton?" A message buzzed back immediately, none too surprising. He was the type to keep his phone glued to him until I responded. "I love you."

"Goodnight, Brax." He would know by my tone and lack of response I was not happy, even if it was a text. So when my phone rang, and I saw it was Brax, I wasn't surprised. "What do you want? I'm in bed. Your daughter and I are tired. We had a few hours of travel to get to her imbecile father, only to arrive and find him fucking around on pain relief *with* Chester!"

Before I could hold it back, the verbal diarrhoea began, not that Brax would notice in his state. "Hi, Cutie!" *Ridiculous*! He was so gassed up! I'm surprised he hadn't passed out already. He sounded like he had been on a week-long bender. "Don't you 'Hi Cutie' me!"

"I love you."

"Was that all? I want to go to bed."

"I love both of you." he slurred.

"Ugh! You impossible asshole! We love you too. Go to sleep, but don't think for one second we won't have words tomorrow."

"I can't sleep without you." He tried being cute.

"Well, try! Goodnight, Braxton." I finally got him off the phone when I felt baby girl move and looked down at my stomach. "I tell you what, princess, your Father is going to be the death of me! And if not him, your damn Uncle!"

As I was saying this, I heard a knock on the door, and my phone buzzed. I saw a message from Mark, letting me know it was him. I got up and waddled over to the door, opening it. My mouth watered when I smelt the pizza he was carrying. "You're my hero, Mark."

"Glad you're as hungry as I am. I thought we would never get Chester out of there."

"Well, Brax has already phoned looking for a bed buddy. You should have left the fools together to sleep it off. Mark and I sat down and ate some food while he filled me in on what had happened today. "I have to say, you don't seem too shocked?"

"Nothing would surprise me with those two. I think Brax and Chester would marry off any future kids we had to each other. Just so they could tell people, they really were related."

"Seems legit." I chuckled as I reached across and took Mark's hand.

"Thanks so much for today, Mark. You guide me through the tough times."

"I keep telling you, babe, you're family." Mark and I chatted while we ate and I asked how things were going with April. I felt for him when he said they didn't get to talk as much as they would like, but I understood. We had lived such busy lives by the time you got home. You just wanted some peace and sleep.

"I miss the days of quiet. I live with Brax now. Oh hell, who am I kidding? I live with Chester too." Mark laughed before his face turned serious, and I knew what he was about to say. "Look, don't think I'm making excuses for them. I promise you I'm not, I really am sorry you turned up to find them in that state, but I can honestly say the way they were beforehand... I wouldn't have wanted you to see that, Charlie. It rocked me, and I don't think I will ever forget it."

"I was just so mad at him, you know?" He sympathised with a small head nod. "I was freaking out that whole time, and then I walked in, and he's just pissing around like it was nothing?" The tears fell again as Mark pulled me in for a hug.

"I know, babe, but what you heard on the phone wasn't the worst. I don't want you to have that memory either, alright? Give them hell, like I know you will, but just know you didn't need to see him in his previous state, either." He rubbed my back carefully, pulling me in tighter, saying, "remember we love you too and are glad you are here for him."

"Thanks, Mark, but no promises yet. I wanted to shank him earlier." I looked up at him as I tried to sniffle back a tear, and Mark threw his head back, laughing. Did he think I was joking? "I know you did, Midget!" Not long after, I saw Mark out, and I headed back into the bedroom. Seeing Brax's suitcase, I opened it and grabbed one of his shirts. I quickly took my own off and replaced it with his before I crawled into bed.

The exhaustion kicked in, and I was out to it before my head hit the pillow. Something woke me the following day, and peeling my eyes open, I realised it was my phone buzzing on the bedside table, quickly answering it. When I heard Mark's voice, I promptly replied and said good morning. "We can head back to the hospital in an hour if you are ready?"

"Thanks, I will be." I raced around, and sure enough, an hour later, I heard the knock at the door. I grabbed my bag and headed out to meet them. When I opened it and stepped out, Chester was on my ass like a fly on shit. "I'm so sorry, Midget."

"You shh! I'm still mad, not about the accident. I get that. But you promised to keep me updated, and you both acted like a pair of tits last night." I explained my frustrations so he could really think about what they did. "Remember, I'm low on caffeine these days. Do not test my patience today." I walked past him down the hallways as I heard the others snickering at his expense.

Arriving twenty minutes later with traffic, we moved through the hospital and I got eager to see him. When I opened the door, I didn't expect the words that came out of my mouth to be the first I spoke. But when I saw him sitting in the hospital bed with his Manchester United jersey on, pain relief hooked up to his arm, face puffy from the abundance of medications they had pumped into him and his hair all over the place, I just blurted it out. "If I wasn't so pissed at you right now, wearing that shirt would be painful enough for you."

Chapter Forty One

BRAX

The moment my Cutie walked in the room, I could see it still pissed her what happened, and no smooth-talking under the sun would get me out of this one. So I had to go a different angle. "Hi Baby, I feel like shit today. You're a sight for sore eyes."

"Your eyes are probably so sore because you were high as a fucking kite last night."

"I can't really remember." She raised her eyebrows, arms crossing over her chest as she glared back.... yeah, no angle would fix this one, so it was better to bite the bullet. "Alright, baby, I'm sorry! If you had been here, you would have given it to him too. The fucker just wouldn't shut up!" When Mark, "that's true at least," I appreciated the backup. "He was so wound up about the accident, and he wouldn't stop stressing, so I shoved the mask in his face." I continued.

"You know he promised to call me and keep me updated?"

"I-" She cut me off. "You know I was stuck waiting an hour and a half to get on my flight, then another hour and a half flying time. Then an hour's drive from the airport... but hey, I'm so fucking glad Chester got high with you. All the while not taking *one* of my calls. Thankfully, Mark had more brains than the pair of you put together."

"Fuck! I'm so sorry, babe."

"Finally! A genuine apology." She threw her hands up. "At least that sounded sincere, unlike the rest of the bullshit coming out of your mouth today. Now, how are you feeling?" She finally walked over and sat on the side of my bed as I stroked her stomach, trying to say hello to our baby girl. "A little sore still, babe, but much better than I was feeling."

"I'm glad. Also, Liverpool won this morning."

"Really?"

"Yes," she snapped. "If you think I will stop at that, you are sorely mistaken. It was our under twenty-three years that played."

"This is my punishment, isn't it?"

"This is nothing yet. Now say hello properly to your daughter. You panicked her as well." I moved forward and gave her stomach a flurry of soft kisses while she ran her hand through my hair. When she felt me try to snake my hand up the inside of her thigh, she smacked me on the back of the head, much to the amusement of the guys. "Fuck! Charlie!"

"Problem, Brax?" She stared at me, a very stern warning.

"No, Cutie."

"Can I come in yet?" Chester asked.

Without turning, she replied, "Speak when spoken to today, Chester." We heard Shane, Liam and Mark chuckle, and when I tried to shoot Chester a sympathetic look, she leaned across in my line of vision, forcing my eye contact.

"So, what did you end up doing last night?"

"Well, I finally went and rested for our daughter's sake. Her father scared the living shit out of us, then pissed me off, leaving us tired, annoyed, and hungry. But while you and Chester were getting high, Mark was kind enough to take my calls, text, and update me. He even brought your daughter and my dinner on his way back last night. What do you have to say, Braxton?" *Fuck*, I thought mum's first degree as a teenager was bad. She had nothing on this crap. I turned to look at Mark, "thanks, brother, I owe you one."

"It's live, mate. Just don't fucking be that obnoxious again… the pair of you." He inclined his head to Chester.

"Pretty sure we've done worse," I countered, earning a huff from Charlie. "Believe me when I tell you, Brax, that is not a conversation you want to be bringing up in your defence right now, because I was on the verge of cutting you myself last night."

"You'd have allowed Pebbles to grow up without her father?" She straightened up and glared at me, then I heard Mark ushering the rest out of the room. "And on that note, come on, guys. Let's go get a coffee and return soon. None of us wants to witness his murder."

"Thank you, Mark." She turned around and watched as the guys headed off for a while. Mark closed the door, giving her a wink before walking off. *Oh, he knows I'm about to get reamed out.* When she turned back to me, I stayed quiet while she moved up to sit closer. I put my hand back on her stomach as she ran her fingers through my hair. "I love you, but don't like you right now."

"I know, baby, and I deserve that."

"I was so worried, I didn't even know what was wrong with you and I had to navigate myself through a situation I was completely blind in." When I saw the tears fall, I shuffled myself up and pulled her across my lap. "Brax, your ankle. Be careful."

"Fuck it. You need this more. Besides, it's fine." I held her to me as she sobbed into my chest. With one hand wrapped around her waist, I softly stroked her stomach, feeling the occasional movement from our baby. I used my other hand to caress her hair back off her face, holding her close to my heart. Neither of us said anything for several minutes, just holding her tight, and truthfully, I was finding comfort in this as well. "You got me through last night. Your voice soothed me in the most fucked up situation I've ever been in. I'm so sorry you had to see me like that when you arrived. It wasn't fair to you or our baby girl."

"I understand why you were like that, Brax. Initially, I was so pissed with Chester because he promised to let me know. But then I had a good chat with Mark last night." I kissed her forehead, saying, "I'm so thankful

Mark was with you."

"Me too. He explained Chester's state, and while I don't know if I agree, I can understand why you gave it to him."

"Even still-" she cut me off.

"I know, and never again! From now on, I'm ordering those marijuana suppositories you can get online and shoving one up each of your assholes to prevent this. It's more tolerable than that shit mess last night."

"I want to argue, but I won't."

"That's a smart choice."

I brushed her hair back as she looked up at me. "Can I push my luck?" Her brow raised, shifting backwards.

"What, Braxton?"

"I just need your kisses, baby." She glared at me and questioned the need? "Desperately need them. I'm a starving man."

"Well, if you weren't a dickhead last night, you wouldn't have gone to bed hungry, would you?"

"You know you're literally killing me?"

"You hate the word literally, and you just used it."

"Now you see my point." So what did she do? Laughed in my face! This little thing just cackled, so I took the chance to seize my prey. I grabbed her head and shoved her face to mine as we started making out like crazy. Our hands were fumbling, desperate, and needy. I couldn't get enough of this woman.

I started kissing her neck and feeling her breasts and ass. She rubbed her hands across my chest and softly brushed them across my now-tight boxers, bursting at the seam. I finally had some luck when she let me slide my hand up between her thighs, and I couldn't believe what I felt. Her panties were soaked!

She was damper than I had ever felt before. The inside of her thighs were so slippery that I almost couldn't help sliding my hand up to her fiery core. I had never felt Charlie this hot before, and any notion of where we were or the fact the guys could come back at any second flew out the window. I just knew we needed this.

I edged my hand higher until it reached the top of her panties, then gently peeled the waistband away from her skin, sliding my hand inside to feel her, pressing my fingers harder to her skin, slipping them further, trailing for the holy grail. All the frustration, anxiety and prolonged arousal had us both about to explode in a fiery passion. I rubbed her centre, and she shuddered and moaned in my ear. My two fingers easily slid to the knuckle right into her soaking hole.

I raised my palm and started making the come hither motion to stimulate her g-spot. At that point, she was gripping me for dear life, so I took the chance to get her to turn in my lap, that way she knelt across the top of my thighs, facing me. First, this gave me better access to her, but second, if the guys came back in, they wouldn't see shit. They would assume and probably know, but wouldn't see what was mine. I opened her up with my fingers again by pushing her panties aside; she leaned into me, panting and moaning, so worked up like she had been for most of her pregnancy. It didn't take long before she was moaning without abandon into my skin. Her juices were freely flowing out, soaking my hand and legs. She was so tender down there, I loved the feel of her warmth and wetness as Charlie convulsed around my probing fingers. With arms wrapped around my neck, practically squeezing the life out of me, her climax hit. Her legs shook fiercely, but I suddenly realised how wet my lap was, with her noticing at the same time. I saw the look of fear on my face reflected in her own. "*Fuck*! Did your water just break?"

"Oh my god, Brax!"

"Stay calm. I've just hit the buzzer to call a nurse. It's okay, they'll be able to help."

"Brax! They'll know what we did!" I knew the look on her face, but now wasn't the time. "I love you, Cutie, but that is the least of our worries. You and Pebbles are the priority, alright?" She nodded as I hit the buzzer several times when they didn't turn up as fast as I would have liked.

Finally, the nurse came running in. "Mr Carson, will you—" she stopped seeing our faces. "What's wrong? You both look panicked?"

"I think my fiancée's water has broken."

The nurse was very calming as she asked Charlie her name and said they would have a look. "Are you in pain or discomfort right now or just before it?"

"No, none." When the nurse asked about cramping or spasms, I saw her go bright red. "Ahh… define spasm?" The nurse looked at us, confused. I loved mine and Charlie's sex life. There was nothing reserved about her. But when it came to talking about it? She went as red as a beetroot.

"She had an orgasm. Her legs were shaking much more than they normally do." Charlie buried her head in my chest, but not before giving me a quick slap.

"Oh, don't worry, love. I've been in this job long enough to see it all. When you stand there for three hours holding a broomstick handle stuck up a twenty-six-year-old's backside—because they "dared him to do it"— you question your sanity." In unison, Charlie and I both asked, "was his name Chester?" We chuckled, and the nurse looked at us again with a comical look. "How about I get a Doctor and we can take you down to the examination room and see what's going on, alright? Are you comfortable staying here for the moment?"

Charlie thanked her and said "yes," before asking, "can Brax come too?"

"I will bring Mr Carson a chair back with me to wheel him down."

We sat nervously, waiting for the nurse to return, when she did, she had two orderlies assist me into the chair while she wheeled it down, not before checking Charlie was fine to walk. On our way, we ran into the guys coming back, and Liam asked, "where are you going?"

I saw Mark look at Charlie, and it took him only seconds to realise. "Is Pebbles coming?"

"We don't know, maybe," she explained. "The staff are taking us down to the examination room now."

When Chester said, "we're coming," Charlie and I looked at each other, but the nurse spoke up for us before we could say anything. "Only as far as the waiting room. If the baby is on the way, we need a sterile environment. That means Mum and Dad only." Shane thanked her as we followed them through, directing the boys to wait, before showing us to the examination room. She had Charlie change into a gown, and the nurse returned, lowering the bed, and helping her up. The midwife soon joined and explained the Doctor was finishing with another patient, so she would conduct the examination, ready in assistance.

Charlie lay back, and I sat by her head, holding her hand as the midwife conducted the checks, while asking her a few questions. "Ahh… interesting." Charlie shot up on her elbows as she wondered what was wrong? "It's fine, dear, but may I ask what you were doing when this happened?"

Charlie couldn't even think about getting embarrassed as the nurse answered for her. "Her partner gave her an orgasm."

"Well, now, that makes sense."

"What does?" Charlie looked at the midwife, then to the nurse, before back.

"Your water is still intact, my dear. What you experienced was a female ejaculation."

"Oh, my god! I squirted!" My laughter rippled out as if it were a million petals of warm sunlight. I heard the guys in the waiting room crying in hysterics as well. "Fuck! Why did I yell that out?" I fell sideways as I roared in amusement.

Chapter Forty Two

BRAX

I was in tears from laughing so hard, positive I would bust a rib or two if I couldn't stop soon. Whenever I thought I had calmed down enough, I would hear the guys start in hysteria and lose my shit all over again. "Shut the hell up, Brax!"

"Oh god, I'm sorry, Cutie but…." And I was chuckling my head off again. I tried unsuccessfully to stop when Charlie turned to the nurse and asked her to kick me out.

"Go fuck yourself, Braxton! Shit! I'm sorry…." Her hands flew to her mouth as she turned back to the midwife, apologising.

"I've heard much worse, dear. How about we get you both back upstairs, and I will have the nurse check on discharge papers for Mr Carson? I would recommend bed rest to you. Note the use of the word rest." I couldn't help it and started chuckling before apologising to the midwife. "Dear, I wouldn't worry about me. It is she that is going to beat your arse."

"See! Even the midwife understands!" Charlie squealed at me as she pointed. They helped to get her sorted before she slowly stood off the bed.

"Wanna push me, babe?"

"You don't want to ask me that, especially after you laughed. I will push you down a flight of stairs."

Still finding it amusing, she slapped me when I choked back a laugh. "Fuck, I love your temper. Wanna have angry sex later?"

"Brax!" she wailed, and the nurse stepped in. "Alright, kids, break it up. You still have the chimpanzee's out in the waiting room."

"Oh fuck, Monkey is going to have a field day with this, babe." I laughed as Charlie stopped and pointed her finger firmly in my face.

"If you encourage him even once, Brax, I swear to-"

I cut her off, "I love you," grinning, while grabbing her finger. Charlie snatched it back and sucked her teeth at me. I saw the eye roll, too, as she turned and started walking out with the nurse who held the door open for us. The guys all standing there, heads down, bodies vibrating with trapped amusement, begging to be released, but knowing the moment they did, all hell would break loose. I was the first cave, falling forward in my chair as I started trembling again. She flipped my hat off, storming out. "Eat a dick, Brax!" They waited until she was out of earshot before they finally released their laughter.

"Been nice knowing you, bro. She's going to fuck kill you." Mark was right, nothing new there.

"I can't help it, man! I fucking tried to stop laughing so many times." The nurse spoke up for me, but only briefly. "In his defence, he tried, not that it made much difference. Also, I am sure your fiancée just left the hospital."

"*Fuck!*" Being stuck in this chair and not discharged yet, Mark knew I was trapped and offered to go. "Thanks, Mark!" I shouted as he raced down the corridor, turned left, before we heard the sliding front doors go a second later.

"You should stay in the hospital another night, bro." I looked back at the boys.

"Why the fuck would I do that, Liam?"

"Because if you return to the hotel with her tonight, she will put you straight back in here." Chester finished for him.

"I know I shouldn't be finding this so funny, but I can't stop. I need to get out of here." The nurse escorted me back up to the room, the guys waited with me while she organised the doctor to come and do a last check and manage my discharge papers and medications. "Why haven't Mark and Midget come back yet? Can someone call him? My phone's in the drawer, and I can't reach it." Liam pulled out his phone and rang Mark. I heard them speaking, but I could only make out a little of what he was saying until Liam said goodbye. "Why are we meeting back at the hotel?" I immediately asked.

"Mark sent you a message when they left. She insisted she wasn't coming back in, so he jumped in the cab with her instead of-"

"Being her normal stubborn ass and storming off on her own?" I asked. When Chester pulled me up and told me to "settle the fuck down," I shook my head. "Sorry! I get it. Okay, we laughed at her. I probably should have stopped sooner. I know that. But heading off on her own, heavily pregnant, in a city we don't even live in! Sorry, but that's my fucking child, too. I'm not comfortable with that." I saw all the guys looking at me, unsure and nervous about speaking. "What?"

"Agh... mate, I probably wouldn't say that to her."

"And why not, Shane?"

I watched him try to find the right words when I challenged him. "It appears... how do I say this?"

"Shane's trying to say you sound like a baboon." Chester said it for him.

"Fucking wanker!" I spat at Chester. "You started this by being a pain in the arse. If you had shut up for once, I wouldn't have had to get you high."

Shane and Liam cracked up now, saying this was just as good. "See, there you go again. Being a baboon. If you stopped for a moment, I would explain." Chester threw it back at me.

"Go on then, if you think you are such a genius with women..."

"You go in saying that shit, and she will put you straight back in the hospital, rightly so." *Really?* "She's still a grown-ass woman, Brax. Yes, she's pregnant, but not incapacitated. You can't speak to her like a child, she'll whoop your ass all over that hotel suite, and bro, I'll light a blunt and watch her do it."

"It'll probably be more entertaining than anything on television, right?" Chester turned to nod a 'yes' in response to Shane's question.

I flipped them both with the middle finger as Liam sat in the chair beside me. "Try going in and explaining to her how angry she was with you. She panicked last night when she got stuck on the flight and couldn't reach us. She just did the same thing to you today by taking off, knowing you couldn't leave and had no intention of letting you know what she was doing if Mark didn't go after her."

"Yes, do what Hippie Boy said and reverse psychology the hell out of that Evil Midget." My jaw ticked as I thought about it. "Do it, man, don't be scared!"

"You better be right. I'm not taking another slap upside the head because of you."

"Nah, you're already brain-dead enough cockhead." I looked at Chester and told him, "continue being a bitch, I dare you. Remember, my ankle will heal."

After finally being discharged, the guys hired a chair for me to make it easier to get around for the moment, we headed to the taxi rank and got in a maxi towards the hotel. "For real, can we get some decent food when we return? I feel like I am wasting away."

"Thought you had a filling breakfast?" I punched Chester in the arm, but of course, he just laughed at me. Liam agreed he could go for food as well. "I was just fucking with him. Of course, we are getting food."

I texted Mark to let him know we were back once we got out of the taxi, with him replying almost immediately that he was at my suite with Charlie. The guys paid the cab, wheeled me through, and went straight for the lift. Liam pushed me down towards the door, and when we got there, Shane knocked before Mark opened it and let us through.

Charlie stared at us in the doorway, Liam asking where I wanted to sit. "Bed please, mate, I'm pissed off, so I wouldn't be good company." Chester's mouth twitched, and he quickly tried to hide the smirk when he realised what I was doing.

"Let me help you," Chester offered.

"It's fine. I can do it." Charlie stood up.

"All good, don't get up for me, it'll be easier for one of the boys, anyway." Chester walked around, took the handles on the chair, and started pushing me to the room. Once inside, we both had to hold back, so she didn't hear. "Man, we're so fucked if she finds out!"

"True. It's a little cruel, but it's also a valid point. And Midget does it all the time without thinking." He pointed out in my defence.

"You're right. I'll let it go for a bit but then explain to her we are both assholes, but I love her asshole, so she needs to bend over."

Chester cracked up as he helped me slide up onto the bed. "Yeah, alright, man. Let me know how that works out for you."

"Do you want to order some food now?" I asked once settled.

"Fuck yeah, I do!" We fist-bumped as he asked, "what do you feel like?"

"Mexican mate! I want my ass to burn so I can finally do a shit. My stomach feels like it will explode from all that medication they pumped me full of."

"Gassy as fuck, right?"

"Yeah, see you know!"

"Better do a shit before you get a blow job from Midget. You fart during that, and I'll see you at your funeral." I pushed him away as he patted my back before heading to the lounge.

I heard him shout out to the others that he was ordering food, and I didn't have to wonder how long it would be before Charlie came in when seconds after he left, she opened the door, slammed it behind her, walking in. "So, you're pissed off, hey?"

She sat on the bed next to me, eyes glued to mine. "It doesn't matter now, Charlie. Besides, I'm tired and hungry."

"You're a fucking funny guy, aren't you, Brax? Now, because you've had enough, it's no longer amusing?"

"Okay, so you want to play that angle? Let's look at you then, shall we?" I barked back.

"Go on then." She gestured for me to continue, crossing her arms over the top of her stomach.

"You went off your nut at me for causing you stress and worry last night, and rightly so. I accepted that. Yet you did the same thing to me today by taking off on your own and not even having the courtesy to let me where you were going? Thankfully, I have wonderful mates who look out for both of us."

I sat back and watched her think about it for a few minutes. "Fuck you, stop speaking sense." She offered quietly after a long beat, "we're both assholes, huh?"

"We are. But babe, I love you. I honestly worry when you wander off on your own like that. Especially now that I have you both to worry about." I reached out and touched her stomach, rubbing it softly.

"Alright. And I worry when you and Chester get yourself into that state. There is no reasoning with either of you."

"Okay, little Mumma. I promise to keep that in mind as well. You gonna kiss me now?"

"I'm going to kiss you now." I pulled her closer by her shirt as our lips met, and we embraced one another. Just as my tongue entered her mouth, I heard the door open.

"Yo! Food is five minutes away... you pair of bitches! I knew you wouldn't stay mad long." We both chuckled as she shook her head, and I wrapped my hand around her neck, kissing her forehead. "Hey, Midget! I got you a present earlier while waiting for Brax's discharge."

"Really? And what's that, Chester?"

I saw him throw something through the air, and when it landed on the bed, I fell sideways, laughing. There next to her was a pink plastic kid's water pistol. "A fucking squirt gun!" I muttered.

"I swear I'll strangle you one of these days, Chester!"

We had been back home for a few weeks, and Charlie was thirty-three weeks along. She was getting more agitated by the day and uncomfortable.

For me, well, I loved seeing her like this. She'd always been unworldly to me, but this was the next level. Given that I was still in the boot with my ankle and Charlie was heavily pregnant, we had been home bound the last few weeks, meaning the guys had been spending much more time in the studio I had downstairs.

Marcus was due back from Canada this morning, so he would have a few hours of sleep before we all caught up tonight. We chose to meet here as it was easier than trying to get about, and Charlie could go to bed when she needed.

I had been awake for about half an hour and lay in bed watching my two girls sleep soundly. When I reached out and stroked her stomach, I felt her hand come up over mine. I moved closer; she lifted her arm up, wrapping it around my back as I lay on her side, resting my head on her shoulder. I felt our baby girl move, so I gently pushed down, seeing if I could get baby Pebbles to give me a kickback. "Quit tormenting your daughter."

"I enjoy feeling her movement."

"I know you do, but once she does, she's going straight to my bladder, and you know what that means?"

"Wait! Are you saying what I think you're saying?"

"Yes, Brax, that's exactly what I am saying." She answered, pushing me on my back while ripping my boxer shorts down. It captivated me as she slid her panties off, straddled my hips and lowered herself on to my ready dick, riding me. After a few minutes, she was sliding along my dick in our favourite position at the moment, where I could still feel her chest over her stomach, without putting too much pressure on it. I didn't know about Charlie, but having her slide up and down me like this drove me crazy. Seeing her on display, her body full of my baby, engorged breasts so plump and juicy and the pure desire painted all over her face.

Our hands explored more, but our stares at each other were electric. When she tried to kiss me but couldn't quite make it because of her stomach, I leaned up to meet her as our lips locked in ecstasy. This was the first time we had kissed all morning, but we both made it worthwhile.

I wanted to get on top, so I hugged her and rolled us over, placing her gently on the bed. I stepped off it carefully, getting my balance first in the boot, and moved her legs to the edge and apart to accommodate me. Now I'm a sucker for many things, but seeing my girl naked on our bed with her hair all messed up and feeling her insides just drives me wild. I leaned down to give her a sumptuous kiss, and we made out with each other tenderly. She wrapped her legs around my ass and pulled me into her. I got the hint and began slowly pumping in and out, holding myself up as I pulled her ass off the bed, slightly into me. We kept on kissing as our bodies moved, making her breasts and stomach rub against me. We fucked like this for a sweet eternity, playing with each other and ensuring our needs were met.

I then did a trick I read about, where you can get all the way in and get her off. I hadn't tried it yet, so I wondered if it would work. Given how exceptionally aroused she had been the last few weeks, I figured it was a perfect time.

I fucked her with short, quick pumps—supposedly this relaxes her, making it easier to open up further. Trying it for a few minutes, with just barely the head in—which seemed like hours, probably days, to her, as she begged me. After the tease, I braced up and rammed it in as far as possible. My cock went to the hilt, and I could feel Charlie go crazy. She started moaning wildly, and hearing her do that made me try to go deeper. "Oh fuck, Brax! What are you doing to me?" Her body fell limp, eyes rolled back, before she tightened and heated. She started cumming, her walls gripped my cock, and the reverberations ignited my soon to be fate. I rode her out, following her commands to go faster and more profound. She screamed so loudly I was afraid that even our neighbours would hear and wonder what was up. "*Brax!*" Feeling her vibrate all over me was enough to push me over. I pulled out and straddled her hips, landing my cock on her stomach as she lifted her head up, ready to watch, and I started pumping myself furiously over her. I felt that familiar twitch and aimed down towards her skin.

"Agh fuck!... Fuck, Charlie!" The final straw was her face, watching me finish myself off, waiting for me. I shot my load and painted the tight skin along her stomach and down over her breasts. Her head rolled back, and I saw a single rope of my cream paint across her neck. The feeling literally knocked me backwards. I fell to the side of the bed, a few more loose shots landing on her, our sheets and my legs. By the time I stopped, I was on my back, covered in our love and sweat, ready to die from the feeling.

Charlie was a sexual creature when it was just us, so she started licking me clean, and I went wild. When she came to my groin, taking it in her mouth and tonguing me clean, I wanted to nut again, but I was so spent from the explosion I just experienced. She crawled up and collapsed beside me as I rolled on my side, wrapping my arm and a leg over her. I fell into a light sleep as we lay there, spent but mostly satisfied. Unfortunately, she got me up again, but this time not with her mouth, and told me she needed a shower from my 'accident'. I could still smell myself, so I joined her, making sure I had put the waterproof bandaging over the incision on my ankle, and removed the boot.

We washed and dressed before getting everything downstairs for tonight when we realised we hadn't got the fucking meat for the barbeque. After a brief battle of words, with Charlie insisting she was okay to drive and me wanting to get a taxi, I finally chucked her the keys, and we got in the car. After pulling up at the butchers, I ordered while Charlie said she was heading across the road to grab an iced tea. I snatched a photo while something distracted her when I saw her walking back. I wanted as many pictures of my babies as possible to remember these moments. She looked like a goddess right now. A white full-brimmed sun hat, knee-length beige shirt dress, and strappy sandals. Her hand rested safely over our precious cargo with her drink in the other hand.

While it took longer than normal, we eventually got back home and unpacked. The guys were heading over at four thirty, so they could carry the heavier stuff out for us. Plus, Liam and Shane insisted on doing the barbeque, as they didn't want us standing for too long. It surprised me I hadn't heard from them all day, primarily from Chester. I'd half expected him to turn up early, wanting to get stoned already. When they finally rocked up at the agreed time, Charlie had left the door unlocked to make it easier. Hence, I text them to let them know to come straight through rather than either of us trying to hobble up the stairs.

I heard the door go, and Chester yelled out. "Yo Brax!"

"Downstairs Fuckface!"

"Alright, Midget Fucker!" The stairs creaked, and I heard Liam ask Chester, "so you're always going to greet him like that now?"

"Or until Charlie twats them both." Mace was right; honestly, it surprised me she hadn't already. Charlie joined me as we waited to greet everyone… quickly squealing when they reached the bottom.

"Chrissy!" she raced over for a hug.

I laughed, as it all made sense. "Now I know why you didn't call me all day, bro! A naughty little monkey was jumping on the bed!"

Chapter Forty Three

CHARLIE

There stood Chester, happier than I had seen him in weeks, like the cat who caught the mouse, with Chrissy standing right beside him. After saying "hello" to everyone and Chrissy asking how the pregnancy was going, we headed outside to sit down. The guys were fussing in the booth over a new recording they did today when I heard the front door go again, followed by Marcus' voice. "Charlie? Brax?"

"Down here, Marcus. Sorry, but fuck those stairs." I heard him holler back, "don't worry, I'm coming down." Footsteps thumped against the wooden internal staircase and seconds later there he was... and Tessa! "What is with all this secrecy? First Chrissy and now you?" They both laughed at me.

"Wow!" she smiled sweetly. "Look at you, girl. I swear, it wasn't that long ago I saw you."

"Tell me about it!" I agreed. "What's going on here? Did I miss the memo you were all coming back with Marcus?" He explained, "it was a surprise. When I heard of Chester's antics, I figured Chrissy needed to pull Monkey's head in."

"Well, this is true. He assisted Brax in breaking his ankle."

"Shut it, you little squirt, or is that big squirt?" Brax and the boys laughed, I turned to Chester and warned him. "Whatever, shut up, Midget! I love you too!"

"I will ban you from my daughter Chester if you carry on."

"Our daughter, Charlie." Brax interjected.

"You'll also be on that ban list if you continue to laugh!" After catching up and the drinks flowing freely, the guys looked thick as thieves and up to something. Brax got up and hobbled inside on his boot, I watched Liam and Shane grab the shot glasses and a bottle of fireball while Monkey grabbed a can of Lemonade and put it down. "What's this for?"

"We are playing, 'Pissed the game.' But before you say you can't because it's a drinking game, we agreed you can shoot that lemonade instead."

"Or I can just watch?"

"Nope, I have already decided, Cutie." I turned and looked at Brax and asked, "who died and made you boss?"

Before I could answer, Marcus said, "you seem awfully cocky, Brax, for someone who just a few weeks ago was on the verge of getting a divorce."

"She gave me ammunition back." Marcus laughed, and Brax came over and sat beside me, pulling my chair closer as he wrapped his arm around my shoulder. "You alright?"

"Fine for the moment. I had a bit of a nap this afternoon."

"Alright, just let me know when you are ready for bed, and I will make sure they keep the noise down," I told him it was alright, he looked at me quizzically. "It feels like our group is whole again. Do you know what I mean?"

"I get it, babe. It is moments like these I remember how damn lucky we are. We have an amazing family around us."

"We do. Which reminds me, do you think we should tell everyone we decided on a name?"

"*Yes!*" We swung our heads around to Chester, who was glaring at us.

Brax cracked up as he leaned over and kissed my temple. "I think you just shot yourself in the foot, baby."

"Yea, but in my defence, I figured it would distract him with Chrissy being here."

"You just got called out," Kendall chuckled.

"I know exactly what my Little Hottie said to me, and I also heard what Brax said." Liam and the rest had missed it, so he turned and asked Chester, "what?"

"They've decided on a name for our niece," he explained to the group.

"Ooh! Tell us, please! Then we can start spoiling her and get special things with her name on them." Mace gushed with love.

Kendall was quick to get excited as well. "Yes! I'm absolutely with Mace on this."

"Agree! We definitely have to get the little princess something special." Chrissy and Tessa joined in also, the boys all turned and said, "thanks a lot, Midget!"

"What did I do?"

"Now all the girls' ovaries will burst, and we'll need to double wrap." That earned him another slap, not that he cared.

"Not my problem. I'm shooting blanks at the target range for the moment." Brax quipped, taking a sip of his beer.

"You pig!" He laughed and started trying to cover my face in kisses as I giggled. "Get off, you creep."

"Right, let's play this game." Chester pulled out one card as Brax kissed up to my ear and whispered, "you're bloody lucky he has the attention span of a gnat."

"Excuse me! When you two are finished tongue fucking, can we start?" Chester drew attention when Brax covered my lips.

Rolling my eyes, I told him, "get on with it already."

"Drink if you piss in the shower. More fluid for your next crime against sanitation."

"Who doesn't pee in the shower?" I asked as Brax turned to me and said, "what the hell? We shower together most days."

"And you thought you weren't a fan of golden showers, bro." Everyone took a drink. Who doesn't pee in the shower?

Chrissy drew next and read out her card. "Drink if you've ever had a threesome. You and your two hands don't count."

"That rules Chester and Mrs. Palmer out." Mark, Liam, Marcus and Chester all drank. Mace's eyebrow raised at Liam, no shit, I was side-eyeing Brax to see what he would do.

"Drink if you've got a big or small booty. No middle ground here." Everyone sat there looking around the table… Finally, Chester spoke up. "All the girls need to drink." The boys agreed before Tessa asked, "what the hell? Are they ganging up on us?"

"I don't know how to take this one." Brax turned and answered me, "Think of your ass like a battery, I know I shouldn't, but one day I'm gonna stick my tongue on it." He tapped my glass. "Drink."

"Get out, now." I pointed towards the door.

We laughed when Shane said, "I'm stealing that argument," and held Kendall's drink up, telling her, "take it." Kendall drew next and skimmed over the card. "Drink if you've ever had worms. Don't worry. Lots of people were street beggars at one stage." Mace gasped, her jaw dropping as she choked on a giggle, poor Kendall going bright red. "Oh my god, no! No, I swear it's the card, look." She turned it around to show us.

Shane saved her. "We know babes," much to her relief.

Taking the focus from Kendall, who had her face buried in Shane's chest, Marcus handed Chester a drink. "You still have worms now, Monkey. You can never sit still."

No one drank, as half of them probably couldn't even remember last week, let alone their childhood. The others lit up a few blunts and passed them around as Brax took up a card. "Drink if you've ever made breakfast for a one-night stand. Were they eggs? Fertilised? Fucking boom!"

No one drank, I chortled, to everyone's amusement. "Savage fucks! Can't even offer a feed!"

Chester turned on me, asking, "Are you serious?"

"What?"

"You're one to talk, didn't you leg it on a guy because he was a dud root?" Liam laughed and said, "I remembered that, it was the night we played 'Never Have I Ever' on the Regional Tour."

"Yep, and the first night Brax tried to move in and bang her." Chester highlighted for everyone's benefit who didn't already know.

"Shut up, Fuckface!" They flipped each other off. This went on for a few more rounds, with Chester getting walloped by a slurry of hard truths, I noticed he was getting increasingly wasted by the second. When I saw his eyes squint, I couldn't help but be the evil shit I am, packing him a joint, chucking it over, while telling him to "catch."

"Ooh, thanks, baby." Before he could even get the word finished, Brax threw his cup at him. "Hey! Don't wet my joint, you fucking Caveman prick!"

"As if I wasted a drink on you, fool. It was empty. And you…." He turned around and stared straight at me.

"What did I do?"

"You make him a joint and not me? What do I pay you for, woman?" I giggled as I got up and sat on his lap like he loved. He pulled my chair closer to put his broken ankle up, relieving the weight pressure on it. I found it amusing to watch his inner conflict, trying to decide what he wanted to rub first… my legs as he always had, or my bump. I eventually grabbed his hand and placed it on his daughter before I leaned into his neck.

"He's gone. Look at his eyes. A few puffs on that, and he'll be on the floor." Brax cracked up as he whispered back his love for my evil side. The guys all took a break for a few and had a joint while I went inside to get some more Fireball for them to use the next round. I put the kettle on and made myself a tea when I heard footsteps and looked around.

"Need a hand, babe?" I smiled at Brax, saying, "I'm fine," showing I was just making a cup of tea. "Chester is off his trolley."

"I told you he would be, didn't I?" I giggled when Brax asked, "how much green did you put in it?"

"I think the question you meant was, did I remember to put any spin in it?"

He came closer when he realised I had given him a straight blunt. "Fuck I love you. That's hilarious, babe." His hands slid to my hips, it didn't take long before one of them moved up my side, pulled my hair out of the way, and his lips suctioned to my neck.

"Mmm, Brax."

"Yes, baby?" His hands reached the front of my stomach, mine making its way up behind his neck and into the nape of his hair, playing gently. He rewarded me by pushing his hips into my butt, running his hands down my stomach until his fingers rested and splayed across my hips.

Soon his groin was grinding against my ass, creating a beautiful friction. "You feel so good, baby."

"It is probably for the same reason you thought it would be clever to walk over here in your boot without your crutches." His warm breath skimmed my skin as he quizzed, "Mmm, and why's that?" He gripped me firmer as he started increasing his speed against my butt, nipping at my neck now. My knees weakened, thirsty for my man and high off the arousal he was showing me. "Because you're stoned, baby."

He laughed against me, before raising his hand and turning my face. "You're right, you do feel more sensitised when you are high, but baby... I always feel this way about you. I'll never get enough."

"Even when I look like an extra in the movie Aliens, my insides spewing out on a hospital bed as your kid stretches me wide open?"

Brax cringed, a grimace on his face. "That's actually fucking gross the way you explained that."

"I know, but it's also true." I shrugged.

"Please don't kill that moment for me, too."

"Okay, but I will bet you one hundred dollars, if you look down there, you will faint."

"I will not!" he was indignant.

"I'll take that bet." He shook and agreed as the kettle whistled, I switched it off, pouring the water into my cup. We heard Chester's voice as I worked around Brax, who was still wrapped around me, trying to rub himself up on my butt. "Don't make that Midget squirt there, bro. No one has cream in tea anymore."

Brax's humour reverberated against me when I told Monkey, "Eat a dick."

"You will, Midget!" Chester hollered back. Brax picked up my tea and carried it outside as we sat down so the game could start again.

I was getting sleepy, curled up as best I could these days in Brax's lap, when I heard Tessa ask a question. "If your name starts with a vowel, then drink up your legend, fuck those consonants." Chester shook his head, confused, and asked her what she had just said. "Does your name start with a consonant or a vowel, Chester?"

"No." The moment he said it, I lost it and nearly fell off Brax's lap from laughing so hard. The penny finally dropped for everyone else who cracked up, as well. "What? What's so funny?"

"Chester, you just said no, man...." I had to stop as I giggled again, thinking about it. "Tessa asked you, does your name start with a consonant or a vowel?"

"It starts with a C?" That was me done, and I had to hop up, trying to squeeze my thighs so I didn't pee myself from hysteria. Finally, Chester realised what he had done. "Fuck off! I'm off my face right now, you Evil Midget."

The guys carried on playing the game, but after laughing so hard at Chester and having to make a quick pit stop at the toilet, I soon sat back down with Brax and curled up, falling asleep. I often felt him stroke my legs or rub my stomach as he shuffled to make sure we were both comfortable. I must have fallen into a deep sleep when I felt him trying to ease me awake. "What's up, Batman?"

"Someone just rang the doorbell, Cutie." Before I could move, Mark said he would go. The stairs would be more accessible for him at the moment. We thanked him as I snuggled back down into Brax, not taking too much notice of it. I was so tired, and I just wanted to sleep.

I heard Mark come back down, and then I listened to her familiar voice. "Charlie?"

"Tina!" I was wide awake. "What are you doing here, babe?" The moment I saw her face, I knew she had been crying, I tried to get up as quickly as I could with some help from Brax. I walked over, wrapping her in a loving hug. "Come on, babe, you need a drink?" She nodded and hugged me back as we made our way inside.

I could see Brax looking, concern plastering his face, and I tried to silently communicate that she would be alright. Of course she would, she was my best friend. I would do everything I could to protect Tina. He turned around and told the guys to carry on so we could have some privacy. After a few minutes of hugging Tina, we finally pulled apart. "You know it's hard to hug you properly these days."

"Tell me about it, babe." I agreed, flicking the kettle on again, before turning back. Softly I asked, "What's wrong? Talk to me?"

"He's been cheating on me, Charlie."

"What! Alex?" It shocked me, I followed up with, "Are you sure?"

"I saw them," she sobbed. I picked her hand up in comfort. "His tongue was still down her throat when I tapped on his shoulder."

"Holy shit! I'm gonna cut his dick off and throw it to the sharks in the Harbour." Tina choked back a laugh before the tears fell again, asking, "what am I gonna do, Charlie?"

"You're going to get smashed with us right now, as well as stay here for as long as you need." She went to interrupt, so I covered her mouth with my hand. "And there is no discussion on the matter."

"I love you, girl, but you and Brax are about to have a baby."

"Tina, you're staying," I insisted. "You're my best friend, and you were the one that helped me through a similar situation. There is no argument… plus, a live-in babysitter would be good." She laughed before sniffling back her tears.

"I love you," she promised. "I love you too," I soothed her. "Do you need anything? Clothes? Vodka?"

"I've got a small bag of essentials in the car." She pointed to the driveway where her car was.

"Help yourself to anything of mine you need, and I'll organise the guys to go with you in the morning to get the rest of your belongings." Tina went to say something, but I continued quickly. "Mumma Bear has spoken. Grab one of the spare bedrooms, babe, and claim it as yours. I just don't recommend the one downstairs. Chester usually has that, so you know it's nasty in there." She laughed, patting her eyes dry, thanking me. "Have you eaten?" she shook her head. "I'll order some food for everyone all while you get sorted."

"Thanks, Charlie. I will freshen up my face, change, and be down."

"I'll have a joint ready for you." Tina headed up to get sorted, I went into the kitchen and ordered some pizza. Brax leaned across the stone top bench as I was on the phone. Moving closer, so our faces were only inches apart, I bent the rest of the way to kiss him as he pulled my top down, having a look. "Quit it, you pest!" He let it go before stroking my cheek. Giving me a quick kiss, Brax sat back. "What are you doing?"

"Ordering some Pizza."

"You're going to be a great Mum, always putting everyone else first." I chuckled as I told him to "shut up."

"Is Tina alright?"

"It's her business to tell, baby. She will be okay but staying with us for a little while if that's alright?"

"You don't even need to ask. Of course." He nodded positively.

"Could you see if Chester, Mark, Liam and Shane would mind helping tomorrow morning so she can get her stuff from Alex's house?" Brax put his finger to my lips and told me, "say no more. I'll sort it out now."

"Thank you. I'll just finish this order and be out." He wandered over to the boys outside and I assumed he was asking if they were free in the morning when I saw them all nod, and Chester lifted his head up, looking at me and giving me the thumbs up. I blew a kiss, mouthing 'thank you' as I finished the order and headed outside. Brax automatically opened his arms for me to sit, and of course, I did.

"All good, Sweet Cheeks?"

"Yeah, thanks, Monkey. Tina is going to be staying with us for a little while. She's just getting sorted now and will be back out shortly."

"Just tell us what time, Midget, and we'll be here."

"Thanks, Shane, I appreciate it."

"Does this mean we earned the right to know our niece's name now?"

We cracked up as Chester said it. "Yeah, I didn't forget you fuckers. I was just buying my time."

"You realise that is technically extortion, right? And it's illegal."

"Only if you can prove it, Midget."

"I agree with Chester this time." Mace shocked me with that, adding. "Tell us, pretty lady. I'm dying here!"

"Tell what? Oh, and Hi, everyone." Tina let her presence known, moving out to join us, grabbing a seat close by me. I reached out, holding her hand, giving it a gentle squeeze.

"Here, chick." Chester passed her the bong with a cone already packed. "You look like you need this more than I do now."

"Like you wouldn't believe," she smiled, "thank you."

"Well, once you get that down, enjoy this, too." Mark chucked her a blunt, Brax and I smiled at the guys trying to help her through this, knowing how important she was to me. Thankfully, it also distracted Chester again, buying us some more time.

The guys and girls were helping Tina forget what happened tonight, and I was nodding off in Brax's lap. I felt him lean down and kiss my lips softly. I opened my eyes and stared back at him as I ran my hand up his cheek. When he realised I was still awake, he moved across my right cheek as he gripped the left, he reached my ear and whispered, "It should be illegal to be this in love with you." I pulled my head to the side and looked at him, not expecting those words. Usually, when he was in this state, he was just horny, not romantic. I smiled, before asking, "what's gotten into you?"

"Can you do something for me?"

"Maybe. It depends on what it is?"

"You remember that first tour, and we snuck off together?"

"I remember. Please don't ask me to repeat what happened that night when we got back to the hotel. This beach ball could create a problem," I said as I rubbed my stomach.

"This beach ball…" he placed his hand over mine, "as you called it, is everything I ever wanted with you. And no, that wasn't what I was going to ask. Do you remember what I told you my two fantasies were that night?"

I thought about it, but it didn't take me long. "I remember."

"Well, one is my daily living dream because it was you." I nodded, because I already knew that. "Well, given your sex drive lately with the hormones, have I got a chance of getting that second from you?"

I looked at him and asked, "you still think about it?"

"Aww god, Charlie, I really do."

"All you had to do was ask. Of course." He captured my lips forcefully, his tongue sliding dominantly over my own. I was lost in our passion when Tina sighed. "Ugh, are they always this sickly sweet?"

"I heard that, Tina!" I said, smirking at her as I pulled away from Brax.

"Well, I'm sure your hearing is fine. It was your ability to communicate with your tongue down Brax's throat I was talking about."

Chester laughed and told Tina this was constant. "Hell, I have her specific moans pegged out now, depending on whether he's being a caveman or loving." The boys laughed when Chrissy slapped him, and I told him, "you're sick."

"Now that you came up for air, I remember you mentioning something about our niece's name when I returned?"

Mark shot up in his chair, shooting his finger at Tina as she said this. "You can stay, girl. Unlike Monkey nuts, you stay true to the cause. What's the name, guys?"

Everyone turned on us while we smirked back. I looked up at Brax, and he shrugged his shoulders, waiting for my direction. "You can tell them, Batman."

"Really?" I nodded 'yes' to him, and he gave me a quick kiss on the forehead. "We have decided to name our baby girl Molly."

"*Yes!*" Chester jumped from his seat in excitement. "I knew you loved it, Midget when I told you!"

Chapter Forty Four

BRAX

Tina had been living with us for a few weeks, and we were now thirty-five weeks pregnant. I was finally out of that ridiculous boot, but had to continue wearing my ankle splint for a few weeks yet. This meant we didn't have to wait much longer until baby Molly joined us. The boys had been around nearly every day. Charlie was working from the office downstairs, as she had some things she wanted to complete before she was on maternity leave. I'd promised to stay upstairs, so she wasn't disrupted and could get through it quicker. This also gave me the perfect cover for Tina to keep her distracted this week. The boys and I had organised, with the voucher from Richard and Carole, to have the nursery ready. I had a good idea of what she wanted from everything we'd discussed — neutral with coloured decorations so that if we had any more children; we didn't have to redo the nursery each time, just change the decor. We had sent Chester and Liam downstairs on an operation to distract and annoy Charlie, as I had Tina come up and check the last touches. Now we waited in the nursery. Chester and Liam had set themselves a target to see how quickly they could annoy her because she came up the stairs ranting at me to get them to fuck off. It took less than five minutes, and they highly impressed me with their efficiency to the task. "Brax! Where are you?" she whined.

"Up here, baby, what's wrong?" I shouted back, not moving. The aim was to have her come to us.

"Where is here? Can you sort these two out? They're pissing me off, and I need to get this work done, Brax!" I could hear her voice getting closer. "Control your children, please." I chuckled and said, "sorry," but did not move, so it did not surprise me when she called out a few minutes later. "Brax! Where are you?"

"Up the hallway, babe."

"Have you gone back to bed, you lazy shit?" I could hear her padding down the hallways towards our room, but I was in the one directly across from it and made my way to the doorframe to greet her. "What the fuck are you doing in there?"

"Nothing!" Yeah, I deliberately made that sound suss to pique her interest.

"What did you do, Brax? Your face gives you away. You know that, right?"

"Alright... look." I paused, scratching the back of my neck, playing the rogue game. "I might have done something, okay?"

"What did you do?" She flapped her hands about. "That room is supposed to be for the nursery!" *And there it was.*

"I know.... so I made it a nursery."

"You did what?" I saw her eyes bug out of her head as she pushed the door behind me, and I helped her open it. The others were all inside and shouted out, "Surprise!" I chuckled when her hands flew to her mouth. Charlie stepped around, taking it all in. I'd had new timber slat-flooring laid, the same as the rest of the house, and went for a pale grey on the walls, not being a fan of white myself, especially with children in the house soon. A white crib sat on one wall with pale pink blankets the girls had sorted, one with Molly's name embroidered. The other side had a cupboard with a built-in change and dresser table next to it for Charlie to put out the things she needed. In the corner, I had a grey teepee added with a matching grey recliner cushion and an assortment of white and pink star pillows. A carousel of clouds hung from above it. In keeping it consistent, I had let the girls convince me to add metallic decorations to the wall behind it in silver and pink hot air balloons and a moon.

"Oh, my god! I don't know if I will burst into tears or pee my pants." I saw Chester sneak up behind her and lean into her ear. "No more squirting from you, missy."

"Chester!" Of course, he just laughed as she tried to slap him. Grabbing her wrist carefully, he pulled Charlie back, wrapping his arms around her shoulders, and hugging her as he asked, "So what'd you think?"

"Holy shit! You guys did this for Molly?"

"Of course, babe, that little girl will be the glue that holds this family together." Charlie turned to look at Mace, eyes filled with tears now as she told her to "shut up before I cry." Of course, the gang just laughed at her as Shane yelled out, "group hug."

"Definitely! I love you all!" We came in when Charlie said that and hugged her as she tried to contain her emotions, taking the room in.

"So, how did we do, Cutie?" I asked.

"It's perfect. But you guys are our family. You know us better than anyone else. There was no way you could go wrong."

"Right, this was fun, kids, and I love you, Charlie, but I need to get ready. I have a date tonight." Charlie's head turned to Tina in shock when she spoke. This was news to her as well. "You dirty, stop out! How am I not hearing about this before now?"

"No time, babes, sorry. Gotta run." Tina tore off into her room. Charlie squealed after her. The rest of us looked on, amused. "Yeah, I might also head, guys, and get sorted. Let you both enjoy this moment together." Mark drew our attention back to the room. "Thank you so much, Mark. I love you."

"Love you too, Midget." He hugged us both before heading out, once we heard the front door shut, Charlie turned to us all, pointing out where they both had just left.

"Okay, so that was weird, right?"

"Yeah. Maybe they are porking or something." Chester shrugged his shoulders as he spoke, none too perturbed by it.

"Chester!" He looked at her unphased, saying, "it could be true."

"No way! Mark has April. He is not a cheat, and Tina has just gone through that. She wouldn't hurt another woman in that way."

Shane started shaking his head, saying, "no," asking, "you didn't hear?"

"Heard what?"

"Shit! Sorry babe, I meant to tell you when I came home last week, but you were already asleep. April and Mark called it a day. A couple of reasons, the main being the distance and heavy work schedules."

"But they are still good friends and have talked since," Chester added, which relaxed Charlie. "Mark is taking it fine. Probably because he is already all up in Tina."

"Can I send him home now, please, Brax? I don't want to hear this."

I chuckled at her and said, "sure."

"Although I was going to ask, does everyone want to stay for dinner since you're here already and helped out this week?" She offered.

"How about we head down the road to the new burger joint to make it easier? Then we can all shoot off home from there. I wouldn't mind getting an early night, to be honest. Those paint fumes have made me higher than half that green we smoke." Kendall looked at Shane and asked, "are you alright?"

"I'm fine, baby. Just getting a bit of a headache, so some fresh air would be good."

"Chrissy and I were just saying the same. You're ready to get into your pyjamas and bed, babe."

"Like you wouldn't believe. Must be something in the air lately. I feel like someone has zapped all my energy."

Charlie chuckled as we all turned to look at her. "I remember that feeling well. Around the time we first found out we were pregnant."

"Midget!" I lost it when Chester yelled at her this time and had to remind her, "don't give a bloke a heart-attack babe."

"Shit! Did I say that aloud? I'm sorry, guys, this fucking baby brain. I speak before I think."

"No, that's just you Sweet Cheeks." She smiled sarcastically, flipping Monkey off. Not long after, we all got into our cars and headed down to get dinner.

By the time we returned, Tina had already left, so Charlie and I set the alarm and headed to our bedroom for an early night.

"I'm just going to grab a shower after all that painting, babe. Won't be long."

"Alright, Batman." It surprised me when Charlie didn't follow into the shower, but I thought little of it. I just figured she was ready to put her feet up. After showering and drying, I brushed my teeth and hung my towel around my shoulders as I returned to our bedroom. I finally looked up as I was drying my hair with the towel. "Fuck, Charlie!"

"Hi," she blushed at the heat radiating from my eyes. Sat on her knees on the bed, wearing nothing more than the matching white lingerie set I got her for our engagement, her hair falling wildly over her shoulders and back. Her plump breasts popped out the top of her bra, that beautiful baby bump standing out proudly as she stared back at me intently. I noticed pretty quickly she was looking entirely flushed, and that is when it hit me.

"Are you?"

"Come see for yourself." When she said that, my dick swelled under my sweatpants and didn't waste any time walking towards her on the bed, slowly climbing on, laying on my stomach in front of her, my head close to her sweet spot as she continued kneeling in front of me. I looked up for a minute and saw her staring straight back. I reached out and carefully hooked my fingers under her panties.

Sliding a finger inside the damp material, I felt her legs shift to give me better access. My finger ran down the length of her already wet slit. Finally, I found what I was looking for. A vibrator tucked between her legs, buried deep inside, and when I felt the button on the end, I quickly pressed it to increase the speed, not once but twice. I had longed for this fantasy. "Aww.... fuck, Brax!"

"It's time to play, Cutie."

CHARLIE

When Brax finally realised what I had done, and that the vibrator was inside me, I could see the immediate shift in his composure. He looked up, I wondered what he was going to say. "You want me to fuck you, don't you?" All I could do was gasp an unconvincing rebuff as he brought his broad and handsome face close to mine, sharp eyes twinkling with lust and confidence looked into mine. "Come with me." Before I could question him, Brax had helped me up off the bed carefully.

"Brax, what are you doing?"

"Shh, baby." When he placed me down in the kitchen, I didn't know what to expect. When I saw him stalk towards me, I backed until I felt the kitchen units to my bottom. *I was trapped.* I closed my eyes and prepared my lips, but he didn't kiss me, his hands just rested on my breasts. Slowly, he pressed his palms against the top, my nipples grew hard in the cups of the bra.

For a moment he just held me like that, then he slowly rotated his hips, I trembled with excitement. In an easy but swift movement, his hands were on my naked stomach, pushing the negligee to the side. I gasped at the sensation of his large, rough hands pressed against my nipples. I let out a deep groan and rolled my pelvis forward when he enclosed my cherry sized stiffness between his thumb and forefinger.

I opened my eyes to look into his stillness, the beads of excited perspiration trickled from my every pore. His cool and dry fingers teased my hapless hard nipples until every tiny bud of them was erect... He stopped the wonderful torture and slipped over my nakedness, pulled the bra away from aching stiff breasts as I leaned back and his lips found my taught little buttons, lashing them with his tongue.

What sensations his fingers had achieved were nothing compared to the new passions radiating from my hard, very swollen nipples. How could one man know so much about my pleasure? I wanted him desperately right this minute, his naked, manly flesh on mine. I pulled at the drawstring on his track pants, loosening them quickly. When my nails scratched up his stomach before digging into his chest, he roared at me. "Fuck! That's so damn sexy." I fell into him as my knees buckled under the vibrator still inside me, our lips meeting in a gasping, rasping kiss, as his hands found my ass. My breasts felt so soft when crushed against his hard, muscular chest. In a rapid gathering movement behind me, he pulled my panties up into my crack, exposing my ass cheeks, now naked but for the thin panties. His hands entered the back of them, and instinctively, I pushed my ass out. Cupping and squeezing the flesh, he made me grind my pussy onto the knee he brought up between my legs, making it easier for me with my stomach to grind against him. He had the advantage also of pushing his leg up against the vibrator inside of me.

I felt a glow of pride, feeling his stiffness there and knowing I could still do that to him. His fingers tickled the sensitive inner crack between the buttocks, then moved his hand lower, found my most erotic hole and toyed with it, putting pressure on the vibrator to go further then back out again. "Please-" A gasp cut me off, "stop teasing me, Brax." I wanted to draw my thighs together to relieve the achy clammy feeling between my legs. But his mouth went to my nipples again, and I had to spread my legs to brace myself against the unit. I felt the cool air to my stomach as I was now exposed fully for him to take. His hand pressed to my stomach, then slipped down and into the tight elastic of my panties. I arched backwards and spread wider as he ran his fingertips, through the pubic hair down, onto my moist, yearning lips.

Slowly rubbing, the lips yielded to his fingers. One found my emerging clit at the same time as his mouth teased and devoured my nipple. He rubbed vigorously, just a few minutes of his expert hands and mouth sent my body into blissful convulsions—exploding into waves of almost painful release. "Mmm yes... more, Brax!" "Go baby, I've got you. Cum for me." He didn't stop until I sank down, panting with the effort of so many waves of pleasure. Our mouths met, tongues darted and lashed like fighting snakes. With my hands, I felt every rippling muscle in his back as I pressed myself hard into him. My naked legs rubbed against his track pants, pussy slickly pressed against him.

"Aww fuck me Brax, please! Take me now!" I knew how much he loved making me beg, so I couldn't help myself when I all but ripped at his track pants pushing them to the floor. He was naked in my arms, his hard shaft pressed into my stomach with a burning desire. In one swift and firm action, he had me face down over the kitchen table, one foot on the floor and with the other knelt on the chair, being careful to make sure it did not squash my stomach on to the table. I cried out in joy as he pulled my panties to one side and quickly tugged the vibrator out. His cock pressed into me, I was so wet that despite his size I took his entire length on the first penetration. "*Yes,*" I cried out feverishly.

"Fuck Charlie yes! Damn it… yes! I remembered too… Sometimes you just want it rammed in there… isn't that what you said?" He mumbled between heavy thrusts, each word emphasised with a powerful stroke.

"Yes!" With each deep pounding, I felt his balls bump against me. He pressed his hand into the small of my back carefully, making sure we did not press my baby bump against anything, but I knew he was trying to arch my ass more towards him, meeting every powerful shafting.

I felt myself trembling, soon my body was shaking in a glorious orgasm. The intensity of my pleasure seemed to multiply into an all-embracing body-quake as he pushed his thumb into my backside and fucked it in time with him. "Holy shit Brax! Oh, God!" I panted like a woman possessed. "Fuck, yes, yes… *Yes!*" I was sobbing for breath and shouting out obscenities when his body went very taut against me, his cock swelled, then pulsed as he paid me the ultimate compliment, filling my depths. I slumped my face onto the cold table, panting like a sprinter as my head made its way back into my body.

He hadn't shrunk much when he pulled out. Slowly, I pulled myself from the table and onto a chair, looking at the massive glistening dick swinging between his legs. I stood, walked over to the washing basket waiting to go downstairs and pulled one of his shirts on. I walked into the lounge and Brax was fast to follow me. He watched as I poured him a very large whisky and he downed it in one when I handed it to him. "Get my shirt off." His voice was that of 'he who should be obeyed' and it was driving me wild. I slowly peeled it off and stood naked in our lounge, my heart pounding, blood racing as my man eyed me up like his prey. I went to him, my mouth dry, feeling as if I were about to be devoured. His lips found the most sensitive parts of my stomach, as his tongue drove me wild. I opened my thighs as his fingers slipped over my clit, making it swell to a new hardness. I reached for his cock, still wet and coated with my juices.

As I slowly rubbed it, he grew hard against my palm. It felt so big in my feverish hand. He looked into my eyes and smiled lustily as his hands gripped my bottom and pulled me to him. I spread my thighs to sit astride his lap, holding him to my entrance, then sinking, impaling myself on his wonderful dick. He pressed deep into me, filling me again. His mouth found each nipple and brought them to their extended hardness. Fuck, how I loved riding this man, feeling him grow thicker each time I impaled his dick!

The noises of our lovemaking filled the room. I did not know which was more deliciously disgusting; his lips and tongue lapping at my nipples, the slurping noises as he filled and emptied me, or my growls and moans mixed with obscenities I wouldn't normally say. Either way, Brax was driving my body wild tonight. Suddenly he rolled us over as he knelt up, pulling my hips on to his legs, my back comfortably against the couch and cushions. He plunged in and out of me, hard and fast. My body lifted into his, pushing up to meet his harder thrusts. My climax swept through like a bush fire, causing my body to go rigid and mouth to gulp significant chunks of air. It was as if I'd entered another dimension where the only sensation was sexual pleasure.

The sexual haze had me lost in exquisite sensations that swept through my body from head to toe. It was timeless, and I wanted it to go on forever. Suddenly, as this wonderful feeling intensified, I felt him leaving me and I cried out in anguish. "Brax, no!"

"Shhh," he hushed me. "Shit babe! Shhh!" I suddenly shot up on my elbows, eyes opening fully as I saw lights coming down our driveway. My hand immediately flew to my mouth as I looked at him, horrified, realising we got carried away and Tina was now home.

"Brax!" I whisper shouted at him.

"Babe, shhh! Just sit here still and quiet, it's too dark and if she doesn't turn the light on, she won't see us.

"Oh my god, Brax! What if she does?"

"I'll cover you, baby, I promise."

"Holy shit! I want to die, this is my worst nightmare." I buried my head in my hands as Brax rubbed my arms, still sitting up watching her movement.

"Babe, just be really quiet, okay, she's about to walk in." I lay there completely freaking out as Brax carefully rested over the top of me, being careful not to lie on me fully and crush my stomach. When I heard the door lock, I gasped, and he placed his hand over my mouth as he whispered in my ear. "Baby, trust me, just be really still for a few seconds."

I heard the door open, then shut and lock before a lot of shuffling... huh?! Is that kissing sounds? "I think we are safe. Looks like they have already gone to bed." *Is that — her reply cut my thought process.* "Mmm good, then they won't hear what I am about to do to you, Mark."

We heard a lot of moaning and scuffling, after a few minutes the door shut, Brax sat up and I followed him. We both looked at each other as best we could in the dark before whispering. "I didn't hear things. That was *our* Mark's voice, right?"

"It was Batman, and Tina definitely said his name!"

Chapter Forty Five

BRAX

After nearly getting caught ourselves, Charlie and I had to wait quietly before we could sneak back to our bedroom. The moment we did, I fell on it, dying of laughter. "Brax! Did that seriously just happen?"

"Which part?" I chuckled at her. "Are you referring to where we nearly got caught fucking or when we sprung Tina and Mark?" *Oh my god, Tina and Mark!* "Holy shit! I need to tell Chester."

"Stop being such a gossip!"

"You know what babe, I have to say this. For someone pretty open with having sex, you really seem to hate the idea of people knowing we have it."

"I do not!" I cracked up, laughing at her indignant face when she said it.

"Really? So you didn't just say it was your worst nightmare? I'm pretty sure they know we have sex. First, they have heard us, and second, you have my baby inside you."

"Shut up, Brax." She pushed me away as I chuckled again. "I just don't like the idea of our friends seeing us have sex."

"Liam has." I laughed at her again.

"Shut the fuck up, Brax!" She picked my pillow up, belting me over the head with it before shuffling into the bathroom. I followed her not long after so I could brush my teeth and get ready for bed. "Brax, out! I'm trying to pee!"

"So? Don't let me stop you. I've seen everything down there anyway, and ate out on it regularly." I couldn't help tormenting her. It made me laugh at how easily embarrassed she was. "I swear you are impossible sometimes!"

"I still have a hard on, just thought you should know." She laughed and told me to "stop it," so I turned to look at her as she wiped herself and stood up from the toilet. "Well, what's the alternative? You can listen to Mark and Tina instead?" I still couldn't help but say it without laughing. The fact Chester had just shit stirred Charlie earlier today and then we had caught them killed me. "Fine! Just hurry." She gave in. After heading back to bed, we finished what we had started in the lounge room before I raced out to the kitchen and grabbed the vibrator we'd left on the floor before jumping back into bed. I was lying on my back splayed across our mattress with Charlie's head resting on my arm while we both tried to suck in some much needed breaths. "I have an idea." She tilted her head up at me and asked what it was. "We should get up early and catch him trying to sneak out in the morning."

"You're assuming she's going to let him spend the night?" How she said it so matter of fact cracked me up.

"Brutal babe! Worth the try, though, don't you think?" When Charlie told me "set the alarm," I rolled over to the bedside table and sorted it before switching the light off. As I cuddled down into Charlie's back, I leaned over first and planted a flurry of kisses across her stomach. "Goodnight Molly, Daddy loves you."

"You're seriously cute sometimes."

"No, masculine."

"Okay Caveman. I love you." I whispered back the same as I curled up behind her, wrapping my arm around her stomach, clasping my little girl as I rested my head back. Waking up to the alarm, I felt Charlie move in my arms and I kissed her delicately as she reached around to my neck, stroking her nails across it.

"Morning Cutie."

"Morning baby... I need to pee." I chuckled back at her and I wasn't surprised. "It's your daughter's fault."

"I have a feeling that's a phrase I will get used to hearing a lot of." We got up, and she headed through to the bathroom before chucking a jumper on, coming out to lie on the couch. I made coffee and a black tea before I came and sat behind her. She lay back in my lap as we scrolled our phones and played the waiting game. I was watching her fall asleep in my lap and I kept staring at her stomach, finding myself drawn to it like a magnet. It still hit me when I realised that was *my* baby. All I ever wanted was this girl, and now she was so close to giving me a daughter. I reached around and angled my phone down as she opened her eyes. Her head shot up, looking at me curiously before asking, "what are you doing?"

"I took a photo of Molly." I showed her the picture; she smiled up at me, hand reaching to my neck, pulling me closer. I saw her eyes full of love, she pressed on my neck firmer, gifting me the sweetest kiss, slow at first, but it didn't take long for our love to turn into long mouthwatering strokes. I ran my hands over her beautiful stomach as our tongues explored each other lovingly.

Finally, Tina's door opened and it was showtime! We sat on the couch that faced the front door and waited until we saw them both heading towards it. Mark with his shoes in hand, trying to be quiet. As they approached the door, we saw him turn and pull Tina into a sumptuous snog. I couldn't hold back a second longer when Charlie giggled, so I asked, "You don't want to stay for a coffee, mate?"

"You fucking wankers!" We burst out laughing, he shook his head as he straightened up again, still holding on to Tina's waist. "You scared the living shit out of me."

"Smile!" I swiftly lifted my phone and took a photo of a stunned Mark and Tina as Midget burst out laughing in my lap.

"Don't you dare!" I exaggerated, hitting send on my phone. "You fucker!"

"No need to worry, bro. I only sent it to Chester." I paused while he hid his face behind his hand. "And Liam, Shane, Mace, Kendall, Chrissy… Oh, and Marcus and Tessa." Charlie was completely tickled and vibrating in humour.

"Get me that coffee already, you asshole." Mark threw his shoes on the floor near the door as they headed over. I gave Charlie a quick kiss on the forehead and got up to get everyone a cuppa. As I was in the kitchen, I heard her start the Spanish Inquisition.

"So, something you want to tell us?"

"You know guys, if you had of been less obvious about it yesterday, Chester wouldn't have picked up on the fact you two were fucking!" I heard Mark swear under his breath when I said that.

"Fuck that guy!" I cracked up at Tina's response, having heard it many times before from Charlie. I felt my phone vibrating in my pocket and pulled it out to see Chester was calling. I headed into our pantry to make it look like I was getting sugar and coffee, but also so the others couldn't hear me. "Be quick, they are just in the next room."

"He's still there?"

"Yeah, mate. Just making him a coffee now."

"We'll see you in ten minutes." I disconnected and pocketed my phone, making the drinks, carrying them out to the lounge room. Mark and I stepped out the front to have a blunt while the girls talked.

"So?" I looked over at him as I lit up the blunt. When he didn't answer, I raised my eyebrows at him.

"Ha, shut up, man. What do you want me to say? She's brilliant company, we both have just gone through a breakup, we got talking, and we both had needs. Let's just see what happens. No pressure, right?"

"No pressure, brother, but I have one question?"

"What's that?"

"Why the fuck didn't you just take her back to your house?" We both laughed, which caused me to cough on the smoke as I passed it to Mark. "We would have been none the wiser if you had just done that, mate."

"Aww man, shut up, I know, alright. I was trying to be polite and not assume. I said I would get the uber to drop her home on the way through—"I finished that for him. "Then it became 'Do you want to come in for a drink' right?"

"Something like that." I raised my brow again, he just smirked and took a toke. We finished the blunt and headed back inside, having a chat, when the front door flung open and in walked Chester, with Liam, Shane, Chrissy, Mace and Kendall in tow.

"Hey fuckers!" He said as he pointed finger guns at Mark and Tina, winking. Charlie and I nearly fell off the couch laughing all over again.

CHARLIE

A week ago, we caught Tina and Mark, everyone taking the piss each chance we got. I was thirty-six weeks pregnant tomorrow and I won't lie, fuck me, I was over this shit! What kind of idiot gets pregnant and then times it so she is giving birth during an Australian forty degree celsius summer? Charlie does! I swear to god our electricity bill was going to be ridiculous by the time the baby came out. Between the air conditioning running constantly on twenty degrees for my sake—while most of the time the others walked around wearing sweaters inside the house before stripping off to go outside again—the band had to practise here because Brax wouldn't leave me. I'd repeatedly told him I was fine, but he firmly dug his heels in like the stubborn git he was, not having a bar. It was early morning, and the sun hadn't even fully risen and where was I? In the kitchen because Molly decided we needed to have some boysenberry ice cream. I was stuffing my face straight out of the tub when Mark walked in. "Molly wanted ice cream for breakfast?"

"Correct." I answered as I shoved another spoonful in. He walked over and flicked the kettle to boil, then grabbed a bottle of water from the fridge, sitting at the kitchen island across from me as he took a sip and

I continued to hoover my ice cream. I know most people would wonder who the fuck he thought he was coming into someone's home and making himself so comfortable. But we had always told our friends to treat our home as theirs, and for all our antics, they had respected it like their own, as we had theirs. So I had no issue in opening my door to any of them.

However, I drew the line at sharing my ice cream. So when he tried to reach over and take the spoon to have some, I smacked him on the knuckles with it. "Aww," he shook his hand out. "What the fuck, Midget? That hurt!"

"It was supposed to. Don't touch my baby girl's ice cream."

"One spoonful won't kill you," he protested.

"But you will end up dead." He turned when he heard Brax enter and asked, "is that the voice of experience?"

"Correct, bro," he answered, then turned to me. "Hey baby." He came over and kissed my neck as he wrapped his arms around my stomach.

"Why are you up so early?" I wondered while demolishing another big spoonful of ice cream. He looked at me for a minute before he moved in and slid his tongue into my mouth. He pashed me deeply for a few seconds before pulling back just as fast.

"That's the only way I can get ice cream in this house now, bro." The boys laughed before they fist bumped and as he pulled his hand back, I smacked him on the knuckles as well. "Aww you fucking Evil Midget of death! That hurts."

When Mark told Brax, "I said the same thing," I sucked my teeth. "And like I told you, it is supposed to! Also seriously? You did all that for a tiny taste of ice cream?"

"Nah baby, just a taste of you." He smacked me on the ass as I waved the spoon at him and mumbled, "that it was a lucky save." I asked him again, "why are you up?"

"I rolled over and couldn't find you, so came to check you were alright when you didn't return."

"Got hungry." I shoved another heap in my mouth while he checked the kettle. Bringing a cup back for Mark and himself, he stood behind me, they chatted while Brax rubbed my belly and I leaned further on to the bench as I ate my ice cream. When my butt pushed into him more, his hands moved around to my back and started rubbing over my hips and sore muscles. "Aww, god that feels good. Do it harder."

Mark's head shot up and he burst out laughing in my face. Before I could register, he snapped a photo with his phone. He looked down at it and now had wrinkles forming under his eyes from humour. "That's fucking gold!"

He turned his phone around and it looked like Brax was fucking me from behind… while I stuffed ice cream in my face. "Send me that, please. I want it as my screensaver." I nudged Brax with my ass, as I called him "wanker."

"How could I not, babe? You have a mouth full of cream and you look like you're about to be filled with mine."

"You're fucked!" I rolled my eyes. Ignoring them, I went back to eating as Mark asked, "what the fuck was that, anyway?"

"He was rubbing my lower back and hips, as they have been really sore lately. I told him to do it harder, that was all." I explained exactly what had transpired.

"Midget, are you being an asshole right now and trying to make me feel guilty for making a joke out of it?"

"Do you feel like an asshole, Mark?" He cracked up and told me, "shut up," as I smiled at him and he went back to his phone, taking a sip of coffee. Brax continued to work on my back and hips for me to the point I was now stuffed full of ice cream, feeling a bit more relaxed and ready for a nap. "Alright, I'm going to sleep now."

"Really?" Brax looked puzzled. "You just got up, grazed, had a massage and now you are going to nap?"

"I might even stop to pee too, before I go back to bed. Are you coming?"

"Am I allowed to? Or are you offering?" I glared at him. "See you in a bit bro, make yourself at home. You know the score, chop bowl is in the studio downstairs, with the bong."

"Safe man. I might go rip a cone, then head back to bed myself. What time are the others heading over?"

"Eleven. Chester had to push it back as he had an appointment first up this morning. He wasn't sure how long he'd be." Brax followed me up to bed, once settled, asked, "Are you okay, baby?"

"Yeah, of course. Why do you ask?"

"I just," he paused, "noticed it seems…" Scratching the back of his neck, his face was creased in concern. "I'm trying to say this without sounding insensitive."

"Then just say it babe, I'll let you know if you sound offensive or not." I grinned at him cheekily to help ease the tension I could see on his face.

"I'm just worried about you. You seemed to struggle a lot this last week."

"Thank you for noticing, babe. I appreciate that, it could never be insensitive. It's nice that you see the little things too, it reminds me how loved I am." I gave him a soft kiss as he stroked my arm. "The honest answer, I feel like my stomach wants to pop. The skin is so sore and tight, it feels really stretched." I observed as he leaned over to my bedside draws and grabbed out a bottle of body lotion. He gestured for me to lie on my back, as he sat across my thighs, straddling them. He pushed my shirt up to just under my breasts, opened the bottle of lotion and put a bit on his hands before he started rubbing my stomach carefully, letting the cream soothe my sore skin and his hands massage me as well. "Keep talking, baby, I'm listening. I just wanted to make you as relaxed as possible, too."

"I know, and that's why I appreciate you." He continued to rub my stomach for me while I tried to explain. "It's weird because I feel like every day now I get bigger, but it isn't just her growing. I can feel her getting herself ready too, if that makes sense?"

"As in turning? I remember them mentioning that."

"Well, yes… that, but making her way down, too. My hips are a lot sorer, sometimes moving can be a genuine struggle. The moment I feel a pee coming, I have to go straight away because it can take a while to get up out of the chair."

"So I will carry you?" I smiled as I held my giggle in and replied to him. "Are you going to find a solution to all my whims?"

"I'll try my best to do whatever to ease the burden on you." He leaned over me, supporting his weight on his arms, kissing me. As he went to sit back up, I held his neck and snogged him deeper. "Mmm... not that I'm complaining, but what was that for?"

He put some more cream on his hands before continuing to rub my hips and stomach. "Hormones Brax. Enjoy the good ones when you can, don't question them."

"Yeah, my knuckles already met the alternative this morning."

"Come, lie with me? I'm ready to sleep."

"Okay, Mummy Midget."

"Hey!" He grinned as he lay down, pulling the blankets over us. I smiled as he reached over and put the air conditioning back on before I felt him press into my back, resting his head between my shoulder blades as he wrapped his arm around my stomach, laying one extended above his head, stroking my hair. I reached down and ran my fingers along his arm and soon found myself fast asleep. I hadn't slept this good for the last few days, just that bit of care from Brax had made the world of difference, so I hadn't a clue how long I'd been out for it when I woke up feeling the need for the bathroom. I sat up feeling Brax's arm still over me and lifted it gently to get up. Turning to head to the bathroom, I shook in quiet humour when I saw Chester had snuck in and was spooning into Brax. I had to put my hand over my mouth to stifle the laugh as I went to the bathroom and came back grabbing my phone. I took a photo first before I pressed it onto the video and shouted, "Brax! What the fuck are you doing?"

His eyes shot open, glancing around the room before sensing the dead weight wrapped around him and seeing me standing. He looked down and immediately freaked out. He threw Chester's arm off as he started kicking until he fell to the floor. Brax jumped out of the other side of the bed towards me. It was only when he heard the laughing Monkey on the other side and saw me in tears of hysterics he realised what had happened. "Fuck! You wanker!"

Chapter Forty Six

BRAX

So apparently Charlie still enjoyed taking the piss at my expense, even after I was nice to her earlier. Okay, game on Evil Midget! "Aww baby, where are you going?" I heard storming out of the room.

"Eat a dick, Midget!" Chester's laughter rang out behind me.

"I didn't do it. It was Chester," she protested.

"Did you film it?" She didn't answer, but I heard Chester cackling, so I turned around to them both, "go fuck yourselves." Shutting the door, I walked down the hallway, leaving the two shit stirrers, making my way to the kitchen to grab a coffee…. then an idea hit. I could hear 'double trouble' coming, a pack of hyenas, thick as thieves, until she looked up and saw what I was doing.

"Agh!" she growled, "you're dead to me, Brax!" I continued, taking another spoonful while watching the smoke coming out of her ears.

"Who's laughing now?" I asked, eating another generous helping of her precious ice cream.

"Not cool bro! You can't steal your daughter's food." Chester took up the battle for her.

"Exactly! It isn't for me!" I saw her stomp her foot as I continued.

"I can see why Molly likes it so much." I took another giant mouthful and ate it as Charlie twitched, her anger boiling over. "Mmm, it's so good."

"I hope you choke on it, wanker!" Of course, being the shit I am, I stood there and ate the whole bowl while she death stared at me before I headed up and got dressed so we could start working. Of course, not before I smacked her on the ass for good measure.

Once I returned, the boys were ready to go, so we headed downstairs, getting stuck in. We'd been working for a few hours and were in a zone, so I had noticed nothing but what I was focused on. Charlie came to the studio door, waving the house phone at me. "Brax! Marcus is on the phone."

"Why didn't he just ring my mobile?"

"He did... four times."

"Shit! Sorry, I was in a zone." I checked my phone, "no sorry, it was on silent, my bad." She passed me the phone and said, "I'll sort everyone some lunch."

"You'll make a great house wife yet, baby." I joked.

"Asshole!" I chuckled as she flipped me off as she left.

"Hey Marcus, what's up?" I returned to the call.

"You have to go to Melbourne next week."

"I can't do that, sorry. Charlie will be thirty-seven weeks pregnant. I'm not leaving town."

"Same day flights, in and out." I flatly said "no," again. "They already booked you in for a television interview."

"Fuck off, Marcus!" I spat, "Are you serious? I already had this conversation with you, man!" The boys all looked, noticing my anger increasing.

"I know Brax, and believe me, if I'd been involved from the onset, I would have flatly said no. I only found this out myself when I tried to call you." I asked "when do they want me to go?" and when he said, "next Thursday," I stood up out of my chair and paced across the acoustic flooring of my studio.

"M, I need to speak to Charlie and call you back. I can't have this conversation without involving her."

"I'm really sorry, mate. Like I said, I'll make sure it is the same day. Whatever it takes."

"Yeah, alright. I'll call you back." I hung up and saw the guys all staring at me. When Liam asked, "what did you do?" my brows knitted as I shook my head. "What do you mean? What did I do?"

"You have that look on your face that says Midget is about to ream you."

"She probably is, Shane." Chester asked, "how bad, mate?"

"The fucking studio booked me in for a television interview next Thursday... in Melbourne! They didn't even consult with Marcus first!"

"Fuck!" Yeah, that about sums it up Chester, the same thought I initially had. "Any way of getting out of it?"

"The best Marcus has done is get same day flights, in and out."

"Do you want me to come and babysit the Pregnant Midget of Tour?" When Mark laughed, he added, "or Mark could, since he will probably be here banging Tina, anyway." He flipped Chester the bird, I thanked them both, pointing to the bong, telling them to have a hit while I went to speak to Charlie.

I jogged upstairs and found her in the kitchen, making some lunch. She looked up and smiled when she saw me coming. That was until our eyes met and she put the utensils down, wiped her hands on the towel, coming around the counter to meet me. I sat down at the bench and Charlie walked over to me, running her hand across my cheek as she gripped my shoulder. "What's wrong, baby? Is everything okay?"

"Marcus' phone call, babe." She looked at me and stepped closer as I rubbed her hips. "He just found out the studio booked me in for a television appearance next Thursday, in Melbourne."

I couldn't quite make out her expression, but mostly she seemed to be more worried and upset about me. "Babe, we always knew this was a risk. I'll be alright. How long do you have to go for?"

"Marcus sorted fly in and out the same day for me." She smiled and said, "that's good then," but I noticed it didn't quite reach her eyes.

"I don't want to risk leaving you at the moment, Charlotte." I sighed.

"I understand that, baby. I promise that Molly and I will be fine. Tina is here and before you know it, you'll be back home with us. It's just a few hours."

"I thought you might have ripped me a new asshole, you know."

"Maybe Marcus." She winked as I smirked and pulled her in for a hug. Her tiny arms wrapped around my neck as she kissed the side of my face.

"I love you. Thank you for always supporting me and making life that bit easier."

"Your girls love you." Charlie pulled me into her and I kissed her sweet lips, her hands holding my neck tighter, tongue pressed against my lips until I opened giving her the access she wanted. Tilting my head to the side as I deepened the embrace, I felt her rubbing herself against me. My hand immediately roamed down her body, settling on her beautiful backside that I grabbed a handful of. "Mmm, we should stop Brax."

"We should, but no." I kissed her harder and with a renewed passion as our hands explored, desperately wishing we were alone to enjoy this moment further. "Let's go away this weekend, the two of us? Have some time to ourselves before Molly gets here?"

"I would love that baby, but we're restricted to where we can go at the minute." She pointed to her stomach.

"It doesn't matter, Cutie, as long as we are together. We can get in the car and drive down or up the coast. An hour, two hours, it doesn't matter. Just find a quiet little town for the weekend."

"Sounds perfect. I've got some hormones I need you to take care of before you go."

"Really? And just how might I do that?" I wiggled my eyebrows.

"Don't be stupid bro, she wants you to fuck her." Charlie rolled her eyes and glared at me as I turned to Chester, who had just spoken from the top of the stairs.

"Don't fuck with me man, you timed that one on purpose."

"Fuck yeah, I did." All I could do was laugh at that honest asshole. What more could I say?

CHARLIE

So there we were, sitting in Brax's car, windows down, stereo up, overnight bags in the boot, his hand in my lap, rubbing my stomach as I had mine up behind his neck, stroking it. We'd headed down the coast for a quiet weekend. I knew this was in part because he was feeling guilty for having to go to Melbourne, but I honestly didn't understand why he felt like that.

This was his job, it's what he did, and I had never once begrudged him for his successes because I knew how hard he worked for them. Sure, the timing wasn't ideal but with people like Marcus in his corner to fly the flag for Brax; they had minimised his time away and got him in and out the same day as promised. Tina was still staying with us, which also meant when she was home and not at Mark's house, he was staying at ours as well. Plus, the rest of the gang had promised to come over, so he had nothing to worry about. All that aside, though, I couldn't be disappointed as we got this time together. I was ridiculously in love with this man, and our entire world was about to change. We would be responsible for a little human, it would no longer just be about us. I wanted one last time, not the band and our friends and family, but just Brax and I.

We finally found a town that looked homely and stopped to get out of the car for a bit, strolling to a nearby cafe for a drink and to check the vibe. We sat outside, taking in some views. "Do you think we could live somewhere like this, Brax?"

"I think we would get terrified of the quiet, babe."

"True, neither of us really knows what that is." I looked up and saw the stunning mountain setting behind him and pulled my phone out. "Stand there babe, let me take a photo?"

He stood as I fussed over the angle, I wanted the perfect shot. Being the dork he is, the moment I took the picture, he stuck his tongue out and threw me a peace sign. "You Gronk! You know Namaste means my soul recognises yours, not that I got high on acid at a music festival once or twice?

He cracked up, and I looked at him, confused for a moment. "God, I haven't heard you say Gronk in so long." I smiled and rested my head in my hand as I asked, "do you remember the first time I said it?"

"To Chester," he immediately replied. "When he came running into your office and tried to hide under your desk to get away from Lizzie."

"To get away from Lizzie?" I raised my eyebrow.

"Well, that and he later admitted he was trying to get a look up your skirt, too."

"Sounds more legitimate." Brax smiled as he said, "we've had an incredible year or two, haven't we?"

"We have babe. We've some amazing memories and incredible friends with us, or that we met along the way."

"The cluster fuck in Canada?" he asked.

"Not all bad, but hardly expected to see Calvin there."

"I still wish you had let me mess his face up." I smiled, reaching for his hand, telling him, "there's no need. We already won. Look at us now."

"When I think of him, I still can't help but laugh that you really thought they would believe you belted him and not Marcus." I threw my head back laughing, remembering it like yesterday, "Baby, he would have been sporting some sore ribs if you gave him an uppercut. Let's be honest, you are that short."

"You never complain?" I smirked at Brax.

"Why would I? It's like my walking blow job. I can just slip it straight in." I called him a "wanker," and rolled my eyes as he chuckled.

"Laugh all you want, what about plastic barbie who tongue fucked you to high heaven the night you tried to take me out on our first date on the Regional Tour?"

"Fuck, don't remind me of that, Cutie! If that chick had any more work done, I would have had to call Mattel to come and box her up and put a warning label on the box for kids." *And he thinks I am brutal!* We sat in silence for a few minutes before Brax asked, "what's your favourite memory of Liam?

"That's easy. When we caught him talking to his reflection in the mirror." Brax agreed and added, "the toy story incident," also, before I pointed out Molly could never watch it now.

I asked Brax what his favourite memory of Shane was. "When we caught him and Kendall buck naked on the couch, and she didn't realise Chester was awake watching them."

"That poor girl, he's so wrong!" I shook my head with a grin. "Mine was when he said if she told him about her sherbet addiction, he would have let her lick it off his balls." Brax finished laughing. Then he said Mark. "I will never forget what he did for me that night you were in surgery. He's like the brother every girl wants."

"I hear that, babe. The day I walked out on you in Canada, I would have fucked that up badly if it wasn't for him."

"He's an amazing guy. I'm glad after things ended with April, he and Tina have some happiness. Whatever that is, since neither of them are saying."

"It's sex baby." I choked and told him to "stop it," as he moved on and said Marcus.

"Oh, absolutely when he punched Calvin!" Brax agreed. There was no way he wouldn't. "Chester?"

"The snapchat fail was pretty epic. Then when he schooled that reporter about it."

"I loved when he grilled you over your feelings for me." He clicked his teeth. "When he spent nearly twenty-four hours using every chance possible to call us fuckers." Brax laughed and said, "That psycho Claire he shagged?"

When I said "porn hub, and his constant wanking before Chrissy." Brax lost it.

He said, "Pregnant Midget of Tour. It still kills me every time." When I said, "I'm glad he's stopped listening to us," Brax lost it as we both said, "You're a good girl, baby."

We finished up our drinks and drove down the road a little further until we found a nice motel to get checked in. I was standing on the balcony watching the sunset, I felt Brax come out behind me, wrapping his arms around my waist and resting his head on my shoulder. His lips softly brushed my neck as his hands rubbed my stomach and hips; I reached one arm up, cupping his neck as I pulled his face into me more. When his fingers carefully cupped my breasts, I turned my face to his, quickly using my tongue to open his mouth up, searching out and finding his. He cupped my neck, gripping me possessively as our passion turned feverish. "Thank you for giving me everything I ever needed, Charlie."

"Brax?" He stroked my face as he softly said, "yes?"

"Take me to bed. I want to be whole with you."

BRAX

What an amazing weekend away we had, and the rest of the week had gone relatively quiet. I was now getting ready to head to Melbourne tomorrow for this bloody television interview, and to say I wasn't happy about it was an understatement. I locked up the house and got ready for bed, when I saw Charlie waiting for me and my breath hitched. There was my heavily pregnant fiancée, waiting for me in nothing more than a tiny pair of lace panties and a gorgeous satin teddy falling over her ample breasts and stomach. Every time I truly looked at this woman, it took me aback. I still could barely believe she was mine. I had known nothing like her.

Every ounce of my being throbbed for her—in places, I sometimes didn't even know existed. "Brax, do you want to take care of my needs?" Knowing she had the upper hand, she began sliding off the teddy as I approached. Her stomach popped out, while her breasts, cradled in a similar white bra, came into view. She spread her legs as I stood between them and started working on my clothes. Soon enough, she had my shirt off, undid my pants, allowing them to drop to the floor, along with my boxers. I stepped out of them as she removed her bra and laid back on the bed. I tugged her panties down, discarding them among our pile of clothes. The beauty of what was before me struck like a lightning bolt.

The exceptional side of her huge areolas were striking against her skin. Her tits drooped to the sides but were full enough to defy gravity, with her large nipples pointing skyward. Her stomach looked incredible, but it was so different at the same time. It jetted out from her tiny body and was capped by her bellybutton, straining against the forces behind it. After that, her belly suddenly sucked back, leaving her pubic mound flat, reflecting what was once a tone, tight stomach. Her pubic hair was light and showed a few weeks of growth. I had offered to help her many times, but she wouldn't let me. Despite that, it didn't hide her beautiful lips that showed a glint of wetness on them with a little creamy button peaking from her clit's hood. "You like?" She asked as she spread before me on the bed, seeing my intense stare.

"How could I not?" I responded as I soaked up my woman. Large breasts capped with bursting nipples, perfectly rounded stomach exhibiting my shot that got by and impregnated her, beautiful pussy ready to be loved by my tongue, and ass crying to be cradled. With that, she twisted a nipple in each hand playing with them softly while closing her eyes and letting out a sigh of ecstasy.

I knelt on the floor as I started kissing her inner thigh. I worked my way up until my cheek pressed against her centre, then turned my attention to the other leg doing the same thing. She was wiggling and moaning softly as I teased my way around where she wanted me. "Please don't play, Brax!" With that, I lowered my face into her and sucked a long lip into my mouth. "Yes, baby!"

She sighed as I sucked her in, then released it, before pulling both lips in while she ground onto my face. They were long, delicious and felt like they were filling my mouth perfectly. With her still flooding my senses, my tongue darted out and I let it slide inside.

Charlie gasped as my tongue entered the muscles contracting around me, pulling it in further. Focusing my attention on her hole, I repeatedly reached in as far as possible, curling and drawing back out a mixture of my saliva and her juices. My thumb searched for her clit while my other hand rested against the bottom of her stomach. The second my thumb made contact, Charlie gasped, and her thighs squeezed around my head. She became silent as her body stiffened with the only movement being her muscles repeatedly contracting around my tongue. "*Brax!*" She groaned as she finally drew in a breath of air and released her grip on my head.

"Damn! I forget how amazing you taste." Normally I would look up during this point to enjoy the afterglow on her face, but all I could see was the underside of her stomach heaving up and down with her strained breaths. My cock twitched at the sight, so full of lust. On either side of the protruding bundle, I saw a pair of hands extended, motioning me up. Giving her clit a quick French Kiss, causing Charlie to shudder, I stood up and took her hands, helping to pull her towards me. Our mouths met, tongues exploring as our hands roamed each other's bodies.

I worked my way down her neck to her tits and inhaled her nipple. Despite having it fully engulfed in my mouth, I could still see how large the surrounding areola had become. I sucked down, feeling a little liquid enter my mouth. It was warm, tangy and did not remind me of milk. "Och! Careful Brax. My nipples are so sore." I was thankful because I really disliked that taste, but I didn't want to be inconsiderate to her. With less aggressiveness, I gave her breasts the attention they needed, being mindful of her nipples. Holding my head, she commanded my attention. "I want you now."

Charlie leaned down to kiss me as I shuffled her to the end of the bed and stood up. I positioned myself against her opening and pressed forward. My head entered her as she spread her legs further, giving me free access. "Why do you feel so good?" she sighed.

I held my position initially to enjoy the feeling of her wrapped around me, like I always did. Her muscles contracted as I entered, but they relaxed as her tunnel embraced the feeling of me filling her. In this position, I could enjoy the sight of my cock sliding in and out, seeing her clinging around my intrusion and withdrawal. Her juices coated me, making my dick shimmer in the light.

I reached up with one hand to massage her chest while my other hand found her clit rubbing in a circular motion. "Fuck me Brax, more!"

Initially, I was concerned about hurting her, especially knowing how much she had been struggling lately, but the feeling of her around me as well as her demands quickly quashed that. I began taking fast little strokes, knowing the depth wouldn't hurt her. I also knew this rubbed her just the right way, accelerating her pleasure with the bed soon squeaking with each thrust. "Aw, yes! I love your cock, Brax!" I couldn't believe my ears as her screams increased in volume. "Fuck, your mouth is driving me wild tonight, Charlie!" To steady myself and provide additional leverage, I grabbed the tops of her thighs, pulling her carefully into me with each thrust. She groaned and grunted with each push as her hands searched for something on the bed to clench. The pillows, sheets, handfuls, crumpled into her fists. That's when I knew, while not as hard as she liked to be fucked, I had hit the spot she needed me to.

After several minutes, sweat dripped from my brow as her screams for my cock intensified, I knew I was done. "I'm coming, Charlie. Fuck!" I shouted through clenched teeth.

"Give me it baby, please." My first load shot up my shaft as I stayed inside her, stroking furiously. She squealed and contracted around me, as I stood pressed inside while the third, fourth and fifth spurt of my love juice raced through her. I continued to twitch through our orgasms while her muscles tried to milk more from me than I offered. I slummed carefully on to her, caressing her heavy tits as I caught my breath and slipped out with a heavy sigh.

"I needed that, baby."

"Me too, Cutie." We curled into each other and after that, it didn't take long to drift off to sleep. By the time Charlie woke in the morning, I had already showered, dressed and was downstairs having a coffee before I had to leave. When she walked down in those panties from last night and my shirt, I almost didn't want to leave at all, heading back to bed looked much more appealing. "You look better than my breakfast. Wanna come feed me?"

I wiggled my eyebrows, she giggled and came over giving me a kiss before making a cup of tea. We enjoyed a drink and when I heard the front door go; I tapped her on the butt and told her to put some pants on. I went to the door and saw Chrissy and Chester on the other side. "Yo! What are you doing here, bro?"

"I said we would come and babysit the Pregnant Midget of Tour, didn't I? I keep my word."

"Thanks, man." I hugged Chester before I went to Chrissy and welcomed them both inside.

"Want me to drive you to the airport to meet Marcus? Chrissy is happy to stay here with Charlie?"

"That would be a massive help, mate." I soon had everything in Chester's car, giving my girls a kiss, promising I would be back before she knew it. "Please take care, baby, and call me if you need anything."

"I promise, I will. We love you." I gave her another pash and got in the car where Chester dropped me off, telling me to call him tonight and he would race out to pick me up. Marcus met me at the airport and we made our way efficiently through the check-in and to our boarding gate.

The flight from Sydney to Melbourne was over in the blink of an eye, we disembarked, and made the long drive from Tullamarine to the Network Studios.

After an afternoon of getting prepped and sorted for the interview, it went fantastic. The response from everyone overwhelmed me. Barely off stage, and waiting in the dress-room to come back out—they had persuaded me to do an acoustic solo for them—I felt my phone vibrating in my pocket and pulled it out to see Chester. "Hey bro, all good? I'm just in between the show."

"Charlie's water broke. We are on our way to the hospital. Get home now, Brax!"

"Fuck! Don't be joking with me, man." My heart was pounding outta my chest. "I'm about to freak out!"

"I swear I'm not. Brax, get home!" *Fuck*! I knew something like this was going to happen! This is *why* I didn't want to do it!

"Chester, don't leave her side," I begged. "Promise me, bro. Please do not leave her until I get there."

"I won't mate, I'm not going anywhere. You have my word, Brax."

"Can you travel with her to the hospital? I don't want her going alone."

"I've got you, brother." I relaxed slightly, if there was anyone who I would trust to look after her, it was Chester. "Besides, I'm gonna need practice."

"What?"

Fuck! I guess this is where the real journey begins.

Epilogue

BRAX

So there you had it, our lives forever changed. Thirty-six hours of labour, Charlie trying to break every bone in my hand, swearing if I ever came near her again with my dick she was going to serve it to me for dinner, millions of profanities, many tears and finally nothing but pure unconditional love as we held our baby *Molly* in our arms.

My daughter.

My tiny precious little baby girl had finally joined us, and of course, being our child, she did things the difficult way.

When I got that call from Chester in Melbourne, I immediately had a feeling something was going on. So when I heard Chester say that she'd gone into labour, I knew this was the life I'd have to get used to—best laid plans, never going the way we wanted them to.

Thankfully, we'd already gone to air with the interview, so I quickly apologised to everyone and explained what was happening as I raced out the studio, Marcus in tow, as he made the relevant calls to get me home.

The whole time I was on and off the phone with Chester, as I had him promise not to leave her side until I got there. While we waited for the agonising 50 minutes for the earlier flight we'd secured, I was relieved when he finally called me back.

They had her booked in and confirmed she was in labour. Unfortunately, for Charlie's sake, she was in the *very* early stages and as much as I would *never* admit this to her; I was so thankful when he told me that, as I was praying, I would get to her in time. The thought of her being in so much pain scared me, breaking the one promise to be there, possibly missing my daughter's birth, was killing me right now.

I was getting more agitated the longer we waited, and I could tell Marcus sensed it. He grabbed his phone, stood up and walked away talking while I sat looking at my phone, waiting for an update. He'd not long sat back down when my phone rang and I saw Chester calling. What I didn't know was Marcus had called him, advising I wasn't in a good way, so Chester had done the one thing he knew would soothe both of us.

As I heard her tired, exhausted and pained voice come over the speaker, I felt a lump in my throat form. Desperate to be there helping her through this, I could hear already what a toll it was taking. I tried to comfort her in the best way I could and promised to be there soon when she had another contraction, and while I tried to help her through it, it only proved to heighten my frustrations.

Finally, we boarded the plane, and while the flight was a relatively short one, it felt like a lifetime. We disembarked and raced through the airport, Marcus searching for the car he organised to pick us up and raced us to the hospital.

Arriving, I was thankful to have my manager as I honestly was not thinking straight right now. He got information on where Charlie was and before long, a nurse came out and ushered us through.

I quickly raced into her room and when I saw Charlie burst into tears, I forgot everything else in that moment as I cradled her in my arms, soothing and promising I was here, I wasn't going anywhere. Once she calmed down and I helped her through another contraction, I got up, finally having the chance to thank Chester because if she had to go through this on her own, I would never have forgiven myself.

Chester and Marcus left to give us some privacy and headed home to shower and wait for the call. I thanked them both watching as they left, before it was just Charlie and me, facing the biggest moment we would ever share in our lives. I watched her—exhausted but determined—and all I kept thinking was I would rather go through that much pain and work myself than watch her go through it. Seeing the person you love be in that much suffering and knowing it was partly your fault was horrible. There were simply no other words for it.

I heard several people say that they couldn't bear to watch their partners give birth, so I did not know what to expect. Blood? Poop? Blood and poop? As I watched our daughter come into the world, though, I experienced the following emotions in this order.

One—Tears. So many. I had never cried like that, and I don't think I will ever again, unless, of course, we are blessed with more children.

Two—Why is my child blue? Is she supposed to be? Can we get a doctor in here who will acknowledge the fact that my daughter is blue? Is she okay? Oh, she's crying, okay, we are good.

Three—Holy crap, my fiancée is a badass! She just pushed a human out of her body! Thank god men aren't the ones giving birth, because we'd have gone extinct millennia ago.

I used to look at parking spaces and wonder if I could squeeze my SUV between a badly parked station wagon and a pole. If you've seen a baby come out via a tiny space, your perceptions changed forever. Women are tough. I carry on like a soccer player when I stub my toe. And let's not talk about my face when my daughter's head popped out.

I remember once reading about Robbie Williams' perception of childbirth and all I can say is Robbie, you're wrong. He described watching his wife giving birth as being like seeing his favourite pub burn down. This thought didn't cross my mind once. It was the most amazing thing I have ever witnessed. You're seeing life begin. Seriously, how amazing is that? Besides, it's such an incredible effort to carry the child and give birth that you're just filled with pride for your partner. Also, it's about the destination rather than the journey with childbirth.

I was holding my daughter in my arms when I realised that life, as I knew it, would never be the same. No longer was it just about me. I had to put this tiny human before myself. The universe was on mute for a while as I stared at this little girl who depended on me for everything. What an enormous responsibility and the greatest honour I'd ever been given.

Just me and my little game changer, dealing with an everyday vampire-style baby attack.

The End

Acknowledgements

There was a time last year when life was throwing one curveball after another and I questioned if I would ever be writing this page... yet here we are. We *finally* did it! I say we because I have been blessed with some incredible people who have encouraged, supported and poured their own sweat and tears into my art, so bear with me here as I pay my gratitude forward...

My editor and developmental team— Fuck me! Where do we start here....J, Tara, Stacey, Christina, Alisandra, Marly and Riley thank you for painstakingly sticking with me through the ups and downs, dedicating as much of your time, love and care to me and my art as you do to yourselves. How fucking lucky am I to be surrounded by an army of women who help me stand when I can't do it myself, but have no issues getting down in the trenches with me also. Thank you for always pushing me to be the best person and artist I can be.

Cat and Anastasia - None of this would be possible without you both, and unfortunately that means you are stuck with me now. Cat, you know me better than I do myself some days, you have come through for me in more ways than I can remember, and without you my vision wouldn't be here as it is written today. Ana... take the fucking compliment! You give my head a wobble when I need it, help me to clear the fog when it becomes overwhelming and remind me of what I am capable of. You are both loved, respected and adored. This is as much a part of you as it is me.

My team of Devil's Advocates - Emily, Kristine, Alice, Marci, Cari, Ellie, Felicity, Alisandra, Tara, Chrissy, Jessica, Ashley, Lauren, Mandy Kim, Robin, Dearna, Karla, Sam, Mandy, Marly, Tess, Cat, Ana, Riley, Ree, Dai, Tina, and Lis... appreciate you all being apart of this crazy little world I created, dedicating your time and love to supporting me, but most importantly for the laughs, love and great times we get to share along the way. Thank you for never being scared ;)

Aaron Matts - (IG: @aaronmatts)

You fucking amazing human being. Appreciate you putting a face to Chester, and the moment I saw you fighting monkeys in Kenya there was never a question you were the epitome of Monkey Nuts. My eternal gratitude. Keep rising, you got this!

Aaron Berkshire - (IG: @aaronberkshireofficial)

My sincerest appreciation for allowing me the use of your phenomenal art and photography to grace the cover of my book. It was a joy to work with you on this project.

Jess at The First Chapter Book Store and Sara at SXB Design - Loved being able to work with other Australian businesses to make the release of this book extra special. Thank you for working collaboratively with me, and taking a chance with my crazy art and personality. You are both appreciated and adored.

My Hot Mess - C, J, C How lucky am I to have three incredibly strong women who I adore, appreciate, and look up to (literally and figuratively). Our little piece of insanity is my sanity. Infinite love to you all.

To two of my closest friends - Wayde and Paul - having you both in my life makes me feel like there is nothing I can't do. You understand me, push me, and aren't afraid to always speak your truth to me. You make me a better person and I wouldn't be doing this without you. My love now and always.

To my family - you are my crazy little thing called love.

And finally my readers - You are the reason I do this. Much love, LF x

Made in the USA
Las Vegas, NV
07 January 2024

84023748R00291